Praise for Dee Davis

After Twilight

"Dee Davis pours on the atmosphere and cranks up the danger in this terrific new thriller. Perfect pulse-pounding reading for a cold winter's night."
—*Romantic Times*

"Dee Davis provides her fans with a powerful romantic suspense. *After Twilight* is an entertaining tale that works because the characters seem real and their interactions quite genuine."
—*Affaire de Coeur*

Just Breathe

"Rising star Dee Davis returns with a new story of sizzling romance and danger. *Just Breathe* is sure to please Ms. Davis's growing list of admirers."
—*Romantic Times*

By Dee Davis
Published by Ivy Books:

AFTER TWILIGHT
JUST BREATHE
DARK OF THE NIGHT

DARK OF THE NIGHT

Dee Davis

IVY BOOKS • NEW YORK

This book contains an excerpt from the forthcoming edition of *Midnight Rain* by Dee Davis. This excerpt has been set for this edition only and may not reflect the final content of the forthcoming edition.

An Ivy Book
Published by The Ballantine Publishing Group
Copyright © 2002 by Dee Davis Oberwetter
Excerpt from *Midnight Rain* by Dee Davis copyright © 2002 by Dee Davis Oberwetter

Ivy Books and colophon are trademarks of Random House, Inc.

www.ballantinebooks.com

ISBN 0-8041-1976-7

Manufactured in the United States of America

First Edition: March 2002

10 9 8 7 6 5 4 3 2 1

To my brother, Dick,
who's always known me better than anyone.

"Only in the dark of the night
can one really see the stars. . . ."

Prologue

THE SEPTEMBER SUN sat lazily in the sky, its shimmering heat almost visible as it began its descent toward the horizon. Despite the calendar, Atlanta was hanging valiantly onto the last vestiges of summer, defiant to the last. Douglas Michaels leaned back in his chair with a sigh, wishing he could emulate some of its arrogance— knowing that he couldn't.

He'd gone too far. There was no turning back. He'd danced with the devil one moment too long, and now it was time to pay the piper. He glanced at his answering machine, the black box mocking him. Even though the light wasn't blinking, he knew there was a message. Knew what it said. The very fact that he'd started recording his phone conversations was revealing, in and of itself.

He should have erased it, but he hadn't, some perverse part of him needing it there in front of him, a reminder of exactly how far he'd fallen. But now even that luxury was more than he could afford, and so, with the touch of a button, he erased the words that he'd take to his grave.

Gracie's picture called to him, her eight-year-old smile gap-toothed, endearing. She was his life, and yet, in his quest for power, he'd risked her future. And her respect. The thought that he'd never see her again ate at him, but it was preferable to the alternative.

He reached for the picture next to Gracie's. *Julia*. His beautiful Julia. After fifteen years, he still woke in the mornings amazed to find her lying there beside him. If he'd met her sooner, perhaps his path would have been different. The point was moot.

He picked up the photo, tracing the line of her face. She was his rock, his light in the darkness. And yet, he'd betrayed her. Just as surely as if he'd taken a lover or stabbed her with a knife.

She trusted him. Believed in him. But it was all based on lies. And once she knew the truth, once she understood the magnitude of what he'd done, she'd never forgive him. It was the thought of her horror, her rejection, that made his choice easier. He would, with this last act, protect them as much as he could.

Looking out the window again, he tried to convince himself that he was being noble, that in the end he was finally taking responsibility for all that he'd done. But in truth, there was nothing noble about him. He was a coward. Plain and simple. And at the end of the day, there was nothing more than that.

He'd let other men, and his own greed, bully him into betraying his values and his family. He'd fixated on the prize and ignored the cost. And now he was taking the easy way out. If he were a better man . . .

But he wasn't.

With a sigh, he closed his eyes, his trembling fingers tightening around cold steel. Even in this he was afraid. Taking a deep breath, he opened his eyes, centering his thoughts on his family—on the freedom he was giving them. Everyone had choices in life.

He'd simply made the wrong ones.

Staring at the photographs of his wife and daughter, Douglas Michaels lifted the gun to his head. The report echoed through the empty house and out the open window, the sound a brief discordant undernote to the soft singing of the cicadas in the hot Atlanta sun.

Chapter 1

Atlanta, Georgia

SHE WAS ONE hell of a looker. A hot body encased in ice. Pure ice, if her demeanor was any indication. But that didn't stop him from assessing the sleek line of her hair, the full curve of her breasts. Oh, she was hot all right. She just needed the right man to set her free.

Not that *he* was the man. Jake Mahoney shifted his large frame in the folding metal chair, wondering why in hell press conferences were always held in places without proper air-conditioning, and with seats that could easily pass as torture implements. Maybe to keep the reporters from staying too long.

He suppressed a smile and turned his attention back to the ice queen. Mary Catherine "Riley" O'Brien looked every inch the part. Slim and aristocratic, she'd give Jackie Kennedy's memory a run for her money. Especially if Carter O'Brien managed to win the election. But that remained to be seen.

In the meantime, he was stuck temporarily on the political beat, trailing the senator's daughter. And pretty package or no, she was the kind of woman he'd just as soon be on the opposite end of the planet from. He'd been chewed up and spit out by better. And he had no

4

intention of making the same mistake twice. Especially not with someone like her.

"Want to meet her?"

Jake pulled his gaze from the podium and turned toward the sound of the voice. Edna Winston's smile was crooked. "Of course I want to meet her. Why the hell do you think I'm here?" He tried to hide his embarrassment with gruffness, but he could see by the twinkle in her eye that she wasn't buying. She'd seen his reaction to Ms. O'Brien.

"Well, actually, I've been sitting here wondering just that. I mean this isn't your usual stomping ground."

"Politicos, murderers," he shrugged, "is there a difference?"

Edna didn't bother to answer, just sat with one eyebrow raised, waiting.

"All right. I'm subbing for Walter. He's indisposed or something. I didn't ask." Walter Finley's affair with the bottle was a well-known fact.

"So this is a onetime shot?" She tilted her head toward Riley, and despite himself he looked.

"Oh yeah." The words came out with more force than intended.

"Well, then I suggest you make the most of it." Again there was a hint of amusement in the older woman's eyes. "I have a meeting with her immediately after this. It'd be easy enough to introduce you."

Edna Winston was a tough old bird. Been around longer than anyone could remember. She was a hell of a reporter, gutsy and tenacious. She could ferret out information when it looked as if there wasn't any.

"And why would you want to do that, Edna?" He eyed her cautiously. She wasn't exactly noted for her charity.

"Because I like you, Jacob."

Nobody called him Jacob, except his gran, and she'd been gone for a long, long time now. Still, he was here to do a job, and there was no sense looking a gift horse in the mouth. Even if it was more likely a gift cobra.

Her lips curled up at the corner, sort of a half smile.

If he didn't know better, he'd say the old broad had read his mind. "All right, Edna. I'm game. When this is finished, take me to the ice queen."

Riley O'Brien smiled politely, watching the crowd. Cannibals, every one of them. Carnivores. Waiting for the opening. One misstep, one misspoken word, and they'd be on her, devouring her, leaving nothing but bones behind.

The general public was gone, escorted out of the tent by members of Atlanta's finest. The risk of speaking at an abortion clinic had been calculated carefully against the gain of pushing forward her father's pro-choice agenda. The end result being Riley's presence as her father's emissary.

So it was one down, one to go. She'd survived the public speech, escaped the demonstrators, and gotten her father's platform across without incident. Which left the press. And given the choice of facing off with the protesters outside or the press corps in here, she'd take the pro-lifers any day.

She'd been in the spotlight most of her life, and she knew the drill, but that didn't make it any easier, any more palatable. Serving oneself up for slaughter every day was not her cup of tea. It was, however, unavoidable, and like everything else in life, she accepted it as a fait accompli. Part of the game.

"Miss O'Brien." The voice was decidedly male, deceptively soft and silky, southern steel encased in velvet. She shivered despite the warmth of the room, and her gaze collided with the deep indigo of his. Blue on black. His smile was slow, insolent, the hunter moving in for the kill. "You're a Catholic. And yet you're standing here at an abortion clinic, supporting reproductive rights. Don't you find that a little hypocritical?"

Daily.

Never.

There wasn't a simple answer. And even if there was, she wasn't about to share it with a room full of vipers who didn't give a damn about what she really felt. They were looking for headlines. Something to titillate the public, to make a name, to garner ratings.

She held tight to her guarded facade. There was no sense in letting them smell blood. With a deep breath, she smiled, keeping all her emotion safely locked away. He waited, his dark eyes knowing. The son of a bitch was baiting her. But she'd played this game with far more worthy opponents—and won.

With a glacial smile, she broke eye contact, her gaze encompassing everyone there. "I am a practicing Catholic, yes. And as a Catholic, I try to hold to the tenets of my faith. . . ." She paused, trying to order her thoughts, her eyes drawn unbidden back to the stranger.

"However, I also believe that life is about choices, Mister—" she glanced down at the seating chart and then back at the reporter. "—Mahoney. And I cherish a person's right to make their own. And that includes all people. Women as well as men.

"My father also supports a woman's right to choose. And in so doing, he is not considering the definition of life, he is, rather, considering the definition of freedom. Intellectual as well as physical. And that, Mr. Mahoney, is what America is all about."

There was a smattering of applause, and although

she couldn't be certain, she thought she saw a flash of amusement in the murky depths of his eyes.

"Ladies and gentlemen, I'm afraid we're all out of time. . . ." Maudeen Drake, her father's press liaison stepped up to the podium, and, with an almost imperceptible sigh, Riley stepped away, Maudeen's words fading to a hum. She'd survived one more round unscathed.

Her father would be pleased.

"Well that was a classic nonanswer." Jake watched as the lithe blonde exited through the curtained proscenium.

"You were expecting what—a heartfelt confession? Riley O'Brien has been successfully dealing with the press since she was old enough to stand behind a podium." He followed Edna as they wound their way among the emptying chairs.

"That's just the point, isn't it? She's been programmed. There's probably not an original thought in her body. Daddy's little girl through and through."

"Spoken like a true cynic." Edna's voice reflected her amusement.

"And you're not? Christ, Edna, I don't see how you deal with these people day in and day out. They're one hundred percent plastic."

Edna shrugged. "It beats your predilection for the dead."

"Homicide is a puzzle, Edna. You have to put the pieces together. But once you do, the motivations involved are pretty straightforward. Give me a corpse over a politician any day."

"As usual, Jacob, you're oversimplifying. Politicians aren't all bad, you know. And I wouldn't classify Riley O'Brien as a politician anyway."

"Politician's offspring, even worse."

Edna turned to face him, her look turning serious. "She's not Lacey."

His ex-wife was a real piece of work, and the fact that her father had been a career brown-noser hadn't helped anything. "There's only one Lacey, thank God. But it's pretty obvious Riley O'Brien is cut from the same cloth."

"I'd be careful about jumping to conclusions, if I were you." Edna's gaze was smug. "You never know when they're going to jump up and bite you in the butt."

Riley resisted the urge to run a hand through her hair. It wouldn't do a thing for her image and, frankly, probably nothing for her peace of mind either. The press conference had been over for an hour, and this was her last interview.

They'd abandoned the tent for the clinic conference room, its subdued pastels at odds with the muted sound of the protestors outside. She'd be grateful to get out of here, away from prying eyes and intense scrutiny.

"You ready?" Maudeen Drake was a beautiful woman; even the fading of youth couldn't change that fact. She was a valuable asset to their political team, and, at least as far as Riley's father was concerned, a valued personal one as well. It was the latter that led Riley to keep the woman at arm's length.

Her father had a right to his own life. And as women went, Maudeen was a good one. But Riley couldn't seem to get past the feeling that her father was somehow being disloyal to her mother. Ridiculous thought—considering her mother had been dead for almost nineteen years—but still one she couldn't seem to shake. With a lift of her chin, she forced herself to focus on the task at hand. "Let's get it over with. It's Edna, right?"

As if in answer, the reporter walked into the room, looking ready for battle, but Riley knew that underneath the razor edges there was a softness. She'd seen it once, a long time ago, at a cemetery in the rain. And she'd never forgotten. Edna was her friend. And Riley knew she couldn't claim many of those.

She relaxed, her smile genuine as she rose to greet the woman.

"Riley, I've brought someone to meet you." No by-your-leave or apology, but then, that was Edna.

Riley's smile froze as the man in the doorway stepped into the room, blue-black eyes mocking her. It was the stranger from the press conference. She struggled to remember his name. It came in a flash. Mahoney. Jake Mahoney.

He wasn't handsome in the classical sense. The lines of his face were too harsh, his jaw already dark with the shadow of his beard. His inky hair was curly, a little too long, and not cut in any discernible fashion. His shirt was expensive and perfectly creased, at odds with the faded softness of his jeans. She had the feeling the contradiction reflected the man himself. And despite herself, she was intrigued. There was an undeniable sense of authority about him. As if he'd been there already and done it all.

She told herself that he was just a man. A journalist at that. But there was no denying the effect he had on her. She felt like a schoolgirl with her first crush. Blood pounded through her veins and Riley fought to hold on to her forced calm. She wasn't a child, and she didn't have a crush. She didn't even know this man.

Maudeen reacted instantly, her face tightening into a polite mask of determination, her eyes meeting Riley's, waiting for a signal. Riley started to nod, to evict the man, to let him know who was really in charge, but somewhere along the way the message missed a nerve ending and she shook her head, holding her hands out to Edna. "Any friend of yours is welcome here."

The woman smiled, taking both of Riley's hands. "Well, I don't know that I'd call him a friend exactly. But I like the boy." She shrugged. "What can I say, I'm a sucker for a pretty face."

Riley didn't believe a word of it. The woman was listed in the dictionary under shrewd, but there was nothing to be gained in arguing the point. And besides, Mr. Mahoney was already in the room, his presence filling it, his strength of will almost palpable.

She met his eyes, keeping hers purposefully cool. "Mr. Mahoney." Her smile slid into candidate's daughter position. No sense in letting him see how much he unsettled her. "I don't believe we've met before."

"We don't exactly move in the same circles." He took her offered hand, and it was everything she could do not to jerk it away. Hot sparks danced along her skin. She blinked, trying to stay focused, confused by the intensity of her reaction to him.

"Meaning?"

"Meaning I don't have much time for the hollow platitudes of politicians." He was dismissive. Almost scornful.

"I see." She frowned. "I'm sorry, then, that you're stuck here with me."

"Don't be." His smile was slow, sultry, his eyes raking over her, his hand tightening on hers. "There are benefits to everything, Ms. O'Brien. One simply has to find them."

"And I'm sure you're very good at that." She narrowed her eyes, her voice one degree colder than frigid.

"I haven't had any complaints."

She swallowed, trying to wrench her gaze away from

his, to find a way to gain the upper hand against this man. Which was probably laughable considering the fact that he'd managed to charm Edna Winston into introducing him. Edna was anything but an easy mark.

"I'd volunteer to leave," Edna interjected with a wry smile, "but I have an article to write."

Riley pulled herself together, embarrassed at the turn of her thoughts. She never let anyone get to her. Not romantically, not sexually, not any way. Ever. And certainly not a reporter. Heavens, she might as well commit political suicide, and take her father right along with her. She was made of sterner stuff.

"Do sit down." Waving at the sofa, she settled herself into an overstuffed chair, keeping her face pleasant, noncommittal. "I've only got a few minutes, so why don't we get right to it."

She sat back, firmly in control again, feeling regal in the wing back. It had been purposefully arranged at just the right angle, the soft light accentuating her to perfection. Sometimes she wondered what the world would think if they could see the real Riley, without the makeup, lighting, and scripted words. Fortunately, it was an idle thought. They wouldn't. They couldn't.

Not the world. Not Jake Mahoney.

No one.

Not if her father was going to be the next President of the United States.

Jake fought for breath, wondering what it was about her he found so compelling. She was a gorgeous woman, but beautiful had stopped doing it for him a long time ago. It was something more, something there in her eyes. Something that called to him.

He shook his head, aware that he was behaving like a befuddled adolescent. Edna was almost smirking. Observant old biddy. He reached into his breast pocket and pulled out a little notebook. All he had to do was keep his focus, get the damn interview, and he was finished with the lethal Ms. O'Brien. Next time Walter called in sick, someone else could pick up the slack.

"Jacob writes for the *Atlanta Journal-Constitution*." Edna shot him a look he couldn't read and waited, eyebrows raised.

"Really?" Riley's comment was polite, her interest obviously feigned. "I thought Walter Finley covered elections."

"He's—indisposed." Jake studied her, wondering if there was fire under all that ice. "I'm subbing. I usually cover homicides."

"More comfortable with the dead?"

"They rarely talk back." He lifted an eyebrow, watching the muscles in her neck contract as she swallowed. He was making her nervous. The thought amused him.

Edna shot him a look, and took control of the interview, launching into a series of questions about Carter O'Brien's plans for Social Security.

Jake took notes by rote, dutifully writing down Riley's answers, his eyes still studying her face. At close inspection it more than lived up to the promise it had held in the larger arena. She was beautiful, all right. Her skin flawless, her long blond hair swept back to reveal a natural widow's peak.

Her eyes were by far her most arresting feature. Large, almost dominating her face, they were a peculiar shade of gray, so pale they were almost devoid of color. Like silver—quicksilver. He frowned, staring at the gibberish he'd written on the page.

Son of a bitch.

He looked up in time to see the corner of her mouth quirk in a half smile, her eyes knowing. She obviously thought she had the upper hand. A challenge if ever he'd seen one. With a slow smile, he took a deep breath, and aimed for the jugular. "Has it ever occurred to you, Ms. O'Brien, that your father is using you? Exploiting your relationship in an effort to gain the presidency?"

There was a moment of shocked silence, Edna's gaze unreadable.

Riley flushed red, then turned white, her silver eyes flashing first surprise, then hurt, and finally anger. "My father is an honorable man, Mr. Mahoney. And he loves me very much. We are a family. And that means we make sacrifices for one another. Make no mistake, I do what I do because I want to."

Riley paused a moment, fighting for control, a calculated mask of polite indifference replacing her anger. "I can't imagine any life other than the one I have. And I know there are thousands of women in America who would love to trade places with me. There is nothing exploitative about our relationship, Mr. Mahoney." Her face remained composed, but her eyes shot daggers. "He's my father. And if I can repay him in some small way for giving me such a wonderful life, then you can be certain I do so voluntarily and with great pleasure."

The lady had spunk, he'd give her that. And Edna was right—she was a pro. Which only made him admire her more. Damn it.

Edna stood up, closing her notebook. "I think that's enough for today." There was censure in her voice. Censure for him.

Jake scrambled to his feet, in shock. Edna should have been applauding him. In fact, had it been anyone but Riley O'Brien, she'd have been right in there with a follow-up. Edna wrote a hard-hitting political column for *Georgia Today*. And her usual mode of operation was to take no prisoners.

Obviously, her friendship with Riley was more than superficial.

"It's always a pleasure to see you, Edna." Riley's smile started out genuine—and dazzling—but when she turned to him, it faded, her eyes turning glacial, her distaste clear. "Enjoy your bodies, Mr. Mahoney."

Who the hell did she think she was? The fucking queen of England? *Christ*. He shook his head, pushing his anger aside, reminding himself that in the grand scheme of things it didn't matter what she thought of him. It didn't matter at all. He didn't need her kind of trouble. What he needed was to stay as far away from the woman as possible.

"Perhaps we'll run into each other again." Her words were emotionless, politically correct. A dismissal.

"Not if I have my way, lady," he mumbled under his breath.

Her eyes widened, unguarded for just a moment, and what he saw there almost took his breath away.

"Interesting man." Maudeen Drake steepled her fingers, elbows resting on the arms of her chair. "Wonder why in the world Edna brought him here?"

Riley shrugged. "With Edna there's no telling."

Maudeen's eyes narrowed in thought. "True enough, but she never does anything without a reason. And I, for one, would like to know what it was."

"Well, I think we can safely assume it wasn't due to Mr. Mahoney's charm."

Maudeen's eyebrows rose. "Were you in the same room I was? I may be over the hill, Riley, but the sparks between the two of you could have lit up a third world country."

"Your imagination was working overtime, Maudeen. I hardly gave the man the time of day." Riley waved a hand airily, pretending disinterest, knowing she wasn't fooling the older woman for a second.

There had been sparks flying, but Riley wasn't about to admit it. Jake Mahoney was trouble of the worst kind. Not that it mattered, because, despite what she'd said, it was unlikely they'd ever run into each other again. They were from different worlds. Which was all for the best, she reminded herself firmly.

"I thought your speech went pretty well, all things considered," Maudeen said, judiciously changing the subject.

Riley pushed aside her tangled thoughts of dark-eyed reporters, focusing on the here and now. "It's always hard for me to tell. The place was packed, but the question is how many were there to see me, and how many were there hoping for some kind of political cataclysm."

Maudeen smiled. "An equal number of both, I'd imagine. I think we can thank the Atlanta P.D. for preventing the latter. Anyway, it's over. And it's time for us to head home."

"Fine by me." Riley turned, rubbing the small of her back. "I'm exhausted."

Maudeen's cell phone rang, the noise jarring after the quiet of the conference room. Holding up a finger, she flipped the phone open. "Maudeen Drake."

Riley glanced out the window at the placard-waving protesters, grateful that the car was parked behind the building. The press was out there now, scrounging for sound bites. She searched the crowd for dark hair, but Jake Mahoney was nowhere in sight. Despite her earlier resolve, she was disappointed.

"Riley." Maudeen had a hand over the mouthpiece of her phone. "Why don't you go on to the car. I'll be right behind you. This'll just take a minute."

Riley nodded, and headed for the door, more than ready to get out of there.

A bored police officer standing outside the conference room came to attention as she walked through the doorway. "You on your way out, ma'am?"

"Yes. The car is just out the back."

"I'll see you out, then." They walked together down the hall in silence, Riley grateful that the man wasn't into small talk. She'd had about as much of it as she could take for one day. Maudeen's car was visible from the back door and Riley felt herself begin to relax.

Almost home.

"Do you want me to walk you to the car?"

She focused on the policeman. "No thanks. I think I can manage on my own." She smiled at him and stepped out into the sunlight.

The days were starting to get shorter, although the heat had still not abated. After the stale frigidity of artificially cooled air, the warm sunshine felt wonderful. Riley tipped back her head and let the rest of her facade drop away. A slight breeze ruffled the trees, the shushing sound comforting, set against a symphony of insects.

She walked toward the car, her thoughts settling on the pleasures of a hot bath. She reached for the car door and was pulling the handle open when she remembered she didn't have Maudeen's keys. With a sigh of frustration, she released the handle and turned back toward the clinic, her thoughts still centered on Rivercrest and a nice soak in the tub.

"Hey, lady, stay the hell away from my car."

The voice was familiar, and she frowned as she recognized the angry figure of Jake Mahoney striding toward her, his eyes widening as he realized who she

was. She continued to walk toward the clinic, trying to
ignore him, but it was impossible to avoid his gaze as he
narrowed the distance between them, his mouth opening with no doubt another angry retort.

He stopped suddenly as sound exploded through the
parking lot, a wave of heat crashing into her from behind. Jake's eyes shifted to something over her shoulder,
fear stark and compelling etching itself across his face.
Her skin prickled with foreboding and she spun around
to look behind her. The car, the parking lot, even the
trees had disappeared, obliterated by a roaring wind of
heat and fire careening across the pavement.

She took a step backward, raising her hands in pitiful
defense as her feet attempted to find the traction to run.
The ground was literally trembling, and just as she
thought the fire would consume her, something hard
and solid hit her from the side, the world exploding into
a cacophony of sound and light.

Chapter 2

"ARE YOU OKAY?" Jake's voice was low and gruff, his breath grazing her ear.

Riley fought against dizziness, trying to remember exactly what had happened. One minute she had been standing in the parking lot, and the next she was part of an asphalt sandwich. And at the moment the top layer of that sandwich was Jake Mahoney, his body warm and hard against hers.

She swallowed against traitorous feelings. "I'd be a whole lot better off if you weren't crushing me."

"Pardon me, princess." His voice was mocking, but he didn't move. "I thought I was saving your life."

Her breath caught in her throat. "Saving me from what?" The minute the words were out of her mouth, she realized how stupid the question sounded, considering the size of the fireball they'd managed to duck.

"The explosion." He rolled off of her, his eyes scanning the fiery debris all around them.

She grimaced, separating herself from the pavement, her breathing gradually returning to a normal rate. "Something blew up?" Again with the stupid response. The man had reduced her to babbling like an idiot.

"No shit, Sherlock." He eyed the smoldering heap of car with something akin to agony. "My *car*." He somehow managed to put enough emotion into the last word to make car-loving men everywhere stand up and salute.

She suddenly wanted nothing more than to reassure him. To take away the pain in his voice, no matter how testosterone-laden the reason for being there. "It wasn't your car. It was Maudeen's."

"Maudeen?" He turned to face her, his eyes narrowed in confusion.

"Yes. My father's press secretary. It was her car."

"I saw it happen, and I think I can recognize my own car." They stood face-to-face now, his blue eyes almost black.

Sirens wailed in the distance. Confusion swept through her. "A black Saab?"

"Yup. Two thousand. Leather seats, turbocharged. Fully loaded. No longer in existence."

Riley frowned at the smoking car. "Maudeen's is a 'ninety-nine."

As if mentioning her name had conjured the woman, she appeared at Riley's elbow, her face ashen, eyes locked on the burning car. "What in God's name happened here? Are you okay?"

"I'm fine. But your car isn't."

Maudeen shook her head, a frown creasing the skin between her eyes. "It's not my car."

Jake turned, his gaze locking with hers. "I told you— it's mine."

"So it's your fault I was almost blown up?"

Jake shot a look at the police officers already crowding around the remains of the car, then turned back to her. "Look, lady, I had nothing to do with my car blowing up, and it sure as hell isn't my fault that you can't tell the difference between your friend's car and mine. To put it succinctly, if it hadn't been for me, you might very well have ended up blown to kingdom come. So I don't think blaming me is exactly appropriate."

She sucked in a breath, moving to stand toe-to-toe with him. "My name isn't *lady,* it's Riley. R-I-L-E-Y. And I didn't mean to accuse you of anything, but I'm working at a disadvantage here." Her voice broke on a sob, and she angrily choked back tears. "It isn't every day that I almost get blown up, Mr. Mahoney. No matter whose car it was. So forgive me if I'm not at my social best."

He reached out and ran a finger along her cheek, his touch almost burning her skin. She shivered and resisted the urge to cover his hand with hers. "We'll find out what happened, Riley. That much I promise you." The words were whispered. Almost intimate. Their gazes collided and held, then a policeman called his name and the spell was broken.

"He's something, all right."

Maudeen's words filtered through Riley's already beleaguered brain as she watched him walk away. He was more than something, actually, but that wasn't a thought she was going to share with Maudeen.

"Come on. Let's get you back inside, and we'll call your father."

She started to tell the woman that she was fine, that there was no need to worry her father, then she realized it wasn't about her at all. It was about the campaign.

Always, it was about the campaign.

"Where the hell have you been?" Leon Bronowsky set the file down on his desk, his eyes on the man in the door. "Pete Rodman has called three times, and Senator Haskins needs your decision on S.468."

"Rodman's an old coot, and Haskins is well aware of

my position. He's just hoping I'll change my mind." Carter O'Brien shot him a crooked grin, his boyish good looks at odds with his age. The man looked absolutely perfect. Not a hair out of place, not a wrinkle in his suit. Which was amazing, Leon thought, when one considered what he'd spent the afternoon doing.

"You didn't answer my question." Leon fought to hold on to his temper. The only way he was ever going to realize his dreams was to keep Carter O'Brien in line. And to do that, he had to keep a civil tongue in his head. No matter what inane things the man said.

"I was just out for a little light recreation." Carter shrugged.

"I wish you'd be more careful." Leon's sigh was staged. He knew better than to try and control Carter's dalliances. "You have an image to uphold. And if that isn't enough for you, there's always Maudeen."

The man's grin widened. "Yes, there is, isn't there?"

Leon sighed again, this time in genuine exasperation. "If she finds out about any of this, there will be hell to pay, and you know it."

Carter sobered, crossing the room to drop gracefully into one of a pair of chairs in front of the desk. "She won't find out. That's why I sent her with Riley. Besides, it isn't as if I'm married to the woman. Hell, the press doesn't even know we're sleeping together."

"My point exactly." Leon reached for a little black ball beside his computer, but stilled his hand before it got there. "A scorned woman is not something to trifle with, Carter."

The smile was back. "I'm not trifling with anyone, Leon. Just having a little fun. While the cat's away and all that."

"I think you have the metaphor wrong way 'round,

my friend." There was nothing mouselike about Carter O'Brien. "More important, you need to think before you act. Now more than ever."

Carter shook his head, laughter creasing the corners of his eyes. "I've been behaving exactly the same way for most of my life, Leon, and I always seem to manage to stay out of trouble."

With a hell of a lot of help. Leon grabbed the ball, flexing his fingers around it. "Just promise me you'll be careful."

"All right. If it'll make you feel better, I'll promise."

"And you'll keep the promise?" Leon hated pushing, but they simply couldn't afford any more mistakes.

Carter shrugged, dismissing the conversation, his handsome face taking on a more serious tone. "Have you talked to Riley?"

"No." Leon kneaded the ball. "But Bill talked to Maudeen and everything went fine."

"Like father like daughter." Carter smiled. "I knew she could handle it."

"It was a risk sending her into that kind of situation, Carter. The whole abortion issue is a powder keg waiting to blow."

"Which is why Riley was perfect for the rally. She never loses her cool, and she appeals to a broad base of constituents."

"And she's Catholic."

"There is that." Carter swatted at a nonexistent speck of dust on his sleeve. "The point is, she's got the innocence and grace to pull off a speech on reproductive rights without seeming heavy-handed. Just what we needed."

"Yes. And according to Bill, she handled it all perfectly."

"Then why are you frowning?" Carter's blue-eyed gaze met his, and Leon broke eye contact. The man simply saw too much.

He sighed. "Nothing really. Bill said there was a reporter baiting her."

"Nothing new in that," Carter said.

"No. But there was just something about the way Bill said it."

"So who is this guy?"

"An AJC reporter named Jake Mahoney."

"I thought Finley covered the political beat for them?"

"Apparently not today. Mahoney usually covers crime. Bill thinks there was some sort of angle because of the clinic. I'm sure it was nothing, Carter. I just wanted you to know."

Carter nodded. "We'll keep an eye on it. I don't want anyone hounding my daughter."

"She can take care of herself."

"Well, as long as she's got me, she doesn't have to, does she?" Carter smiled, but the gesture didn't reach his eyes. "Let's make certain Mahoney doesn't become a problem."

Leon almost felt sorry for Riley. Almost. At the end of the day the only thing that mattered was the campaign. And Riley at her father's side was a crucial part of the package. "Push comes to shove, I'll—"

Carter cut him off with a wave of his hand. "I don't want to know. You do what you have to do, but please, do not bring me in on any of your little espionages."

"Fine. I'll keep you in the dark." Leon dug his fingers into the ball, fighting his anger.

Carter nodded absently, his mind already turning to other things. "So we're clear for the next couple days?"

Leon laid the ball next to the computer, drawing a cleansing breath. "We are."

"Great. I need the time to relax before we storm the Midwest."

"Well, I couldn't justify three days of nothing, Carter. I scheduled the odd reception. But except for that, it'll just be you and your daughter."

Carter's smile was genuine. "That is something I can never get enough of. Just what the doctor ordered, Leon. Rivercrest, Riley, and my roses. The calm before the storm."

"Maybe not." Bill Weasley, Carter's personal secretary stood in the doorway, his face carefully neutral. A redhead, Bill worked hard to keep his emotions under lock and key, and for the most part managed to do a good job of it. But sometimes, like now, there was a hint of something beneath his seemingly calm exterior. "I just got finished talking to Maudeen. There was a bomb at the rally."

Carter's face drained of color. "Is Riley all right?"

Bill nodded. "She was there when it happened, but escaped with nothing more than scratches."

"Thank God." Carter closed his eyes, relief blending with gratitude.

"Was anyone else hurt?" Leon reached again for his ball.

"No one. But it was evidently a close call. According to Maudeen, if it hadn't been for Jake Mahoney, Riley would have been killed."

Leon nodded absently, his mind already trying to sort out the implications of what had happened. There was simply nothing easy about life. Nothing at all.

"There's got to be a way we can figure out who the hell the target was." Jake ran a hand through his hair, frustration threatening to boil over. He glared at the police detective, willing the man to fork over answers.

"I think we've already established that there are a number of possible scenarios and no way to narrow the options down without more information." Riley sounded like a damn telephone recording. Or a primary school teacher.

In the face of everything that had happened, she looked amazingly unaffected. A few scratches and a torn skirt did nothing to detract from the calm serenity she radiated.

He wanted to shake her—among other things.

He closed his eyes and then opened them again, rubbing his face wearily. "So we're left with the fact that someone blew up my car, but we can't say for sure whether it was really *my* car they meant to blow up."

"That's about it." Detective Ferguson looked faintly apologetic. "We'll know more when ATF gets through with their investigation, but the truth is, even then we may never know why it happened."

"I think it's pretty obvious why they did it." Maudeen Drake studied the detective through narrowed eyes. "I mean, this is an abortion clinic, and there were protestors out front. Surely that's motive enough. These people kill all the time for their cause."

"Surely if they'd planted the bomb they'd have given some sort of notice." Riley stood up and walked to the window, the fading sunlight highlighting the gold in her hair. "Or taken credit for it or something. Isn't that the way it works?" She waited expectantly, her attention focused on the detective.

"Something like that. But there aren't any rules, Ms. O'Brien. And the variables here confuse things. First off, there's the possibility it was a random bombing. That would support your pro-lifer theory." He glanced toward Maudeen, who nodded. "But there's also the fact that the owner of the bombed car is an investigative reporter—"

"And I suspect you have your fair share of enemies." Riley shot Jake a telling look.

"No more than a politician's daughter." He tried but couldn't keep the ire out of his voice. How dare she look down her aristocratic nose at him?

"Exactly." Detective Ferguson smiled at them all as if they were prize pupils, totally missing the undercurrent. "Which leaves us nowhere."

"But not for long." David Mackenna strode into the room, his presence dwarfing everyone else. "We found remnants of the bomb." He was a hard-looking man, solid steel with flint for eyes, his straight black hair gleaming almost blue in the conference room's fluorescent light.

"Which means you can figure out who set it," Jake said, studying his friend. The two men had met playing football at the University of Georgia, and been fast friends ever since. While Jake had pursued journalism, David bounced around law enforcement, finally finding his true calling working for the ATF.

There wasn't a bomb made that David couldn't find and defuse, his talents taking on legendary proportions. But more important, Jake trusted him, and quite frankly, he didn't trust a whole hell of a lot of people.

"I don't understand." Riley turned to look at Mackenna, her gaze appraising.

"There's always a fingerprint." David shrugged.

"Fingerprint?" Riley's brows drew together in confusion.

"Not literally," Detective Ferguson explained. "But in most bombings there's something left behind that acts like a fingerprint."

"A signature of sorts?" Maudeen sat on the edge of the table, her interest obviously piqued.

"Exactly," David said. "Every bomber, just like an arsonist, has an M.O.—a preferred methodology. And with careful analysis of the scene, it's usually possible to find something that will help identify the perpetrator. Sort of a calling card."

"And you think you can find this 'calling card' in what's left of the bomb?" Riley sounded doubtful.

"Mackenna is very good at what he does," Ferguson said.

"But in the meantime, you're thinking that this was a random act related to the clinic." Maudeen shifted so she could see the detective.

"I can't say anything for certain, ma'am." He looked to David for confirmation, and the big man nodded. "I don't think you're in any immediate danger, if that's what you're asking. Odds are, whoever did this has already hightailed it out of Atlanta. But you can never be too careful."

"But it was *Mr. Mahoney's* car that was bombed." Riley glared at him, stubborn lines settling around her mouth and eyes.

"A car that just happens to be the spitting image of Maudeen's car," Jake spat out, glaring right back. "Not to mention the fact that my being here was a last minute thing. There's no way anyone could have known I was coming in time to plan a bombing."

Riley continued to frown, but before she could say anything, Maudeen interrupted. "I'd say the best plan is for us all to be careful over the next few days. Until Mr. Mackenna can tell us something more definitive."

"We'll find out who did this," David said. "It's just a matter of time. In the meanwhile, just lay low and watch your backs."

"Laying low is not exactly in the cards for me right now, Mr. Mackenna." Riley's eyebrows rose in wry amusement, almost as if she were laughing at the situation—or herself. Jake's estimation of her rose slightly. Not that it meant he'd let himself be suckered in by a pretty face. He'd played that game before and was still paying for it.

"Just do the best you can," David said.

Maudeen stood up with an authority that implied the interview was over. "It is all right for us to leave now?"

Detective Ferguson rose too, holding a hand out to Maudeen. "We're almost finished here. I see no reason for you to stay. If we have any more questions, we can contact you later."

"Fine." Maudeen shook the detective's hand then turned to Jake. "Thank you for what you did today. I know that Senator O'Brien will be eternally grateful."

Jake doubted O'Brien would be pinning any medals on him, but there was no sense in being rude to Maudeen. "I'm just glad I was there."

"Me too." Riley's voice teased his ear, and he turned to face her, surprised to see an impish quality to her smile. "You certainly know how to show a girl a good time." Maybe there was more to Ms. O'Brien than he was willing to credit her.

He took a step closer, his gaze locking with hers. "I aim to please."

The smile disappeared, and she sucked in an audible breath, her tongue moistening her lips. "I suspect you're quite capable of fulfilling that promise Mr. Mahoney." In one second her look changed from playful to haughty. The ice queen was back with a vengeance. "Unfortunately, it looks like my dance card is full."

He traced a hand along the line of her jaw, satisfied to see a flicker of reaction. "Pity." Dropping his hand, he stepped back, then watched as she swept from the room, Maudeen and the detective following in her wake.

"I know that look." David Mackenna eyed him with an expression somewhere between amusement and exasperation.

"What look? I was just saying good-bye."

"Right. And I'm a shrimpy little guy from Des Moines." David disentangled his six-foot-four frame from the conference room chair, his look telling. "I think she's a little out of your league, kimosabe."

"Maybe." Jake stared at the closed door, his mind's eye picturing blond hair and silvery eyes. "And then again, maybe not."

Fact was, he'd never been able to resist a challenge.

"What's the matter, pretty boy? Having a hard time with the washing?" The burly inmate poked a mop handle in Haywood Jameson's face, making it impossible for him to reach the machine without losing an eye, or at least seriously damaging it.

The man stepped closer, his stance menacing. Haywood sighed, wondering if there was ever going to be an end to the nightmare that had become his life. "Come on, Foster, I've got work to do."

"Yeah. But I ain't certain I'm going to let you do it." The man smiled, revealing a slew of missing teeth. Haywood suppressed a shudder. Nothing in his sheltered southern life had prepared him for men like Foster. Nothing at all. Still, the Jamesons were survivors, and if he wanted to make parole, he had to avoid any kind of disagreement.

"Look, Foster, give me a break. I just want to get this laundry done and get out of here."

"So you can kiss some more shiny white ass?" Foster shoved the mop handle into the soft skin of his throat, and Haywood took an involuntary step backward. "Boy, the way you brown-nose, I'm surprised you ain't covered in shit."

Actually, there was truth to that statement. Haywood wanted to stay alive. And to do that, a man needed protection. And to get *that*, he either had to make nice with the guards or make nice with the prisoners. And frankly, the way the prisoners made nice scared the bejeesus out of him. So guards it was.

Unfortunately, at the moment there wasn't a uniform in sight.

"Back off, Foster." Another inmate, a wiry black man, with chocolate eyes, laid a surprisingly gentle hand on Foster's arm. "No use in starting trouble over that worthless piece of highfalutin trash. It's not worth the risk. I mean, look at his bony ass. Nothing there anyway."

The big man lowered the mop and stepped away. "You right. Ain't no time for trouble." He blew a kiss in Haywood's direction. "Maybe next time, pretty boy." He sauntered off, and Haywood released a breath he hadn't realized he'd been holding.

"You need to be more careful, Jameson. Foster's not a man to be toying with. He's in here for real murder, not some pansy-assed vehicular homicide. Christ, you can't even murder anyone right."

Haywood flinched, but didn't lower his eyes. There were rules in here, and by God, he didn't have a Harvard degree for nothing. His learning curve was damn high. It had to be. Or he'd wind up queen for a day . . . or worse.

"How much time you got left anyway?" Bryce Daniels was no slouch in the crime department either. He'd knocked over a convenience store a while back, leaving three of the employees dead in his wake. But for all that, he was an oddly peaceful man. A live and let live kind of guy. And for some unknown reason, he'd taken a shine to Haywood.

"A year and some change. But the parole board is meeting in a couple of days." He sounded like a school-boy hoping for a date to the dance. A fat one with pimples. As long as Douglas Michaels was the chief of the Atlanta Police Department, he didn't have a chance in hell of ever getting out.

Not that he deserved it.

Daniels narrowed his eyes, seeing far more than Haywood wanted him to. "Who knows, maybe this time it'll be different."

"Maybe so." Haywood tried but couldn't keep the re-sentment out of his voice. "You being considered this round?"

"Yeah, for all the good it'll do me." If possible, Bryce sounded more desolate than Haywood.

"But you're practically a model prisoner."

"Doesn't have anything to do with that, and you know it. Hell, it doesn't even matter that I didn't kill anyone. It's all about who wants you to stay on the in-side." Daniels ground out the words.

"But they told me . . ." Haywood frowned, trailing off, uncertain how to continue, not wanting to offend his only friend. And yet, with startling clarity, he real-ized how very little he really knew about the man.

Daniels jerked his arm in the direction of the other inmates in the laundry. "*They* don't know anything. I didn't murder anyone. I was just in the wrong place at the wrong time." His words were bitter. "With the wrong color skin."

"So we're both stuck here?"

"Looks that way. Which means we best keep our heads down and not make any waves."

Haywood nodded, staring at the tops of his shoes. "I don't know what I'd have done in here without you." He looked up to meet the man's liquid brown gaze.

Daniels face softened, a hint of gentleness in his eyes. "You'd have found your way with or without me."

"Maybe. But I still owe you a lot."

Daniels shrugged, the gentleness swallowed by something harder—almost dangerous. "Just watch yourself, Haywood. There're folks in here who'd like nothing better than to chew you up and spit you out again."

Haywood shuddered, closing the washing machine lid and starting the monstrosity. "I'll be careful. Truth be told, though," his voice cracked with emotion and self-loathing, "there are days when I think I'd almost be better off dead."

Daniels shook his head, his eyes narrowing. "No you don't, Haywood. Believe me, you don't."

Chapter 3

"I'M FINE, DADDY." Riley twined the telephone cord around her finger, leaning back in her chair. "A few scratches here and there, but otherwise unscathed."

"I can be there in an hour, if you need me."

"I know. But there's no point. Besides you're scheduled to meet with Frederick Weatherby, aren't you?"

"It's nothing I can't cancel, darlin'. I don't like the idea of your being there all alone with a bomber on the loose."

Riley laughed. "Hardly on the loose. In all likelihood he's probably out celebrating somewhere, high-fiving with the other right-to-lifers, end of story."

"Honey, a bomb is nothing to be joking about. You could have been seriously hurt."

"But I wasn't, Daddy. I told you, I'm fine. And I'm not alone. Maudeen hasn't left yet, and Adelaide is here. Besides, I'm off to a meeting in just a little while."

"Probably do you good to keep busy. Something to do with the campaign?"

"No, it's for the mayor's council on teen pregnancy. I told you about it."

"I remember." His voice indicated he clearly did not. "So how did the rest of the event go?"

Riley smiled. "Nothing to report at all. The speech went well. The press conference held no surprises.

Mainly questions on reproductive rights. A few others. Mike Brewer asked a lot of questions about tax cuts, and Harvey Mann wanted to know if we were planning to revisit the issue of an equal rights amendment."

"What about this Mahoney fellow?" His voice was casual, too casual. Maudeen had obviously been shooting off her mouth.

"Nothing to tell, really. He was subbing for Walter Finley."

"The old sot." Her father's voice was derisive. "Maudeen thought Mahoney might have upset you."

"Hardly." The man made her light up like a Fourth of July fireworks display, but that wasn't the kind of thing her father was talking about.

"Good. Mahoney isn't a novice."

"You know him?"

"No, but he has a reputation. Let's just say he's been around the block a time or two."

"But not on the political beat."

"True, but a barracuda is dangerous in and out of the water." As usual, her father was talking in analogies.

Anger flared. "Well, he's not a danger to me. I'm not about to get sucked in by a—" She stopped herself. No need letting her father know exactly how much Jake Mahoney had already gotten to her. "—someone like that," she finished lamely.

"I know you won't, darlin'. It's just that I worry. A father's prerogative."

"I know you worry, but you don't have to. I'm a grown woman, Daddy, and there isn't a reporter alive who can get the best of me."

"That's my girl." She heard the pride in her father's voice. "And as much as I hate to admit it, I guess I owe him my thanks."

"I suppose so." She admitted it grudgingly, not liking the idea of being in Jake Mahoney's debt one little bit.

"Well, I'll have Bill send him some scotch or something. That ought to take care of it." Leave it to her father to put a material value on her life.

"At least make it single malt," she said, grinning.

"Done." The smile in her father's voice answered her own. "So I'll see you tonight?"

Riley felt a surge of delight. The house was so empty without her father there. "Wouldn't miss it."

"Good. We'll have dinner. Leon is coming."

Leon Bronowsky was her father's oldest friend and closest adviser. "You, me, and Leon. That'll be nice."

"Maudeen too."

She sighed, resigned to the fact that Maudeen was a fixture in their lives whether she wanted it that way or not.

"Riley, you there?" Now her father sounded annoyed, signaling that he knew exactly what she'd been thinking.

Despite the fact that she was alone in the kitchen, she felt the hot stain of a blush, and ducked her head, feeling all of about twelve. "I'm here, Daddy. Dinner will be perfect."

"I'm glad you're all right." His voice had softened now, and Riley basked in the warmth of his love. "And despite my misgivings, I'm glad Jake Mahoney was around to help. Just watch out for him, all right? Reporters like him are dangerous."

"Only if we have something to hide. Which we don't. Besides, unless I'm dead, he's not going to be interested."

"That's not funny, Riley."

"I know. I'm sorry. I promise I'll stay out of his way, okay?"

"That's my girl." His voice swelled with pride.

" 'Bye, Daddy. I love you." She placed the phone back on the wall, remembering the way Jake's hard body had felt against hers.

He was dangerous all right, but not in the way her father was thinking.

Jake walked into his office, juggling his mail and a Burger King sack, almost tripping over his trash can in the progress. It hadn't exactly been a banner day. First, he'd misplaced a key source, sending the man running for deep cover. Next, he'd had to cover for Walter, bailing the man out yet again, forced to trail around after the ice princess.

And, to add insult to injury, his hormones had mutinied with one look at her holiness, leaving him on testosterone overload. Then, as if his day wasn't already perfect, his car had been blown to smithereens in what appeared to be a bad case of mistaken identity.

Hell, the lady hadn't even been grateful. He'd torn his favorite jeans, lost a hell of a car, and she'd acted like the whole thing was his fault. *His fault.* He sat down in his chair, his traitorous mind happily trotting out images of Riley O'Brien. Silvery eyes and golden hair. A goddess with an attitude he'd just as soon live without.

To hell with that.

She was just a pretty face, and anything else he'd seen was simply imagination. It was over, and he'd escaped practically unscathed, fragmented Saab not withstanding. He should be kissing the floor and thanking his lucky stars. Instead he was mooning around like a lovesick basset hound.

Christ.

He dropped the food on the desk and began sorting

through the pile of envelopes. He'd started having his
mail sent to the office after the divorce. He was never
home enough to remember to pick up his mail, let alone
read any of it. This way at least it stood a fighting
chance. He grinned, lobbing a stack of catalogues at the
trash, the weight of the magazines making the plastic
bin rock.

Propping his feet up, he reached into the sack for his
cheeseburger. Protein, dairy, vegetables, and carbs. The
perfect meal. He took a bite and leaned back, his gaze
settling on the remaining stack of mail. With a sigh, he
set his burger on the desk and reached for the envelopes, opening the top one.

Bill. He tossed it onto the desk and opened the next
few; more bills. What he needed was to win the lottery.
He made a comfortable living. Enough to keep him in
cheeseburgers and beer. But with Lacey always whining
for more money, he was hardly getting ahead.

As if to prove the point, the last creamy envelope was
addressed with his ex-wife's familiar scrawl. If handwriting could talk, this one would definitely sound
southern. Soft and sensual, dripping with honey. Lacey
was a Dixie belle to the core. And to hear her tell it—a
destitute one.

He sent alimony religiously, but it never was enough.
He might not have been good enough for her, but his
money certainly was. She contacted him at least once a
month with a sob story designed to play him like a vio-
lin—and usually she got her way. He was a pushover.
But not today. Today he was ending the cycle once and
for all.

Carefully folding the antique laid envelope into an
airplane, he shot it off toward the trash, grinning. It
arced across the room and dropped neatly into the can,

joining the catalogues. Whatever Lacey wanted, she could find some other sucker to provide it for her. He picked up his cheeseburger and took another bite.

Women were dangerous. If he hadn't already been convinced, spending the morning with Riley O'Brien had certainly proved it. And there he was full circle again. Back to silver eyes and golden hair. He threw the remains of his cheeseburger at the trash can, his stomach tightening painfully.

Damn it all to hell.

"Glad to see you're still among the living." Tim Pierce poked his bald head around the edge of Jake's cubicle, his face reflecting concern despite the flippant tone of his voice.

"Unfortunately, I can't say the same for my car." Jake tried to sound nonchalant and failed.

"I guess it's totaled?" His editor ambled into the cubicle and sat on the folding piece of metal that passed for a guest chair.

"I'd say one step beyond that, actually."

Tim peered at him speculatively through his glasses. "Any idea what it was all about?"

"Logic says it was something to do with the rally, but the police are hedging. So I guess until David makes the bomber, we won't know anything for certain."

"And maybe not even then." Tim shrugged. "So you're left with a hell of a lot of coincidences. Any chance this somehow ties into the Larsen fire?"

Jake reached for his french fries. "I'm thinking not. But never say never. I'm hoping maybe Douglas Michaels will be able to clear things up for me."

"You've actually got an appointment with him?" Tim raised his eyebrows, obviously impressed. "I thought after your phone call he'd run for cover."

"He did." Jake shrugged. "But his secretary told me he was working at home today."

"So you figured you'd just drop by for a little visit with Atlanta's finest." Tim smiled. "I like the way you think."

"Well, let's hope Michaels feels the same way. With Larsen dead, the police chief is our best shot at the truth. And he wasn't exactly forthcoming the first time around."

"I take it there wasn't much left of Larsen's house."

"Nothing usable."

"You're sure?" Tim reached for a fry.

"Positive. I managed to have a look-see right after the fire."

"What about his office?"

"I'm being stonewalled in the regular channels, but I pulled in a favor, and with any luck I'll be getting access to his case files in the next day or so."

"And the girlfriend?"

"Still out if town. But she's due back any day. I'll talk to her then. In the meantime, I need to crack Michaels. If Larsen was right, the man is dirty up to his eyeballs. All I have to do is prove it."

"Drink some more lemonade." The O'Briens' house-keeper hovered over Riley's shoulder, pitcher in hand. Adelaide firmly believed lemonade could bring about world peace if drunk in quantity.

"If I have another sip, I'll float away." Riley smiled up at the woman. "I'm fine. A few scratches here and there, but otherwise unscathed."

"What did your daddy say?"

Riley rolled her eyes. "He said I should have had more protection. Honestly, Adelaide, he acts like I'm a toddler sometimes."

"I think at the moment his concern is more than justified. Someone just tried to kill you."

"No they didn't. It wasn't my car, remember? I was just in the wrong place at the wrong time. And frankly, I think everyone is making way too big a deal about this."

"We just care about you, honey, that's all."

Riley smiled up at the older woman. "I know that. And I can't imagine what I'd do without you. But I'm fine, Adelaide. Honestly. You and Daddy can both just stop your worrying."

"He coming home?" she asked, setting the pitcher on the table, golden bangles tinkling with the movement.

"Not now. He's got a meeting over in Marietta, and I didn't see any point in his canceling just to come hold my hand."

"Wouldn't hurt him to miss a meeting." Adelaide frowned, disapproval coloring her voice.

"We're too close to the prize. He can't afford a misstep at this point, and you know it."

"Canceling a meeting to be with his daughter after she was almost killed is hardly a misstep."

"You're making more of it than is necessary. Daddy will be home tonight. I'll talk to him then."

"Fine. We'll leave it at that." Adelaide raised her hands, shaking her head. "So tell me about Jake Mahoney."

Riley shrugged. "There's nothing to tell. He's a reporter for the AJC. Homicide, which is certainly apropos. He was at the rally covering for someone else. That's it."

"That is not *it*." Adelaide crossed her arms, her look inscrutable. "The man saved your life."

Riley frowned. "Because he happened to be in the

right place at the right time. I'm telling you it's no big deal."

"So who are you trying to convince, me or you?"

Riley blew out an exasperated breath. The woman was too damn observant for her own good. "Neither. I'm stating facts. The man was a boor. He wouldn't know the ballet from the Follies Bergere."

"And that matters?" Adelaide's eyebrows shot up.

"No. Of course not." Riley ran a distracted hand through her hair. "It's just that we have nothing in common. He's a reporter, for God's sake."

"Edna's a reporter."

"Well, it isn't the same and you know it." She felt cornered, as if her emotions were naked for view.

"It's just not like you to be so ungracious."

Now she felt chastised. "I'm grateful, of course. But that doesn't mean I need to grovel at the man's feet."

Adelaide laughed. "I never said anything about groveling. In fact, all I did was ask about the man. Seems to me your Mr. Mahoney affected you a little more than you're willing to let on."

"He's not *my* anything, Adelaide. And he didn't affect me one way or the other." There, she'd said it to Adelaide and she'd said it to herself. Jake Mahoney was just a man. A reporter, at that. Anything else she felt was surely the result of overactive adrenaline or something.

"Far be it from me to nose into your business."

Riley smiled. "That's a laugh. You've been butting into my life since I was old enough to walk."

"I just want what's best for you."

"I know. And right now what's best for me is business as usual." She stood up with what she hoped was conviction. "And to that end, I've got a committee meeting to go to."

Adelaide frowned. "Do you think it's wise to be going out on your own?"

"How many times do I have to say it? There is nothing to worry about. I'm not in any danger. Not from fringe group terrorism and not from Jake Mahoney. In fact, if anyone should be looking over his shoulder, it's him, not me."

"You don't know that for certain."

"No." Riley fought against rising exasperation. "I don't. But it's the logical conclusion. It was his car, after all."

"But it looked like Maudeen's," Adelaide insisted stubbornly.

"Yes. But why would anyone want to hurt Maudeen?"

"They wouldn't. But you're another story entirely."

"I fail to see what blowing me up would accomplish. The sympathy vote alone would get Daddy elected by a landslide. It just doesn't make any sense. I'm sure in a day or so we'll find out the culprits were some overzealous right-to-lifers."

"That certainly doesn't excuse what they did."

"Of course not. But it does mean that I'm in the clear. So, please, stop worrying."

"I can't help myself. I just want you to be safe and happy." Adelaide's eyes were dark with something more than just concern over the bombing.

Riley covered the older woman's hand with hers. "I love you, Adelaide, and I appreciate your concern, but I'm a big girl, and I can take care of myself. Besides, my meeting is at Douglas Michaels's. How much trouble can I possibly get into at the chief of police's house?"

Riley reached for the file in the backseat, grateful for the mundane task. Given the excitement of the day, she could use a strong dose of normal, despite what her father said. And meeting with Douglas Michaels about the teen pregnancy council was just the ticket.

She slammed the car door shut and turned to face the house. Michaels had done well for himself. The two-story colonial was a pristine white, the black shutters adding just the right touch of color. She'd been here once before, but it had been nighttime; so she stopped for a moment to admire the trellis-shaded porch, perfectly accented with pots of colorful geraniums. Gracious living.

With a smile at her own whimsy, she started toward the door, only to stop again when something in the street behind her backfired. Heart pounding, she spun around, her mind replaying the instant inferno of the bombing.

The street was placid, the asphalt road shimmering in the heat. Releasing a breath, she smiled weakly, her concern fading as an ancient car wheezed to a stop, its faded blue finish almost blending into the pavement— except for the splash of red paint near the rear bumper.

She didn't have a clue what kind of car it was, but it had obviously seen better days. And just as obviously, it didn't belong in this neighborhood. Another shiver of apprehension tickled her spine, but she pushed it firmly aside. She'd had a hell of a day, but that didn't mean everything that happened was suspect.

She started to turn away from the dilapidated vehicle, but something about the driver, now emerging from the car, caught her eye. Blue on black.

Jake Mahoney.

And he was scowling.

"What in hell are you doing here?"

She fought against a surge of irritation. Really, the

man was too much. "I think the question is more aptly aimed at you."

"I'm here doing my job." He came up the path, his eyes narrowed against the sun, even his walk challenging.

"Hounding yet another public official?"

"I'd hardly say I was hounding you, Ms. O'Brien. And even if I were, I've paid for it in full." He gestured toward the Rent-a-Wreck.

"I take it your insurance didn't cover a replacement car."

"It didn't cover bombings period. That," he jerked his head toward the jalopy, "was all they had available."

She swallowed laughter, struggling to keep a straight face. "Well, it suits you."

"Thank you so much, your worshipfulness." His manner was anything but grateful. In fact, the word curmudgeon sprang to mind. Curmudgeon with pheromones to spare. The man made her slap-happy.

"So, Mr. Mahoney, what have you got in mind for an encore? Snipers? Napalm?"

"An interview, Ms. O'Brien. All I'm here for is an interview. I'll leave the pyrotechnics to you."

She raised an eyebrow but refused to rise to the bait. "Is Douglas expecting you?"

"First name basis, huh? I had no idea Michaels ran in such exclusive circles." He grinned, neatly deflecting the question.

"I'd hardly call my circles elite, Mr. Mahoney."

"Well, from my point of view, I'd say it doesn't get much snootier."

"Why is it everything you say comes out as an insult?" she queried as they stopped in front of the door.

"Maybe because I mean it that way?" He rang the

bell, and they waited in silence, the tension between them building with every breath. The door remained steadfastly shut.

"I don't understand it." Riley frowned. "We had an appointment."

"Rounding up campaign contributions?" He reached for the doorknob, giving it an experimental twist.

"I'm here for a meeting." She bit out the words, surprised at the level of emotion he raised in her.

He shrugged and pushed the door open. "So let's see if the man's home."

"You can't just go in there," she hissed, wondering if she sounded as priggish as she felt.

Jake's grin was wicked. "But I already told you, I'm good at what I do." He stepped across the threshold. "Coming?"

She squared her shoulders, giving him what she hoped was a glacial look. "I am not."

"Fine." He shrugged, and disappeared into the entry.

She stood at the doorway, debating the wisdom of being anywhere in the same country as Jake Mahoney, then, with a sigh, followed him inside.

"I thought you weren't coming?" His whisper caressed her ear, sending spikes of something she wasn't ready to identify shooting through her middle.

"I thought someone ought to protect the man."

"Oh, and you're just the woman to do it, princess." There was an underlying meaning to his words that set her to shivering all over again.

"Douglas?" She called loudly, shooting a narrow-eyed look in Jake's direction. "Julia? Is anyone home?"

"You know his wife as well?" He sounded amused.

"Of course. What did you think? I was shacking up with Atlanta's police chief?"

He shrugged. "It wouldn't be unheard of."

"Anything for the campaign, is that it? Well, you've got me figured all wrong, Mr. Mahoney. And I'll thank you to quit jumping to unwarranted conclusions."

"Whoa there, princess. Didn't mean to get you all riled up. It's just that in my business we usually call a spade a spade."

"In your business, Mr. Mahoney, everything is a spade if it suits the story."

He touched his hand to an imaginary hat. "And in yours if it isn't a spade, you'll spin it into one."

"Touché." She stopped in the hallway, suddenly aware that she was standing uninvited in the middle of Douglas Michaels's house. "This doesn't feel right."

"Well, nothing ventured, nothing gained. We might as well continue with the tour since we're in."

"Nothing's sacred, right?" She tried but couldn't keep the sarcasm out of her voice.

"Plenty of things are sacred, Ms. O'Brien. But public officials aren't on the list." His tone saw hers and raised the ante. "Does he have a study?"

"It's over there." The words came out before she had time to think better of them. "But you can't go in without his permission."

"Riley, I'm in the man's house. Besides, the door was unlocked. He's bound to be here somewhere."

"Douglas?" She called again. The house remained stubbornly silent. "Maybe he's out back."

"Or maybe he's got the television on." Jake moved to the door of the study, already reaching for the doorknob. "Michaels? You in there?"

Riley took a step forward, only to collide with the muscular steel of Jake's back.

"Holy shit." The expletive was whispered, and the

tone in his voice made the hairs on her neck prickle to attention. She tried to step around him, but he held out an arm, effectively blocking her from entering. "Call 911."

She fumbled for her cell phone, her heart beating a staccato symphony against her ribs as she tried to peer over his shoulder. "What is it?"

"Michaels is dead."

Chapter 4

"OKAY. SO DO you want to tell me what this is all about?" Riley sat down on the front steps of Michaels's house, watching as technicians loaded the plastic-clad body into the ambulance.

They'd spent the last hour answering questions, or rather, Jake had. For the better part of that time Riley had been huddled over the bushes, reliving her lunch, the vivid image of Michaels's splattered remains still making her stomach heave.

"I don't know any more about this than you do." Jake leaned against a pillar, his eyes narrowed in thought.

"Like hell." Anger rocketed through her. "In less than eight hours, I've nearly been blown up, I've broken into a house, I've discovered a dead man, and I'm on a first name basis with a homicide detective. To add insult to injury, all of these truly wonderful events have been tied, in some capacity, to you. So don't you dare tell me that you don't know anything."

"I think you're exaggerating things just a bit. I was here to see Michaels, just like you. And, your opinion of me not withstanding, I hardly think a visit from me would drive a man to suicide."

"I think you underestimate yourself." She shot him a tight smile, anger still churning. The man made her crazy.

49

"Well, no matter the cause, the fact remains that Michaels is dead, and we were the ones to find him. Not an easy thing even for someone with experience in homicide, and certainly not something someone like you should have to deal with."

She lifted her chin defiantly. "I am not made of glass, and I assure you I'm handling all of this," she waved a hand in the direction of the ambulance, "just fine."

"Easy, princess, I was only trying to make nice."

She ground her teeth together to swallow back her retort. Nice, her ass. The man was going for the jugular all the way. "All right. Let's take it one step at a time, shall we?"

He nodded, crossing his arms on his chest. The motion made his biceps tighten, and she found herself staring at the black hair on his forearms.

Riley swallowed, forcing herself to abandon lascivious thoughts in favor of the dilemma at hand. "You told me you were here to interview the man. So, despite what you want me to believe, that means you had something on him, right?"

"I was following a lead, yes."

"A man of many words." She closed her eyes, counting to ten, then opened them again. He was grinning. Damn the man. He thought this was a game.

"Look, reporter boy, whether you like it or not, I'm in the big fat middle of this. And while Douglas Michaels is nothing more than a quarry to you, he's an acquaintance of mine, and I'll thank you not to make light of what happened here. If you know something that might explain why a perfectly normal man would suddenly decide to end it all, I think you owe me that explanation."

"Let me make something perfectly clear, your worshipfulness." He grated out the words. "I don't owe you anything. If Michaels was a quarry, then you can damn well put odds on the fact that he deserved to be one. I report it as I see it, Ms. O'Brien. And if the fat lady sings, then I'm betting someone's pinching her."

"What in the world are you talking about?" She stared up at him, wondering if Michaels's death had affected him more than she'd realized.

He sighed, and sat down next to her, running a hand through his hair. "I don't know. You make me crazy. So I said the first thing that came into my head." It was the first time he'd spoken to her without a sarcastic edge, and she was surprised at how much it pleased her.

"If it helps," she shrugged, "you make me crazy too."

He smiled. "Well, at least that's something."

"So you want to tell me what's really going on?" They were back where they started, but at least there seemed to be a temporary truce of sorts.

He tipped back his head, his look resigned. "I honestly don't know much. A couple of weeks ago I got a call from an assistant D.A. named Hank Larsen. Said he'd stumbled onto something that involved Michaels."

"Something shady." Riley frowned, trying to picture Michaels breaking the law.

"Yeah. Something to do with fixing a trial. Larsen said he had evidence to prove it."

"But he didn't?" Riley asked, confused.

"I don't know." Jake shrugged. "He died before he could meet with me."

Riley's eyes widened in surprise, her breathing suddenly becoming more difficult. "You think someone killed him?"

"Well, officially his death was ruled an accident. His house burned down, with him conveniently in it."

"But you don't believe it was an accident?" Things were rapidly spinning out of control, and even though she wasn't directly involved, it scared her.

"My business is based on the knowledge that everything isn't always what it seems. So I have my doubts. Especially in light of Michaels's death."

"But he killed himself."

He shrugged. "That's certainly what it looks like."

"You're a very cynical man, aren't you?" She studied him through narrowed eyes, noticing for the first time the fine lines around his mouth and eyes.

"Too many years in the newspaper business has a tendency to do that to a fellow, I guess."

Riley had the distinct feeling there was more to the story, but knew better than to ask. Their truce was fragile at best, and she found herself wanting it to last. There was something about Jake Mahoney that reached out to her.

A kind of kinship. Which was a ridiculous notion when one considered the fact that they worked opposite sides of the street. Still, it was there, nevertheless, demanding that she pay attention. She shook her head, forcing herself to focus on the issues at hand.

"So what you have are a lot of unanswered questions and nothing but dead ends."

"Literally."

She winced. "I didn't mean—"

He smiled, the gesture softening the harsh edges of his face. "I know. And you're right. I've got more questions than answers, and not many places left to turn."

"So you quit?"

"No way. In this business, you've got to pick your path and stick to it until you find your story—or until you're positive there's nothing to find."

"And then?"

His smile broadened. "You pick another path."

"So basically you're saying you dig in for the duration."

"Something like that. Investigating can be slow going. It's a matter of asking and reasking questions until you get the right answer. Sometimes that can take a while. But eventually someone lets something slip. All it takes is one little chink and the mountain comes tumbling down."

"What about the bombing?" She turned to meet his gaze. "Do you think it's tied into all this somehow?"

"It doesn't seem likely, but without definitive proof, I can't rule it out completely."

"Another path?" She returned his smile, surprised to find she was enjoying their banter.

He shrugged. "Anything's possible."

"Ms. O'Brien, Mr. Mahoney." Detective Ferguson walked out onto the porch. "You all can go now if you'd like. I don't have any more questions. And if I do," he smiled, "I know where to find you."

Riley scrambled to her feet, suddenly feeling guilty. "Has anyone contacted Julia? And what about Grace?"

"It's all been taken care of. They've gone to her mother's house. I sent a couple of detectives over to talk to them. We'll try and get this," the detective tipped his head toward the house, "all sorted out before they come home."

"There's no need for them to see it like . . ." Riley trailed off, shivering, the image of blood-spattered walls making her physically ill again. Jake's arm slid around her waist, warm and strong, and she leaned against him gratefully.

"I'll see that Ms. O'Brien gets home safely."

The detective nodded, his mind obviously already turning back to his case.

Riley pulled in a breath, letting the motion soothe her rebelling stomach. She swallowed, relieved to be in control again, images of Michaels firmly banished from her mind. *For now.* "Thank you." Her voice was soft, and she was surprised to hear it quiver.

"Not a problem." He dropped his arm, as if noticing their intimacy and rejecting the notion entirely. "You've been through a lot today."

She nodded, keeping her eyes on her shoes, feeling all of about twelve, and sorely missing the contact.

"Shall I drive you home?"

She shook her head, struggling to find her voice. Emotion threatened to overwhelm her, and she felt tears pricking the corner of her eyes. Now was not the time to fall apart. And she certainly didn't need Jake Mahoney to baby-sit her. "No, I'll be fine. I can see myself home, but thanks for the offer."

Everything suddenly felt awkward, as if they were poised somewhere between being strangers and friends. She found herself wishing for the latter, but knew it was impossible. "So I guess this is it. I'm not sure what one says to someone in your line of work." She looked up, her breath catching at the look in his eyes. "Happy hunting?"

His lips curled into a lazy grin, the gesture spreading across his face to his eyes. "Why thank you, ma'am." He doffed an imaginary hat. "Truth is, I always get my man."

She smiled despite herself. "I'll bet you do, at that."

They stood for a moment, gazes locked, saying things that couldn't be said with words. Promises that couldn't—wouldn't—be kept. Then, with a nod, he spun on his heel and walked away. She watched him, his gait confident and sure. He didn't look back. Didn't have to.

He knew she was watching him. Probably knew she wanted him.

But Riley found that she didn't care, because the fact was, he wanted her too.

And even though they weren't about to act on the knowledge, it was something to hold on to in the dark of the night.

"What the hell were you doing at Douglas Michaels's house?" Leon Bronowsky bellowed. Her father's right-hand man was also his oldest friend, and Riley knew that his bark was much worse than his bite, his anger caused by his concern for her.

"I had a meeting scheduled. We're on a committee together. Daddy knew about it." She shot her father a look, but he made a play of pouring his scotch, pretending that he didn't hear. So much for his help. "It wasn't like I planned to find the man, Leon. Believe me, if I'd had a choice in the matter, I wouldn't have been within a hundred miles of the place."

Leon blew out a long breath and steepled his fingers, elbows resting on the arms of his chair. "I suppose in some twisted sort of way it's providential. A police chief's suicide trumps a little bombing any day."

"You sound so callous, Leon. A man died, for God's sake." Carter sipped his drink, eyeing his old friend over the edge of the glass.

Leon raised a hand in defense. "I'm not trying to make light of a tragedy, but at the same time, I can't help but see it as a temporary godsend."

"Temporary?" Riley and her father spoke almost in unison.

"Absolutely," Leon said. "Once they clue into the connection between you, Jake Mahoney, the bombing, and the Michaels death, there will no doubt be rampant speculation."

Riley frowned. "There's nothing to speculate about. There's absolutely no connection between me and anything that happened. Best I can tell, it's just a matter of having abysmally bad timing."

"Doesn't matter." Carter leaned against the living room mantelpiece, the perfect picture of the politician. "Leon is right. For the moment, Michaels's story is enough. But as soon as they catch wind of your involvement, all bets will be off."

"Meaning they'll try and make something of nothing." This was the part of politics Riley hated, and in particular this was why she hated the press.

"I'm afraid it's inevitable," Leon said. "Once they do start to circle 'round you, the trick will be to parlay it into some sort of favorable sound bite."

"It's not just about sound bites." Carter drained his glass in a single swallow, his eyes narrowed with worry. "Riley's been through a tremendous ordeal, and I, for one, won't stand by and see her hounded by the press because of it."

"I don't think there's anything you can do to stop it, Carter." Leon sipped his whiskey, his look resigned. Riley hated it when they talked about her like she wasn't present.

"I won't tolerate it," Carter continued. "We were part of a media circus when Riley's sister died. And I don't want her to go through something like that again."

"Daddy, it's all right." Riley spoke soothingly, more than aware of her father's propensity for loosing his cool. "I don't remember much about Caroline's death, honestly. And as far as this is concerned, it's part of the territory."

"You were almost incinerated today." Carter waved

his glass in the air, the gesture punctuating his words. "That's hardly within the norm."

"That's not what I meant, Daddy, and you know it. Anything that happens to you or to me is public fodder. I don't have to like it, but I do at least accept it. And in the case of something as big as a car bombing, I'd be shocked if the press wasn't interested."

"Especially when you add finding a dead man to the list." Leon reached for the decanter to pour another drink.

"Well, technically, I didn't walk in on him. Jake Mahoney did."

Her father met Leon's gaze, his hand tightening around the smooth crystal of his glass. "And that's another bone of contention. What the hell is the man doing, following you around?"

"I don't think he was following her, Carter." Leon spoke soothingly, but her father ignored him, his attention fixed firmly on Riley.

"Is there something I need to know about this man?"

Anger flashed through her. "Daddy, if there was, it would not be any of your business."

"So there is something." His eyes narrowed speculatively.

"No. I'd never met the man until today. And quite honestly, what I saw wasn't all that appealing." She pictured his probing blue-black eyes and the strong line of his jaw, willing her words to be the truth, knowing they were not. She was lying to her father, and she was lying to herself. Jake Mahoney was attractive on all sorts of levels.

"What do we know about him?" Carter turned to Leon, his gaze now shrewd.

"Nothing that should be cause for alarm. According to my sources, he's a good reporter. Divorced. Worked for the AJC seven years, on the homicide beat for five. Word on the street is that he's tenacious as hell."

"And arrogant," Riley added, unable to stop herself.

Carter nodded, crossing to the drinks table for a refill. "That seems to go with the territory. Reporters are an arrogant lot by nature. They have to be to spend all their time sitting in judgment of other people."

"Well, if you ask me, the press in this country has gone too far." Leon's tone was condemning. "They have no sense of decency. And frankly, if the story will sell papers or bring in ratings, I don't think they give a good goddamn about how much truth is involved."

"I can't argue with that," Carter added. "Truth is an irrelevant commodity in today's hyped-up world, and the press is leading the debaucherous parade."

"Well, then it's all the more important that we get Daddy elected." Riley smiled at the two of them—her family, such that it was. "Maybe he'll be able to stop some of it."

"Stop some of what?" Maudeen Drake stood in the doorway looking coolly elegant in a black silk dress.

"The press's rush to misinform," Carter said. Riley watched as her father crossed to the older woman, holding out both hands. "You look beautiful as always."

"Thank you, Carter." Maudeen's smile was luminous.

Riley bit back a comment. It wouldn't do to start a fight. Besides, part of her was ashamed of her animosity. Her father deserved someone in his life. She watched as they settled side by side on the sofa, and wondered for the millionth time how different things would have been if her mother and sister were alive.

"We were just telling Riley that she should beware of Jake Mahoney and his ilk."

"Daddy and Leon think he's going to eat me alive."

"Nonsense." The older woman smiled. "You've been handling reporters since you were little."

An image of mocking blue-black eyes begged to differ. Riley blinked, clearing her head. "Of course I have," she answered, with more conviction than she felt.

"Well, I think it best for everyone if you stay away from Mr. Mahoney." Her father leaned forward, his eyes intense. "If nothing else, he seems to invite trouble."

"Daddy, I've only talked to the man two times. You're overreacting."

"Maybe so, but we're awfully close to winning this thing. And I don't want anything to upset the apple cart."

"Fine. It's not likely I'll see him again anyway." Leon and Carter exchanged a look, and Riley was immediately suspicious. "I don't need you to go fighting my battles for me." Leon opened his mouth to answer, but Riley held up a hand. "I mean it, Leon. I'm a grown woman and a seasoned political veteran. You've got to stop handling things for me, and let me take care of myself."

"It's only that we love you." Leon's tone was sincere, but Riley had her doubts. Leon loved her, all right, but she knew he loved winning more. Fortunately, they played for the same team.

"I know that. And I'm grateful that you want to watch out for me. But Jake Mahoney isn't a risk. There's nothing he can do that will hurt me or endanger this campaign."

Well, there was some truth in that.

Sort of.

Jake Mahoney had the potential to do lots of things to her, but they had nothing to do with her father or the campaign.

Chapter 5

"YOU'RE GOING TO clog the few arteries you have left."
Jake sipped his beer, watching his friend pour extra
gravy on his chicken fried steak. It was past dinnertime
at the OK Café, but the place was still hopping.

David Mackenna stabbed a forkful. "If it's worth eating, it's worth eating right."

"I'm not sure your doctor would agree." Jake
grinned, then sobered. "I suppose it's too soon to have
any news on the bomber."

"It hasn't even been twelve hours. I'm good, but not
a miracle worker."

"I know." Jake ran a hand through his hair. "I'm just
frustrated. The world seems to be falling apart and I
can't explain it."

"You're talking about more than the bombing, I take
it?"

"Yeah. Michaels. His death has got to be tied to
what Larsen found, but I'll be damned if I know how.
Nothing Larsen told me can be substantiated. It's innuendo at best. And Michaels's death is just another damn
door closing." He slammed a hand down on the table,
then blew out a long breath. "God, I didn't mean that the
way it sounded. Maybe I am a cynic."

David raised an eyebrow. "Been doing some soul
searching lately?"

Jake shook his head. "More like I've been searched. Riley O'Brien practically accused me of manipulating tragedy for a story."

"Well, there's probably a little truth in what she says." Jake opened his mouth to retort, but David held up a hand. "But you're a reporter. Taking the facts and turning them into a story is what you do. If that means playing off of tragedy, then so be it."

Jake suppressed a smile. "Now you sound like the cynic."

"Well, in my line of work, it's hard not to be." David lifted his glass in a mock toast. "So I guess that makes us two of a kind."

"And one of us without any answers. I tried to talk to some of the chief's buddies this afternoon, but no one had anything helpful to say. In fact, truth be told, some of them were downright hostile."

David shrugged. "Law enforcement is a private club, especially when something like this happens. I'll see what I can find out."

"Thanks. Maybe there'll be something there. All I got was the party line. To hear them tell it, the man had a perfect life. Nothing at all that would suggest thoughts of suicide. Which doesn't change the fact that he's dead. Tomorrow I'm going to talk to the M.E."

"You're thinking Michaels was murdered?" David buttered a piece of corn bread.

"It seems within the realm of possibility. Not that it changes anything. Suicide or murder, the truth is, I don't know for certain that Michaels's death is related to any of this. To hear Larsen tell it, I wouldn't have thought his information was that damning, but now I'm not so certain." Jake sat back, draining the last of his beer. "You still investigating the fire?"

"Unofficially. Something about it just doesn't feel

right, and I won't rest easy until I have the full picture." David pushed back his plate. "But I've got to say, odds are the whole thing was exactly what it appears to be."

"An accident." Jake sighed. "Which leaves me back at square one."

"Larsen."

"Exactly. And the first thing I've got to do is try and figure out what the hell it was he found. He was working on six cases when he died, so maybe it was through one of them that he stumbled on the information about Michaels. Hopefully by tracing his steps, I'll be able to put it all together."

"Sounds pretty impossible to me."

"Well, for a start I've got an appointment day after tomorrow with a guy I know at the D.A.'s office. I need to get a look at Larsen's files. And there's the little matter of his girlfriend. Seems she headed for the islands almost before Larsen's body was cold. She's due in tomorrow, and I'm hoping maybe her hasty departure has something to do with what she knows." He stopped, staring into his beer glass, frustration cutting through him with the precision of a butcher's knife.

"What about the bombing?" David sat back, his gaze appraising.

"I honestly don't think it's related, but I guess I can't afford to rule it out without at least checking on the possibility. Maybe Riley O'Brien knows more than she's telling."

David frowned. "You don't seriously think she's involved in any of this?"

"She was present at the bombing and then at Michaels's house. It bears examination, at least. Bottom line is, I can't know anything for certain until I talk to her, and to do that I've got to find a way to get the woman to open up to me."

David took a sip of his beer, eyeing Jake over the rim of the glass. "Then I'd say you have your work cut out for you."

"She isn't an easy person to talk to," Jake agreed. Riley O'Brien was more prickly than a porcupine with a dog on its ass.

David laughed. "I was referring to *your* less than stellar record with women."

"Hey, Lacey screwed me, not the other way around. And as far as Riley O'Brien is concerned, she's a potential source of information, nothing more."

"Right." David leaned back, crossing his arms, the smug look on his face making Jake want to punch him. The man didn't miss much.

"Look, I'm telling you, any interest I have in her is purely job related. She was present at the bombing and she was at Michaels's."

David's smile grew to a full-fledged grin. "I still think your interest goes beyond professional."

"Think what you want. But I guarantee you're on the wrong track. I've been there and done that. I was married to the empress of ice, remember?"

"And you think Riley is made of the same stuff?"

"I know it. Pure ice." And fire. Sweet, sweet fire. Jake fought the image his mind was conjuring. An image of Riley lying on his bed, hair flowing around her, eyes wide with passion.

"I don't know, there are worse ways to go." David had been reading his mind for years. It was a habit that made him very good at what he did, but rather annoying as a friend.

"Look, I'm not taking that kind of chance. I've got no desire to repeat my mistakes."

"Sounds to me like the woman got to you, ice queen or no."

He pictured silvery eyes, and his hand clenched as he thought about the soft gold of her hair. Silver and gold. All the riches a man could possibly want. He shook his head, banishing his ridiculous thoughts.

"No way. The woman's untouchable. I couldn't reach her even if I wanted to—and I'm telling you, I don't."

"Fine. I get it. Your interest in her is only related to your story."

"Exactly."

"So follow your gut then and find the story." The right side of David's mouth quivered, jerking upward into a half smile. "And who knows, maybe somewhere along the way you'll figure out how to rescue the princess."

"Christ. It's midnight." Carter O'Brien rolled onto his back, oblivious to the fact that he pulled the covers with him.

Maudeen Drake sighed, and pulled the sheet firmly back to her side of the bed. For a woman who'd spent the last two hours in the arms of the man she loved, she felt oddly empty. Depleted in a soul-deep kind of way. "I didn't know you were watching the clock." The words came out on a pleading note, and she hated herself for it.

Carter sat up and shot her one of his megawatt smiles. A smile designed to win over an electorate. "Come on, darlin', you know that I'm not. It's just that I've got an early meeting in the morning." It was his way of telling her to go home. Maudeen fought against her resentment. "You shouldn't have stayed this long."

"No one cares that I'm here, Carter. Leon and Adelaide have gone home, and Riley isn't a little girl anymore. She's a woman now, well able to accept the fact that we're together."

"It's not that." He caught sight of himself in the mirror, brushing his hair back with careful fingers. "She's had quite an ordeal. I should be there for her."

"She's asleep, Carter." Maudeen swallowed her exasperation, pasting on what she hoped was a pleasant smile. "But if you think it best, I'll go home."

Again she had a fleeting moment of melancholy. She'd been with Carter for years. Loved him most of them. Slept with him for at least half of them. And yet, in some ways they were no closer than when he'd hired her thirty years ago.

"That's my girl." Carter patted the sheets absently. "I knew you'd understand."

She didn't, but now wasn't the time to press the point. She pulled on her clothes, heedless of whether she was doing buttons right or wrong.

Oblivious of her distress, Carter propped himself up against the pillows. "First thing in the morning, I want to have a word with the security folks."

She slid the zipper of her skirt closed. "I thought you'd refused an escort." Since winning the primary, Carter had had the option of Secret Service protection, and, at least until now, he'd summarily dismissed the idea, valuing privacy over security at all costs.

"I did." The sheet dropped as he shifted, and she sucked in a breath, as always, awed by the sheer physical power of him. He wasn't a big man in the traditional sense, but he was solidly built. No middle-age spread. Middle age. Who was she kidding? They'd both seen middle age a long time ago. "But after last night's scare, I think it's worth revisiting the issue. At least when we're away from Rivercrest." He shrugged, sighing.

She reached for his brush. "So you're telling me from now on we're going to have Secret Service men following us?"

"Just Riley and I." He smiled, his grin almost impish. "And not for a few more days. I think we deserve a swan song." There was more to his words than Secret Service. Maudeen fought against a shiver.

She pulled the brush through her hair. "A swan song." She tried but failed to keep the sarcasm out of her voice. She loved Carter O'Brien. Loved him with everything that she was, but she wished that there were a way to separate the politician from the man.

She smiled at her own foolishness, knowing full well that the politician *was* the man.

"Ah, come now, Maudeen." He reached over to pat her, his smile contagious. "Everything I do has to be for the good of the campaign."

"You're preaching to the choir, Carter." She tried for a smile but missed.

"In just a few more months it'll all be over, and I'll be standing at the podium taking the oath of office." He wasn't even listening to her.

She leaned over, placing her hands on his shoulders. "You'll need somebody by your side."

"I've got Riley." He pulled away—distancing himself. "You know that's the way of it. You've known it from the beginning."

And so she had. Still, there were days when the subterfuge of it all got to her. Days when she just wanted for them to be a normal couple. When she wanted to shout to the world that she loved him, and that he loved her.

But that was a pipe dream. Stuff and nonsense. She swallowed her bitter thoughts. Unless something dramatically changed, it was obvious they were on the fast road to nowhere. And she, for one, wasn't about to sit by and watch Carter's rise to power destroy their relationship. She'd given Carter her best years. Riley wasn't the only one who deserved to stand at that podium.

Carter leaned over to kiss her, his lips starting fires deep inside her. She reached up to pull him closer, but with a lithe twist he was free, swinging up out of the bed. "You're talking to the NBC folks tomorrow, right?"

He disappeared into the bathroom without waiting for an answer, his voice rumbling through the doorway, sounding strangely disembodied. "Make certain Leon is aware of the agreement. I wouldn't want any problems with our favoring one network over the other. And will you help me to remind Bill to make sure Senator Hutchinson gets the flowers we talked about? She came through for us when we needed it. And I'll not have her thinking I've forgotten." He appeared in the doorway, his thoughts already centered on tomorrow.

Her lover was gone, consumed by Carter O'Brien, presidential candidate.

And, God, how she hated the candidate.

It was dark. Deep, impenetrable black. And cold. Icy cold. Riley shuddered and tightened her arms around Mr. McKafferty, the little bear offering comfort, his ragged fur and tattered bow a reminder of all things safe and good.

She wasn't certain where exactly the little bear had come from. She hadn't seen him in years, but just at the moment she was grateful to have him here with her. At least she wasn't alone. She fought back a sob, her eyes frantically searching for even a glimmer of light.

Nothing. She might as well be blind.

The wind whistled and moaned, stirring the soft hair around her cheeks, the sound almost human. A keening wail. Or a scream. It whipped at her nightgown, icy fingers trying to shred the cotton. She shivered again and tried to move forward, but her fear kept her bound in place, surrounded by wind and darkness.

She closed her eyes, and then slowly opened them, hoping against hope she would find herself safely in bed, away from the blackness—the wailing. But she knew it wasn't possible.

She had been here before.

The pounding of her heart echoed in her ears, a strange counterpoint to the moaning of the wind. The fury of the storm increased, its presence reaching through the night, surrounding her with malevolence. She shivered and clutched the little bear tightly, eyes straining into the darkness.

"Caroline?" Her voice was lost in the sound of splintering glass.

She sucked in a breath and tried again. "Daddy?"

White light stabbed through the darkness, hurting her eyes with its brightness, and she took a hesitant step forward, knowing that light meant safety. Escape from the dark.

But something stopped her. Something deep inside. A newfound terror that was greater than anything she'd felt before. Time stood still as she focused on the bar of light that spilled into the dark corridor. She sucked in a breath, her fingers digging into Mr. McKafferty's soft reassuring fur, and took another step, and another.

A clap of thunder split the night, and the light dimmed then brightened, white turning red. Deep crimson. The color of lipstick. The color of blood. The light reached for her, oozing forward, more frightening than the dark had ever been. She stood frozen, unable to run, waiting for the light to find her, to destroy her.

Clutching the bear, she summoned the last of her strength, and opened her mouth to scream. . . .

"Riley, honey, wake up." Maudeen sat on the side of the bed, reaching over to shake the sleeping woman, the gentle green glow of the clock casting pale illumination across the room.

Riley moaned, then slowly opened sleep-clouded eyes. "What happened?"

"You had a nightmare." Maudeen sat back, uncertain what to do. From the time Caroline died until shortly after her mother passed away, Riley had had horrible nightmares, but they'd stopped almost as abruptly as they'd begun, and, as far as she knew, they hadn't returned. Until now. "Are you all right?"

"I think so." Riley sat up, running shaking fingers through her hair, and frowned. "What are you doing awake?"

Maudeen contained a smile, noting that Riley wasn't surprised to find her at Rivercrest, only that she was awake. Carter seriously underestimated his daughter. "Actually, I was just going home. Shall I call your father?"

"No. Leave him be. I'm fine now. I'm sorry if I worried you."

"You're sure?" She searched Riley's face for some sign that she was really all right.

"Positive." The younger woman smiled weakly, nodding, almost as if she were trying to convince herself. "It's just been so long since I've had the dream."

"So it was the same?"

Riley nodded, her beautiful face clouded with pain. "Why would it come back now—after all this time?"

"Honey, you've had a hell of a shock to your system,

and even though you're pretending everything is all right, the truth is, you almost died today. And that's enough to make anyone have bad dreams." She reached for Riley's hands, giving them a squeeze. "And when you factor in what you witnessed at Douglas Michaels's, well, I'd be shocked if you weren't having nightmares."

"I just don't want it all to start again. I thought it was behind me."

"Caroline, you mean?"

She nodded. "And my mother. I love them, Maudeen, but remembering is so painful. It's easier just to forget." Guilt washed across her face, and Maudeen wished she could take it all away. Riley had experienced too much pain for someone so young.

"My father always said it's best to face things head on. Maybe that's all your dream is trying to tell you." She gave Riley's hands another squeeze, then reached over to turn on the lamp. They both blinked, then laughed awkwardly, the intimacy of the moment vanishing with the light.

"I'm all right now, really." Riley's voice sounded calmer. "You go on. I'll read awhile and then try to sleep."

"All right then." Maudeen reached over to give her a last pat. "I'll see you in the morning."

Riley nodded, closing her eyes, and Maudeen turned to go, wishing she could do something more, something to help set Riley free of her nightmares once and for all.

Chapter 6

THE MEDICAL EXAMINER'S office smelled of death and formaldehyde, the sweet stench hard to stomach first thing in the morning. Jake followed Megan Green as she walked across the room to a cubicle in the corner.

"There's no question, he killed himself." She pulled back the curtain, exposing the lifeless form of a teenage girl. Jake swallowed to keep from gagging. "There were powder burns on his fingers, and the trajectory of the bullet and the angle of the entrance wound are consistent with a self-inflicted gunshot." She picked up a scalpel and Jake fixed his gaze on a water stain high on the wall. "An open and shut case, actually."

"Did you establish a time of death?"

"Somewhere between eight and ten, I'd say. He'd been dead about half a day when you discovered the body. So what's your interest with the police chief anyway?" She paused, scalpel in hand, curiosity crinkling her forehead.

"Well, aside from the fact that I found him, he has a connection with another case I'm investigating. You did the autopsy on Hank Larsen, right?"

"Not much to autopsy." She leaned over the girl's body, and Jake concentrated on the water stain.

"But you established cause of death as suffocation."

"Right. It takes longer than you think for a human to

burn. In most cases, when someone is trapped in a fire, the victim smothers long before he burns to death."

"And there was no sign of foul play?"

"Jake," she stopped and turned to face him, "we've been through this before. The man's house caught on fire and he died before he could get out. End of story."

"Cut and dried."

"Nothing is cut and dried. But sometimes things are more straightforward than they seem. Did somebody set the fire that killed Larsen? Maybe. Can I prove that through his autopsy? No way." She resumed her work with the body. "I heard you had your own brush with pyrotechnics yesterday."

"Yeah. My car decided to spontaneously combust."

"Way I heard it, it was supposed to be Riley O'Brien's car."

"Her father's press secretary's, actually."

"So you think it was a pro-life thing?"

"I don't know. I guess the trick now is to try and find out."

"If anyone can do it, I suspect it'll be you. I'd lay odds the bomb wasn't for Riley, though."

Jake raised his eyebrows in surprise. "You know her?"

"Slightly. Mainly by reputation. But she's well thought of in Atlanta. Done a lot for the city."

"That's what politicians want you to think, Megan. It's called spin."

"Cynical this morning, aren't you?" She dropped an unnamed body part into a bag, sealing it with a quick twist.

"It seems to be a common opinion."

Megan shot him a questioning look, then turned back to the table. "Well, Riley O'Brien is more than a politician, Jake. I sit on the mayor's council for teen pregnancy with her."

He tried to contain his surprise. "Seems to be a popular committee."

"It's important work," she said, continuing to work. "Bartlett wanted a cross section of the community."

"More like a roll call of Who's Who in Atlanta. You, Michaels, Riley."

"You've really got a stick up your ass, don't you?" She waved her scalpel at him. "The council is important, Jake. And without heavy hitters like Riley, we'd never have any success. She's been phenomenal. Knows who to push and just how far to push them. Half the things we've accomplished were due directly to her involvement. Maybe in your mind that's political, but in mine it's about caring. And Riley really cares."

"All right already. So you're an O'Brien supporter." Jake held up his hands, taking a step back.

"Not across the board. I'll take the daughter, but pass on the father, if you don't mind. Carter O'Brien seems more interested in Carter O'Brien than anything else. In my opinion, he's the one to be cynical about." She turned back to her work. "But then, I'm a Republican."

"I won't tell anyone." Jake laughed. "And I wasn't maligning the council, honestly. Just curious about the connection between Riley and Michaels."

"Because she was at his house yesterday?"

"Yeah. She mentioned the council to the police. I was just curious."

Megan looked up with a frown. "You're not 'just' anything, Mahoney. You're thinking there's some kind of connection between what happened to Michaels and the council. Or maybe between the bombing and the council."

"I'm not thinking anything. I've just got a hell of a lot of pieces and nothing that seems to fit together."

"I'm sorry I wasn't able to help."

It was Jake's turn to shrug. "You can't tell me more than they tell you." He nodded at the girl's body.

"I only wish I could." Megan waved absently, turning back to the job at hand. Jake walked down the hall, trying to keep his breathing shallow, his mind still on the senator's daughter. He was grasping at straws, trying to make pieces fit into places they probably didn't, but the next order of business seemed to be a talk with Riley O'Brien.

The pertinent question was whether it would help matters or only make them worse.

And based on his physical reactions to Ms. O'Brien, he had the uncomfortable feeling it was definitely going to be the latter.

It was one of those in between days, a last hoorah for summer with an insistent push from fall. There was a storm building off toward the west, the air heavy, humid and warm, but there was also an undernote of autumn, a hint of chill, a different smell. Riley walked through the towering pines breathing deeply. This was her favorite time of year. The world was peaceful, beginning to settle down for a long winter's sleep.

If only she could capture some of that peace. But she couldn't. She was trapped somewhere between the past and the future. There was so much riding on the next few months. Everything her father had worked for was coming together in one single moment. One vote. And even though there would be another day, this was the moment. The moment when all the press conferences, the strategizing, the dreaming would come to fruition.

And Riley would be the First Lady. After a fashion.

She wondered if her mother would have liked the job. Probably not. Deirdre O'Brien had been a fragile fairy of a woman. Barely five feet in her stocking feet, she'd been the heart of their family. But when Caroline died, everything changed, the balance shifting to the macabre, her mother wasting away, certain that with the loss of her firstborn, life simply wasn't worth living.

The fact that there was a second, *living*, daughter hadn't mattered at all.

Riley fought against a wave of bitterness. It was over, part of the past. And she'd moved on—or at least tried to. Until last night. And the dream. Nebulous and abstract, it still reeked of a time she wanted to forget. As long as she lived, and remembered, a part of her sister and mother lived on, but if she let them, the memories would consume her. So the trick was to keep the painful memories separated from the pleasant ones.

She pushed open the gate, stepping into the tiny graveyard. Her sister's grave was off in a well-tended corner, the stone startling white against the creeper-laden fence. Riley felt a rush of sadness—for all that had been, and for all that could never be.

Her mother's stone was almost in the center of the cemetery, next to an open space intended for her father. She swallowed tears. The pain of the past suddenly seemed overwhelming.

She'd needed her mother. Wanted her. But her mother hadn't been able to let go of Caroline, and in the end had chosen death rather than to live on without her. Riley knelt by the headstone, running her hand over the smooth face of the marble. So many things would have been different if her sister had lived.

But she hadn't.

And there was nothing Riley could do to bring her

back. Or her mother. They were gone. And she and her father were here. And *because* of everything that had happened, they shared a bond that couldn't be broken. They were survivors.

Riley frowned. Not just survivors. Winners. She and her father had risen above tragedy. They'd made a life together. And now they were on the eve of reaping all that they'd sown. Her father was going to be the next President of the United States.

There was still the matter of the election, but the polls were clear. Barring catastrophe, Carter O'Brien would win. She traced the carving that spelled out her mother's name. The cost had been high, but they remained winners. She should be ecstatic. But she wasn't. She leaned her head against her mother's headstone.

Truth was, all she wanted to do was cry.

The house was stately. A remnant of an era gone by. Jake stepped out of his car, his reporter's mind taking in the graceful sweep of its columns and white painted facade. There was an understated style to Rivercrest, evident from the moment a visitor turned into the magnolia-lined drive. Not exactly the porticoed magnificence of a southern plantation, but still an elegant reflection of the grandeur of the old South.

According to his research, the house had been built by Neel Reid in the 1920s for one Elliott Riley. From there it had passed from family member to family member until it reached the last of them. Deirdre. Upon her death, it had passed to Carter, and would one day, no doubt, belong to Riley.

Riley.

He shook his head, trying to banish the image of honey hair and silvery eyes. He sucked in a breath, buried his hands in his pockets and considered the best approach. The idea was to breach the mansion and capture the ice queen. Or at least catch her unaware.

And hopefully keep his wits about him in the process. The divine Ms. O had a habit of setting his blood to boiling, and he wasn't certain he could keep his cool indefinitely. Still, nothing ventured nothing gained. And if Riley could shed light on his investigation, it was worth a little discomfort.

He strode to the front door and rang the bell, plastering on what he hoped was an irresistible smile.

The woman who opened the door was a cross between regal and pixie. Her short gray hair curled around her head in a riot, framing a surprisingly unlined caramel-colored face. In her day, she had been a beauty, and the aura of it lingered still.

But it was her eyes that held his attention. Soft brown with a hint of something more. A woman one did not trifle with.

"Who are you?" she asked in a take-no-prisoners kind of voice only certain women can affect. Something to do with progesterone, he guessed.

He swallowed and, if he'd had a hat, he'd have whipped it off his head. "Jake Mahoney, ma'am."

"The reporter." She tilted her head back, her dark eyes surveying him critically. "Why are you here?"

"To see Riley." That seemed obvious.

"I know that." She shot him another look. "But why?"

He took a deep breath, trying to look charming. "I have to talk to her."

"As a reporter or a man?" The woman waited, and he knew this was secret password time. Unfortunately, he didn't have any idea what game they were playing at. *If in doubt, boy, tell the truth.* He could almost hear his father's voice.

He met the sprite's gaze full on, holding his steady. "Both."

The woman studied him for a bit and then smiled gently, evidently liking what she saw. "She's out back." She cocked her head toward the back of the house. "With her mama. You go on and find her." Then, still smiling, she closed the door in his face.

He stood there for a moment, bemused. The woman was definitely an enigma. Or a nutcase. Shaking his head, he started to walk around the house, hoping the old gal hadn't tricked him into rottweiler territory.

The house looked even larger from the back. A long wing ran perpendicular to the main structure, an obvious addition, and off to his left, amid overgrown vegetation, he could just see the top of an outbuilding of some kind. There were roses everywhere, some pruned to prize-winning perfection and others tangled together in wild masses of color.

The yard itself was cropped to golf green quality, broken only by circles of chrysanthemums edging strategically planted trees, nature held at bay by a rickety looking hurricane fence. The gate lay open invitingly, and although there was no way to be certain, Jake's instincts told him that Riley was out there somewhere.

But not with her mother. Despite the older woman's words, he knew better. Deirdre O'Brien was dead. He frowned at yet another puzzle and walked through the gate. At least there hadn't been a dog.

The forest was silent, the only sound the slight rustle of the wind high in the pines. Even with all the years he'd spent in Atlanta, he hadn't gotten used to the trees. They were so tall. And, unchecked, so dense it was hard to maneuver. Having spent the better part of his life in the coastal plains of Texas, he found any trees at all amazing, but Georgia pines were awe-inspiring.

He strained to see a flash of something human among all the green and brown, but nothing jumped out at him, and it occurred to him that perhaps the old gnome had sent him on a wild goose chase.

Gullible.

So much for trusting one's elders. He almost turned back, but a spot of white caught his attention. He moved forward, trying to keep silent. There was a sort of clearing here—and a fence. He could just make out the solid line of the creeper-covered stone. No kudzu in the O'Brien woods.

The white spot took on substance. A gravestone. He shivered. Her mother—Riley *was* talking to her mother. He stopped at the gate, suddenly feeling like an intruder. Hell, he was an intruder. She was kneeling in the far corner, her head against a stone. There was something so lost and lonely about her that he wanted to reach for her, to somehow make everything all right.

He shook his head, realizing it was only an illusion. She was made of ice; he'd seen her in action. Still, something deep inside him, something more powerful than reason, drew him forward. He wanted to go to her, to pull her into his arms. He'd actually taken a step when she heard him and looked up.

Tears glistened on her face, and there was nothing cold or forbidding about her. Instead, the haunted look was back. Like a doe trapped in a hunter's sight. He felt a wave of revulsion. *He* was the hunter. She rose slowly to her feet, her eyes never leaving his. Leaves and grass clung to the long lines of her jeans-clad legs, and her hair hung loose, almost to her waist, gold highlights flashing as she moved.

"What are you doing here?" The transformation was almost instant. Peasant to royalty with only a sentence. Her eyes cleared, her face hardening, locking her soul inside. The ice queen was back.

"The woman at the door told me you were back here." He leaned against the gatepost, waiting to see what she'd do next. There was something compelling about her, no matter which persona she adopted. With the one, he found he wanted nothing more than to chip away at the ice until he revealed the woman underneath. With the other, well . . . if he ever had the chance, he knew exactly what he'd like to do with *her*.

She shivered, despite the heat, as though she knew exactly what he was thinking, then shook her head, as if dispelling the thought. "Adelaide?"

It took him a moment to remember what they were talking about. The woman at the door—Adelaide—a fitting name for a sprite. He almost smiled, but the intensity of her gaze made him think better of it. "If she's about this high," he raised a hand to his chest, "and looks like a gnome."

The corner of her mouth quirked upward, but she quashed it before it could turn into a full-blown smile. "I don't think she'd appreciate being called a gnome." She lifted her chin in an imperial sort of way, and Jake fought the urge to bow. "And she'd never send you back here, unless . . ." She stopped, her eyes searching his.

"Unless she thought I could be trusted." He took a step toward her, and she took one back, her progress stopped by the slab of marble behind her.

"This is private property." The threat came out on a whisper, her silver eyes flashing in the dappled sunlight.

He held up his hands in supplication. "I just want to talk."

"Then make an appointment." She edged to the side of the gravestone, one slim hand resting on the top.

"But I'm here now." He took another step toward her, close enough now that he could see the rise and fall of her breasts beneath her sweatshirt.

She took another step backward, this time stopped permanently by the cemetery wall. Her pupils were huge, and he thought for a moment that she was afraid, but then he saw her tongue dart out, nervously tracing her bottom lip, and he knew. Knew that she was as attracted to him as he was to her. And that she was fighting it every bit as hard as he was.

Their gazes met and held, the tension between them almost tangible. One step, one tiny little step, and he could touch her, taste her. One short step and he'd probably regret it the rest of his life. He sucked in a ragged breath, purposefully moving back. "Is this a family cemetery?"

Confusion flashed across her face, then something that looked like disappointment, but before he could be certain, it was replaced by relief. Pure unadulterated relief. "Yeah, it's been here since before the war."

He frowned. "But I thought the house was built in the twenties?"

"It was." She had gained control of her emotions now, her mask securely back in place. "But the land has been in my family a lot longer than that. There've been Rileys on this land for over a hundred and fifty years."

"Is that how you got your name?" He glanced around the cemetery with renewed interest.

She nodded, running a hand absently along the marble of the gravestone. "It's a family thing. Someone's always called Riley. Usually a boy. But since I was the end of the line, it had to be me."

"That's your mother?" His eyes dropped to the stone under her hand, and she pulled it back nervously, twining her fingers together in front of her.

"No, mother's buried over there." She tipped her head toward the center of the little cemetery. "This is my sister."

"It must have hurt losing your sister and your mother so close together." He watched the emotions chasing across her face.

"It was a long time ago." She drew in a deep breath, smiling tightly. "We survived."

He tried to think of something flippant to say. Something that would erase the intimacy between them. But, somehow, in the quiet of this place, he couldn't do it. "I used to visit my mother's grave too."

Her gaze met his, questioning. "She's buried in Atlanta?"

He shook his head. "Texas. She died when I was a kid." He should have stopped there, turned the subject to the reason he was here, but his mouth obviously had ideas of its own. "I used to go there to talk to her. It made her feel closer somehow."

She shot him a tremulous smile, her facade cracking just a little.

"So who is this?" He pointed at another stone.

Riley moved so she could better see the marker. "That's my great-uncle Cyrus. Never knew him. According to my grandmother, he drank himself to death."

"Not a bad way to go."

"If you want to go." Again there was a hint of a smile, and he found himself wishing he'd been the cause of it. She sobered, her eyes searching his again. "You still haven't told me why you're here."

He almost hated to ruin the moment. Hell, there wasn't supposed to be a moment. He was here for information—on the off chance that Ms. O'Brien could somehow help him get to the bottom of things. He narrowed his eyes, trying to ignore the regret churning in his gut. "I came to talk to you about your connection with Douglas Michaels."

Chapter 7

"WHAT CONNECTION? I barely know the man." Riley clenched her fist so hard she could feel her nails digging into her hand. He was a reporter, for God's sake. Anything else she was feeling about him was insignificant compared with that fact. With a concerted effort, she forced her fingers to open, ignoring her stinging palm.

"You were at his house yesterday." His eyes were nearly black, and in the shadow of the trees it was almost impossible to read his expression.

"For a committee meeting. I told you that."

"A committee meeting for two?" There was an edge to his voice, an implication she couldn't possibly ignore.

"I thought we covered this ground yesterday. I was at Michaels's for a meeting about teen pregnancy. We're working on setting up day-care centers in area high schools. The presentation for the city council is next week. Douglas had some statistics he wanted to go over."

"I see."

Exactly what he wanted to see. She wished she had the nerve to wipe the smug look off of his face. "Look, Mr. Mahoney—"

"Jake. After everything we've been through, the least

84

you can do is call me Jake." He smiled, the gesture slow and sure.

She took a step away from him, the distance giving her strength. "*Mr. Mahoney,* it was an innocent meeting. I was simply in the wrong place at the wrong time."

"Like the bombing." His eyebrows rose, his look appraising.

"Exactly. I chose the wrong car, and almost got blown to bits."

"Well, it's possible you weren't the only one to choose the wrong car." His voice softened, his eyes narrowing in thought.

"So you're still maintaining that the bomb was meant for me."

"I just find it interesting that you and Michaels sat on a council whose purpose involves reproductive rights."

"Teenage pregnancy and reproductive rights are not the same thing."

"Well, there's definitely a relationship. And when you add that to the fact that you seem to turn up with regularity where there's trouble, I think you'll have to agree that it's possible there's some sort of connection."

"You think I had something to do with Michaels's death?" She tried but couldn't keep the shock from her voice.

"No. The man committed suicide. And I certainly don't think it was because of you. But maybe there's something we're not seeing."

"Something about the council?"

"Maybe." He frowned, pulling himself up to sit on the wall of the cemetery, looking oddly at home despite the circumstances. "It's certainly a connection between you, the bombing, and Michaels."

"I think you're making it into something more than it

is. I serve on a committee that works to help out-of-wedlock mothers, and you think someone tried to exterminate me because if it?"

"Well, when you put it like that, it doesn't make a lot of sense."

"It doesn't make sense at all. And even if it did, there's the fact that no one is taking credit. If the bombing was related to the clinic and/or the council, you'd think there would have been more hoopla. Extremist groups love fanfare. Usually when something like this happens, groups fall all over themselves trying to take credit."

"Which puts us back to the target being either you or me."

She shouldn't have been pleased about his use of the word us, but she was. There was something intimate about it. Something that joined them together. She shook her head, pushing the thought aside. Jake Mahoney was not a friend. "Well, at the risk of sounding like a broken record, it was *your* car."

"Yes, but you were riding in an identical one. And looking at the two of us, who is a more likely target—the daughter of a presidential candidate or a local investigative reporter?"

"I'll admit, on the surface, it would seem like me."

"But . . ."

"But looking at the two of us on a more personal scale, I'd think that you were the more abrasive person, and therefore much more likely to have enemies who'd want to see you dead."

"I suspect I rub a few people the wrong way." He smiled, his teeth white against his tan, and her heart did a crazy little flutter step. "But even at my worst, I doubt I inspire murder."

"Well, I'm not exactly known for my controversial views."

"Maybe you're just the means to an end."

"You're talking about my father." She frowned.

"The man has certainly made his share of enemies. And even if he weren't controversial, the truth is, he's close to obtaining one of the most powerful positions on earth, and I find it conceivable that someone might want to stop him."

"By killing me? That's ludicrous."

"I've seen people killed for a hell of a lot less."

"But what would it accomplish?"

"Your father can't win this election without you, Riley. The country is hooked on the idea of a new Camelot. The dedicated father and his doting daughter. Another beautiful couple. Hell, you exploit the fact every time you appear together in public."

"You make it sound sordid." She fought against a wave of anger. He was twisting things around to suit his purposes.

"If the shoe fits—"

"I've told you before, my father is an honorable man. He will win this election on his own merits. The nation will vote for *him*, Mr. Mahoney, not some perverted concept of me as First Lady."

"Come now, Ms. O'Brien." He hopped off of the wall, closing the distance between them, his tone mocking. "Surely you're not naive enough to believe that."

"I am neither naive nor stupid, Mr. Mahoney." She sucked in a breath, fighting to keep her emotions at bay. "I think we've just come to the end of our interview. My father was right about you."

"Really?" The steel was back in the blue-black depth of his eyes. "And what exactly did he say about me?"

"He said that you were a barracuda." She hadn't wanted her father to be right. She hadn't realized it until right now—this very minute.

"And what do *you* think?"

She swallowed, trying to sort through her thoughts. She wanted Jake Mahoney to be different from the others. She wanted him to be honorable. She wanted him— period. And there wasn't a damn thing she could do about it.

She didn't have any choice. Not if he was a threat to her father. She lifted her chin, keeping her face still, glacial. "I think you'd best get the hell off of my property."

He stood for a moment longer, just watching her, his eyes locked on hers, and then he turned and made his way out of the little cemetery, disappearing into the dark shadows of the whispering pines. Riley stared at the spot where he disappeared, trying to remember when she'd last felt so desperately alone.

"What were you thinking, sending him to me? He's a journalist, for God's sake." Riley took a sip of coffee, the chicory blend pungent and hot, liquid comfort.

"Honey, I'd say that man is a heck of a lot more than just a reporter." Adelaide lifted a pot lid and spooned broth over the simmering roast.

Riley made a face at the housekeeper's back, ignoring Adelaide's implication that Jake Mahoney was something special. He wasn't. "He was certainly in reporter mode today."

Adelaide popped the roast back in the oven and then turned to the kitchen island, wooden spoon in hand. "Well, that's understandable. The two of you have been through a lot. I'd say he was just trying to understand what happened."

"I suppose so. But there was no reason for him to malign Daddy."

Riley reached for the biscuit cutter, handing it to Adelaide, their movements choreographed from years spent in the kitchen together.

"He's just doing his job, Riley. That doesn't make the man the devil," she said, picking up the extra dough and balling it together.

"Adelaide, you don't even know him, and you're defending him like he was family." Riley frowned at the woman, and started to line the cut biscuit dough up in the pan.

"I got a feeling about him." Adelaide's face took on a stubborn cast. "Besides, Edna likes him too."

"What the hell does Edna know?"

"You watch your mouth." Adelaide shook the rolling pin in Riley's direction. "Edna's been a good friend to you."

Riley felt the heat of the flush staining her face. "I know."

"Of course you do." Adelaide smiled, her look softening. "Besides, it's more than just Edna's opinion, and you know it. I told you I've got a feeling, and I'm always right about these things."

Adelaide had a way of reading people. Seeing into their souls. If Riley hadn't grown up around her, she'd probably have thought it strange, but Adelaide had always been an important part of her life, and Riley trusted her instincts. Still, everyone was wrong now and then. And Riley told herself that this was just one of those times.

She met the housekeeper's eyes, knowing hers were narrowed in disbelief. "Whatever you 'feel' about Mr. Mahony doesn't change the fact that he's trying to make trouble for Daddy, and I won't stand for that."

A shadow crossed Adelaide's face, gone almost before it arrived. "Your daddy's perfectly capable of taking care of himself. You'd do better to watch out for yourself. It's not normal for a girl your age to be spending all her time on other folk's dreams."

"It's my dream too, Adelaide. Daddy and I are a team. And I won't let someone like Jake Mahoney interfere with that."

The housekeeper stopped rolling the dough and studied Riley's face. "Honey, I know you love your father, and he loves you, but you've got to find your own way in the world."

It was an old conversation, and Riley knew there was no way they'd ever agree on it, so it seemed prudent to just ignore the comment. Besides, there were more important things to talk about.

"Adelaide, I don't want you to let Jake Mahoney past the front door again. He's not a friend, no matter what you and Edna have in your twisted little minds." She used her icy voice, the one that stopped most folks cold, but of course it had absolutely no effect on Adelaide.

"Whatever you say, honey." She smiled benignly and put the biscuits in the oven.

"Adelaide, he's trouble, and right now that's the last thing I need."

"Seems to me he might be just what the doctor ordered." Adelaide's voice was soft, no more than a murmur, but Riley heard her loud and clear just the same.

She sighed. Once Adelaide got something into her head, it was impossible to dissuade her, and for whatever reason, she'd made up her mind that Jake Mahoney was one of the good guys. If Riley had to call it, she'd say her old friend had made up her mind about more than just his temperament. She'd all but pasted a sign on the wall: This one's for you, Riley.

She smiled. The idea should have been repugnant. They were from opposite worlds. The man was practically the enemy. But if she was honest, she'd have to admit there was something kind of appealing in the idea. Okay, damned appealing.

And the thought scared her to death.

Jake stood inside Strictly Yours trying to pull his thoughts together amid a riot of wool and angora. It might technically be summer outside, but it was nor'easter type fall in the upscale boutique. He had never felt more like a fish out of water. There was a dowager in one corner complete with poodle, and over by a display of scanty underwear, a little man in Armani. Other than that, the store was empty.

"May I help you?" The shop woman's forced smile sized him up in about a nanosecond, dismissing him as a low-dollar prospect. Which wasn't too far from the truth. The store was the kind of place his ex-wife had liked to frequent. Long on attitude and short on style.

"I'm looking for Amber Northcott."

The woman relaxed slightly, dropping the chi-chi accent for a backwoods drawl. "You can find her in the back." She pointed toward an opening decorated with iridescent sixties-style beads. "Amber, someone to see you."

Jake nodded his thanks and made his way toward the back of the store. So far he hadn't managed to move his investigation forward one iota. Megan had been friendly, but unfortunately had only confirmed that Michaels had committed suicide. Riley had been downright hostile, but there didn't seem to be anything between her and Michaels beyond the council and bad timing. All he could do was hope the old adage "Things come in threes" wasn't in effect today, because he needed information, and Amber Northcott was practically his last hope.

The beads parted as a redhead walked into the shop, her eyebrows raised inquisitively. "I'm Amber. How can I help you?"

She was probably somewhere between thirty and thirty-five, the kind of woman his father would have said had been "rode hard and put to bed wet." And he wouldn't have meant it as a compliment. She was hardly the type he'd picture with an ADA, but then, to each his own. In a harsh kind of way, he guessed she'd be called a beauty.

"I'm Jake Mahoney, with the AJC." He stuck out his hand. "I'd like to ask you a few questions about Hank Larsen."

She took his hand briefly then released it, her eyes moving slowly from his head to his toes, evidently liking what she saw. "Hank's dead. I can't imagine I'd have anything new to tell you."

He cupped her elbow, shooting her his most charming smile. "Why don't you let me be the judge of that."

She shrugged. "Suit yourself. We can talk back here."

He followed her through the swinging beads, to a folding table with chairs. "I'm sorry for your loss."

"It's been hard." She didn't look particularly broken up. But then, maybe she just hid it well.

"How long were you and Larsen involved?"

"A little over a year." She sat down and reached for a packet of cigarettes. "Want one?"

"No thanks." Jake pulled the notepad out of his pocket and sat in the other chair.

Amber lit a cigarette and sat back, watching him through a haze of smoke. "Look, Mr. Mahoney, I'll be honest with you. I cared a lot about Hank, but I wasn't in love with him. And he wasn't in love with me. We had more of an arrangement."

She lifted her eyebrows in punctuation of the last word. "He needed someone to attend legal functions with, and I enjoyed being wined and dined. It worked well for both of us. And while it makes me sad to think of him dying like that, I'm not all broken up over it or anything." She exhaled a perfect smoke ring. "I just didn't want you to have the wrong impression."

"Your arrangement with Hank Larsen is none of my business, Amber. What I am interested in is his state of mind before he died."

"State of mind?" She frowned at him, her expression blank.

"You know, was he agitated, upset, worried about something?"

She considered the question for a moment. "I don't think so. In fact, if anything, I'd say it was just the opposite. It was almost like he was excited about something."

Jake looked up, his senses tingling. "What makes you say that?"

"Just the way he was acting. Hank was a good guy, but a little tight with his money. And all of a sudden he's babbling on about a trip to the islands. St. Bart's no less. He kept saying our ship was about to sail and that we'd be riding the tide, or something like that." She stubbed out the cigarette and leaned closer, waving a hand in the air. "Next thing I know, he's dead."

"Did he give you a clue as to how this proverbial ship was going to come in?"

"Not a word." She cradled her chin in her hands. "I'm sorry."

"Can you tell me why you left so quickly. After his death, I mean?"

"I suppose it'll sound silly. It's just that Hank's death made me realize how—" She bit her lip, obviously struggling for the right words. "—fragile we all are. And suddenly I had a need to live life a little. You know, prove that I was alive. Like I told you, we'd talked about St. Bart's. It seemed the obvious place to go." She looked up, her green eyes bright with tears. "I know it probably seems callous, but at the time it seemed like the right thing to do."

Disappointment surged through him. Another dead end. He stood up. "I appreciate your talking to me."

Her eyes ran up and down him again, and a smile tugged at the corners of her mouth. "My pleasure."

He handed her a business card as they walked back through the swinging beads. "If you think of anything else, give me a call."

"I'll do that, Jake." Her grin had turned flirtatious, and he resisted the urge to laugh. Any other time, he might have been tempted. But not now. Not with a woman like Riley O'Brien out there.

God, he had it bad.

Tendrils of fog curled in and out of the chain link of the prison yard fence. Normal people weren't outside on an evening like this. But then there was nothing normal about felons.

The men were split into groups. Like teenagers at school lunch. A group at the far end was engaged in a basketball game, their cheers echoing eerily through the mist. Another group was huddled near the gate, their talk muffled and low.

Haywood Jameson leaned back against a fence pole, marveling at how far he'd fallen. One minute he was the golden boy of Atlanta, and the next he was watching convicts play ball. He sighed, closing his eyes, trying to block it all out.

His father had been to visit. Well, visit wasn't the right word, actually. The meeting had only lasted long enough for him to sign paperwork that effectively cut Haywood out of the family business, and symbolically out of his family's life. Still, in a perverse kind of way, it had been nice to see him. To remember what it had been like to belong somewhere.

He supposed he should be grateful they hadn't cut off funds until after his trial. At least he wasn't in debt. But he'd hit bottom, and best he could tell there wasn't anyone standing in line waiting to help him up.

He was a convict. And a murderer. And no one gave a damn about him.

He opened his eyes. Bryce Daniels was walking across the yard with the lean grace of a dancer, or maybe a panther. There was just something about the man. Something far removed from the world they were living in. Grace. That was it. The man had grace. Which was quite an accomplishment in here.

Haywood raised a hand in greeting and started forward, tired of being alone with his thoughts. A man had to take his friends where he found them. As he crossed the exercise yard he suddenly noticed that everything had gone quiet, almost as if the mist had swallowed all sound.

The group on the left had split into two units, the larger one unmoving—waiting. A smaller one, comprised of two men, strolled leisurely toward the center of the yard. In the distance the faint noise of the basketball game filtered through the wet fog.

The hairs on the back of Haywood's neck stood on end, and noise splintered from the group on the left. A fight. Haywood swerved away from the confrontation. If there was one thing he'd learned in here, it was to keep low and stay out of trouble's way. Bryce evidently had the same idea because, with only a cursory look at the escalating brawl, he continued forward.

The other two men were obviously of the same mind, continuing to distance themselves from their compatriots. They stopped when they came to Bryce, one gesturing to the fray behind them.

It happened in the blink of an eye, and yet to Haywood it seemed like slow motion. The first man slid neatly behind Bryce, pinning his arms, the second ramming a fist into Bryce's gut.

Haywood's first instinct was to run. To get as far away from the violence as he could. But another more powerful emotion held sway, surprising him. Loyalty. And with it came a flood of anger.

He ran forward, knocking the first man aside, wondering where the hell the guards were. Bryce fell to one knee, and the second man reached for him, something flashing in the watery light.

Swinging his elbow up and to the right, Haywood caught him in the chest. The man scowled, then stepped back and disappeared into the swirling mist. Haywood fought for breath, his eyes searching for the other man, but he too, was gone.

The noise of the fight was fading. And Haywood's beleaguered brain pulled forth an image of the huddled group carefully splitting apart. The fight had been staged. To cover the attack on Bryce. He swallowed convulsively, the implication hitting him hard.

He knelt beside his friend. "You okay?"

The older man opened his eyes, pain stark against the pallor of his face. "Stabbed me." The words came out on a hiss.

"Where?"

"Chest." The word was hardly more than a whisper.

Haywood fumbled with the zipper on Bryce's canvas jacket. The damn thing wouldn't open. Grabbing the collar, he jerked the coat downward, tearing it. Where were the guards?

Blood pulsed thick and black through a jagged tear in Bryce's shirt. Haywood pulled off his own jacket, folding it into a pad, holding it firmly in place over the wound. "It's going to be all right. Just hang on."

His mind was running in crazy circles, trying to decide what to do. He'd never seen a man die. Never been this close to death. Except for the accident. And then he'd been too drunk to know what had happened. What he'd done.

He pressed harder on the wound. He wasn't about to let someone else die.

"Go." The word came out of Bryce's mouth on a whoosh of air. His eyes fluttered, then closed.

Haywood shook him. "Don't you dare die on me."

Bryce's eyes opened again, life flickering there. Dim, but alive. "Dangerous."

Haywood marveled at the fact that this man, in this place, was probably dying, and yet Bryce's last thoughts were for him. For his safety. Misplaced loyalty in here was a death sentence. But Haywood didn't care. Maybe tomorrow, but not now. Not while Bryce needed him.

He searched the yard for signs of help. The mist had thickened, turning to rain, and it soaked into his clothes like icy fingers. Bryce's breathing was shallow and fast. He had no idea if that was good or bad, but decided that breathing in any capacity was preferable to the alternative.

Suddenly, out of the gloom, he saw two guards. Making certain to keep one hand on the makeshift bandage, he raised his other hand and waved, yelling for help. The rescue team, such as it was, was on its way.

Bryce's hand tightened on his arm. Haywood leaned close, trying to catch his friend's whispered words. "Keep quiet." He tilted his head toward the approaching guards.

"But—"

"No point in signing a death warrant." Bryce's words were faint but clear. It was understood that matters inside were settled without interference from prison staff, but this was different, surely.

"What happened here?" A burly guard knelt down beside Haywood, his companion keeping watch.

Bryce squeezed his arm. Haywood sucked in a breath, feeling like a coward. "I don't know. I found him like this."

"Call the infirmary," the guard barked, taking control of the situation. His partner was already on the radio.

Bryce tugged on Haywood's sleeve. "Watch your back." The words were barely a whisper. Spoken soft and low. For Haywood's ears alone.

He shivered and pressed harder on his friend's chest, the man's blood sticky on his hand, reminding him that even in hell, people could die.

Chapter 8

Rⁱˡᵉʸ TWISTED HER hair into a French knot and reached for a hairpin. It had been a long day, and it was going to be an even longer night. The last thing she wanted to do was spend an evening schmoozing with her father's supporters. What she needed was a day off.

What she needed was a lifetime off. Guilt washed through her as she slid her dress off the hanger. She owed her father better. These rebellious thoughts had to stop. She was just overtired. Too many things had happened over the last couple of days. The bomb, Michaels—Jake.

She smiled at the thought. She'd never met anyone who could push her buttons quite like he did. He could make her run the gamut from anger to confusion to desire in about eight seconds flat. She closed her eyes, giving in to thoughts of him, imagining what it would feel like to have his arms around her, to have his lips on hers.

She sighed, and opened her eyes, pushing her traitorous thoughts firmly aside. There was no sense thinking of the man like that. No sense at all. He was a reporter. A cantankerous one at that. He was more comfortable in a morgue than in a stateroom. And any dealings they had would most likely be adversarial, not romantic.

Which was a shame and inevitable all at the same time.

She knew she couldn't have a relationship with anyone. She had more important things to accomplish. Global kinds of things. She was going to be the First Lady of the United States of America.

And all she could think of was Jake Mahoney. His eyes, his mouth, his hands . . . She drew in a shaky breath and stepped into her dress, reaching behind her to pull up the zipper, the tab staying stubbornly out of reach.

Sometimes she needed her sister so much. Caroline would have known what to do. About Jake, about her father, all of it. Her sister had always known her own mind. She'd been as strong-willed as their father. A blonde with a redhead's temperament. An O'Brien all the way.

They'd shared so much, she and Caroline. Secrets and dreams. Caroline paving the way for her younger, shyer sister. Riley smiled with the memory, finally sliding the zipper home. Caroline had been the light of their existence. And with a ten year difference between them, she'd been Riley's idol. A magical fairy princess.

Hot tears welled in her eyes, and Riley brushed at them angrily. How long would it be before the pain went away? Her sister had been dead for twenty years, and still it hurt as though it had happened yesterday.

She'd tried to lock it all away—to keep it out of her heart and mind—but it always surfaced again, picking at her, eating away at her reserves. She sat down on the bed, wrapping her arms around her waist, revisiting the terror of the night before—the dream. It was almost as if it were a symbol. An echo of those awful days. But she failed to see any logic in the abstract images.

There was fear, certainly, and pain. But nothing concrete. Nothing that meant anything. Her therapist had said it was a manifestation of her grief. And when it had vanished, she'd put it aside, pretending to forget. But now it was back. And with it came her memories, her grief, and a longing for her sister so acute it threatened to break her heart.

Without realizing what she was doing, Riley found herself standing at the door to her sister's room. Or what had been her sister's room. It had been a long time since she'd come here. Even with remodeling, she could still feel her sister's presence.

She took a step forward, shadows shifting across the floor, misty twilight bathing the room with an eerie half-light. The furniture was carefully neutral. Chosen purposefully as the antithesis of what Caroline would have chosen. Beige instead of rose, pleats instead of ruffles, stripes instead of the floral prints her sister had loved. There was nothing left to indicate the room had ever been hers. But still the essence of Caroline remained, a hint of sandalwood on the breeze, the memory of her laughter hanging in the air.

Thunder rumbled in the distance, and Riley shook her head, banishing her morbid thoughts. There was no sense in being overly dramatic. The past was just that—the past. Her sister was dead and gone. Her mother too. And nothing—not desire, not need, and certainly not a dream—was going to bring them back.

She walked over to the open window and reached up to close it, her eyes dropping to the table by the armchair, the hair on her arms rising as gooseflesh chased along her skin. A book lay open on the table, a half drunk glass of lemonade sitting beside it.

With shaking hands she reached for the book, knowing already what she was going to find. The book was Caroline's. Mary Stewart's *My Brother Michael*.

Riley turned to the first page, her heart pounding against her ribs. Caroline's name was scrawled across the page. The handwriting loopy, the *i* dotted with a heart. She turned the pages randomly, the words leaping off the page, the story more than familiar.

Caroline had been reading it to her the spring she died. Riley could hear her voice, see her face. They'd sat together in the garden reading—and drinking lemonade.

"Caroline?"

She whirled around, her heart threatening to break through her rib cage.

Her father stood just behind her, the room's shadows making him seem smaller somehow, lost, his pain almost palpable.

"No, Daddy, it's me." Riley dropped the book back on the table and reached out for him, wanting to soothe the pain she saw reflected in his eyes. "I'm sorry if I startled you."

Her father stared at her for a moment, confusion fighting with the last traces of fear. "I thought . . . I thought . . ."

"It's okay." She pulled him into a hug. "It was just a trick of the light."

He nodded, his expression clearing. "I don't know what I was thinking. I walked in and you were silhouetted against the window. I guess I just lost it for a moment."

"I understand. It's easy to do. She's still here somehow, isn't she?"

He gave her a hug and then let her go. "She's in our hearts, if that's what you mean. But if you're implying she's here in some metaphysical way, I'm afraid I can't buy into that."

"But you thought I was her."

"I reacted to the moment, Riley. Nothing more."

She didn't believe him. Not completely, anyway. There was something there, something in his eyes. He had believed she was Caroline. Even if it was only for a moment. He'd felt her here too.

"So what are you doing in here? Reading?" His eyes dropped to the book on the table. "You were supposed to be getting ready for the party."

"I was. I just came in here for a minute. I guess someone else was taking advantage of the light." She shifted, blocking the book from view. No need in upsetting him further. "What time is it?"

"Almost seven. We're going to be late." He shot her a stern look as he guided her toward the door. "Leon will have our heads." His voice held a hint of laughter, his emotions obviously firmly back in control.

Riley shot a look over her shoulder, her gaze settling on the book and the lemonade. Shivering, she turned to follow her father, the scent of sandalwood still hovering in the air.

"You're kidding." Jake glared at his editor. "You want me to back off the investigation?"

Tim Pierce rubbed his balding head, looking decidedly uncomfortable. "Only the part that has to do with Riley O'Brien."

"You were just saying yesterday that there were too many coincidences. What if Riley is the key?" Jake scrambled for some sort of explanation. Something that made sense of his friend's edict.

"But you've just told me you weren't able to establish a connection when you talked to her this morning."

"I wasn't able to establish anything, Tim. The woman threw me out."

"Well, what do you say we leave it at that? After all, you're not on the political beat. By all rights if there's a story it should be Walter's."

"Walter's?" Jake tried but couldn't keep the incredulity out of his voice. "Walter can't write his way out of a paper bag—and that's when he's sober, which we both know is only about ten percent of the time. What the hell is going on here?"

Tim sighed, leaning back in his chair. "Orders from on high. I got the call about an hour ago."

"How high?" The paper was top-heavy with managers, but something like this had to come from higher than the editorial staff.

"The very top. Apparently there was a phone call today concerning your visits with Ms. O'Brien. There was talk of harassment, Jake. The big brass isn't taking this lightly."

"I wasn't harassing anyone, Tim. Hell, I saved her life."

"And then you followed her to Michaels's."

"I didn't follow anyone. I told you I was going over there. How the hell was I to know that *Ms. O'Brien* would be there too?"

"I know that. And you know that. But between the bombing, the body, and her throwing you off her property, I can see where someone might get the wrong idea."

"Yeah, if it's presented in that kind of light. Hell, Tim, all I did was ask the woman a few questions. No one told me I had to use kid gloves. So maybe I touched a nerve. That's what reporters are supposed to do." Jake stood up, his hands clenched at his sides, his mind on Riley O'Brien and her lying silver eyes. How dare she call the paper?

Tim held up a hand in placation. "I'm not accusing

you of anything, Jake. But there's nothing I can do about it. I was ordered to pull you off of anything having to do with Riley O'Brien, and that's what I'm going to do."

"What if there's an overlap between the Michaels case and the bombing?"

"You said yourself that isn't likely." Tim shrugged. "If there is, you'll just have to work with Walter."

"Oh joy." Jake sat back down, reining in his temper. It wasn't Tim's fault. There was no sense shooting the messenger.

"Maybe it's not a complete wash." With a slow smile, Pierce pushed his glasses to the top of his head, making him look an odd cross between Benny Hill and Yoda. "I can't ignore the edict, but I don't have to like it. And since I haven't seen you tonight," his smile grew broader, "there's no way to stop you until tomorrow."

"But I don't see how—"

"It just so happens that there's a fund-raiser tonight—at Victor and Marietta Wilbine's. And unfortunately," Tim shook his head regretfully, "Walter still isn't feeling well."

Jake shot a look out the office door window to where Walter was working at his computer, then turned back to Tim, an enlightened grin spreading across his face. "A last hurrah, so to speak."

"I think you can make it whatever you need it to be, but make it count. We're talking final quarter here. Anything beyond that and you're on your own."

Jake nodded, already heading for the door. It might be fourth down and ten, but he had no intention of punting. Riley O'Brien had better ready her defenses.

Marietta Wilbine's house was the result of an abundance of money and an overreliance on Martha Stewart.

Marietta's theory was that if a little was good, then a lot was even better. The result being a house that resembled a flower mortuary. There were dead flowers everywhere. In wreaths on the doors and windows, in vases scattered about the large foyer, even framed on the walls.

And to make it worse, the flowers smelled. A wild cacophony of scents that reminded him of a head shop. Jake tried to breathe shallowly, already certain that his sinuses would never be the same.

A woman in uniform took his overcoat, while a severe-looking man in black checked his credentials, his earpiece targeting him as Secret Service. This was the moment of truth. If Riley was thorough, she'd have barred him from attending. If not . . .

He shook his head, clearing his thoughts, determined to ignore the warmth flooding through him. Riley O'Brien had a way of unsettling him even when she wasn't in the room.

With a nod, the Secret Service agent handed back his press pass and invitation. He'd obviously passed muster. Riley hadn't bothered to have his name removed, confident that her call to the newspaper had been enough. He suppressed a grin. She'd seriously underestimated him.

She might be officially off limits, but there were other ways to get information. And he wasn't above using them. He had that itch deep in his gut—the one that meant there was a story to find.

Besides, he had a few things he wanted to say to the senator's daughter. No one hamstrung him without a fight. And this was as good a place as any. He straightened his tie, moving through the foyer, trying to resist the urge to sneeze.

Damn flowers.

The room was full to bursting with people. It was a

night to see and be seen. The potential President was being feted by the best of the best. Or at least that's the kind of crap magazines like *Georgia Today* would be selling tomorrow.

Senators mingled with industrial magnates, old money mixed with new. There was a ballerina in the corner talking to a man who made his money raising hogs, and an artist laughing at a joke being told by a professional football player.

Georgia's elite.

Not his cup of tea. Frankly, he wasn't an elite kind of guy. A fact his ex-wife had never let him forget. His gaze swept over the crowd, absurdly disappointed when he couldn't find Riley.

Her father was over in a corner, deep in conversation with Leon Bronowsky and a local congressman, two Secret Service agents standing watch nearby. He studied O'Brien's right-hand man. Leon Bronowsky was a shark, and he guarded his empire fiercely. Still, Jake had no beef with the man. He was a kingmaker, a high roller. Men like that took risks. Big risks.

But the payoff could be equally big, and it looked like Bronowsky had hit the jackpot with Carter O'Brien. In an odd kind of way, Jake almost admired him. *Almost.* Men like Bronowsky also tended to destroy anything that got in their way. To hell with the consequences. People were commodities. Nothing more. And Jake had no intention of being a casualty.

Bronowsky looked up and their gazes met. Jake tipped his head in acknowledgment. The older man's eyes narrowed for a moment, sizing him up, then, with the slightest of shrugs, he returned his attention to Carter and his entourage.

Thoroughly dismissed. Not that that was a bad thing, as far as Jake was concerned. It only confirmed what he already knew. Riley was the one who got him pulled from the story. *Riley.* He glanced around the room, searching for a glimpse of her.

Where the hell was she?

"She's not in here." At Edna's whispered words, Jake jerked around, embarrassed that the woman had once again read his mind.

"Who?" He strove for nonchalance, knowing full well that he wouldn't fool anyone, least of all Edna.

"You know who." Edna smiled, and took an offered glass of champagne from a passing waiter. "I thought you'd been warned off."

It was Jake's turn to smile. News traveled fast among journalists. "I wanted to go out with a bang."

"You watch yourself." Edna's tone turned serious. "I've no idea what you think you're playing at, but the people surrounding Riley are playing for keeps."

"I know how to play hardball, Edna."

"I know you do. I just want you to be careful." She spoke lightly, but her eyes reflected genuine concern.

"You're the one who threw me at her."

She eyed him over the top of her glass. "I arranged an introduction. What you make of it is up to you."

"I don't intend to make anything of it, Edna." His gaze collided with hers.

"You trying to convince me, or yourself?" Her smile was slow and sure. "She's out on the patio."

"What the hell is he doing here?" Carter kept his smile in place, but his voice was icy. "I thought you handled it."

"I did." Leon shot a glance around the room, guiding his friend farther into the corner. Carter was a loose cannon when he lost his temper, and this was not the place for a public display. "If anything, this is just his way of saving face. If he values his job, he'll stay away from Riley."

"And if he doesn't?"

"Then we'll have to do something else, won't we?" Leon's words were meant to placate.

"Fine." Carter downed his scotch. "Just keep him away from my daughter."

"I keep telling you, she can take care of herself." Maudeen came to stand beside him, laying a gentle hand on Carter's arm. Very subtly, he stepped away from her touch. She flinched, but immediately covered her reaction.

"I know that, Maudeen. But for some reason, this man is fixated on Riley."

"I don't understand what all the fuss is about."

"Well, I wouldn't expect you to. She's not your child, after all." He was speaking through clenched teeth now, his anger seething just beneath the surface.

Maudeen dropped her eyes to the floor, the slight shaking of her hand the only visible emotion. "But I care about her, Carter."

"Of course you do." Leon forced his voice to reflect a calm he didn't feel. "But I'm telling you there is no cause for alarm. Mahoney is being taken care of."

Carter blew out a slow breath, and Leon was relieved to see his friend relax. "You're right. I'm sorry. I over-reacted."

Maudeen bit her lower lip, Carter's snub obviously hitting home. "I shouldn't have said anything."

"No. It's all right," Carter said. "I know I'm overprotective when it comes to Riley, but she's all I have. If anything happened to her . . ." He paused, his words hanging between them. Carter only loved two things in this world: his daughter and himself. And God help the person who threatened either one.

"Nothing is going to happen to her," Leon insisted, shooting a warning glance at Maudeen. He could see that Carter was riding the edge. He had been since they'd arrived. Leon had attributed it to Riley's misadventures, but suddenly he wasn't so certain.

"See that it doesn't," Carter barked, then walked away, his candidate's smile firmly back in place. Leon released a breath. Disaster averted.

For now.

The misty day had turned into a misty night. Lightning to the west meant rain was on its way. A storm. God, how she hated storms. They reminded her of . . . of bad things. The wind had picked up, swirling the first leaves of fall across the patio with a soft shushing sound. Riley shivered, wrapping her arms around herself.

She ought to be inside, courting her father's supporters. But she was tired. Tired of the plastic smiles and fawning people. Tired of pretending to be something she wasn't. All she wanted was a moment's peace. Surely that wasn't too much to ask. The distant sound of thunder echoed through the undulating trees.

"There's a storm coming."

His voice was soft, edged with something more. Something dangerous. Predatory. She didn't turn, only stood, her fingers clutching the stone wall that divided the patio from the manicured grounds. "It's still a long way off."

He moved closer. She could feel his breath against her bare shoulder. "Distances can be deceiving."

Lightning flashed. She counted. One one thousand, two one thousand . . . The distant rumble of thunder filled the air. She shivered again.

"You don't like storms." It was a statement, not a question. His hands settled on her shoulders, the heat from his body radiating through her, igniting flash fires deep inside her.

She shook her head, not capable of saying anything. They stood like that, watching the trees twist in the wind, listening to the distant sounds of the coming rain. His warmth seeped through her, and when he slowly turned her around, it seemed the most natural thing in the world.

She met his gaze, black like storm clouds, the hint of blue disappearing with the night. There was definitely danger here. She was lucid enough to know it. But there was the promise of something else. Something totally outside the rigid world she lived in. Something she wanted more than anything. Despite the danger.

He bent his head and brushed his lips against hers. With a muffled groan, his touch became more insistent, and the coming storm was obliterated by a maelstrom of their own making—the pounding of her heart replacing thunder, the touch of his lips on hers igniting white, hot lightning.

She'd never felt like this. Not in twenty-nine years of living. Good sense and years of caution faded under the onslaught of this kiss. She opened her mouth, welcoming him inside, reveling in the feel of his tongue, entering, possessing.

She pressed closer, feeling the heat of his hands as they caressed through the smooth silk of her dress. His mouth moved, tracing the soft skin along the inside of her neck. Shivers racked through her, and his hand slid below the neckline of her dress, his fingers unerringly finding the soft swell of her breast.

His mouth closed over hers again, the heat inside her

building to a fever pitch. When his thumb rasped across her nipple, she moaned, the sound swallowed by his kiss. This was heaven—or hell.

Somewhere, beyond the magic of his touch, she heard voices.

Her father's party.

Reality came crashing in. Mortified, she pushed away, her face burning, her breathing coming in gasps. Without meaning to, she stepped back, only the wall keeping her from total escape.

He reached for her, his eyes black as obsidian. She held up her hand and whispered the word no, putting all her years of training behind the single syllable. She was her father's daughter. Steeling herself, she held her head high, her gaze locking with his. "I can't do this. It's wrong. You're a journalist, for God's sake."

His reaction was immediate, indignation replacing concern. His dark eyes flashed and he stepped back, distancing himself from her. "Toying with the commoners, your majesty?" The anger in his voice was leashed, barely in control.

"I'm not royalty." The words came out against a rumble of thunder. The storm was nearing. "You don't know anything about me." She pressed closer to the wall, struggling to understand what had just happened—why he was so angry.

"Oh, believe me, I recognize the type. You lead a man on, take what you want, and then put him firmly in his place. Well, let me tell you, sweetheart, I've been there and done that, and I'm not doing it again."

She paused, searching for words, staring at the tiny muscle twitching along his jaw. "I have no idea what you're talking about."

"Don't you?" He stepped closer, his breath caressing her ear. She shivered. "It's all a game to women like you, isn't it? Trap the poor schmuck and then make him pay. Do you get together with your girlfriends afterward to count coup?"

"Jake, I didn't mean . . . it's just that my father . . ." She trailed off, not knowing how to finish. Not knowing exactly what had brought about this lightning change. She'd never met anyone who could throw her, but this man could take her breath away with just a look.

"Your father wouldn't like it, would he, princess? After all, you're daddy's little girl to the bone, aren't you?" His words were intended to cut, and they did, deeply. "Everything is about him. Protecting him. Worshiping him. Living for him. And you don't care who you hurt in the process, do you?" He was yelling now, but the escalating wind whipped his words away.

She fought against tears. This man was nothing to her. She didn't care what he thought. "I haven't hurt anyone." She spit the words out, enunciating each one for emphasis. She slid sideways, preparing to run. Anything to escape the disdain in his eyes.

His hand snaked out, wrapping around her wrist, holding her in place. "Give me a break. You know exactly what you're doing. You wave your royal hand and the world does your bidding. Your call to my paper could have cost me my job, and I don't take that lightly."

She went still, trying to understand his words. "What call?"

"Don't play stupid with me. I know it was you. You called the paper and had me reassigned. Said I was harassing you." He leaned forward, his grip tightening on her wrist. "Believe me, princess, when I'm harassing you, you'll be more than aware of it."

She swallowed, confusion warring with fear. "I'm telling you, I didn't call anyone."

He paused, a flicker of something washing across his

face. If she hadn't known better, she'd have thought it was hope.

"Take your hands off of Miss O'Brien this instant." Leon Bronowsky stepped out onto the patio, flanked by two Secret Service men.

Instinctively, Riley took a step toward Jake, wanting to protect him, not understanding why. But he'd already turned away, his eyes narrowed as he took in her father's friend and the two armed bodyguards.

"It's all right, Leon." Her voice was shaky, the sound diminished by the wind. "We were only talking."

All four men ignored her, and she felt a flair of resentment.

"Escort Mr. Mahoney from the premises," Leon barked.

The two Secret Service agents took a step toward Jake, who held up his hands, his face full of scorn. "I can see myself out."

"Well, you won't mind then if we make sure that you do." Leon's voice was just short of dismissing.

She opened her mouth to say something. To explain things, to try and defend herself. But he was gone without giving her a second glance, Leon and the security men following in Jake's wake.

Pain racked through her, surprising her with its intensity. Lightning illuminated the empty patio, the promised rain finally starting to fall. And, to her great horror, she started to cry.

Chapter 9

"I'VE NEVER BEEN so embarrassed in all my life." Riley stopped pacing around the library long enough to glare at her father and Leon. "I am not a child."

Leon held his hands up in placation. "We're well aware of that, Riley, but part of my job is to make certain you aren't harassed by the press."

"He wasn't hounding me. He was just talking to me." And kissing her, but she'd think about that later. "It was meant to be a private conversation."

"We could hear him yelling inside the house." Her father's voice was tight with anger.

"We had a misunderstanding. He believes that I'm responsible for some phone call to the paper." For the moment that was all she was willing to admit to her father. The rest of it she would deal with on her own.

Her father and Leon exchanged a glance.

"You placed the call?" She waited, her gaze locked with her father's.

"Leon did. At my instigation."

"Why?"

"Because I don't trust the man's intentions, and because I don't want to see you get hurt."

Too damn late for that. But of course she couldn't share that with her father. "Well, he blames *me*."

"I don't see how that matters. He's hardly important

in the grand scheme of things." Leon's tone was cold and dismissive.

Riley wondered what he'd think if she told him just how important Jake Mahoney had become to her. She shook her head, clearing the thought. It had been one kiss. Nothing more. And if she was tempted to make it into something else, she had only to remember their conversation afterward to know what he really thought of her.

Still, there was a principle here.

"The point isn't whether Jake is a player, Leon. The point is that you lied to me."

"We didn't lie, Riley. We just didn't tell you. It didn't seem relevant."

"Well, it was relevant. First, you accused the man of something he most definitely did not do, and then, to make it all worse, you let him believe it was me that did it. I will not tolerate being manipulated in that manner, Leon. Do I make myself clear?" The statement would have had more power if her voice wasn't quivering.

Damn it.

"Darlin'." Her father reached for her hands, his eyes soft. Some of her anger dissipated immediately. "Leon and I only want what's best for you. And I was worried that this man might cause trouble."

"For the campaign, you mean." She tried but couldn't keep the bitterness out of her voice.

"Well, unfortunately the campaign is our life at the moment. There simply isn't any way to separate the two. But that doesn't mean I'll let it intrude on your life to the point that it puts you in harm's way."

"Daddy, you're acting like there really is some sort of threat out there. Is there something you're not telling me?" She looked first at her father and then at Leon.

"No, but someone blew up that car, Riley," Leon

answered. "We can't ignore that. And there's the little matter of Michaels's death."

"Both of which are not related to me. I was simply in the wrong place at the wrong time, and if it hadn't been for Jake Mahoney, I might be dead."

"And we're grateful to him for that." Her father's words were meant to pacify, but they only agitated her more.

"Of course you are." She glared first at Leon, then at her father. "So grateful that you practically got the man fired."

"Riley, we are trying to do what's best for you and for the campaign," her father said. "I'm sorry we didn't tell you about the phone call. But the stakes are too high for us to take chances. Maybe Jake Mahoney is an innocent bystander in all this, but then again, maybe he's not. Until we know which way the wind is blowing, I want you to stay away from the man."

"Daddy . . ." She tried but failed to keep the exasperation out of her voice.

"I'm probably being overprotective, darlin', but you're my baby and I'm not taking any chances."

"We're all under a lot of stress." Leon moved to stand by the window, looking out into the night. "It'll be over soon."

"And we'll have a whole new set of problems." Riley tipped back her head, closing her eyes and rubbing her temples.

"Part of the game, princess." Her father's words were low, soothing.

Jake had called her a princess too. But he hadn't meant it kindly. She shivered, remembering his touch, wondering suddenly if there was truth in the things he'd said to her at the party.

She opened her eyes, smiling at her father. Jake

Mahoney was a stranger. He didn't know her at all. There was no reason to believe anything he said. Her place was here with the people she loved. They only wanted to protect her—even if they were a bit over-zealous.

"Next time, tell me what you're going to do. I hate being blindsided. And maybe, while you're at it, have a little more faith in me. I'm tougher than you think."

It was Leon's turn to smile. "Of course you're tough. But old habits die hard. And we love you."

"I know you do." She sighed, hugging first Leon and then her father.

"Things will seem better in the morning." Her father held her close, his familiar scent comforting.

The wind rattled the glass in the window, and through it she could see the balcony railing, stark against a flash of lightning. She wanted her father to be right. But somehow, she had the horrible feeling the storm had only just begun.

"Sounds like it was a hell of a party." David Mackenna sipped his beer, his lips twitching as he struggled to contain his laughter.

Jake frowned at his friend. "I lost my temper. I admit it."

"It seems to me that's not all you lost." David's grin broke out in full force.

Jake was surprised to feel the heat of a blush. "It was just a kiss. I got carried away in the moment. It sure as hell isn't going to lead to anything else."

"Not if her henchmen have anything to say about it."

"I've taken on henchmen before. They don't scare me. It isn't leading to anything else because I don't want it to."

"Right." David's look turned mocking.

Jake frowned at his friend, determined to change the subject. "Look, as much as I'm enjoying your clever innuendos about my love life—or lack thereof—that's not why we're here. On the phone you said you'd found something."

"I did." David sat back, crossing his arms over his chest. "Hank Larsen's fire wasn't an accident."

The beginnings of excitement curled through Jake's insides. "You're positive?"

David smiled. "Oh yeah. The accelerant was a tricky little bastard to find, but I'm a persistent son of a gun."

"There's an understatement." Jake lifted his beer in a mock salute.

"Now all I have to do is figure out who put it there." David drained the rest of his beer and squinted at the empty glass. "Another round?"

"Sure. If nothing else, we can celebrate my inability to think with anything besides my—"

"Jake." Lacey Anderson, late Mahoney, smiled benignly at them, her voice carrying across the crowded bar.

"Case in point," Jake groaned. This was rapidly turning into the week from hell.

"Any idea what she's doing here?" David asked, his face expressing the revulsion Jake was feeling.

"None. But then when the hell did she ever tell me anything?"

"Long time no see, darling." Lacey sidled to a stop in front of their table, drink in hand, and bent to kiss him full on the lips. There was a time when he'd lived for her touch, but not anymore. He leaned back, distancing himself, wondering what the hell had possessed him to ever get mixed up with her in the first place.

"Out slumming, Lacey?" Jake tried but couldn't contain the contempt in his voice.

"As usual, Jake, you're behind the times. The Dugout has turned into quite the hot spot. A wonderful place to see and be seen, if you know what I mean."

"I never know what you mean, Lacey."

"Anyway," she said, ignoring his barbs, "I'm here with friends, and I saw you across the room. I should have known you'd be here." She tilted her head, her smile crooked, inviting. "You are a creature of habit after all."

He had no idea if it was a good thing or a bad thing, but coming from Lacey, he suspected the latter. His ex-wife had never been one for the status quo. Lacey wanted the best life had to offer, preferably served to her on a silver platter. Jake's blue collar tendencies had always been a bone of contention, and when it had become apparent he wasn't going to shed them for Lacey's upper class ideals, she'd dropped him like a hot potato.

"Yeah, well, I like life to be predictable." Not that it had been of late.

"Apparently that applies to your choice of friends. Same old, same old." She shot a disdainful look at David. The two of them had never gotten along. And it looked as if nothing had changed.

David frowned. "Hello, Lacey."

Her smile faded slightly, but she held his gaze steadily. "David." She nodded in his direction, then dismissed him, pulling up a chair, her attention centered on Jake. "I'm glad I've run into you, actually. We need to arrange a time for me to come by."

"Come by where?"

"The apartment, silly." She smiled, her perfect face dimpling in all the right places. "Didn't you read my letter?"

"Haven't had time to read any mail lately." No sense

in admitting he'd eighty-sixed it without even opening the thing.

"Well," she smiled, drawing out the moment, "I'm getting married." She held out her hand, flashing a diamond that was bigger than her knuckle.

David whistled. "That must have set some poor sucker back a tidy sum."

"It's one of a kind." Lacey twisted her hand, studying the ring, oblivious to everything else.

Jake swallowed his surprise, not certain how he was supposed to feel. Relieved, delighted, hell, he felt like buying a round for the bar. "So who's the lucky guy?"

"Martin Schlembauger."

"The industrial tycoon? Isn't he pushing a hundred?" David was trying hard not to laugh.

Lacey straightened her shoulders, her eyes shooting sparks. "He's only seventy-five."

"And incredibly rich." David's voice dripped sarcasm.

"So," Jake said, determined to pull the conversation back to a civilized level, "you said you wanted to come by the apartment?"

"Oh. Right." She turned her attention back to him, her plastic smile turning coy.

What in hell had ever made him think that Riley O'Brien was anything like Lacey? They were nothing alike. Lacey was money-hungry and shallow. Riley was the real deal. Class all the way. He suddenly felt ashamed of his earlier outburst. He'd hurt her. And with no good reason. He'd let his pride get in his way.

She shouldn't have called the dogs on him, but that hadn't been an excuse for him to launch into her the way he had. There'd been pain in her eyes. Pain that he'd put there. And all because he'd let himself believe she was like his ex.

Damn it to hell.

"Jake . . ." Lacey covered his hand with hers, pulling him back to the present. "You're not listening."

"I'm sorry. I was distracted. You were saying . . ." He forced a smile, feigning interest. Behind her head, David was rolling his eyes.

"I was saying that I still have some boxes at the apartment. And I'd like to get them, if you don't mind. We're moving to Savannah, and I want all my things."

"I thought you'd want to buy everything new." He unsuccessfully tried to keep the sarcasm out of his voice.

As usual, Lacey missed the undertone. "Oh, I am. But there are still things I'd like to keep. There are some things about our time together that are worth remembering."

He couldn't think of a single one. "Well, you're welcome to come get whatever you want. I'll have the boxes brought up from the basement."

She patted his hand like he was a prize poodle. "I knew you'd understand." She sat back, her look turning appraising. "That was some picture in the paper—you straddling Riley O'Brien. It must have been quite exciting."

"The woman was almost killed, and my car was destroyed; I hardly think that qualifies as exciting."

"Well, you rescued the senator's daughter. Seems like you ought to be able to turn that into an opportunity for advancement."

Leave it to his ex to see the mercenary angle. "I don't want to advance anywhere, Lacey. I'm perfectly happy just as I am."

"Well, it just seems to me like the perfect chance to maneuver yourself into something a little more impressive, Jake. I mean, the man is going to be the next President. And he ought to be incredibly grateful. You should be able to parlay that into something."

God, some things never changed. And Lacey was one of them. He wondered suddenly if old Marty knew what he was getting into. He probably ought to warn the guy. But then again, it really wasn't any of his business. And that in and of itself was a wonderful feeling.

"I didn't rescue the woman from terrorists, Lacey. I just tackled her."

"The picture in the paper made it look quite intimate." She raised one perfectly sculpted eyebrow.

"There was a bomb going off. And the woman is practically a stranger. There is nothing intimate about that." But there had been. Despite it all, there had been.

"I see." There was a world of innuendo in the remark.

"No, you don't see anything at all."

"Or," David added, "more likely, you only see what you want to see."

Lacey laughed. "I'd forgotten how blunt you are, David." She pushed back from the table, fixing her attention on Jake. "I really should be getting back to my friends. It was lovely to see you, darling. I'll be by for the boxes in the next day or so." She leaned over and planted another kiss. This one sensual, designed to excite.

It left him cold.

His mind focused instead on another kiss. One that, despite his wishes to the contrary, had rocked his entire world.

The question was, what was he going to do about it?

Maudeen lay back against the pillows of the guest bed, trying not to fret. Carter should have been back by now. The hands on the clock indicated that it was late. Very late. So either he'd come back and she'd missed the sound, or he was still out.

She knew she shouldn't borrow problems. She had nothing conclusive to go on. Nothing except woman's intuition. But she put a lot of stock in that. Things were spiraling out of control. Carter and his dalliances were becoming a threat.

She was aware that from time to time he had sex with other women. He'd done it from the beginning. The reality was, Carter's wandering heart had brought him to her in the first place. To date, his indiscretions had been few and far between, and she'd never doubted that she was the one he loved.

But that was changing. She could feel it. Feel him slipping away. There was a woman in D.C. One of the staffers. She was half their age, all tits and hair. And until now, only a nuisance. But suddenly she wasn't feeling so confident.

The door to the room opened and Carter stood there, looking perfectly pressed, despite the hour. His handsome face curved into a grin. "Hello, darlin', miss me?"

He'd been drinking. There was a slight slur, almost undetectable if you didn't know him. But she did. Really well. He crossed the room, sitting on the bed, leaning over to kiss her. She smelled Shalimar, sweet and cloying, and not her fragrance.

Damn him.

"I couldn't sleep." She fought for control, not wanting a confrontation.

"Well, maybe I can help relax you." His voice was warm and lazy, his breath warm on her face.

"Where've you been?" As soon as the words were out of her mouth she regretted them.

His face changed, shuttering. "Just out. I needed to think."

Unless she missed her guess, thinking had not been on the agenda. "I see."

"Ah, Maudeen, give it a rest, darlin'. I'm here now. That's what matters, right?"

She supposed in some absurd sort of way he was right. But this wasn't how she wanted things to end between them. Stolen moments when he was between lovers. She wasn't about to give up all the years she'd invested in him simply because he couldn't keep his zipper up.

She reached for the buttons on his shirt, easing his shirt open, running her hands over the broad expanse of his chest. He growled his approval and, after removing the rest of his clothes, climbed into bed, his warmth radiating out to envelop her. She laid her head on his chest, conscious of the strong beat of his heart.

He sighed, closing his eyes, his arms wrapping around her.

"Carter?" She sucked in a fortifying breath. "Do you love me?" She lay in the dark, waiting for his answer, knowing it wasn't going to come. And not because he'd fallen asleep. No, the answer wasn't coming because Carter O'Brien didn't love anyone but himself.

Riley. Where are you? Riley . . . Riley?

Riley jerked out of sleep, her heart hammering. Caroline. She sat up, swinging out of bed, her eyes searching for her sister, her ears straining into the darkness.

There was nothing.

She drew in a shuddering breath, trying to gain control of her emotions. It had only been a dream. Caroline was dead.

Dead.

She was overwrought. And so she'd imagined her sister's voice. Maybe even willed herself to hear it. She needed someone to confide in. Someone who could tell her what to do. Everything was so confusing.

Especially her feelings about Jake.

She walked to the window, looking out at the rainswept night. The storm had never fully materialized, although the occasional flash of lightning still held promise. With a sigh, she leaned her head against the cool windowpane.

All she could think of was the kiss. The kiss and the man behind it.

One moment he seemed gentle, almost cherishing, and the next, he had sucked her soul through her lips, only to spit it back at her in a swirl of anger. He confused her, entranced her, and generally made her furious. Not the least of it, the fact that he believed she'd been the one to call his paper.

It shouldn't matter. Leon was right. In the grand scheme of things he wasn't likely to impact her life, but she couldn't stop wishing that he would. The thought was crazy, but it was there nevertheless. Haunting her.

Like Caroline.

She shivered at the thought. She was acting like a loon. Seeing things. Hearing things. Making mountains out of molehills. She turned back to the room, determined to go back to sleep. To push all thoughts of Jake Mahoney firmly aside.

She was a grown woman, and there was no point behaving like an adolescent. If Caroline *were* here, she'd no doubt tell her to get a grip. Jake had made his feelings for her perfectly clear. He thought she was shallow and opportunistic. And he believed she'd betrayed him.

But she hadn't—she hadn't.

She sat on the edge of the bed and reached to turn on the lamp, the flash of light blinding her for a moment. She closed her eyes and then slowly opened them again, her breath catching in her throat.

Sitting on her bedside table, open as though she'd only just been reading it, was Mary Stewart's *My Brother Michael*.

And the air suddenly smelled of sandalwood.

Chapter 10

Rⁱˡᵉʸ SAT IN her car staring at the brick building in front of her. Rain spattered against the windshield. She'd been driving around for what seemed like hours, and she still couldn't make heads or tails of what was happening.

There had to be a logical explanation for finding Caroline's book. Maybe her father had put it there. Or one of the maids. Certainly there was nothing sinister in the act. She was just letting her imagination carry her away. With everything that had happened, it was understandable.

Anyone would be a little jumpy.

Or at least that's what she kept telling herself.

She'd been too spooked to stay in the house. She'd wanted perspective. That's why she was sitting in her car, in the middle of the night, in front of an apartment building, in the rain. The fact that Jake Mahoney's apartment was in the building had nothing to do with anything. Nothing at all.

Well, okay, it had something to do with it. She sighed. If she were being completely honest with herself, she'd have to admit it had everything to do with it. She simply couldn't stop thinking about him. Which was why she was trying to build up the courage to go and talk to him. Even though he clearly despised her.

She sucked in a breath and opened the car door. Might as well get it over with. At the very worst, she'd have said her piece. And who knew, maybe something positive would come of the whole thing. At least, for once in her life, she was doing what she wanted to. Not letting anyone else dictate the way she should handle things.

She stepped out into the rain.

It was her life, and just for the moment she was going to live it. Besides, the man might throw her out. Or yell at her again. The thought almost sent her running back to the shelter of the car, his angry words still echoing through her head.

What was she doing? Committing political suicide, that's what. If the man didn't rip her to shreds, the newspapers would if they got hold of the fact that she was standing in the rain in the middle of the night mooning over one of their own.

And that was nothing compared to what her father and Leon would do when they found out. Her newfound independence vanished. She wasn't being brave; she was being incredibly stupid. No man was worth risking her father's career. Was he?

She pulled her jacket closer, indecision holding her immobile. She wanted to tell him it wasn't her fault. That she hadn't done anything to endanger his precious career.

Oh, who was she kidding? She wanted to feel his arms around her again—to be lost in his kisses. And that was exactly why she ought to turn around and go home. There wasn't any room in her life for complications. She belonged at Rivercrest with her father. Not here in the rain, dreaming about a stranger.

She turned to go, dipping her head to avoid the worst of the downpour. She shouldn't have come, but at least she'd realized it before she'd done anything foolish. What she needed now was a hot bath and a warm bed.

Tomorrow this would all be a bad memory, and no one would be the wiser.

A crash of thunder announced that the storm had finally arrived in full force. She tried to hurry, suddenly feeling afraid. A sound echoed through the storm. A car door maybe. She glanced back over her shoulder in time to see the silhouette of a man illuminated by the lightning.

She sped up, trying to keep from breaking into a dead run. There was nothing to suggest that the man was after her. Dressed in a mackintosh and carrying an umbrella, he was probably just going home. She was letting the storm scare her, allowing her imagination to run away with her again.

Her car loomed out of the dark, and with a sigh, she pulled her keys out of her pocket, fumbling with the lock, cursing herself for her stupidity. She had no business being out here at this time of night alone. What the hell had she been thinking?

She shot another glance in the direction of the stranger. He'd passed the entrance to the apartments and was closing the distance between them. She squinted against the rain, trying to force her now shaking fingers to ram the key into the lock. Between the rain and the dark, she couldn't make it fit.

Finally, the key slid into place and she wrenched the car door open, just as two strong hands closed on her shoulders.

She tried to jerk free, to run, but her legs had deserted the ship. As she buckled forward, her last thought was that in this storm no one could hear her scream.

• • •

"Riley, it's me. Jake." He was kneeling in front of her, his worried face blurry in the rain.

"You scared the hell out of me. I thought . . . I thought . . ." She stood up, trying to regain her composure.

"I just wanted to make certain you were all right. And it's a good thing I did. You weren't." He gestured to the open door and the keys dangling from the lock.

Resentment boiled to the surface, accompanied by anger. "I wouldn't have been so frightened if you hadn't been stalking me."

He frowned, raindrops dripping from his hair onto his face. "I'm hardly stalking you. I was coming home. I live over there." He gestured in the direction of his apartment building.

"I know that. But you passed it up and f-followed me over here. And I didn't kn-know it was you, so I panicked."

His frown turned to a scowl, and she took a step back. "Someone was stalking you?"

"Y-You." She fought to contain a shudder as the icy rain pelted her.

He gripped her shoulders again, his look intense. "Riley, I came from that direction." He tilted his head away from the building.

"But—" She stopped as her beleaguered brain registered the fact that he wasn't carrying an umbrella or wearing a raincoat. "I guess I let my imagination run wild. I've been doing that a lot lately." She smiled weakly, the shivering starting in earnest now.

Jake's look changed to one of concern. "You're soaked. We've got to get you inside."

She shook her head, still bemused by everything. "I should go home. Sh-Shouldn't be here."

"Don't be ridiculous," he said, reaching across her to close and lock her car. "We need to get you dry first."

Her mind insisted that she say no, but evidently her body hadn't received the message. She leaned into his warmth, grateful for his strength as he steered her toward his apartment. The storm had increased in intensity, the lightning and thunder crescendoing around them.

Jake lowered his head so his words could reach her over the wind. "What are you doing out here, anyway?"

"I was coming to see you." The words were out before she had a chance to think better of them.

He stopped, his gaze probing hers. "Why?"

"To tell you I didn't set you up."

"I believe you."

"Then why?" Anger seared through her again.

"Why did I come down so hard on you?" He paused, his eyes still searching hers. "It's complicated. At first, part of me honestly believed it was you. But another part of me knew you wouldn't do something like that."

"So you went with the Riley's a bitch scenario?"

"Something like that. Look, this isn't going to make sense, but the truth is that I wanted you so badly it was easier to believe you'd betrayed me."

"And now?" The words were soft, almost a whisper lost in the wind and rain.

He didn't pretend to misunderstand. "I still want you."

She sucked in a breath, tipping her head back, oblivious now to the fall of rain. What she wanted, what she craved, was the touch of this man. It wasn't wise, it probably wasn't even rational, but at the moment she didn't care.

He brushed his mouth against hers, the touch sending trails of heat chasing through her. The kiss was even more powerful than the one at the party. Elemental. Made more so perhaps by the storm around them.

She wasn't sure exactly how it happened. One minute they were standing in the rain, bodies pressed together, and the next he was carrying her through the lobby of his building, her face buried in the damp wool of his sweater.

She might have abandoned her reserve, but her instincts ran deep, and she'd been playing the politician's daughter all of her life. Only when the doors to the elevator slid shut did she allow herself to relax, to concentrate on the power of the man who held her.

His gaze collided with hers, his eyes hungry. He released her, holding her close, so that her body slid against his, the motion of the elevator enhancing the friction. She arched against him, wanting more, her hands threading through the inky silk of his hair.

His mouth found hers, and she welcomed him inside, reveling in the thrust of his tongue against hers. They parried and dueled, using touch as a silent language, neither advancing or retreating but instead joining together in a tempestuous dance of emotion and sensation.

The elevator abruptly jolted to a halt, the lights dimming then going out altogether. They separated, his arms still holding her, her cheek pressed against his chest, the rhythmic beating of his heart comforting.

"What happened?" She sounded as breathless as she felt. She ought to be frightened, but she wasn't. Not here, not with Jake.

"It must be the storm." Keeping an arm around her, she felt him reach for the elevator panel, heard the soft click as he pressed a button. "The power must be out."

"Are we safe?" She tried to see him in the dark, but the blackness was absolute, the silence surrounding them.

"Absolutely. This elevator has been here as long as the building. I'd say in fifty years it's survived its share of blackouts."

She relaxed against him. "But we're stuck?"

"For the time being." His hands moved in slow, languid circles across her back, his breath lifting the tendrils of hair around her face. She moved closer, pressing against him, feeling his arousal hard against her thigh.

With a groan, he lifted her so her back was supported by the corner of the elevator, his mouth crushing hers, his need for her laid bare with his kiss. Passion rose inside her, and she gave it to him freely, wanting him as much as he wanted her.

His fingers brushed against the satin of her bra, dipping inside, finding her nipple unerringly in the dark. The sensation ignited pools of liquid heat between her thighs, and she arched back, offering herself to him. He trailed hot kisses along the line of her neck and down the slope of her breast, the soft silk of his hair adding torment to the already unbearable heat.

When his lips closed around her areola, tugging gently, she fought to contain a moan, the sound coming out a muted gasp. His tongue circled her nipple, drawing it farther into his mouth. Braced against the wall, she leaned back, her body responding with a fervor she hadn't known she possessed.

His hand reached for the hem of her skirt, easing the gauzy cotton up her thigh, his tongue still licking and teasing her breast. His hand rose higher, and higher still, until all that separated his fingers from the throbbing junction between her thighs was the soft satin of her underwear.

She held her breath as his fingers slid between the satin and her skin, circling lazily, slowly, until she thought she might explode. Then suddenly he was there, deep inside her, moving, stroking, the rhythm increasing as he suckled her breast.

His mouth and his hands possessed her, driving her higher and higher, until there was nothing but the feel of him burning against her, inside her. He moved down, raining kisses along the smooth skin of her abdomen, crossing the divide marked by her bunched skirt, the heat of his lips making her writhe against him.

With amazing finesse he slid down her panties, removing them, raising one leg so it hooked over his shoulder. With a soft cry she abandoned all decency, pushing against his head, urging him on, balanced on the edge of a precipice that scared and excited her beyond anything she'd ever imagined.

His mouth found her, his tongue driving deep inside her. He tasted her, drinking her in, pulling her soul from her body into his. The darkness surrounded her, caressing her as his tongue moved in and out, in and out, driving her higher and higher, until the darkness exploded with light, and she cried his name, reaching to hold him, to anchor herself in the spinning vortex he'd created.

She felt his arms close around her, heard the sweet whisper of her name as he kissed her face, and she let go, allowing herself to soar, to fly, knowing that he would never let her fall.

The elevator lurched with a hum as the lights flickered back on. Riley blinked, startled by the brightness, immediately embarrassed. She ducked her head, mortified at what she had done, but he forced her head up, forced her to look at him. The passion reflected there made her gasp, and her embarrassment faded. Whatever was happening, they were in it together, and there was something absurdly alluring about the fact.

With a ding, the elevator doors slid open with a whoosh. Using his body as a shield, Jake held her close and they walked in silence to the door of his apartment. Once inside, he reached for the lights, but she stopped him, wanting the protection of the shadows, of the dark.

Lightning flashed in the window, washing the room with momentary light. She took a step toward him, reaching for the buttons on his shirt, trembling with the enormity of what she had done, what she intended to do.

His hands covered hers, a question in his eyes. And she stood on tiptoe to press her lips against his. A covenant of sorts. His mouth opened and he pulled her hard against him, accepting what she offered, raising the ante with the fervor of his kiss.

They backed into the room, arms locked around each other, tongues tangling together with need. When the sofa stopped forward momentum, they pulled apart, breathless, laughing like children.

She reached again for the buttons on his shirt, fumbling in her haste. With gentle fingers he helped her until she slid her hands along the satin smooth muscles of his chest, delighting in the contrast.

Steel in velvet. Like his eyes, his voice, the man was a contradiction that begged exploration. She ran her tongue along the edge of one nipple, pleased when it tightened under her touch. Pushing his shirt to the floor, she dropped her hand, stroking first the ridge of his stomach and then shyly reaching for the hard bulge beneath his jeans.

Covering her hand with his, he helped her establish a rhythm, his other hand seeking, and finding, the soft curve of her breast through the thin cotton of her blouse. Heat built as Riley's timidity gave way to passion, and the banked fire inside her sprang to life again.

"I want you, Riley O'Brien." His voice was hoarse, grating against her with the same power as his fingers.

"Good." She slid down the zipper on his jeans, her eyes locking on his. "Because I want you too." Her hand closed around the long hard length of him, and she smiled, reaching up to swallow his groan with her kiss. "Right here. Right now."

He pulled her up into his arms, his mouth branding her as his. In three strides he carried her into the bedroom, laying her on soft cotton sheets. The sounds of the storm were muted by the window glass, but she could see rivulets of water running down the panes.

The lightning was less frequent, but still illuminated them in bursts of icy white, the cool color a contrast to the heat burning inside her. They pulled off their clothes, careless of buttons and closures, their need spurring them into a frenzy.

Riley ached inside, wanting only to feel him fill her, two parts coming together to make a whole. She tipped back her head, welcoming his hands and mouth. He explored every inch of her, leaving nothing untouched, unloved. Trembling with the sheer power of the feelings he evoked, she rolled on top of him, indulging her need to taste him—all of him.

She'd never felt so reckless, so sure of herself, and she marveled at the confidence he inspired in her. Even the storm no longer scared her. Rather, it felt like a symphony. A musical score accompanying the splendor of their lovemaking.

With a smile, he flipped her to her back, pinning her with the gentle comfort of his weight. Catching her gaze, he waited, poised above her, promising everything.

She nodded, opening to him, and with one swift move he buried himself deep inside her, filling her to the bursting point. The pleasure was exquisite, and she pushed against him, taking him even deeper.

There was passion reflected in the depths of his eyes, passion and triumph—and something else, something so tender it almost took her breath away. She lost herself then, in the dark of his eyes, blue on black.

Eyes still locked together, he began to move. Slowly, almost languorously at first, each slow thrust tormenting and delighting. With a moan, she slammed upward, driving him home, and the fury erupted, the storm reaching crescendo. They moved together faster and faster, whirling higher and higher, twisting and turning, locked together in their own special dance.

With a crash, thunder filled the room, the reverberation echoing off the walls. Reaching for the heavens, they touched the stars, rising above the storm, intertwined—intrinsically joined.

Body to body.

Soul to soul.

For the first time in as long as Riley could remember, the darkness was her friend. She felt safe and cherished—protected against the monsters of the night.

Martell Osterman hated his job.

Well, most of it. He had to admit there were times when he liked it. Times when he got to rough somebody up, break bones, or even better, take somebody out. But people were more cautious these days, and, more often than not, it seemed the only thing they wanted to pay him to do was sit on his ass, drink bad coffee, and wonder what the hell he was doing parked in front of a yuppie apartment building on fucking Peachtree Road.

The silhouette of Christ the King rose into the storm-tossed sky, twin crosses illuminated in the lightning. God on fire. Martell wanted to laugh, but instead he shivered, wondering if God was indeed watching—judging. He reached for his cold coffee and took a sip. Surely he was on the side of righteousness, or at least the almighty dollar. A god of sorts. Weren't they one and the same?

It didn't matter. He knew his limitations and that was something. He turned his back on the cathedral and its spires, ignoring his misgivings. He had a job to do. He looked out the car window, eyes scanning the street, careful to keep low in the seat.

No sense in leaving someone with a memory.

He cast another sideways glance at the church across the street, a giant monolith, a testament to man's ego or God's demands. The part of him he hadn't sold to the devil yearned to believe. But it was too late. Too late for anything but the apartment on the sixth floor.

And the man inside it.

Jake Mahoney—and the bimbo with legs to here. He clenched, wishing he was the one in the warm apartment, fucking the blonde's brains out. He'd seen her. Wanted her. But before he could get near enough to confirm that she was as winsome up close as she was from a distance, his mark had arrived.

Damn it to hell.

He replayed the scene in his head. Seeing her indecision, and then her fear. She'd thought he was a threat. In his mind's eye, the lightning flashed and just for an instant her features were illuminated.

His blood ran cold, snapping him back to the present.

His boss was going to shit a brick.

The bimbo with Mahoney was the fucking senator's daughter.

Chapter 11

JAKE STOOD AT the bedroom window, staring out into the Atlanta night. The storm had passed, the morning star shining through what remained of the clouds. The streets shone diamond bright in the lamplight, sluggish morning commuters beginning to head to offices across the city.

He turned around, leaning against the windowsill, his gaze resting on the sleeping woman in his bed. As usual, he'd bitten off more than he could chew. Not that the metaphor was exactly apropos.

The fact was, he'd been wrong about Riley O'Brien. She wasn't made of ice. She was all fire—and something more. A sweetness, almost a shyness, that she buried deep under the hard shell of the candidate's daughter.

And quite frankly, she scared him to death. There was a vulnerability there. A trust that he wasn't certain he could live up to. She made him act crazy. Made him forget all about his resolutions concerning women.

And he wasn't a man who liked being out of control.

The cynic in him said it was all about hormones. Testosterone and pheromones. And the last time he'd trusted those he'd ended up with Lacey. Now there was a smart move. Not that it was fair to compare Riley with his ex-wife. Underneath Lacey's beautiful facade there was nothing. No warmth, no light—nothing. Just a woman who loved no one but herself. A woman who meant to climb to the top, no worries about who she destroyed along the way.

And he should know, he'd almost been a casualty.

But Riley was different. There was a substance to her, a depth that transcended her outer appeal. At least he thought that was the case. But what the hell did he know? Still, he couldn't dismiss the sex. It had been incredible. Frankly, he'd never experienced anything quite like it.

His body responded immediately to the memory of her, hot and willing in his arms. He wanted more. Hell, he wanted Riley. But then once upon a time he'd wanted Lacey too, and look where that had gotten him.

Still, there was a difference. Damned if he could say what it was. But something about sex with Riley transcended the normal. He had the feeling that he'd held something special in his arms. Something that didn't come along more than once in a lifetime.

Unfortunately, it was probably the wrong lifetime.

He wasn't ready for another commitment. And even if he was, there was simply no way—not between his career and her life. The President's daughter and the journalist. It sounded like the title of a bad B movie. One he'd be best off avoiding at all costs.

But he had the distinct feeling it was a little too late for those sentiments.

Riley sighed in her sleep and rolled onto her back, her golden hair splayed out on the pillow, one hand, palm up, on the sheet. She was beautiful even in sleep—and trusting. Despite her take no prisoners attitude, down deep she was soft.

He turned back to the window, thinking about the events of the past few days. He had nothing but questions. Primarily concerning Hank Larsen and what the hell he'd found that had gotten him murdered. Hopefully he'd have more answers tomorrow, after he'd had the chance to go over the man's case files. Something that tied in to Michaels.

Michaels. Another big question. What had made the man commit suicide? There were a million possibilities. And without a note, there seemed no way to know for certain. What he had been able to get out of Michaels's coworkers seemed to imply everything was all right on the job. And although Jake hadn't interviewed the wife, he'd managed to see the statement she gave the police.

She'd claimed her husband was happy. And healthy. Which meant that whatever had happened had come on suddenly. Jake leaned his head against the glass. Surely his phone call hadn't been enough to send the man over the edge? He tried to remember his exact words. He'd implied that he knew more than he did. Had Larsen found something damaging enough to throw the chief of police into complete panic at the thought of the information going public?

But with Hank dead, where was the threat? Which left him right back at the beginning. What the hell had Larsen found?

He blew out a breath, watching the cars below him. Mankind in a perpetual hurry. Going nowhere fast. Behind him Riley moaned, the sound low and frightened. He spun around in time to see her thrashing in the bed, hands extended, caught in a dream, her face tight with fear.

"Caroline?" Her cry was plaintive. The voice of a child. "Daddy?"

He crossed the room, surprised at the depth of his concern.

"No."

The single word sent a chill racing through him. This was no dream. It was a nightmare. He shook her gently, calling her name, but she fought against him, her whimpers of fear edging on hysteria.

Without thinking, he slid into bed, locking his arms around her, pulling her taut body against his. "It's all right, sweetheart, I'm here. You're safe."

She stopped moving, her body relaxing, but her soft whimpering still filled the room. Anger rose inside him, filling him with an overwhelming need to find the source of her pain and exterminate it once and for all.

"I won't let anything hurt you, Riley. I promise."

His soft words seemed to comfort her, and with a sigh, she sagged against him, still caught in sleep. He brushed back her hair and kissed her cheek, the feel of her tears against his skin threatening to break his heart.

Riley opened her eyes, surprised to see dappled sunlight on the ceiling. She remembered closing her shutters last night. To keep out the storm. She frowned as other details began to filter through her sleep-laden brain. The color of the walls was wrong.

Memories of the night came flooding back.

The elevator.

The storm.

Jake.

Oh God. She turned her head, memory becoming reality. He was there. Next to her, in full-blown naked glory. She sucked in a breath, her body doing more than remembering. Sleep had softened the hard edges, leaving the beauty of the man. His hair curled across his forehead, the stubble of his beard shadowing his face. Dark against light, the contrast reflecting the man.

He sighed and shifted, one arm closing possessively

around her. It felt right. And horribly wrong. She'd acted on emotion last night. Following passion instead of common sense. But now the storm had passed, and although she regretted nothing, it was time to face reality.

It was like that movie with Audrey Hepburn—the one about a princess who escaped for a day. She closed her eyes, trying to remember the title.

Roman Holiday.

Audrey Hepburn had been overwhelmed with the weight of her responsibilities. She'd run away. Right into the arms of Gregory Peck. And she'd fallen in love with him.

Riley frowned, trying to remember more, then wished she hadn't. Gregory Peck's character had been a journalist too. And in the end Audrey Hepburn had left him, choosing duty over happiness.

Riley supposed it was meant to seem noble, but it was more than that. She of all people knew that it was far more than that. It was tragic. A woman condemned to loneliness, all in the cause of honor and duty.

She carefully dislodged Jake's arm, thankful when he didn't awaken. It would be easier that way.

She wasn't a princess. But she knew all about duty. Her place wasn't here. No matter how wonderful her time with Jake had been. She belonged at Rivercrest with her father. She slid from between the sheets, gathering up her clothing, her eyes never leaving the sleeping man.

She was taking the coward's way out. She knew that. Running away from something that had the potential to change her life. But things were never easy. And she, of all people, knew there was no such thing as happily ever after.

Everyone had their place in life. And she was well aware of hers.

Her father was going to be President of the United States. There wasn't room in her life for anything else. She had a duty to fulfill.

She'd had her interlude. And she'd cherish it always. But now it was time to go back where she belonged.

No matter how much it hurt.

Haywood stood at the door to the infirmary, trying to screw up the courage to go inside. He'd had to pull the few meager strings he had to wangle the chance to see Bryce. And now that he was here, he didn't know what he wanted to say.

He'd never been a man's man, tending to be a bookish type. Not that he was exactly a ladies' man either. He was more of a loner. The kind of man nobody particularly wanted to curry favor with. Except for the fact that he was part of one of the richest families in Atlanta. Correction—had been part.

Now he was totally alone.

And that's what made Bryce's friendship so special. The man didn't give a damn who Haywood had been on the outside. He was a friend because he saw something decent inside of him. Something Haywood sure couldn't see in himself. But in the moment when he'd seen Bryce being stabbed, he'd known without a doubt that he'd be willing to die for the man.

And that was an amazing revelation. Something he was certain he'd never felt about anyone before. *Never*. Not even . . .

He shook his head, unwilling to go there. She was dead, and for all practical purposes so was he. Dead. Inside and out. And reliving that night wasn't going to bring anything back. He was an empty shell. And nothing mattered.

He shook his head, pulling himself out of the past. Something did matter—*his friend*. And right now he needed to make certain Bryce was going to be all right.

The infirmary, such that it was, wouldn't be winning any good housekeeping awards. There were six beds lined up on each side of the long room, neatly bisecting it in half. No privacy screens here. No amenities either. Except that the sheets were clean and the mattresses fresh.

He walked down the center aisle, grateful the ward was almost empty. There was already talk on the cell blocks. He'd interfered in prison business. Called the guards, no less. It marked him. For some a hero—for others the enemy. Probably more the latter than the former. It should have scared the crap out of him, but instead he felt liberated. He'd taken a stance.

It felt good.

Bryce was in the last bed, his bandages white against the smooth mahogany of his skin. He lifted a hand in greeting, his smile false against his pain.

"You going to be okay?" Haywood tried for cheerful but missed by a mile.

"They tell me I'll live. Took a few stitches, but they patched me up real good." Bryce shifted against his pillows, propping himself up a little higher. "It's good to see you." This time his smile was genuine.

And Haywood felt a burden he hadn't known he was carrying shift and then dissipate. "Glad to see you too. I was afraid for a while that—" He broke off, feeling awkward and uncomfortable.

"Nothing to be afraid of. Takes a little more than a piece of honed Plexiglas to bring me down. Have a seat." He motioned to the battered chair next to the bed.

"Doc says you'll be out of here in a few days." Haywood sat on the edge of the seat, his gaze still locked on the bandages.

"Yeah. They're holding on to me a little longer. Some crazy idea of protecting me."

Haywood suppressed a shiver. "You think the guys who did this would try again?"

Bryce shrugged, wincing with the motion. "Wouldn't be surprised."

"Then it's just as well they're keeping you here."

"No place is safe, Haywood, when someone wants you dead."

"You make it sound more serious than just a prison beef."

Bryce shrugged, the gesture making him wince. "I don't know. There're people who might want to see me dead. But I wouldn't have thought I was much of a threat anymore."

Haywood frowned. "You're talking about the people who framed you?" They'd never really talked about his incarceration, other than the fact that Bryce maintained his innocence.

"Yeah," he sighed.

"Want to tell me what it was about?"

Bryce leaned back against his pillows. "It was a long time ago. Ancient history. No sense dredging it up now."

Haywood leaned forward, patting his friend's hand awkwardly. "We all live with our past, Bryce. It never goes away altogether."

"You talking about you or me?"

Haywood suppressed a bitter smile. "Me, I guess. You never actually murdered anyone. I did. I suppose there's folks who'd like to see me dead too."

"Maybe. But they're playing on the right side of the law."

Haywood shivered despite the warmth of the room. "Here's hoping they stay that way."

"Things gonna happen the way they're gonna happen. Ain't nothing you can do about it."

Haywood pulled out of his self-pity. "You really believe that?"

"Yeah, maybe. Once, a long time ago, I had it all. And then, just like that," he snapped his fingers, "it was gone. Had nothing to do with me. But I paid for it just the same. In an instant everything changed forever." He ran a hand along the edge of his bandage. "After that nothing else mattered."

Haywood's eyes dropped to the bloodstained gauze, then lifted to meet his friend's gaze. "Surely some things matter."

"I suppose so." His response was lackluster. "But I'm not making any wagers on it."

The guard at the door tilted his head, indicating it was time to go.

"Listen, Haywood . . ." Bryce grimaced as he struggled to move closer. Haywood met him halfway. "You shouldn't have helped me. The guys who did this to me will be watching you now. Whoever is pulling their strings will know what you did." He paused, pulling in a ragged breath. "And there's a possibility they'll come gunning."

Haywood nodded. The thought had already occurred to him. "If I had it to do over, I'd do exactly the same."

"I know that." He reached over, grasping Haywood's hand in his. "And for that I'll be forever grateful. But I'm not up to watching your back right now. So be careful. Sleep with one eye open if you have to."

Haywood squeezed his hand and released it, embarrassed at the emotions welling inside him. He hadn't felt anything in such a long time.

It was overwhelming, but it felt good. It felt damn good.

Maybe he'd been wrong. Maybe he was alive after all.

Which was ironic when he considered the fact that, thanks to the altercation in the yard, he was probably marked for death.

Jake smiled, stretching beneath the sheets. He couldn't remember the last time he'd felt this good waking up in the morning. But then, it had been an amazing night. He rolled over, reaching for Riley, surprised when his hands met only the cool cotton of her pillow.

Frowning, he sat up, searching the room. She wasn't there. And neither were her clothes. A flash of panic ripped through him, as he flung the covers aside and ran to the bathroom.

Empty.

She wasn't in the kitchen either, or the living room. She was gone. Vanished as if she'd never been there at all. He sank onto the sofa, his stomach churning. She'd run away. He shouldn't have been surprised. By all odds, they should never have come together in the first place.

But they had.

His heart sank. Maybe she was like Lacey after all. Memories of last night flooded through him, refuting the thought before it was even completed. She wasn't Lacey. But the fact still remained that she'd left without so much as a word. Anger surged through him.

He might not be ready for a full-blown relationship, but he sure as hell deserved more than a drive-by. Maybe she was used to one-night stands, but he wasn't. When he slept with a woman, it meant something, damn it.

And if he had his way, this wasn't going to end here

and now. One way or another they were going to have a repeat performance. Ms. O'Brien had another think coming if she thought he'd give up this easily. He was a fighter to the core. And when he found something he really wanted, he went after it full steam ahead.

He blew out a breath, amazed at the turn of his thoughts. He stood up, needing to do something—anything. Out of the corner of his eye he caught a flash of white near the door.

An envelope. Hope speared through him. She hadn't run away. She'd left a note. He picked it up, ripping it open.

His joy dissolved into disappointment. It wasn't from Riley. He sank down on the sofa, trying to reel in his thoughts. Opening the thin sheets of paper, he glanced down halfheartedly, then jerked back for a second look as his brain registered the significance.

He was holding a twenty-year-old autopsy report—for Caroline O'Brien.

Chapter 12

Riley OPENED THE back door, hoping against hope that the kitchen would be empty.

It wasn't.

"Morning," Adelaide called cheerfully. "Sleep well?" She turned to face Riley, her grin indicating she already had a pretty good idea of the answer.

"How did you know?"

"You were gone all night. You're blushing like a virgin, grinning like the Cheshire cat, and your buttons are crooked." She nodded meaningfully toward Riley's shirt.

Riley look down at the buttons on her blouse, her face burning hotter. "It was nothing."

"Right, and I've been asked to guest host for Regis Philbin. Riley, this is me you're talking to. I know you."

Certain her shirt was suitably straight, she looked up, meeting Adelaide's gaze. "It was a mistake to go."

"Jake wasn't who you thought he'd be?" Adelaide's dark eyes held a serious question.

"It's not that." She shook her head, chewing her bottom lip. He had been so much more. "It's just that I can't . . . it's wrong . . ." She fumbled for words, trying to order her rattled thoughts. "It's just impossible. There's Daddy, and the campaign. It was one night, Adelaide. Just one night."

"Tell that to your heart."

There was wisdom there, and Riley recognized it, but she didn't have the luxury of letting her heart hold sway. "It isn't that simple."

"It's as simple as you want to make it. Honey, we're talking about your life. You can't let other people's dreams be your sole reason for existing."

"I'm not. It's my dream too." She sounded defensive and she knew it.

"Is it?" Adelaide raised an eyebrow in question, looking fierce. Jake was right—she did resemble a gnome. An incredibly wise one at that.

"It is," she said firmly. "Daddy and I have worked hard for this, and I am not going to do anything to jeopardize our chances. Nothing is worth that, Adelaide. Nothing." Some small part of her wasn't buying any of this, but so far she was managing to keep it sequestered.

"I'm glad to hear that, Riley." Her father strode into the kitchen, smiling, but the smile didn't extend to his eyes.

There was an uncomfortable silence as father and daughter eyed each other warily. Riley continued to chew on her lip, not certain where to start. "You know."

"That you went to Mahoney last night? I figured as much."

"And you're angry with me?" It was a stupid question. Of course he was angry. How could he not be? He'd specifically asked her to stay away from the man. And she'd slept with him. Not that she intended to share that little fact with her father.

"I'd best be getting off." Adelaide reached for her purse, shooting Riley a look. "I have errands to run."

Carter nodded absently, his attention focused on his daughter. Riley swallowed nervously. So much for reinforcements.

"I'm not angry, Riley. I'm disappointed. I thought you'd show better judgment." His look belied his words.

Riley felt her stomach drop, but despite the feeling, or maybe because of it, she lifted her chin. "I didn't do anything wrong."

"Maybe, maybe not. Either way, you took a risk."

Her own anger flared. "I most certainly did not. I only wanted to explain that I hadn't been the one to call his paper."

"It doesn't matter a hill of beans who placed the call, Riley." Her father narrowed his eyes and they stood face-to-face.

"Of course it does. I won't have people thinking I can't be trusted. He could have been dismissed from his position."

Carter waved a hand, interrupting her. "The man was asked to stay away from you. Nothing more."

"Either way, it was my integrity. And I don't like having it impugned for no good reason."

Her father sighed, running his hand through his hair in an uncharacteristic gesture. "And that's the only reason you went?"

"Not that it's any of your business, but yes, that's the only reason." Sort of. It certainly was the most obvious choice.

"I see."

She sighed with exasperation. "You don't see anything."

"Of course I do. You went off in the middle of the night, in the middle of a storm, no less, to tell a man you barely know that you were not responsible for his being rebuked for harassing you."

"He wasn't harassing me."

"He most certainly was. You just aren't savvy enough to recognize it."

Well, if talking to her had been crossing boundaries, she thought, sleeping with her would certainly not be within acceptable bounds. Any thoughts Riley'd entertained about coming clean with her father dissipated with his words. "Nothing happened." She clenched her fists at her sides, trying to get through to him.

"You were gone all night." He might as well have been tapping his foot, the proverbial parent.

"I am a grown woman, Daddy."

"Who is about to become the First Lady of the United States."

"First Daughter," she corrected perversely.

"Whatever." He waved a hand through the air again. "The point is that First *Daughters* do not go around cavorting with journalists. Especially barracudas like Jake Mahoney."

"I wasn't cavorting."

He grew very still, his eyes on her rumpled clothing. "You obviously spent the night."

She swallowed, certain there were some things she did not have to share with her father. "It was storming. It seemed safer to stay."

He glared at her.

"Nothing happened." Why was it her father's stare could reduce her to repeating herself? And lying. "And more important, it's over. I will not be seeing him again." And she meant it. "I know how important this campaign is to you. And I won't jeopardize it—I swear to you. Although, to be honest, I fail to see how my seeing Jake Mahoney is a threat to anything."

"He's a reporter."

"Daddy, I realize that there's danger in talking to the press. And I realize that being involved with a member of the press is taboo. But I think you and Leon have gotten a little carried away about all this." If she talked enough, maybe she'd convince herself that it didn't matter.

Her father's face relaxed, concern replacing his anger. "I didn't mean to sound so harsh. But you're my child, Riley, and I love you. . . ." He trailed off.

"It's all right, Daddy. I love you too. But you've got to let me find my own way."

"I'm trying. It's just that I worry." He smiled sheepishly, a lopsided attempt at compromise.

"Well, stop worrying. Jake Mahoney isn't part of the equation." She said it with all the certainty she could muster, knowing that she'd just have to make it the truth.

Somehow.

"You won't see him again?"

She stopped short of out and out lying. "For all its size, Atlanta is a small town, Daddy. I can't say that I'll never see him. But I have no intention of initiating further contact. How's that?"

"It'll have to do." He pulled her into his arms.

She hugged him back, the contact comforting. He'd always been there. No matter what had happened, they'd faced it together. He probably knew her better than anyone on earth, but she still couldn't help wondering if he had any idea what was truly best for her.

How could he possibly know, when she wasn't certain herself?

"Here's the article on Larsen's death." Jake picked up a sheet from his printer tray and handed it to his editor.

Tim slipped on his glasses, skimming the article. "There's not much here."

"That's because we don't know much. Only that the fire was the result of arson. Which means that Larsen's death wasn't an accident."

"Which, considering he was an ADA, probably narrows the list of suspects to a couple hundred, give or take."

"Exactly. Although given what we know, there's a distinct possibility that we can narrow that down. But not on paper. Not yet, anyway. All I've got is the man's phone call."

"And the fact that he's dead. Circular logic. So what do the police say?" Tim frowned, looking up from the article.

"They've upgraded the investigation to homicide, but they aren't ruling out the idea that the fire wasn't intended to kill the man."

"Which would mean manslaughter."

"Yeah, but that doesn't track with what we know. If Larsen really did have something on Michaels, and if Michaels knew about it, then it would make sense that he'd have Larsen taken out of the equation."

"The problem with that scenario is that once Larsen was safely out of the way, it doesn't follow that Michaels would kill himself. So we're back where we started."

"I'm close, Tim, I can feel it."

"What happened with the girlfriend?"

"Not much. Larsen had evidently been bragging about his ship coming in, that sort of thing. But she didn't know where any of it was coming from."

"Did she give you an explanation for her sudden vacation?"

"More or less. Basically, Larsen's death spooked her. Made her realize how quickly it can all end. So she took the first boat out of town, so to speak."

"So another dead end." Tim's eyebrows shot up above his glasses, his expression doubtful. "You going to Michaels's funeral?"

"Yeah. Under the circumstances, it seems appropriate. Then later tonight I'm set to see Larsen's files. Hopefully, there'll be a connection to the trial Michaels allegedly tampered with. It's worth a look."

"All right. For now, we'll hold off on anything more than reporting the ATF's findings." Tim leaned back against Jake's desk.

"Sounds like a plan." Jake glanced down at the envelope lying on the desk, debating the wisdom of sharing its contents with Tim. He decided he owed his editor at least a heads-up. "I came across some other information today. Something to do with Caroline O'Brien."

"I thought you were going to back off." Tim's look turned fierce.

Jake held up his hands in defense. "The information just fell into my lap. And I'm not certain it means anything anyway. But I want to follow through, and to do that, I might need to talk to Riley."

"Jake . . ." There was a world of meaning in just the one word.

"I'll be careful. I promise. But you need to know that Riley wasn't the one who made that call."

"It doesn't matter, my friend. The call was made and the orders came down."

"I'll be discreet, I promise. But this is something I need to do." Hell, he just needed to see her, period, but he wasn't about to share that with Tim.

The editor sighed. "I suppose there isn't anything I can say that will stop you."

"No. But I wanted you to know what I was up to."

"So you want to tell me what it was exactly that got dropped in your lap?"

"Why don't I wait and see if it amounts to anything first."

"Fine." Tim shook his head, looking more like a tolerant parent than a managing editor. "Just don't get too distracted. We need to find out what happened with Larsen. Anything between you and Riley O'Brien needs to remain subordinate to that."

Whatever the hell was going on between him and Riley, he was fairly certain it wasn't going to be subordinate to anything, but it didn't seem wise to share that fact with Tim. "I honestly doubt it will amount to anything. But you know me, I've got to follow up on a lead."

Tim's expression was resigned. "Just be careful."

"Don't worry. I will." Jake smiled absently, wondering exactly how he was going to get Riley to see him. And exactly how he was going to break it to her that someone was interested in her sister's death.

What he needed was an ally.

And he knew just whom to call.

Riley sat on the edge of her bed, staring at the empty table. The book was gone. Or maybe it had never been there. She ran a hand through her hair, trying to understand what was happening to her. In the course of two days, she had abandoned her reserve for something coming close to recklessness.

She'd slept with a man she hardly knew, and now it seemed she was losing her mind. She traced a finger along the finely grained wood of the table. The book *had* been there. She was certain of it.

Sort of.

She'd been in such a state last night. Worrying about Jake and her father. Lost in thoughts of her sister. Maybe she'd just imagined it all. No one would deny that she'd been under a great deal of stress. Her father was running for President, and she'd somehow turned into a magnet for disaster. Or maybe it was Jake who was the magnet, and she was simply attracted to the wrong man.

God. It was all so confusing. And in the grand scheme of things, Caroline's book was nothing. Still, it was unsettling. Maybe she should have told Jake. Maybe there was something to it after all.

She blew out a breath in frustration. Maybe she should just take an ad out in the newspaper: Senator's Daughter Cracks Under Pressure. Squaring her shoulders, she stuck out her chin. O'Briens were made of stronger stuff than that. Someone had probably put the book away. It was no doubt safely back in the library. Back where it belonged.

Just like her.

She belonged here at Rivercrest—with her father. At the end of the day, family loyalty was everything.

And nothing else could be allowed to get in the way.

Especially not Jake Mahoney.

"You're absolutely certain that it's a good idea for us to be here?" Carter stepped out of the town car looking picture perfect. Which was exactly the way Leon wanted him.

"Of course it's a good idea." Leon straightened his jacket and closed the door, nodding to the driver. "Douglas Michaels was a staunch supporter, and he was a major player in Atlanta politics." They began to walk toward the church, Secret Service men flanking them on two sides.

"He also committed suicide, and rumors are running rampant."

"I don't see what that's got to do with you, Carter. You're just a fellow citizen of Atlanta coming to pay last respects." Flashbulbs popped on all sides as they neared the entrance.

"That's all fine and good, unless some overexuberant reporter decides to find fault with our presence."

"You're being paranoid. The man just snapped." Leon leaned closer, keeping his voice low. "I can't say that I'm really all that surprised, given his line of work. Imagine the horrors he's probably been witness to over the years."

"Sorry I'm late." Maudeen pushed through the crowd of reporters, falling into stride with them. "Where's Riley?"

"Inside, I hope," Leon said. "She was coming directly from the Junior League."

"Where've you been?" Carter hissed out of the side of his mouth, his face a mask of sincerity, his eyes still centered on the crowd around them. "I've been looking for you all morning."

Maudeen dipped her head, swallowing nervously. "I had some errands to run."

"I see." Carter sounded anything but happy, and Leon wondered if he'd misjudged the man's attachment for the woman.

"Carter, I went to see Julia Michaels. I thought it was something you'd want me to do."

He relaxed immediately, reaching for her hand. "How's she holding up?"

Maudeen shrugged. "As well as can be expected, I guess. They've been keeping her sedated."

"Did she mention anything about why he did this?" There was a note of disbelief in Carter's voice. "Hell, he wasn't much older than me. And certainly at the pinnacle of his career. It just doesn't make sense."

"I don't think anyone has a clue, Carter. In fact, I doubt we'll ever know for sure." Leon pulled open the church door. "Some people simply aren't capable of achieving greatness without caving in to the pressure."

"I guess you're right." Carter shook his head, obviously dispelling any thought of Michaels's demise, his expression moving back into candidate's position. "And this is certainly one hell of a photo op." He raised his hand in a calculated wave.

"Absolutely." Leon laid a hand on Carter's shoulder. "Front page material. Hell, we ought to be thanking Douglas Michaels."

Jake stood in the crowd of reporters watching Carter O'Brien and his entourage pass. The man actually walked like a President, if that were possible. He was flanked by his press secretary and Leon Bronowsky. They were deep in conversation, and despite their purposeful air of serenity, he would have sworn there was dissention in the ranks.

The thought made him smile, thinking of Riley. Her absence from the little gathering could mean anything. And he was determined not to read anything into it.

"She's already inside." Edna Winston appeared like a phantom at his elbow.

"So what, you've taken to mind reading?" He looked down to meet her amused gaze.

"You're the one who called and said he needed to talk."

"Well, I wasn't implying you had to materialize out of thin air."

Edna laughed. "I think you're just preoccupied. I take it you had a nice evening."

He actually felt the stain of a blush. Damn the woman. "How did you—"

She smiled. "Let's just say I'm in the know."

"Well, that makes one of us."

"These things are seldom easy, my boy, but that doesn't mean they're not worth the effort."

"Do you always talk in riddles?"

"Only when I'm attending a state funeral."

Jake sobered. "There are certainly a lot of dignitaries here. Michaels had a lot of friends."

"Honey, this isn't about friendship. It's not even about respect. It's about political oneupmanship. These people are afraid not to be here."

"Because they have something to hide?"

Edna linked her arm with his. "No, because appearances are everything. And even a funeral can become a political event." She tipped her head toward another entourage making its way toward the church. "The mayor. He didn't even like Michaels. Wanted Fred Abramson for the job."

"I thought it was his appointment?" Jake watched as the little man waved for the crowd. "His and the city council's."

"Hardly. A decision like that comes from the well-connected, Jacob. A favor here, a job well done there. Cultivate the right people, and a low level flunky becomes police chief."

"You're talking in riddles again."

"No. I'm just talking common sense, based on years of political experience. I know how the game is played. And if you want to find out what drove Michaels to suicide, then you need to understand whose palms he was greasing."

"So why aren't you investigating this?"

"Because I don't give a rat's ass. I've got bigger fish to fry. In case you haven't noticed, there's an election to cover. And I'd say things are heating up quite nicely." She smiled up at him. "So tell me why you wanted to talk."

"I'm not sure now is the time."

"I hardly think Michaels will care, Jacob. And other than that, who gives a damn?"

"Well, it's about Riley. I need your help."

Her smile broadened to a grin as they walked to the church. "I thought you'd never ask."

Riley sat in the church, trying to look pious, but the truth was, she didn't feel the slightest bit reverent. She felt more like a hypocrite. She hadn't known Douglas Michaels that well, and though she was sorry he'd died, she wasn't sure how she felt about the fact that he'd killed himself.

Seemed like sort of an easy way out. A coward's solution. But then, who was she to be talking about cowards? She'd run out on Jake this morning, and she'd avoided telling her father the truth.

And now both of them were here in the church with her. Well, not "with her" exactly. She was sitting three people down from her father and half a church away from Jake. Only it felt like he was only inches away. She could literally feel his eyes on the back of her neck.

Damn the man.

She blew out a breath and pretended to concentrate on the service. Michaels's wife was giving the eulogy. What would it feel like, Riley wondered, to tell a church full of strangers about the man you loved? What would it feel like to wake up in an empty bed, knowing he was never coming back?

Maudeen was crying softly into a handkerchief. Her father's, probably. Maudeen and Julia Michaels had gone to school together. Shared their hopes and dreams. Now Julia was alone. And Maudeen was going to be mistress to the President.

Riley bit her lip, ashamed of her bitter thoughts. Her father had the right to be happy. It's just that she wanted to be happy too—with Jake. Despite herself, she turned to look behind her. He didn't turn away. Didn't pretend he hadn't been watching her. Instead, he boldly met her gaze, his blue eyes full of questions.

Questions she couldn't—wouldn't—answer.

But God, how she wanted to.

"So you want to tell me what this is all about?" Jim Bartlett leaned forward, eyes narrowed, his hands steepled together on his desk.

"I appreciate your meeting with me on such short notice. I'm doing a piece on Douglas Michaels and I thought maybe you could help me clear up a few points."

"I'll help if I can." The mayor eyed him warily, his look contradicting his words.

"Michaels's rise through the ranks of the police force was nothing short of meteoric."

"I don't know that I'd say that. He had something like thirty years with the force."

"Most of it fairly undistinguished. But he was still appointed chief. According to my sources, Michaels wasn't your first choice for the job."

"That's true. I wanted Abramson. I don't think there's any secret in that."

"But the council wanted him too. So how did Michaels wind up with the job?"

"Look, Mr. Mahoney, there's a lot of under-the-table deal-making involved in political appointments. Even something as seemingly low level as a police chief."

"So you're saying there was pressure to appoint Michaels."

Bartlett leaned back, his gaze hardening. "I'm not saying anything. I'd be careful who you push, Mr. Mahoney. There are people out there who don't take kindly to having their motives questioned, and they tend to come out fighting when challenged."

"Are you threatening me, Mr. Bartlett?"

The mayor's smile did not extend to his eyes. "Absolutely not, Mr. Mahoney. This just isn't your usual turf, and I wanted to make certain you understood how the game is played."

"Oh, I know how the game is played, Mr. Bartlett. I just don't know who all the players are. But I will, and when I do—I promise you, I'll be the one who comes out fighting."

Chapter 13

"So how was it?" Edna sipped her iced tea, keeping her voice low, so the other restaurant patrons couldn't overhear their conversation.

"God." Riley choked on her salad. "I might as well have taken out a full-page ad in the AJC. I suppose you talked to Adelaide?"

Edna shrugged, not looking the slightest bit apologetic. "She mentioned it."

"Well, she'd just as well not have said a thing. There's nothing going on between Jake Mahoney and me." Riley leaned forward, waving her fork to emphasize her point. "I spent the night there. I probably shouldn't have, but I did. And although it was wonderful, it was a huge mistake. And I can promise you, I will not be making it again."

She stopped, out of breath and angry at herself for revealing so much.

"It doesn't sound like a mistake at all." Edna speared a piece of lettuce and dipped it in dressing.

"Are you crazy?" Riley's voice came out on a shriek, and she quickly reined it in, lowering it to a whisper. "Being with Jake is inviting disaster."

Edna held up a hand. "Look, why don't we agree to disagree. In my humble opinion, he's a good man."

"I believe that too." Her eyes met Edna's, and Riley

found herself wishing her father was a shoe salesman or something. Anything that meant his life wasn't subject to intense public scrutiny. "But the fact remains that my life isn't my own. And the daughter of the President cannot cavort with a journalist."

"Cavort?" Edna's eyebrows rose above the top of her glasses.

"Daddy's word. But he's right, Edna. I can't have a relationship like that. Truth is, I can't have a relationship at all."

"Your father said that?"

"No, not in so many words. But it's true. I need to focus on my father's campaign right now. And later, if we win the election, on what's best for the country. There isn't time for anything else."

"Sounds like a load of horse manure to me." The older woman studied her, frowning. "You look tired."

"I guess I've been burning the candle at both ends. Things have been tense at home, between the campaign and the publicity surrounding the bombing and Douglas Michaels's suicide."

"I saw the picture in the paper. Have they really been hounding you?"

"Considering the magnitude of the situation, they've actually been amazingly reserved. But you know Daddy—any press is bad press unless he's the center of it all."

Edna nodded, taking a sip of tea. "I guess that's understandable under the circumstances."

Riley sighed. "I suppose so. But it gets rather tiring. I can't do anything without examining the potential for repercussions, and sometimes I just wish I could be a regular person and live an ordinary life."

"I'm not sure that any of us really lead ordinary lives, Riley. It's all a matter of perspective."

"Now there's a cheerful thought." Riley attempted a smile, but she missed by a mile.

"Honey, you've got to start living for yourself. And maybe Jake Mahoney is a good way to start."

"You sound like Adelaide. But the answer is still no. I have to put this campaign before anything else. And the simple fact is that Jake's job is always going to put him in the middle of trouble . . . trouble that could ultimately bring bad press for my father. I just can't take that kind of chance. I owe Daddy better than that."

"Sometimes it's more important to put your own needs first." Edna's phone rang, and she pulled it out of her purse, flipping it open. "Winston here."

She listened for a moment, the lines of her face softening as she smiled. "We were just talking about you, Jacob. I'll bet your ears are ringing."

Riley tried to look disinterested, but her heart rate ratcheted up a couple of notches.

"Yes. She's right here. Would you like to talk to her?"

Riley shook her head, waving her hands to fend off the phone.

Edna shot her a look. "Here she is."

There was no way to refuse without being rude, so she took the phone, justifying her actions by telling herself it was the polite thing to do.

"Riley? You there?" His voice was smoky and deep, sending a shiver racing through her as memories of last night tumbled over each other in her brain.

"I . . . I'm here." Her gaze met Edna's, and the older woman nodded approvingly.

"I missed you this morning." There was a lazy curl of something sensual in his words, and her heart threatened to leave the building altogether. "You ran out on me."

"I had a meeting." It sounded lame even though it was the truth.

"I saw you at the funeral."

"I know." She trailed off lamely, words deserting her.

"Riley? We need to talk."

She shook her head, taking a deep breath for fortification. "I don't think that's such a good idea, Jake." She closed her eyes, relieved that she'd managed to force the words out.

"I don't think we have a choice. Too much happened last night for us to ignore it."

"Nothing happened." The words had become a mantra she was repeating to everyone.

"That's bull and you know it." He was angry now. "What we had last night was incredible."

"It was just sex, Jake." God, she hated lying. Last night had been amazing. Beyond her wildest dreams. But she couldn't tell him that. She shouldn't even be admitting it to herself.

"It was a hell of a lot more than that."

"Maybe we just don't feel the same way about it."

"Riley, I was there, remember? You're lying to me and you're lying to yourself."

Her stomach lurched. Now he was reading her mind.

"I need to see you."

"I've already said that's impossible." She looked to Edna for support, but the woman was pointedly ignoring her, sipping her tea, keeping her attention focused on the restaurant crowd.

"Look, it's about more than just last night. It involves something I found concerning Caroline."

"What?"

"Your sister. I have something here I think you ought to see."

"You're investigating my sister?"

There was silence for a moment on the other end. "No, sweetheart, I'm not. I've just found something that I think you should see. All right?"

The endearment hit her with the power of a tidal wave, washing away much of her anger, leaving her struggling to hold on to at least some of it. He sounded sincere, and she wanted to believe him, but she'd been raised to distrust the press, and Jake was first and always a journalist. Still, he wanted to share information. That was something, wasn't it? And if she was honest with herself, she had to admit she did want to see him.

She covered the phone with her hand, her gaze meeting Edna's. "He wants to meet with me. Something to do with Caroline."

It was Edna's turn to frown. "And that's all he said?"

Riley turned a vivid shade of pink. "Well, no. There was other," she waved her hand in the air, "stuff."

Edna sipped her tea, brows drawn together in thought. "Then I think you should go."

"Just like that?"

"Riley, you spent the night with the man. Surely you have some sense as to whether you can trust him."

She did trust him. And that was what scared her. She blew out a breath, moving the phone back to her mouth. "I don't want to meet anywhere publicly."

"You could come here." There was a smile in his voice.

She swallowed nervously, a fire sparking deep inside her. "No. I don't think that's a good idea."

"All right then, how about by the river? The park at Akers Mill."

Riley sighed, realizing she had never stood a chance. Between the sound of his voice, the memory of last night, and her own desire to see him, it had been a losing battle from the start. Throw in Edna and her obvious matchmaking, and that was the ball game.

Reporters 1. Candidate's daughter 0.

"I'll meet you in an hour."

The Chattahoochee River was known for its rafting, but you couldn't tell it from this particular stretch. The water was slow here, brown and lazy, the banks swollen by the recent rain. Trees lined the river, some dipping low, branches trailing the water.

Riley picked her way around the rocks to the water's edge, finding a seat on a large boulder. She'd come here often as a kid—with Caroline. They'd skipped rocks, waded, fished, even run a trot line once. They'd pretended the old mill was the ruins of a grand plantation, and refought the battles of the Civil War among the towering beeches and oaks.

She'd learned history, and discussed the ways of life. Read fairy tales and dreamed. Always with her big sister watching over her.

Tears welled.

She threw a rock into the river, watching as it skipped over the rolling water. It would be so nice to run to Caroline. To tell her about everything that was happening. To ask her about Jake. To get her advice. But that wasn't going to happen. Caroline was gone. And life had continued. Without adventures at the river.

Without dreams.

She lifted her arm to throw another rock.

"Penny for your thoughts?"

The rock spun out into the river, sinking without a bounce. "Jake."

He held out a hand and helped her up. "I didn't mean to scare you."

"It's all right, really." She let her hand linger longer than necessary, taking comfort from his touch. "I was just lost in thought."

He frowned, reaching out, one finger tracing the plane of her cheek. "You've been crying."

"I was thinking about my sister. I seem to be doing that a lot lately." Ducking her head, she struggled for control. "We used to come here when I was little."

He dropped his arm back to his side, moving away from her. "I'm sorry. If I'd known, I would have suggested somewhere else."

"It's fine. Kind of apropos, really." They started walking along the river's edge, shoulders brushing as they moved, each touch sending sparks of fire dancing across her skin.

"Did you come here a lot?"

She nodded, letting the velvet timbre of his voice wash over her. "I wasn't a planned child. My mother wasn't supposed to be able to have more children."

He reached for her hand. "They must have been delighted."

"Not really." She looked out at the slow moving water, watching a branch caught in an eddy. "It wasn't that they didn't want me. But they were used to things as they were. I think the idea of a baby was more than my mother could handle. So she did what she did best—ignored the problem." His hand tightened on hers. "My sister took over taking care of me.

"It was a lot to ask of a ten-year-old. But she didn't seem to mind. I guess I was sort of a real life doll to her. Anyway, I can never remember a time when she wasn't there." They stopped, and Riley turned to face him. "We used to come here on 'adventures.' Caroline had a fertile imagination, and it was heaven for me."

Jake laid a hand against her cheek. "You must miss her very much."

"I do. Always will, I guess." She forced a smile and continued walking. "So, do you have brothers and sisters?"

"No." He tossed a stick into the water, the current carrying it away. "There was only me and my dad."

"You said your mother was buried in Texas. Is that where you're from?"

"A million years ago." She thought she heard a touch of bitterness in his voice, but it was gone before she could be certain. "I'm from Freeport. My dad has a shrimp boat."

"He's still living?"

"Yeah." Jake smiled. "He doesn't go out on the boat much anymore, but he still goes down to the dock every day."

"So who takes the boat out?" They stopped again, and sat down on a fallen log.

"My cousin Hector. He runs the operation now. Just don't tell that to my father." He laughed, and she relaxed in the moment, the intimacy of sharing with another person. She couldn't remember the last time she'd just sat and talked with someone.

"Did you ever go out on it?"

"The boat? Yeah. Every summer until I was grown. It wasn't the easiest of jobs, but my father believes hard work makes the man."

"And does it?"

"Well, you be the judge." His smile was intimate, and she shivered with pleasure. "All I can tell you is that I dreaded those summers."

She couldn't help but laugh. "So you left."

"As fast as I could. I couldn't wait to get the smell off

my shoes, and I still can't stand to look at a shrimp, let alone eat one."

"But why Atlanta?" She tilted her head, allowing herself the luxury of studying his face.

"By default, I guess. I went to the University of Georgia. Football scholarship."

"Wait, let me guess." She closed her eyes, pretending to concentrate. "Tight end."

He smiled. "Safety. But that was pretty close. How'd you guess?"

"Loads of experience. My sister loved football. We used to watch games together."

And just like that the moment faded. They'd come full circle. Back to Caroline.

She turned to face him. "You said you'd found something about Caroline."

He reached into his pocket, producing two pieces of paper, and handed them to her. "It's not so much what I found. It's what found me."

Riley stared at the autopsy report in her hands, rereading it, her thoughts reeling. "This says that my sister was pregnant."

"Wasn't she?" Jake asked, his voice soft, his concern obvious.

"No." She looked up, anger warring with horror. "Of course not."

"The report couldn't be clearer." He reached for her hands, and in her agitation she jerked them away, surprised to see the flash of hurt in his eyes.

"Then it's been doctored or something. Caroline wasn't old enough to have . . . to have . . ." She trailed off, unable to finish the thought.

"I can understand how hard it must be to think of your sister in that light, but she was eighteen, Riley.

That's certainly old enough to have been—" He paused, obviously searching for the right words. "—*in love*."

"Being in love doesn't always have to equate with sexual activity."

"Riley," Jake's voice was gentle, "you were only eight. You wouldn't have known."

"Of course I would." She sounded petulant and she knew it, but this was *Caroline* they were discussing. *Caroline*. "My sister didn't have a boyfriend. And without a boyfriend she couldn't have been pregnant. This has got to be some malicious person's sick idea of a joke."

Jake shook his head, his eyes serious. "If that were the case, whoever wrote it would have sent it directly to your family. I've been doing this a long time, and when someone leaks something, his motivation may be far from noble, but the information generally tends to have basis in fact."

"But the implication would be that someone covered it up." And that someone would have had to be her father. But she didn't believe that. He faced things head on, her father. He wouldn't have lied about something so important.

"Maybe we're jumping to conclusions. The only thing we can be certain of at this point is that someone out there wants us to believe that your sister was pregnant."

She forced herself to concentrate on the facts. "We need to authenticate this. Is there a way to do that?"

"The M.E.'s office should have a copy. We ought to be able to verify it off of that. And failing that, there's always your copy."

She nodded, trying to separate emotion from logic. She couldn't help anyone if she gave in to her panic. "And we can keep what we find quiet?"

"I honestly don't know. If we don't do something, then whoever sent this to me will probably send it somewhere else. And they might not be as concerned about the story's impact on you." His eyes met hers, the message there going well beyond anything to do with Caroline.

Riley looked away, ignoring the implication. "This is a nightmare."

"Maybe not. If we can prove this is fake, then at the very least you'll be ready with a rebuttal if this version becomes public."

"And you'll help me do that—prove it's a fake?" She hated having to ask him for anything, but he was the only one she could trust. The thought brought her up short. But the sentiment was accurate. It might be a mistake. Or it might be only an emotional reaction to the intimacy of the night before. But whatever the reason, she did trust him.

"I can check with the M.E. if you'd like. See if they have a copy. But we could be opening a kettle of worms if the document proves accurate."

She held his gaze, trying to decide what to do. It had been one thing to *say* she was going to find out what this was all about, but it seemed quite another to actually *do* something about it. Still, it was her family they were talking about. She couldn't stand by and do nothing. "I'll look for our copy. It'll give us further authentication."

"I think you're doing the right thing. You need to know what the truth is. And if it does turn out your sister was pregnant, then you can figure out the best way to handle the information."

She studied him for a minute, trying to order her thoughts. "If someone did cover this up, it wasn't my father. I can't believe he could have kept that kind of secret from me."

Jake turned to look out at the water. "People do what they think they have to, Riley."

"So you think he was protecting me?" She shook her head. "I don't buy it. Daddy and I have always been honest with each other. We're a team. If there's any truth to this at all, it doesn't involve him. I'm certain of that much."

"So you're going to tell him what I've found?" Jake threw a stone into the water, his eyes still focused on the lazily moving river.

She ran her hands through her hair, wishing she'd wake up and find all of this a dream. But it wasn't. And though the thought of a cover-up frightened her, never knowing the truth frightened her even more. "No. I need to know the truth first. Then I'll bring it to my father. There's no sense upsetting him, until I have a better idea what this is all about."

Jake nodded, his eyes narrowing. "What can you tell me about the night Caroline died?"

Chapter 14

RILEY TOOK A step backward, needing the distance, suddenly doubting her decision to trust him. His dark eyes were probing, his demeanor seeming to change from confidant to inquisitioner in an instant. The strength of her uncertainty made her dizzy and she stumbled.

Jake reached for her, his strong hands steadying, his touch only confusing her more. Their gazes met and held, and breathing became difficult. "I didn't mean to sound so abrupt." Regret colored his expression. "It's second nature for me, I guess."

"To go for the jugular?" The words came out on a whisper.

"Sometimes." He lifted a hand, caressing the curve of her cheek. "But not with you, Riley." His gaze darkened, and she shivered from the intensity. "Never with you."

There was so much unspoken between them. Far beyond Caroline, and the campaign. But she wasn't ready for that. Might never be ready for that. So she chose the lesser of two evils.

"She loved the balcony. Especially when there was a storm. She'd stand there and watch it come in, watch it cloak the sky. It was raining that night. An awful storm. The railing was loose. Had been forever. My father was always saying he'd fix it. But he didn't. They heard her scream." She trailed off, staring out at the river. "They say she died instantly."

"They?"

She pulled in a slow breath, the motion soothing. "The police. My father. Leon. Everything I know about my sister's accident is secondhand. I wasn't there."

He frowned, and she wondered if it was because of her words or her sudden capitulation. "But you were in the house."

"I was asleep. My room is at the opposite end of the house."

His look was probing again. "But you must have heard something."

She shook her head. "Nothing."

"What happened when they woke you?" He sat down on the log, pulling her with him.

"They didn't." She felt tears again, and wondered if it would ever stop hurting. "I told you before, I was an afterthought in their lives."

"Sweetheart, it would have been awful for them. A parent's worst nightmare. I'm sure they only did what they thought best."

"Maybe, but either way, it wasn't until the next morning that I knew anything was wrong." She closed her eyes. "As I said, there was a storm that night. A bad one. I can still hear the thunder."

"Is that why you're afraid of storms?"

She opened her eyes, startled. She supposed she shouldn't be surprised that he'd noticed. That was his avocation, after all. But even so, she found it a bit unsettling. "I suppose it's part of it." She stopped, unwilling to go any further. "I've honestly never liked them." It was a lie, but she couldn't bring herself to discuss her nightmare.

He nodded, his eyes reflecting his doubt. She sucked

in a breath, waiting for him to ask for more, to push harder. "So they told you the next morning?"

"Told me what?" She struggled to cover her surprise. He hadn't pressed her. Maybe he'd meant what he said. Maybe he wouldn't force her confidences.

"About Caroline." His voice was gentle.

"Oh, I see." She felt foolish—and selfish. She'd been so preoccupied with thoughts of intimacy and Jake, she'd forgotten her reason for being here. *Caroline*.

"So, did they tell you that morning?" Jake repeated.

"No. Not immediately anyway." She stared out at the river, letting the memories wash over her. "When I woke up, the sun was shining. Which surprised me. Daddy always came in to wake me up—so I could get ready for school. It was a game of sorts. He would come in playing reveille."

"On the trumpet?"

She shook her head, smiling. "No, it was all pretend. He'd sing it like he was the trumpet."

"Sounds like a hell of an alarm clock to me." Jake returned her smile.

"It was." She sighed, remembering.

"But the day after Caroline died he didn't come?"

She picked at the moss on the side of the log, the soft feel of it a contrast to the hard edges of her memories. "No. I thought he was probably running late. And since I was the one who usually was behind, I decided to surprise him. So I got out of bed and put on my uniform."

"Catholic school." It was a statement, not a question.

Riley nodded. "Anyway, after I finished, I sat on the side of my bed, waiting for him to come. Excited because he was going to be so proud of me."

"For being on time."

She blew out a breath. "I wanted so much to please him." A piece of bark broke off in her hand and she threw it into the river, watching as it sank and then surfaced, bobbing along in the current. "I waited and waited. But he didn't come. So finally, I went along to Caroline's room, thinking she'd know where Daddy was.

"But she wasn't there. So I sat by the window, and waited some more. Waited until the morning was almost gone, every minute more certain that something was horribly wrong."

"What happened?" His voice was soft, but insistent, pulling her away from the past.

"Adelaide found me. And broke the news. My parents were locked in their bedroom. Consoling each other, I suppose." She swallowed her pain, pushing it firmly away. "So you see, I can't shed any light on her death. I went to bed with a sister and family, and woke up the next morning to find that they were all gone." She shrugged, forcing a smile. "But I survived."

His hand tightened on hers, his look unreadable. "At what cost?"

"I don't know. There's a price to everything, isn't there?" She tried to keep the bitterness out of her voice.

"Some more than others." Again she had the sense that there was more to his words than just talk of Caroline. "I didn't mean to make you go through it all again. But if I'm going to help you, I need to try and understand what happened."

"So that we can unearth some forgotten truth about my sister? That's just what they want, isn't it? Whoever sent the autopsy report. They want me to question my beliefs about my sister. To believe the worst. Well, I won't."

He reached for her other hand. "No matter how much we love someone, no matter how well we think we know them, the truth is, there are always secrets. Things that wait in the dark of the night to show their ugly heads. To prove to us once and for all that there is no such thing as a happy ending."

She believed all that he was saying, believed it with her whole heart. But saying it aloud made it sound so awful, so empty. Like a life devoid of sunshine. Perpetual darkness. She shivered. "You're not talking about Caroline anymore, are you?"

Jake dropped her hands, abruptly severing the connection between them. "I was talking about all of us, Riley. The whole damn human race. We seem intent on believing in fantasy—in fairy tales. But I, for one, know firsthand that, in reality, it's sometimes nothing more than an empty illusion."

"*Sometimes* being the operative word here, Jake." She couldn't believe that *she* was offering him hope. But he sounded so bitter, and something deep inside her wanted only to ease his pain, to wipe the sadness from his eyes.

He smiled, the gesture crooked and endearing. "We've gotten a little off track." He was politely but firmly closing a door. Disappointment washed through her. "The point is someone wants us to find out the truth about Caroline. Whatever that may be."

Riley nodded, pulling her thoughts away from the enigmatic man in front of her. "And we've got to follow the bread crumbs to the answer."

He nodded, his look grim despite the smile. "And if you're right, it will have all been about nothing."

"And if it's not?" She met his gaze, looking for reassurance, for something, anything to ease her sudden doubt.

"Then we'll face it together."

The thought should have comforted her.

But it didn't.

Two trips to the M.E.'s office in one week had to be a record. At least this time he was sitting in Megan's office instead of watching her slice and dice.

"Who gave this to you?" Megan was frowning over the top of her reading glasses at the autopsy report.

"I don't know. I found it in my apartment. Apparently, someone shoved it under my door."

"Was there a postmark?"

"Nothing. Just a plain envelope. No fingerprints."

Megan's eyebrows rose over the frames of her glasses. "You took this to the police?"

"God, no." Jake smiled sheepishly. "I have my own kit."

Megan laughed, the sound filling the small office. "I should have known."

"And I'm trusting that you won't tell anyone either."

"Why would I?" She shrugged. "There's nothing illegal about having a copy of an autopsy report. And this one," she waved at the papers in her hand, "isn't even interesting."

"Except for the fact that it concerns the daughter of a man running for President of the United States."

"Well, there is that." She smiled. "But it's still nothing earth-shattering. According to this, Caroline O'Brien fell from the balcony of her home, and in the process managed to break her neck. End of story."

Jake's mind was whirling with possibilities, none of them panning out. Why the hell would someone give him Caroline's autopsy report? Her death had been well-publicized. A tragic event that had ultimately taken the life of Riley's mother as well. He hadn't been around when it happened, but he'd seen it referenced often in newspaper articles about Carter. The pregnancy, if there was one, had obviously been covered up—but even that wasn't particularly newsworthy twenty years down the road.

He turned his attention back to the M.E. "Can you verify that it's authentic?"

"Sure. We should have the original." Megan grimaced. "Somewhere. Things are a bit jumbled in our archives since we've moved to the new building, and this case is really old. But I can have someone check into it. And if we can't find it, there's always the APD. There should be a copy in the original police file."

"How about the M.E. who signed this? Is he still around?"

She shook her head regretfully. "No."

"The proverbial dead end?"

"The literal one." She shrugged. "He died over eight years ago."

"Perfect."

"Hey, you take what you can get. Right?"

"I suppose." He stood up, ready to go, swallowing his frustration. "I'll count on your discretion of course."

"Jake, I've been out on worse limbs for you before. This one is nothing. I'll keep the search on the QT and call you if we find anything. Okay?"

"Thanks, Megan. Don't know what I'd do without you."

The M.E. smiled. "You'd flounder."

Riley stood in her father's study feeling like a traitor. Which was stupid, because all she was trying to do was protect him. Protect him and find out the truth about her sister.

Hopefully, the two things weren't at odds.

She sat down in front of her father's desk, praying for a miracle. So far the fates seemed to be on her side, which, considering she'd never attempted anything even remotely clandestine before, was something of a relief. All she had to do was find the report, prove to Jake that the other one was a fake, and voilà, she was off the hook.

Sort of.

There still remained her feelings for the man, but now was not the time to examine those. Truth was, between bombs and campaigns, old mysteries and renegade journalists, there might never be a "right" time. She sighed and pulled open a drawer.

As in everything, her father's desk was overly organized. He had a streak of the obsessive compulsive. All the files were neatly labeled, most of them having something to do with the campaign.

Closing the first drawer, she pulled out a second. Again the files were neatly organized, and although the labels yielded more personal titles, there was nothing about Caroline. Or about her. She pulled open the final drawer only to find more of the same. Great. She was on a wild goose chase, tempting cataclysmic disaster.

Or maybe she was preventing it.

At least that's what she kept telling herself.

The whole idea here was to protect her father's campaign. Everything in politics was about spin, and if ever there was a situation they needed to control, this was the one. She honestly didn't believe the report Jake had was real. But if it turned out that her sister had been pregnant, she'd have first shot at the information. *They'd* have first shot, and it'd be easy then for Maudeen, or one of her father's other PR folks, to give the whole thing a positive slant.

Or bury it once and for all.

If Jake would allow it.

And therein lay the rub. Jake was first and foremost a

reporter, and, despite what he'd said, it would be difficult if not downright impossible for him to pass on a
story. And even if he did, there was always the chance
that whoever had sent the autopsy report would take it
to someone else.

This was the right thing to do.

She closed the drawer. Nothing here. She swiveled
around in the chair, searching the office, trying to think
of where her father would keep something as important
as her sister's autopsy record.

She crossed the room to the oil painting of Rivercrest. It wasn't very good. Her mother's sister fancied
herself a painter. Still, it was perfect for hiding the safe.
She glanced out the door, and then carefully pushed the
painting out of the way. It slid back on specially in-
stalled runners, exposing the cold gray steel of the safe.

Twisting the knob first left and then to the right, she
prayed that her father hadn't changed the combination.
A satisfying click indicated he hadn't. She drew in a
breath for fortification, reminding herself that she and
her father had no secrets.

The safe, like the desk, was neatly organized. Papers
in one compartment, other precious things in another. It
was tempting to look at her mother's jewelry, but there
wasn't time. Praying that she was doing the right thing,
she reached for the papers.

There were titles and deeds, report cards and birth
certificates, the little things that marked the life of a
family. Almost at the end of the pile, she found what she
was looking for. Caroline's death certificate and the autopsy report.

She carefully folded the papers and stuffed them in
her pocket, then closed the safe, sliding the picture back
into place.

"Riley? Darlin', what are you doing in here?" Her

father stood in the doorway, leaning against the doorjamb.

She jumped a mile, heat rushing to her face. So much for her undercover skills. "You startled me."

"I can see that." Her father frowned. "Are you all right?"

She sucked in a breath, pasting on a smile. "I'm fine. I was just lost in thought." She scrambled for composure. "I thought you'd already gone."

His face relaxed. "I'm on my way. Just thought I'd give my best girl a hug before I left."

She stood up, moving into his embrace, feeling guilty for deceiving him, but it was in his best interest, and that had to count for something. They broke apart, and this time her smile was genuine. "You're going to be a great success tonight. I just know it."

"Well, I'd better be. People paid good money to attend this thing, and they'll be expecting something wonderful."

"They paid their money because they support you, Daddy. They're expecting to see the candidate, nothing else."

He ruffled her hair. "I suppose so. Sure you don't want to change your mind and come with me?"

"And upset the entire seating chart? I don't think so. Besides, Leon will be there. And Maudeen. You don't need me."

"I always need you, princess."

"I know, Daddy. Me too, you." She blew him a kiss. "But right now you'd best get a move on."

He glanced at his watch and grimaced. "I'm already late. Leon will not be happy."

She grinned. "Or at least he'll pretend that he's angry." Leon's bark was much worse than his bite. "When should I expect you home?"

It was his turn to blush. "I, ah, won't be back until in the morning. It's over an hour's drive from here, and the wine will no doubt be flowing, so I thought it best to stay close by."

Her father always carefully limited his alcohol at official functions, but she wasn't about to call him on it. If he wanted a night away with Maudeen, so be it. She certainly had no right to question his needs. Not after last night.

"That seems prudent. No sense taking chances." She smiled at him, telegraphing her support.

Besides, his absence meant she could take what she'd found to Jake without having to answer questions. Maybe fate was actually on her side. She'd show the report to Jake and have it safely back long before her father got home.

"Thank you, darlin'." Her father hugged her again, then headed for the door. "I'll see you tomorrow."

"Knock 'em dead." She flashed the victory sign, and his smile widened to a grin.

"I love you, princess."

"I love you too, Daddy," she whispered as he left. "More than you'll ever know."

"Megan Green called." Walter Finley waved a sticky note in his face as Jake walked into the newsroom. "Said it was important."

Jake took the Post-it and headed for his office, stopping halfway, turning back to face Walter. "So what happened the day of the rally?"

Walter had the grace to look embarrassed. "I caved. Fell off the wagon completely. So much for the twelve steps."

"But I thought you'd been doing a lot better."

The older man shrugged. "I'd been going to meetings. Obviously that wasn't enough."

"So you just went on a binge?" Jake sat on the edge of the desk, his instincts tingling. Walter was a lush, and he didn't always manage to get to work, but he rarely missed something important. And the rally was big news in Atlanta.

"No. At least that wasn't my intention. I got a call about a tip."

Jake frowned. "From who?"

"I don't know." Walter drummed his fingers against the desk, the staccato sound audible in the already noisy room. "It was a man. Said he had information—something to do with illicit funding."

"For the presidential campaign?"

"He didn't say. But I got the feeling he was talking about local stuff, and given the problems we've had of late, I thought it might be interesting to hear what he had to say. He wanted to meet at the Velvet Hammer."

"The tit bar?"

"I think the tits are a bit long in the tooth, if you know what I mean." Walter grinned. "Anyway, I figured I could meet the guy and still make the rally."

"So what happened?"

"Informant never showed. I waited for about an hour. *Not drinking.*"

"And then something happened."

"Yeah, guy I was sitting next to started buying rounds. What can I say . . ."

"You got wasted."

Walter dipped his head. "I don't have an excuse. I simply couldn't handle it. But at least I had the presence of mind to call the paper." He looked up, his eyes begging forgiveness.

"Yeah. At least you did that." Jake sighed. "You remember what the guy looked like?"

"I'm afraid it's all pretty fuzzy." The older man frowned, obviously trying to force the memory. "He was small, I do remember that. And sort of dandified."

Now there was an archaic word. "What about hair color?"

Walter shook his head. "It's all just a big blur. Why you asking?"

"Because it seems awfully coincidental that you get a call that ultimately leads to your getting drunk, right before I get my car blown up."

"I thought they blew up the wrong car—that it was supposed to have been someone's in the O'Brien entourage."

"Maybe. Or maybe it was a setup."

"You think someone got me drunk on purpose?"

Jake blew out a breath, his mind whirling. "It wouldn't be hard to do."

Walter stared down at his hands. "And since you always cover for me, you'd be called in."

"It's plausible."

"But pretty far-fetched. What if I'd ignored the call? Or been strong enough to resist the drink?"

Jake met the old reporter's rheumy gaze.

"So it was an odds-on gamble. But why would someone want to blow you up, Jake? You investigating something that big?"

He thought about the police chief—about Hank Larsen. Was there something there worth taking him out? And if so, who was pulling the strings? He sighed, returning his attention to the old man. "I don't know, Walter, but I sure as hell intend to find out."

Chapter 15

"HEY, YOU WERE supposed to call me back." Megan Green leaned against the partition that formed the outside wall of Jake's cubicle.

"Sorry. It's been that kind of a day." He indicated the chair across from his. "You didn't have to come over here."

She shrugged and sat down, crossing one shapely leg over the other. "I was on my way home, so I had to drive by here anyway."

"I take it you found something?"

"It was more about not finding, actually. Which raises some interesting questions in my mind." She frowned. "We don't have any record of the autopsy or the report."

Jake opened his mouth to ask a question, but she waved him silent.

"I'm not surprised, really. As I told you earlier, the record keeping in the new building isn't up to snuff, and the older cases seem to be the ones that wind up misplaced. What does surprise me, though, is that there isn't a police record either."

"Maybe because it was an accidental death?"

She shook her head. "Doesn't track. We're talking government bureaucracy here, and we save everything. There should have been something."

"You mean there isn't even a file?"

"That's what I'm telling you. There's nothing. It's as if officially the woman never died."

Jake ran a hand through his hair. "So what does it mean?"

Megan shrugged. "Probably nothing. But I figured it was enough of a coincidence that you'd want to know about it."

"Thanks." His mind was turning over the possibilities, trying to make sense of something that quite possibly didn't.

"How're you coming on the Larsen story?"

"Slow and steady, I guess. I've got an article running in the morning. I guess you heard that the fire has been ruled arson."

"Yeah, word filtered down. David Mackenna is good at what he does. So now you're looking for an arsonist?"

"Something like that." He glanced at his watch. "Shit, I'm due at the courthouse in half an hour."

"A reporter's work and all that." She smiled, standing up. "Kinda late for a meeting, isn't it? It's already after seven."

Jake shrugged, sliding into his sport coat. "Sometimes it's best to meet when there are fewer prying eyes."

"Enough said." She walked with him out of the cubicle, toward the door. "Just be careful that you haven't bitten off more than you can chew."

If only she knew.

"You're looking a lot better, my friend." Haywood pulled a chair up beside Bryce's bed. "I would have brought candy, but my access to shopping has been somewhat limited these days."

Bryce smiled, his face still a little haggard. "I'm gonna live. Not that anyone will care, mind you."

"What about the guys who did this? Any news on them?"

"Come on," Bryce scoffed. "You know as well as I do that in here it's live and let live, and die and let die."

"Still, you'd think someone would have seen something."

"Oh, I'm sure they did, but no one is saying anything."

"So when are they releasing you?" Haywood forced a smile, hoping his concern didn't show through.

"You mean back to the main population?"

Haywood grinned. "Well, the alternative would be preferable, but yeah, I meant back to stripes and bars."

"Don't know. I think they want to give things a chance to die down."

"You don't look like you believe they will."

Bryce sighed. "If what I think is happening is happening, there isn't anything that'll stop them."

"We're back to your past again."

"We're back to people with more power than you can imagine."

"Oh, I can imagine, Bryce. You forget where I come from. So tell me about who's after you."

"The less you know, the better. Suffice it to say that this man makes and breaks people on a daily basis. He builds them up or he tears 'em down, and I don't think he gives a shit which way it goes, as long as he comes out a winner."

"Sounds serious. Maybe I could talk to someone for you."

"Talking won't do no good. We're way past the talking point, believe me. Something out there's scaring the man, and so now he's after me."

"Why?"

"Because I know too much. Trouble is, I don't know what the hell it is I know." Bryce reached for a water glass and drank the contents down. "At least things are looking up for you."

Haywood frowned at the change of subject, confused. "Don't know what you mean."

"Michaels is dead, didn't you hear?"

A feather of hope tickled against his heart. "Someone killed him?"

"The bastard killed himself."

The feather vanished, replaced with sharp pain. "You don't think it was my fault?" He hated the need in his voice, but he'd already killed one person, and he couldn't bear the weight of another death, even indirectly.

"Because your wife is dead? I can't imagine that he'd kill himself over that. I mean not after all this time."

"It's only been five years, Bryce. And believe me the pain doesn't lessen."

"Hey man, I didn't mean it like that. I know it hurts. I just meant that whatever caused the chief to off himself, I don't think anyone can hang it on you. The good news is, with the man dead, maybe you'll be able to get paroled."

The feather was back, this time with a little more life. "You think so?"

"It's surely possible. You said yourself, the biggest reason your parole keeps being denied is that Michaels always attended your parole hearings." Bryce shrugged. "Now he can't."

"Jesus, Bryce, be careful, you're going to give me hope."

They laughed, the sound companionable. Haywood

wasn't certain he'd ever had a real friend. Besides Melanie, that is.

"So what are you gonna do when you get out?" Bryce asked.

"I don't know. Buy a steak maybe. What would you do?"

"My sister has an apartment on Bolton, above a Sack and Go. I figure I'd start out there. Until I could find a place of my own. Then I'd look for an opportunity to do some good."

"Doing what?" Haywood leaned closer, curious to hear what Bryce thought of as good.

"I want to work with kids. Help them find their way. Maybe if someone had been around for me, things would have been different. Maybe I'd have made better choices. Known what it really was to be a man."

"I can't imagine you ever being anything less."

"Things aren't always what they seem, my friend. Don't ever forget that."

"I won't."

Just like last time, the guard signaled that their conversation was at an end.

"Next time I see you, you'll be back in general population." Haywood smiled down at his friend. "It'll be good to have you back."

"There's no place like home. I'll see you in a couple of days, then."

"Count on it." Haywood walked down the corridor, trying to shake the feeling that he'd just said good-bye.

"Mahoney." Jake slowed for a red light as he answered his cell phone, the rental car backfiring in protest.

"Jake, it's Riley." She sounded breathless. And his heart sped up just hearing her voice.

"Did you find it?" Best to concentrate on business. There'd be time to deal with his raging hormones later.

"Yes."

"And . . ." He waited, listening to the soft sound of her breathing.

"Can you come over here? I want to talk about it."

"Not until later. I'm on my way to the D.A.'s office."

"Something to do with Caroline?"

"No. The Larsen case."

"I see. How long will you be?"

"I don't know for sure. But if you want, I'll swing over when I'm finished."

There was silence for a moment as she digested his words. "No. Daddy's at a benefit. It'll run late and I think he has other plans, but I don't want to take a chance."

"So you want to tell me what you found?"

"I'd rather talk about it in person."

"Caroline *was* pregnant." He waited for her agreement.

"As a matter of fact, according to this, she wasn't. The document you have was obviously altered."

"Or yours was."

"Why would my father have doctored his own version of his daughter's autopsy report?"

"If she was pregnant out of wedlock, I'd think that might have something to do with it."

"Oh, grow up, Jake. Teenage pregnancy is not something that ruins a campaign. And even if it was big news, he was only running for state rep at the time, not exactly the big stakes of a national election."

"Then maybe there's more to the story."

"Or maybe the whole thing is the product of someone's twisted imagination. Did you find out anything from your friend at the M.E.'s office?"

"Yeah, the other copies of the report are missing."

"And you don't think it's by accident? Jake, we're talking about something that happened twenty years ago."

"I just find it a little odd that we have two differing reports, and the only other ones in existence have gone conveniently missing."

"I see."

"Riley, you have to at least accept the possibility that something is really wrong here."

"Oh, I accept that all right. Someone is messing with my family and I don't like it, and believe me I am going to get to the bottom of it. Starting with this report."

"I'll see what I can find."

"No," she said. "*We'll* see what *we* can find. I'm coming to you. I'll meet you at the courthouse." It wasn't a question. The woman knew what she wanted.

And he couldn't say the idea of seeing her was unappealing. "Fine. We'll talk when you get there. Who knows, maybe you can help me find proof that Douglas Michaels was up to no good."

"Oh Lord, I'd forgotten you were investigating Michaels." There was silence on the line.

"Riley? You there?"

"Yes." There was another pause. He heard her exhale. "Jake, there's one other difference between my autopsy report and the one you have."

The hair on his neck prickled to attention. "And that would be?"

"There's another signature. Douglas Michaels was the investigating officer the night my sister died."

Chapter 16

"These are the files that were in Larsen's office." Roger Danvers waved a hand toward the boxes stacked on a table. "Unfortunately, he had some at home, and those were incinerated with the rest of the house."

"Don't you have copies?" Jake frowned at the stack of boxes.

Roger shook his head. "Nope. They were the originals. You could probably piece the files together using other sources, but that'd take more effort than the things were worth."

Riley walked over to the table and lifted a lid. A cloud of dust accompanied the motion and she coughed.

Roger laughed ruefully. "Cutbacks in housekeeping. You folks going to be okay?"

Jake nodded, his mind already on the task ahead. "Thanks for doing this, Roger."

"Not a problem. Just don't tell anyone it was me, okay?" He lifted a hand and walked back into the hallway.

"I take it we're not supposed to be here."

"Well, technically these records belong to the people of Fulton County. And since we're taxpaying residents, we have the right to see this stuff."

"But . . ."

He grinned. "There are a heck of a lot of forms to fill

198

out and red tape to finesse in order to actually do that. Having Roger's help saves us a lot of time and aggravation, believe me."

"And Roger is?"

"An assistant D.A. We've been friends for a long time."

"You homicide types obviously stick together."

"It's that predilection for dead bodies, I guess."

"So do you think he recognized me?"

"Maybe. You've got to admit, your face is memorable." He let his eyes drift over the lines of her cheeks, coming to rest on the full curve of her lips. She blushed, the soft pink heightening her appeal. Jake forced himself to look away. "Anyway, if you're worried he'll tell someone, don't be. Roger's as discreet as they come."

"I wasn't worried about that." Her reassurance was too fast—bordering on glib.

"Of course you were. But it's okay. I understand. Being seen with me probably wouldn't win you brownie points with your father."

"Well, he isn't your biggest fan."

"Lady, I got more enemies than a Catholic in Belfast. Might as well add a future President to the list."

"So, we're back to 'lady' again."

"Sorry." He shrugged. "You seem to bring out the worst in me."

They stood for a moment, gazes locked, each waiting for the other to make a move.

Riley broke eye contact first, turning back to the files. "Will Roger get in trouble for helping you?"

Jake sucked in a deep breath, eighty-sixing his desire. "Not if we don't tell anyone."

"I see. And you're certain I'm not doing anything illegal?" She shot him a look, her eyes questioning.

"Not technically."

The corner of her mouth tipped upward. "All right then. Tell me what I'm looking for."

Jake pulled the lid off a box and looked at the files inside. "I'm not sure exactly. Larsen thought Michaels was up to no good."

"Something to do with a trial. I remember." She pulled a file from another box and started to flip through it. "And you think whatever it was he found might be here."

"No, actually I don't. I figure whatever proof he had burned along with his house."

"The fortuitous accident." She looked up from the file she was examining.

"Not so fortuitous, actually. I'm surprised you didn't see it on the news. David found evidence that it was arson."

Her eyes widened. "Which means that Larsen was murdered?"

"Well, that's certainly a possibility. Although the jury is out on that one. It could be that the fire was set to destroy evidence, and Larsen just happened to be in the wrong place at the wrong time."

"His house."

"Right. If I'm on the right track here, then murder looks a whole lot more likely. But without something to prove motive, it's just arson."

"And homicide."

"Yeah. And either way, we're suddenly playing a whole new ball game."

"Do they know who did it?"

"The arson? Not yet."

She chewed on the corner of her bottom lip, her expression confused. "So if you believe Larsen's proof burned, then why—"

"Are we here?" He sat down and opened a file folder.

"Because this is what got him thinking about it. And maybe if we look through it all, we'll see what he saw. We can start by looking for references to Douglas Michaels. You don't have to help me with this, you know."

"Oh, but I do."

He raised an eyebrow, waiting.

"I want to talk to you about my sister, and I want your undivided attention. And considering your propensity for being single-minded, I figure the only way I'm going to get that is to help you find Larsen's proof."

He let his gaze trail over the boxes piled on the table. "Hope you don't have any other plans for tonight."

Martell flattened his back to the wall of the office next to the conference room, turning his head slightly so he could see through the door into the room. Mahoney and the senator's spawn were sitting cozy with a bunch of boxes.

Boxes that potentially could cook his goose.

He cursed under his breath, trying to decide what to do. Seemed that lately everything he did was a dollar short and a day late. Well, maybe not the dollar short part, but he sure as hell was making a practice of being too fucking late.

And no doubt there'd be all kinds of hell to pay for it.

He should have realized there'd be other files. Should have made certain they were destroyed too. But instead he'd managed to only do half the job. And now he was on the wrong side of the damn door.

Maybe, if he was lucky, there wouldn't be anything to find. But luck was something else that seemed to be in short supply lately. Not that anything they found would connect to him. Hell, it wouldn't even connect to his employer. Thanks to Michaels and his timely demise. So maybe he was standing here worrying about nothing.

He hesitated, not certain whether he should stay or go. If he stayed, maybe he could figure out how much they knew, but he was also running the risk of someone seeing him—or worse, getting caught. On the other hand, while it was safer to get the hell out of Dodge, he'd be dropping the ball again.

He was supposed to be tailing Mahoney, and if the son of a bitch found anything, he needed to know about it. It'd be a hell of a lot simpler if he could just take the bastard out. But that wasn't an option anymore. Not while the senator's daughter was glued to his side. His orders in that department had been more than clear.

Personally, he had no problem doing the bitch too. One less holier-than-thou politician wasn't going to hurt the world. But there was no sense in biting the hand that fed him. Especially since it fed him so well.

He leaned back against the wall, his decision made. He'd stay. And maybe, just maybe, he'd be able to report that they hadn't found a thing. But somewhere in the pit of his stomach, he knew that wouldn't be the case. Life was about odds after all.

And Jake Mahoney had a way of making them turn in his favor.

"Any luck?" Riley met Jake's gaze over the top of the file she was reading.

"Nothing that screams problems. The chief is mentioned now and again, but usually only in an official capacity, and there are documents here with his signature." Jake looked as tired as she felt. They'd been at it for what seemed hours, and things weren't going particularly well.

"Anything unusual about the documents?"

"Nothing that I can see. They're all pretty run of the mill. You finding anything?"

"Other than the fact that there are a lot of real scuzzballs in Atlanta, nothing helpful. But we'll find something." She found herself wanting to reassure him, but not knowing how. She was out of her depth, and things were happening too fast. Part of her wanted to retreat. To pretend that none of this had happened. But that was a coward's way out.

And she was not a coward.

She believed in facing things head-on.

She wanted the truth. About her sister. About Jake. About herself.

Jake made her feel things she'd never felt before, and the last couple of days had her questioning the choices she'd made, wondering if there wasn't more to life than just being the candidate's daughter.

But her life was so entwined with her father's, it was difficult to tell where his life ended and hers began. Maybe Adelaide was right. Maybe it was time for her own dreams.

She shook her head and forced herself to concentrate on the case file in front of her. It was older than the rest. The trial concerned an armed robbery and dated back just over nineteen years. The accused was a twenty-one-year-old black man who had shot and killed the owner of a convenience store and three customers. The viciousness of the attack was frightening even on paper.

She shivered, reading the testimony of a witness who'd lived.

"You okay?"

She looked up from the transcripts to meet Jake's

concerned gaze. "Yeah. This is just an awful case. A robbery with four murders. And the whole thing was avoidable. I mean, they were cooperating, and this guy shot them anyway."

"Makes you have new respect for what the D.A.'s office does."

"God, yes. I can't imagine facing scum like that day in and day out." She turned the page. "There's a mention of Michaels here." She scanned the contents of the sheet. "Evidently he was one of the investigating officers." Jake came up behind her, reading over her shoulder. "Looks like Douglas interviewed the county's key witness. His notes are here. According to this, without her testimony, there's no way this Daniels fellow could have been convicted."

"Daniels?"

She nodded. "Bryce Daniels. Margaret Wallace is the woman who testified against him. You ever heard of either of them?"

"No. But then, I would have been a kid in Texas at the time. How about you?"

"Same problem. And I was even younger than you. I wonder why Larsen would have been looking into a case this old?"

"Case law probably. Maybe there's something in this case that he could use to win something else he was working on. Is there anything else?"

She flipped through the file. "Some police records. There's a witness list here." She read down the list of names. "That's odd."

"What?" He read the list over her shoulder. "Do you know someone?"

"No." She frowned. "It's just that there are three witnesses listed here. And only one was called."

"Maybe the others weren't needed."

She shrugged. "Maybe not. Or maybe they just weren't helpful. Michaels interviewed all three though."

"Are his notes included?"

She flipped through the pages again. "No. I guess they're not part of the official record."

"But the notes on the other witness, the one who testified, they're there, right?"

"Right." She frowned at the file, her brain churning. "And so if one set of notes is here, you'd expect to find the others."

"Exactly. Record keeping for trials is meticulous."

"So either they never existed . . ."

"Which doesn't make sense."

She nodded. "Or they were misplaced somehow."

"Possible, but it seems odd in light of all that is here."

"Or—" Excitement shot through her with the power of a cannon. "Larsen kept them separately for some reason."

"Something to do with Michaels."

"But what?" Her excitement faded. They were right back where they'd started.

"I don't know. But one of these people ought to be able to help us." He pointed at the witness list.

"Or Bryce Daniels."

Jake smiled. "You've got a knack for this, you know."

"I'm learning from the master." Their gazes collided, and Riley's breath caught in her throat. Jake leaned forward, and with a will of their own, her eyes closed, her body leaning toward his.

A crash from the next room interrupted the moment, sending a shiver of pure fear racing down her spine.

"What the hell was that?" Jake sprang into action, eyes narrowed as he inched his way toward the open door to the connecting office.

"I don't know. Maybe something fell." She followed him across the room, not particularly wanting to get closer, but not wanting to be on her own either.

Jake grabbed a pointer from a nearby chalkboard, brandishing it like a sword. "Who's in there?" His voice echoed into the office and died, followed only by silence. He stepped through the opening, eyes scanning the room.

Riley stopped in the doorway, holding her breath. The little office was empty, everything pristinely in place. On the far wall, the door to the hallway swung open slowly, as if an unseen hand were pulling it.

"Stay here." Jake sprinted across the room, still holding the pointer, and disappeared out into the hallway.

Riley held her ground for about two minutes before realizing that being alone in the courthouse held absolutely no appeal. She followed Jake, stepping out into the hallway in time to see him sprinting around the corner.

Martell took the stairs two at a time, his breathing labored. Mahoney was behind him. He could hear the sound of his footfalls on the stairs. Son of a bitch. He'd fallen asleep, not fifteen feet from his quarry, knocking over the trash can when he'd jerked awake.

Shit.

He rounded a bend in the stairs and ran across the landing. A large number one was painted on the wall, beckoning him. Almost there. Martell pushed himself forward, using the railing as leverage. Mahoney sounded closer. The man was gaining on him. With a burst of speed, he took the last set of risers, flinging open the door to the garage.

After the fluorescent lighting of the stairwell, the dark of the garage was blinding. And concealing.

Martell blinked and forced his eyes to focus. His car was off to the left. Only about a hundred yards. He swerved down the aisle, anger overcoming him.

He'd had just about enough of Jake Mahoney. And nothing, not even his employer, was going to keep him from putting Mahoney in his place once and for all. He automatically reached for his gun, disappointed to find his holster empty. Fearful of metal detectors, he'd left it in the car.

Son of a bitch.

Sliding between his car and the next, he fumbled for his keys, hearing Mahoney slow down as he rounded the corner into the aisle. If he could just get in the car before Mahoney saw him, he'd have the advantage he needed.

And then he'd make the bastard wish he'd never been born.

Riley stopped at the bottom of the stairs, holding onto her side, her breath coming in gasps. With a trembling hand she pulled open the door to the garage, then stepped cautiously from the stairwell, crouching low to avoid being a target.

The fact that she was even thinking about being a target drew her up short, instinct making her turn back toward the safety of the stairs. Something clattered behind her, and her mind trotted out visions of Jake in trouble. Adrenaline surged and she swung back around, straining in the dark for some sign of where he was.

Off to her left she heard footsteps, and, heart pounding, she worked her way toward the sound, keeping between the cars, using them as a shield. When she reached the end of the row, she inched forward, sticking her head around the rear bumper of the car so she could see down the aisle.

Jake was crouched low, walking slowly away from her, the pointer still clutched in his hand. Relief washed through her, and she stepped out from behind the car, calling his name. He stopped and turned, just as the sound of a car engine split the quiet of the garage.

She whirled around, only to be caught in the blinding glare of headlights. The engine roared as the car accelerated. Frantically, her brain telegraphed the message for her feet to move, but they were having none of it.

The light grew closer, and just when she thought it would envelop her, something hard hit her from the side, throwing her to the ground, as the car hurtled past her, tires screaming like a banshee.

"You all right?" Jake's breath was warm against her ear, his body hard against hers.

Déjà vu.

She'd definitely been through this routine before. And quite frankly, it hadn't been all that fun the first time.

She struggled to find her voice. "He almost killed me."

"He wouldn't have had the chance if you'd stayed put like I asked you to." Jake's voice was laced with anger.

She pushed at him ineffectually, trying to get him off of her. "That's the only thanks I get for coming to your rescue?"

"My rescue?" He lowered his face until they were nose-to-nose, his eyes flashing.

She narrowed her eyes, holding his gaze. "Yeah. If I hadn't come along, you'd have been flattened like a pancake."

"If you hadn't come along, I'd probably have gotten a good look at the bastard who almost ran you down."

Her anger evaporated. "You didn't see what he looked like?"

He shook his head, rolling off her. "It was too dark, and he was too far ahead of me."

Riley tested various body parts, satisfied to find everything in working order. "Then it didn't matter that I was here. You couldn't have seen him anyway."

He grabbed her by the shoulders, shaking her. "Do you have any idea how close you came to being killed?"

"I won't be much better off if you don't stop shaking me."

He released her instantly, his anger replaced by concern. "Did I hurt you?"

She rubbed her arm, watching him resentfully. "Not much."

"It's just that you scared me."

"Well, if it helps at all, I scared myself." In truth, she hadn't thought at all, her brain focused only on the need to protect Jake. "So what do we do now?"

"We get the hell out of here."

"Not that I don't agree with the sentiment, but I was thinking more along the lines of what to do about the man who just tried to kill us."

Jake grimaced. "Considering neither one of us got a good look at him, there isn't a lot we can do. Did you see the car?"

She shook her head. "Just the headlights. And I predict it'll be fairly difficult to identify a car by its brights."

"So, that leaves us back where we started."

"Bryce Daniels."

"And the other witnesses. First thing tomorrow, I'll see if I can find them. Maybe one of them will be able to shed light on all of this. In the meantime, we still need to have our little talk."

In the excitement, she'd forgotten about her sister. "Not here."

"Your place?" His words were tainted by sarcasm.

"Right, we can just pull up a chair and wait for my father to get home."

"My idea of a perfect date," he quipped, then sobered. "I guess it'd better be my place then."

Considering what had happened the last time she went to his apartment, Riley wasn't certain going there was such a great idea. But—she glanced at the skid marks on the pavement warily—going home to an empty house was certainly out of the question.

So it was the lesser of two evils.

She'd just have to behave.

Chapter 17

MARTELL PUNCHED IN the telephone number, his anger making him edgy. He waited impatiently while the other line rang and was answered, then spat out his concerns before there was even time for a greeting: "We've got a problem."

"What do you mean *we*?" His boss's voice was calm, almost bored.

"You're right," Martell ground out. "What was I thinking? I should have said *you* have a problem."

"And that would be?"

"Mahoney. He's getting close. He knows about Daniels."

"What do you mean 'he knows'?" There was a marked edge to the other man's voice, and Martell drove it home.

"He knows that Daniels exists. And that there's a connection between him and Michaels."

"And you know this because?"

"Because I fucking heard him say so. He and the senator's kid were going through records at the courthouse."

"Riley was with him?" There was anger this time.

"All over him would be a better way to describe it. The lady has the hots for your reporter."

"He isn't my anything, Martell, but he is becoming a rather annoying problem."

"So I can take him out?" After their little chase scene, Martell was anxious for a rematch, and this time he wouldn't miss.

"I think the correct question is, can I try *again* to take him out? And the answer is no. It's gotten too complicated."

Martell swallowed his disappointment. "But he's getting close. What do you want me to do?"

"You wait. I'll call you when the time is right. And Martell . . . ?" The voice was mocking. "Don't screw up. We're almost home free. And I'd hate for you to become a liability."

Martell slammed down the phone. Liability his ass. Without his help, this thing would have turned sour months ago. He'd stopped Larsen. With a little help from the man's girlfriend. Greedy bitch. He closed his eyes, breathing deeply. Everything was going to be okay.

He flipped on the television and sat down, trying to force himself to calm down, the opening bars of *Law & Order* making him grin. There was no sense in getting worked up. No sense at all. Everything was fine. He was letting the pressure get to him.

Tonight hadn't been one of his best moments. But no real harm had been done. And there was no way Mahoney and the bitch could have recognized him. It would have been nice to take them out. But a guy couldn't have everything. Jerry Orbach's face flashed across the screen, the irony not escaping him.

Nobody was going to find anything on him.

With a smile, he leaned back, feeling better, changing stations. Larsen's face flashed across the screen and he stopped flipping, turning up the volume, a chill running up his spine. The news anchor was claiming the ATF had discovered evidence to link the fire to arson. Son of a bitch. They'd made him.

Or at least they'd made the bomb. Shit. He stared at the screen. They hadn't connected him to the fire, but they were a step closer than they should have been. Which meant he needed to be doubly certain there weren't any trails that led back to him. He'd been very careful, but it didn't pay to leave loose ends. And no matter what the big brass wanted, he wasn't going to lie low and let this shit bury him.

Fact was, the only person who was going to take care of Martell was Martell. He'd learned that lesson a hell of a long time ago. So he'd do a little housecleaning, and then he'd sit back and ride the fast track to easy street.

"About time you showed up. I was fixing to pitch a tent." David Mackenna was an imposing figure. Well over six feet, he had a quiet manner that made one feel as if he were perpetually preparing to pounce, even when he was just standing at the door.

"We ran into a little problem." Jake shrugged, and Riley wondered what he'd consider a big problem. Almost being run over by a speeding car ranked right up there on her list.

"What happened?" David's eyes narrowed as he crossed his arms over his chest.

"I think maybe we'd be more comfortable inside," Jake said, sticking the key into the lock. "How'd you get up here anyway? This building is supposed to have security."

David flashed his badge. "Credentials get you a long way."

Jake sighed and opened the door, letting Riley enter

first. She settled on the sofa, waiting, not certain how much Jake would be willing to reveal to David.

"We almost got run over." Jake slid out of his jacket, throwing it over a chair. "Some bastard was tailing us. When I chased him, we wound up in the parking garage, and before I knew it, he was barreling across the pavement."

"Whoa." David held up a hand, frowning. "Back up. Let's go through this more slowly. Where did this happen?"

"At the courthouse." Jake sat down next to Riley. "We were looking through Larsen's files."

"Since when did Ms. O'Brien here become an investigative reporter?" David sat on the arm of the sofa, his hard-edged gaze turning to her, making Riley squirm.

"I had something to discuss with Jake, and the courthouse seemed as good a place as any."

His appraising eyes moved from her to Jake, then back again. "I see." And Riley thought he probably did. The man didn't miss much. "So you were looking through Larsen's files . . ."

"And just when it was getting interesting, someone in the office next to us made a noise."

"Actually, *noise* is an understatement." She shot an exasperated look at Jake, then turned to David. "I'd say it was more like a cannon explosion or a wrecking ball crashing into a cement block."

Jake smiled tolerantly. "Suffice it to say it was somewhere between a noise and a cataclysm."

"It was really loud." She shot him a heated look. "And scary."

"It was a wastebasket, Riley."

"Obviously, a loud wastebasket." David interjected, watching them with amusement. "What happened next?"

"The guy ran," Jake said, focusing on the story again, "and I chased him. We wound up in the parking garage, where I managed to lose him."

"Meanwhile, I followed Jake," Riley added.

"Against my orders," Jake growled.

"Well, someone had to watch your back," she snapped, her own anger rising.

"I was doing just fine on my own, Riley." His eyes were shooting sparks. "If you hadn't stepped into the light—"

"You'd have been roadkill." She cut him off with a wave of her hand.

"All right. All right. I get the picture." David's voice shook with laughter.

Riley sighed, and leaned back against the cushions. "I was only trying to help."

Jake reached over and covered her knee with his hand. "I know."

"So did you get a look at the guy?" David asked, trying to gain control of the rapidly deteriorating conversation.

"Not a damn thing," Jake said. "And nothing on the car either."

"The light was really bright," Riley responded, defensively.

"So what did the police say?" David moved to sit in an overstuffed chair.

"We didn't call them."

"Why the hell not?" Even sitting in a chair, David's size made him imposing, and when you added anger to the mix, he was positively frightening. Riley grabbed an afghan and wrapped it around her.

Jake shrugged, apparently unaffected by his friend's outburst. "Because there was nothing we could tell them, and because I didn't want questions about why we were there. Riley doesn't need that kind of publicity. She was only there because of me."

"You could have been hurt." The simple statement said a lot about the man, and Riley realized that David's anger was caused by concern.

"But we weren't," Jake insisted.

"This time." David let the words hang ominously, then turned his intense gaze on Riley. "You should never have been there in the first place."

"I know." He was right, of course. She couldn't remember the last time she'd shown such recklessness. *Sleeping with Jake*, the little voice in her head whispered.

"Look," Jake reached for her hand, "enough with the lecture."

David ran a hand through his hair, its dark length rippling with the motion. "Fine. So tell me what you found."

"Well, it's not conclusive. But one of the files in Larsen's possession involved a robbery/murder. And our friend Michaels just happened to be the officer who interviewed the witnesses."

"So how is that relevant?" David waited, puzzled.

"It may not be," Riley chimed in. "But there were three witnesses, according to the ADA's notes, and only one of them actually testified."

"Which, in and of itself, isn't that unusual," Jake continued, "but the police notes from the original interviews were conveniently missing from the file."

"They could have been lost." David was playing devil's advocate.

"True, and I'd buy it if all the notes were missing. But the notes about the witness who testified were there."

"And there was no mention of the other witnesses at all in the trial," Riley added.

"So who was the perp?" David asked, obviously trying to assimilate all the facts.

"A guy named Bryce Daniels."

"Not a nice man, according to the records." Riley shivered.

"Was he convicted?"

"Oh yeah, the witness did a bang-up job. Daniels was sentenced to life."

"And without the witness?"

"From what we were able to see, the prosecution would have had a hell of a time placing Daniels at the scene." Jake leaned back against the sofa cushions with a sigh. "So, at the very least, we have more people to talk to."

"It's forward movement. And at least Daniels will be easy to locate." David turned his attention to Riley. "I'm still not certain I understand your part in all of this."

Riley looked at Jake, and he nodded. Obviously he thought David Mackenna was a man to be trusted. And just at the moment, she was inclined to believe it. "Jake got a little surprise under his door this morning."

David's smile disappeared and he looked at his friend. "Surprise?"

Jake reached across Riley to grab the autopsy report from the table, handing it to David. "This was delivered in a plain white envelope, no postmark."

David read through the document, frowning, then looked up at Riley. "Caroline O'Brien is related to you?"

"She's my sister."

He nodded and turned to Jake. "So why would someone send you a twenty-year-old autopsy report?"

"We think to stir up trouble. I tried to track down the original, or at least another copy from the M.E.'s office, but Megan says it's not there."

"Did you check to see if there was a copy with the police report?"

"I did, actually. Or Megan did. And it seems that the file is also conveniently missing."

"So this is the only remaining copy?" David looked down at the papers in his hand.

Riley shook her head. "No. I found another copy in my father's study, but the problem is, they're not the same." She pulled her copy from her jacket pocket and handed it to David. "In Jake's version, my sister is listed as pregnant. That information is missing from my family's copy. And on our copy there's an additional signature."

David read through the second version of the report, stopping when he came to the last page. "You realize this last page is the police report."

Jake nodded. "Yeah. And Douglas Michaels was the reporting officer. The point is that if he was involved, maybe there's some sort of connection to everything that's been happening."

"Kind of a big leap, don't you think? I mean, following that train of thought, you'd have to suspect every case the man ever worked on." David sat back, his brows drawn together in a frown.

"I realize I'm jumping the gun a bit," Jake said. "But you can't ignore the fact that something is going on. And that Douglas Michaels seems to be in the big fat center of it. And then when you consider the fact that this little gem just happens to drop in my lap, I can't help but wonder if there's not a link somewhere."

"Before we go trying to establish connections," Riley said, "I think maybe we need to face the fact that we don't even know which of these documents is real." She frowned at the papers in David's hand.

David nodded, holding the two reports so he could

compare them. "They both look authentic. I'll be damned if I'd know which one to pick. Although instinct says the pregnancy one is the original."

"But—" Riley shot a heated look in David's direction.

"Hang on a minute. I'm not trying to malign your sister. But look at the situation. If we're to assume one of these is the real document, then that leaves two scenarios. One, that someone doctored the autopsy report to make it look like your sister was pregnant."

"Someone who wanted to stir up trouble." Riley gave a self-satisfied nod.

"But the problem with that," David continued, "is that it would be easy to disprove. You have a copy of the autopsy report, and the police report."

"But the originals have disappeared." Jake's eyes narrowed as he considered David's words.

"True. But they may still surface. And the point is, it's a defendable situation, assuming Caroline wasn't pregnant."

"She wasn't." Riley almost hissed the words.

"Okay, so assume that someone is doing this to stir up trouble where there is none. Why send it to Jake?"

"Because he's a damn good reporter."

Jake smiled, and she caught her breath at the look in his eyes.

"Not to interrupt the moment," David said, "but there's a problem with that. Jake *is* a good reporter, and he'd never go to press with something unsubstantiated. So if I were going to try and go public with a story I'd fabricated, the last place I'd go is the legitimate press."

"You're saying you'd go to the tabloids."

"Exactly. This is playing out all wrong if this version," he waved the first autopsy report, "is the fake. Which brings us to option two—that someone doctored the original document to make certain that news of Caroline's pregnancy never reached the public twenty years ago."

"That would make my copy the fake." Riley's gaze met David's.

"Right. Given your father's high-profile profession, I think that would be an understandable reaction."

"My father doesn't know about this."

"No one is saying it's your father, Riley," Jake said. "David's just presenting a plausible option. One that would assume that *someone* doctored your copy of the document at the time of your sister's death."

"So you both believe that my sister was pregnant." She forced all emotion out of her voice. This wasn't the time. She'd analyze her feelings about it all later.

"Based on what we have, I'd have to say that yes, I think Caroline was pregnant." David handed her the two reports.

Jake's eyes met hers, his look somber. "I think you at least have to accept the possibility that it's true."

"I don't know what to believe. Everything is so tangled up." She leaned back against the sofa, trying to sort through her thoughts. "You said something about a connection earlier. Are you thinking that Caroline's—" She paused, searching for the right word. "—*situation* is linked to everything else that's been happening?"

"I don't know." Jake stood up, nervous energy making him restless. Riley understood the feeling. "On the surface, it doesn't seem likely, but everywhere we turn we keep running into Michaels. And it seems a bit beyond coincidence that I'd be investigating the man and lo and behold someone delivers a document that connects to him too."

"But whoever delivered the autopsy report can't have

known that you'd be able to get your hands on my family's copy."

David frowned, his eyes narrowed in thought. "It is within the realm of possibility. I mean, the two of you have had your pictures splashed all over the papers. *Together*. It's not that big a leap to think that Jake might share the information with you."

"But for what purpose?"

"Your guess is as good as mine." David shrugged. "Anything we come up with is going to be purely speculation."

"Well, at least for the sake of argument, let's go over what we know." Jake resumed his pacing. "Hank Larsen finds information about Michaels and tells me, but before he can elaborate, he winds up dead. So *I* approach Michaels, who denies the whole thing. And the next thing I know, my car is history."

"But you don't think that's related." Riley frowned, trying to keep up with his train of thought.

"I didn't think so, because I couldn't imagine that Larsen had found anything big enough to warrant my death. And because I wasn't supposed to be there in the first place. But I'm not so sure anymore. I talked to Walter. And from what I can tell, it's entirely possible my being at the rally was a setup."

"You mean someone orchestrated your being there?" Riley stared at Jake, gooseflesh crawling up both arms. This was fast turning into a Robert Ludlam novel.

"Exactly." Jake sat back with a frustrated sigh. "But that's where it ends. I don't have a tie-in to Michaels's suicide. And there's certainly nothing in what we know that would connect to Caroline. So we're stuck."

"Not completely," David said. "The reason I was waiting for you is that I think I've linked Larsen's fire to the clinic bombing. The fingerprint is the same. So all I have to do is ID the bomber, and once I have him, I'll have whoever is pulling the strings. Which ought to give us some answers. Unfortunately, this kind of thing takes time."

"Which is something we don't have a lot of."

"Not with people trying to run you down." David's look turned fierce, and Riley pulled the afghan more tightly around her.

"Evidently, I've developed a penchant for being in the wrong place at the wrong time." She shrugged, trying for lightness, the tremor in her voice invalidating the effort. "Hit and run, car bomb," she ticked off two fingers, "and then there was the man last night."

"Last night?"

"There may have been someone following Riley last night." Jake frowned. "Outside my apartment. I arrived before anything happened."

"Did you get a look at him?"

Jake shook his head. "He was gone by the time she could tell me about it."

David turned to Riley. "How about you?"

She lifted her hands in frustration. "It was dark."

"Well, I'm betting it was lead foot." David's tone was still grim. "Look, the important point here is that whatever is going on, the people behind it all are playing for keeps. Which means that until we find answers, the two of you are going to have to sleep with your eyes open."

Chapter 18

"So TOMORROW YOU talk to the witnesses?" Riley stopped pacing around Jake's living room long enough to ask the question. Since David had gone, she'd felt like a caged cat. All energy and nothing concrete to do with it.

"First I have to find them."

"Well," she smiled, "if anyone can do it, I'd put my money on you."

"Thanks for the vote of confidence, but it's been nineteen years."

She nodded, rubbing the back of her neck. "At least you know where to find Daniels."

"Yeah. But we have to prepare ourselves that he may be less than cooperative. He's a convicted killer, after all."

"I don't see how you do this day in and day out."

It was Jake's turn to smile. "I guess the truth is there's something very satisfying about taking seemingly unrelated bits and pieces and weaving them into something whole, putting it all together after the fact."

"Maybe you should have been a cop."

"No, there's more freedom in journalism. I pursue what I want to. Besides, a cop rarely ever sees the outcome. The end of the story, if you will. If he's successful, he takes it through to an arrest, and maybe an opportunity to testify, but the story doesn't end there. I get to follow through to the very end. I like that."

"You make it sound exciting, but I've just spent an evening reading through some very dry material."

"And almost getting run down by a crazy man."

"Okay, so it was a little exciting." She crossed to the window, looking out on the traffic. Everything seemed so normal, people driving their cars, blissfully unaware of everything that had happened.

"So you really don't think your father knows about this?" Jake came to stand beside her, his presence comforting.

"Caroline's pregnancy, you mean?"

He nodded, his eyes on the traffic below.

She shook her head. "It just doesn't track with the way things played out."

"I'm not following."

"We're Catholic, Jake. Irish Catholic to boot. If Daddy had known that Caroline was pregnant when she died, then there would have been a service for her child." She turned to face him. "But there wasn't."

"I'm sorry. I'm not trying to make this more painful for you. I just want to get to the bottom of what's happening."

Riley sighed, suddenly feeling the full effect of the events of the past twenty-four hours. "I know." Tears welled. "It's just difficult to imagine Caroline in trouble, with no one to talk to."

"Then concentrate on the idea that there was someone. Maybe someone she loved."

She fought to pull her emotions into control. It wouldn't benefit anyone for her to fall apart. "But even if there were someone, we don't know who."

His thumb stroked the contour of her cheek, the

motion strangely soothing. "We'll figure this out, Riley. You just have to give me a chance."

She stared into the blue of his eyes, trying to lose herself, to pretend that none of this was happening. "What I really want is to wake up and find that this was all a dream."

"All of it?" His question had nothing to do with Caroline.

"No." The word came out on a whisper. "Not all of it."

"You're an amazing woman, Riley O'Brien. Do you know that?" He ran a finger across her lips, the touch more sensual than a kiss.

She smiled awkwardly, his words embarrassing her. "I'm not sure you know what you're talking about."

He moved closer, his gaze locked with hers. "I always know what I'm talking about."

She licked her lips nervously, wondering why breathing had become so difficult. He was so close now she could see the gold flecks in his eyes. Lapis lazuli. His breath caressed her, igniting a flame deep inside.

And then he kissed her, his touch hard and demanding. Almost possessive.

Riley pulled away, uncertain of her feelings. She wanted to say no. To tell him there was no future between them. But her heart was overriding common sense. Just at the moment, for now, she needed him. Needed to feel his heart beating next to hers, needed his warmth, his humanity. She needed him to keep the dark at bay, to hold onto her until the storm had passed.

A slow smile lit his face as he watched the parade of emotions that she knew must be playing across her face. Her breathing became difficult again, and he closed the distance between them, his arms circling her waist, drawing her closer.

His kiss was gentle, his lips barely brushing against hers, but there was something sensual in the act. Something spiritual too. She pressed closer, wanting more. With a groan, his kiss became more demanding, his hands sliding under her shirt, fingers massaging, caressing, circling.

"Tell me that you want me." His voice was tight, hoarse with passion, and she felt the fires inside her begin to spread.

"I want you." She was surprised to hear a tremor in her own voice, evidence of the way he moved her.

With one smooth gesture he reached beneath her knees and swung her up into his arms. And just like that all her doubts dissipated. Leaving only Jake, and the naked desire shining from his blue-black eyes. He carried her to the sofa, placing her carefully among the cushions.

When she reached for him, he shook his head, his crooked smile beguiling. "Tonight, I want everything to be perfect. No storms. No chance for regrets. Just you and me, Riley. All the other baggage left at the door. Do you think you can do that?"

She nodded wordlessly, knowing her heart was reflected in her eyes. His smile deepened, and he walked to the fireplace and opened the screen, adding logs to the already blazing fire. Then, with the flick of a switch, the room was clothed only in the soft gold of firelight.

He laid a quilt on the floor, and after adding cushions from the sofa, he reached for her hand and slowly pulled her up, until her breasts pressed against the hard expanse of his chest, their breathing becoming as one. Her legs fit between his as if they had been made to do so, their bodies joining together as if they were halves of what had once been whole.

They danced then, to music no one could hear. Swaying together, gazes locked, making love with nothing more than their eyes. Riley reached up to trace the planes of his face, relishing the contrast between the smooth skin of his cheek and the beard-roughened texture of his chin.

He bent his head, first kissing her eyes and then the line of her nose and the curve of her brow. Then finally . . . finally kissing her lips, the sweet intoxication of his touch almost more than she could bear. She opened her mouth, taking him inside, her tongue tracing the line of his teeth, his taste at once familiar and exotic.

She wondered if she could ever truly get enough of him. Or if she would forever be doomed to wanting more. She smiled against his mouth, realizing there were far worse fates. They moved backward, dancing toward the fire, until they reached the makeshift bed. Together they knelt, still face-to-face, bodies touching, hands joined.

There was magic in the dark velvet of his eyes, and she let herself go, knowing that for the moment there was nothing but the two of them and the soft glow of the fire. Their own special island in the night.

Jake marveled at the emotions rocketing through him. Emotions that *she* inspired. There was desire, certainly, more than he'd ever known, but there was so much more than that. There was a kind of fierce possessiveness, a protective urge as old as time itself. Something he'd never felt before.

And even more surprising, there was a gentle tenderness, the need to cherish, and revere, the power of his need almost unmanning. And finally, there was a selflessness, as foreign to him as breathing under water. He knew in that instant that he would give anything, do anything, if it would make her happy.

She smiled up at him, her eyes like a storm-tossed sea. And with a groan, he captured her mouth with his, telegraphing through his touch all that he was feeling. They fumbled with buttons and zippers, still kneeling together, until they were skin-to-skin, bodies caressing each other. Satin on leather.

With a fluid motion he laid her back against the cushions, watching the firelight glitter in her hair and play upon her breasts. Dipping his head, he took one swollen peak into his mouth, his tongue dancing with her taut nipple until she cried out, the sound filling him with pleasure. Sucking harder, he caressed the other breast with eager fingers, unable to get enough of her, secretly willing the night to last forever.

Her fingers twined in his hair, urging him onward, her body like a fine instrument, primed and waiting— waiting for a musician. Waiting for *him*. He smiled at his own rhetoric, wondering when he'd become a poet.

Slowly, he inched downward, his tongue tasting first the soft skin of her belly and then, lower still, trailing soft kisses along her inner thighs, his tongue stroking her skin, his desire demanding he take more, that he taste all of her, that he make her once and forever his.

Shifting slightly, he pushed her legs apart and bent to kiss her, lapping at her delicate softness, drinking in her sweetness. Her hands tightened in his hair, her body arching joyfully upward, meeting him, wanting him.

Needing her now more than life itself, he rose above her, eyes locked on hers, feeding on the soft sounds of her passion. With one swift stroke he was inside her, feeling her heat as it pulsed around him.

Together they established a rhythm—in, out, in, out, harder and faster, until there was nothing but the motion, the friction, the incredible union of their bodies, their souls. He called her name, and felt her hands in his, felt her tighten around him, felt the spasm of her release, and then the world exploded.

And all he could see was the sparkling silver of her eyes.

It was still dark, which meant he hadn't been asleep long. Riley was sleeping on her side, one arm thrown across him, her hair fanned out on the quilt. She was a beautiful woman. And a feisty one. She held on to her beliefs with a fierceness he envied.

One of the downsides to his job was cynicism, and he had it in spades. But Riley brought something else out in him. Something hopeful. He smiled at his thoughts. Jake Mahoney hopeful. Now there was a laugh. He slid out from their makeshift bed and walked to the window. Stars still twinkled and a pale moon still hung high in the darkened sky. He took a deep breath—a sigh, really—and leaned his head against the cool glass.

Riley's father certainly wanted her away from him. Which, under the circumstances, he wasn't sure he blamed him for. He certainly seemed to be inviting trouble these days.

Any notion he'd entertained that all of this died with Michaels had been put to rest at the courthouse. The man who'd stalked Riley and almost run her down wasn't being paid by a dead man. No, there was someone else out there calling the shots.

And then there was Caroline O'Brien. A pregnant teenager who'd fallen from a balcony to her death over twenty years ago. How the hell did she fit into all of this?

He glanced down at the street below. Everything was quiet. The world asleep. Behind him, Riley thrashed against the quilt, calling for her sister. He spun around, concern knifing through him. It was the same as the other night, her voice sounding childlike, plaintive. It sent chills running down his spine. He dropped down beside her and took her shoulders, shaking her gently.

"Riley, sweetheart, wake up. It's only a dream."

She didn't hear him, her nightmare holding her captive, her pleading growing more intense as she stopped calling for Caroline and began to call for her father. She was sweating, but her body felt icy cold. He pulled up the quilt, wrapping it around her, and tried to wake her again, this time stroking the side of her face.

"Wake up, Riley. You're dreaming." Whatever was tormenting her, it was something awful, and judging from the tone of her voice, something to do with the past. "Riley, listen to me. It's Jake. Wake up." His voice was harsh, fear adding an edge.

Her eyes flickered open, and she reached for him, tears glistening along her cheeks. "Jake?"

He pulled her close, startled to hear the racing beat of her heart. "It was just a dream, sweetheart."

She sucked in a ragged breath and then exhaled slowly, as if gathering strength. "I'm okay."

He doubted the truth of that but admired her resolve. "What happened? What were you dreaming about?"

She shook her head, her face pressed against his chest. "I honestly don't know. It's always the same, but it never makes any sense."

"You've dreamt this before?" He assumed it was the same as the one the other night, but he needed to be certain.

"Yes. Mainly when I was little. But it started again recently." Her voice was muffled against his chest.

"Do you want to tell me about it?" He kept his voice gentle, one hand stroking her hair.

She tipped her head so she could see him, her eyes

still shining with tears, but her breathing was back to normal, and her heartbeat wasn't as frantic. "There's nothing much to tell. It's pretty abstract. I'm walking down a corridor. And it's storming. There's wind and lightning. Everything is black and then white. Blinding white. And I'm alone. Except for Mr. McKafferty."

"Mr. McKafferty?"

She nodded, her voice lost in the dream. "Caroline's bear. She sometimes let me play with him."

"Then what happens?"

"I can see a light at the end of the hall, but as I get closer, everything turns red, and I'm so afraid I can't move. I try to scream but no sound comes out, and then suddenly I'm back in my room, awake." She shuddered at the memory, and he pulled her closer.

"And it started when you were a kid?"

"Yeah. Sometime after Caroline died. I thought it had gone. I mean, I haven't had it in years. Not since I was about ten."

"It just disappeared?"

"Well, I suppose spending a million hours in therapy probably helped." She laughed, but there wasn't any humor in it. "But now it's back. I guess the stress of the last few days has set off my subconscious or some similar mumbo jumbo. The worst of it is that it's got me thinking about Caroline again."

"And that's a bad thing." His tone was somewhere between a statement and a question.

"It shouldn't be. I know that. But it is."

"When did the dream first come back?"

"The night after we found Michaels. Makes sense in an odd sort of way, I guess. Anyway, I decided I needed to face things head-on. Exorcise my ghosts, so to speak. That's why I was in the graveyard. I thought if I went there, if I faced them, maybe the dream would go away."

"But instead I interrupted."

"I don't think it would have done any good anyway. I'm not sure I can ever truly let it go. In some ways everything that I am is built on Caroline's death, and the aftermath."

"Sounds pretty bleak to me."

"I don't mean for it to. It's just that I've never really been able to let it all go. I just manage to keep it sequestered off somehow—out of my day-to-day thinking. But I guess with everything that's been happening, I opened the floodgates."

"You're talking like there's something more than the dream."

She rubbed her hands up and down her arms as if warding off something evil. "No. Not really. It's just that my imagination has been on overdrive because of it. I thought I smelled her perfume. And there was a book—" She broke off, obviously hesitant to continue.

"A book?"

She nodded. "This is going to sound stupid. But it was her favorite book, and it was in her room. Open. As though she'd only just left it there. And the next night—" She paused, moistening her lips with her tongue. "—the night I came to find you, it appeared on my bedside table. Only, the next morning, when I got back, it was gone again."

She stared down at her hands, her fists clenching and unclenching. "I know there are a thousand logical explanations, Jake. Or maybe I just imagined the whole thing. But with everything else that's happened, I feel like I'm going crazy."

He reached out to stroke her hair again, his mind whirling with questions, and for the first time in his life he wasn't certain he could find the answers. "I think maybe you should tell your father about all of this." He shifted so that he could see her eyes.

She chewed on the inside of her lip, her look reminding him all over again how seriously mismatched they were. "I can't." Her voice was soft, but there was resolve. "Not until I understand more about what's happening. God, Jake, this is all so confusing." She sat up, firelight kissing her skin.

"Sweetheart, it's late. Just for the moment, let me take care of you. Keep you safe. We can face the rest of it tomorrow." All he wanted was to hold her, to pull her close and feel her heart beating against his. Crazy thoughts maybe, but he could no more stop them than he could a roaring freight train. He flipped them, so she was underneath, his body hard against hers.

Something flickered in her eyes and then was gone. She nodded slowly, her eyes locked on his, her hand closing around him, kneading gently. "Make love to me, Jake."

He kissed her, his tongue finding passage into her mouth, the moist hot feel of her almost his undoing. God, he wanted this woman. Wanted her with a fury unlike anything he'd felt before. Her hand slid up and down, stroking, squeezing, caressing, the pain sweet, his need burgeoning into white-hot desire. With a groan, he pulled her up, twisting so she was straddling him.

Slowly, she lifted, then slid downward, impaling herself on his throbbing shaft. He sucked in a breath, wondering if there could be anything better than the feel of her, hot and wet against his taut skin, only to lose the thought as she began to move, her hands on his shoulders, her silken hair falling like a screen around them.

Grasping her hips, he helped her set the pace, slow

and easy, each upward motion almost separating them. She licked her lips, her eyes glazing over with passion. "Now, Jake." Her words bit into him, as much an aphrodisiac as her movements.

He increased the pace, driving deeper, harder, with each stroke. She threw back her head, her body glistening in the firelight. Lost in the moment, she rode him for all she was worth, her eyes closed, her face beautiful in her abandonment. He stroked her breasts, his hands cupping, fondling, as they climbed higher and higher.

Then suddenly perched on the precipice, he dropped his hands back to her hips, timing their movements for one last powerful thrust. She screamed his name, her hands covering his, her ecstasy driving him higher, taking him over the edge.

His vision exploded into fire. White on white. Everything going blank, as sensation overrode all rational thought. There was nothing but fire, and light, and Riley. A mind-blowing dance through the stars.

Bryce Daniels leaned back in the prison cot, wishing he had a bottle of Jim Beam. Even after all this time, he still had the urge. A dim light from the corridor illuminated the ward. Most of the beds were empty. Only one other inmate was in residence, and he'd been placed at the opposite end of the room.

From what Bryce could see, the man was sleeping. If only he had the same luxury. But nights had always been difficult for him in here. Nights were for remembering. He rubbed a hand across a beard-stubbled chin and wondered how the hell he'd ever gotten to this place.

He'd had dreams. But dreams were only that. Something to trot out in an emotion-induced haze. Something to wallow in when the world blindsided you. And his had died a long time ago.

He rolled over, staring out the window. Wondering if he'd ever see the outside again. Ever feel the grass between his toes or the water of the Chattahoochee against his skin. He remembered days spent beside its waters. Laughing. Loving.

He sobered, pushing away his thoughts. There was no room for that sort of thing in here. Nothing that could possibly be gained from wallowing in half-forgotten memories. But it was easier said than done. They came anyway. Blindsiding him when he least expected it.

Twenty fucking years had gone by and it didn't even feel like a second. Not one fucking second. He pressed his fingers to his lips, remembering—wanting.

If wishes were horses . . .

With a groan, he turned onto his back and reached for his water, wishing it was whiskey, imagining the sour mash burning its way to his stomach, sending fiery tendrils of heat radiating through his body. Warmth. Blessed warmth.

It seemed he could never escape the cold. It surrounded him, lived in him. God, he was constantly cold. Constantly alone. No matter where he was, it seemed he was always alone.

Alone with his memories.

Alone in his torment.

His mind wandered, echoes of a poem by T.S. Eliot filling his head. That's what he was all right. A hollow man—a goddamned, empty, hollow man.

A sharp click broke the silence of the room, and he stared at the door, watching in morbid fascination as the doorknob slowly turned. The man in the other bed never moved. Not even when the intruder's footsteps echoed softly through the room.

Bryce wanted to fight, to scream, to yell, but there was only a strange sense of unreality, of inevitability. A sense that maybe at last he'd find peace. And if he was lucky, perhaps he'd no longer be alone.

The intruder drew closer, a smile on his face, a syringe in his hand. More of Eliot's words sing-songed through Bryce's head. "This is the way the world ends . . . This is the way the world ends . . . This is the way the world ends . . . Not with a bang, but a whimper."

Chapter 19

Riley rolled over and opened her eyes. Dappled sunlight danced across the bed, filtering through the trees outside the window. She stretched and yawned, sitting up, trying to push off the last vestiges of sleep.

A glance at her watch confirmed what she already knew. It was late. Still early morning, but if she wanted to get home before her father, she'd have to get a move on. Jake was sleeping, one arm thrown above his head, his face relaxed, serene. Which, considering all that had happened to them, was nothing short of a miracle.

Careful not to disturb him, she slipped out of bed, rummaging around for her clothes. It had certainly been a night to remember. She smiled at the memory, her sore muscles a testament to their nocturnal activities. But now that the morning had come, it was time to find answers.

"Sneaking out again?" She whirled around, startled by his voice. He was sitting up, a scowl replacing his earlier tranquillity.

"No, of course not." She fumbled with a button. "At least not on purpose. It's just that you looked so peaceful. I hated to wake you."

His frown deepened. "So you were going to leave without saying good-bye."

"It's not as if I was taking the last plane out of

Casablanca. For goodness sake, Jake, I was trying to be thoughtful." She frowned back at him. "It's late. I have to get home."

"Before Daddy finds out?" There was an edge to his voice.

"Yes." Their gazes locked, and she fought to keep hers steady.

He sighed, running a hand through his hair. The action made him incredibly appealing. "I'm sorry. I didn't mean to snap. It's just that this is the second morning I've woken up to find you MIA."

She smiled, sitting beside him on the bed. "Well, I think missing in action might be a little bit of an overstatement. After all, I'm right here."

He tilted his head, his dark eyes drinking her in. "So you are." He reached for her, moving quickly, pinning her under his weight on the bed. "And since you're still here, what do you say we do something about it?"

"Jake, it's late." She pretended to struggle. "I've got to go."

"I know, duty calls." He planted kisses along the line of her throat, his touch sending hot liquid fire streaking through her body. "First Lady business and all that. But since you're already late, what are a few more minutes going to matter?"

"Minutes?" She grinned up at him, raising an eyebrow.

"Well, if you're game, I think we can arrange something a bit more time consuming."

"No, I have to go." She pulled away, already regretting the loss of contact.

"All right." Jake cupped her face in his hands. "I'll call you as soon as I know anything."

"Why don't you let me call you. There's no sense in upsetting my father needlessly."

"Because of me."

She shrugged, not certain what to say. They were back to *Roman Holiday*.

"Well, for what it's worth, I've got a feeling there isn't a man alive that your father would approve of."

"You're not being fair." She pulled away. "My father loves me. And he wants what's best for me. It's just that we don't always agree on what that is."

"Well, I have some ideas along those lines myself."

"About what's good for me?"

He pulled her back into his arms. "Yeah. And what's good for me."

She traced the line of his lips with a finger. "Oh yeah? So tell me what's good for you, Jake."

He caught the finger, the fire in his eyes sending jets of heat spurting through her. "You."

She opened her mouth to retort, to continue their banter, but it seemed Jake was finished talking. His lips covered hers, his kiss greedy. She closed her eyes and opened her mouth, their tongues dueling, dancing.

The man was intoxicating.

Finally, he pushed back with a sigh, his eyes black with passion. "Go. Before I decide to keep you here forever."

She sucked in a breath, surprised to find that she was incapable of speaking.

He covered her lips with his finger, mimicking her earlier gesture. "Remember that kiss, Riley." She nodded, still trying to find her voice. "It's a promise."

"A promise?" The words were barely more than a whisper.

He nodded, smiling, his teeth white against the black of his morning beard. "The promise of things to come."

She reached for the doorknob, her hand shaking,

suddenly certain that if Audrey Hepburn had met Jake
Mahoney in *Roman Holiday*, she wouldn't have stood a
chance.

"Need help with that?" Jake reached to the top shelf
for a cake mix and handed it to the old black woman.

Lenora Hadley accepted the box without comment,
her look appraising. "You work for the store?"

Jake looked around the crowded grocery store, and
then back at the woman. She was old, but her gaze was
clear, her eyes shrewd. "No ma'am, I'm a reporter. Jake
Mahoney."

"So you're helping me shop?" She pushed her basket
down the aisle, adding sugar and biscuit mix.

"Well, I was thinking more along the lines of buying
you coffee." He shot her his most charming smile,
knowing it wasn't going to do him a bit of good.

"Why?" She regarded him with skepticism.

"I have some questions I want to ask you." He forced
his voice to sound neutral. No sense letting her know
how much he needed to talk to her. If anyone could shed
light on things, he had a feeling it was Mrs. Hadley. Besides, he was getting to the bottom of the list. Margaret
Wallace, the witness who'd actually testified, had been
dead for three years, and the other witness, a fifteen-
year-old kid, had disappeared without a forwarding ad-
dress.

"About what?"

"The robbery you witnessed."

Her eyebrows shot up and then dropped again, her
face a mask. "You sure took your time about coming.
It's been nineteen years. How'd you find me?" She bent
to pick up a bag of cornmeal and then straightened to
face him.

Jake shrugged. "Your daughter told me you'd be here."

She frowned. "Woman talks too much." Pushing her cart, she set off for the next aisle, not waiting to see if he was following.

Why was nothing ever easy? "I just need to ask you a few questions," he called, hurrying after her.

She pushed the cart to one side, her dark eyes skewering him, probably seeing far more than he wanted her to. "You're buying, right?"

"Absolutely. Where would you like to go?"

She added a jar of peanut butter to the cart. "It'll have to be here. I haven't got time to go anywhere else."

"You want to finish your shopping first?" Now that she was acquiescing, he wanted to be as agreeable as possible.

"No." She shook her head, already heading for the coffee bar. "There's nothing in here that'll spoil. I can finish when you're gone."

The guy behind the coffee counter had earrings in places no one should have had earrings—and he had an attitude. None of it fazed Mrs. Hadley. "I'll have a decaf, venti, nonfat, mocha." She leaned down to peer at the bakery display. "I'll also have a slice of the white chocolate macadamia nut torte."

Jake raised an eyebrow.

She shrugged. "Might as well enjoy this."

The boy-toy transferred his bored look to Jake. "What can I get you?"

Jake paused, uncertain. He hated designer coffee, especially all the damn options. "Coffee, black."

The boy frowned, a surly look in his eyes. "Sulawesi, Guatemala Antiqua, or Sumatra?" Jake winced. Evidently, if you didn't order a grande firme mufaletto cappuccino or whatever the hell the hot new drink was, it threw the whole system off.

"He'll have a Columbia Narina." Mrs. Hadley smiled beguilingly at the nose-studded wonder.

Mr. Earring nodded, his disdainful gaze still on Jake. "Tall, grande, or venti?"

Jake resisted an urge to scream "Cup" and looked to the old woman for advice.

"Venti."

Earring-boy repeated the order at the top of his lungs, and another employee, this one with purple hair, served up their drinks, leaving Jake more convinced than ever that one should never buy coffee from rock-star wanna-bes.

He shifted his attention back to Mrs. Hadley. "Thanks. I'm not sure I could have managed that on my own."

She shrugged, smiling. "You just have to know the lingo."

They took their coffee and found a table in the corner. Not exactly the perfect place for a private conversation, but it would have to do.

She studied him over her coffee cup, her expression wary. "I told my daughter someone would eventually come asking about what I saw. But I'd say you're a dollar short and more than a few years late. That boy more than done the time by now."

"You're talking about Bryce Daniels."

"That's the name." The woman's eyes narrowed. "Never saw him before the trial."

It was Jake's turn to frown. "But I thought you saw the murders."

"I did." She took a bite of her cake and then sat back waiting.

"So you're telling me that Daniels wasn't the man you saw?"

"Bright boy." She smiled, the gesture not quite reaching her eyes. "Seems you catch on faster than the police."

"They interviewed you afterward."

"They did. Fellow by the name of Michaels."

"Douglas Michaels."

She shook her head. "Don't know. Just remember his last name. Real arrogant, that one. Claimed he didn't need my testimony. And I was standing not ten feet away."

"You were in the store?"

She nodded. "Hiding in the back."

"What about the other witnesses?"

"Weren't but one. A kid. Mathers or something. He was hiding with me."

"What about this Wallace woman, the one who testified at the trial?"

"I never saw her."

"Why didn't you come forward when you saw the wrong man being prosecuted?"

She squared her shoulders, eyes flashing. "Look at me, Mr. Mahoney. Ain't no one gonna believe a black woman over a white police officer."

He cautiously swallowed some of his coffee, the liquid still scalding. "And no one ever asked you about it again?"

"Not a word. I kept thinking sooner or later someone would come, but they never did. Until you." She finished the last of her cake and sat back, eyes narrowed in thought. "You going to fix things?"

"I'm going to try, Mrs. Hadley. I'm certainly going to try."

• • •

"All right. This is your ten-minute warning." Maudeen stood in the doorway of the hotel suite, clipboard in hand. "Carter, you and Riley will be seated on the dais, and Leon, you're at Ted Turner's table."

"We're ready." Carter gave Riley's hand a squeeze, and she fought against a wave of guilt. As if sensing her thoughts, he turned to give her a questioning look. "You okay?"

"I'm fine, Daddy. Everything is going to be great." She sucked in a breath and pasted on a smile. Candidate's wattage. It was all second nature. "How many people are out there, Maudeen?"

"Around six hundred, give or take. All friendlies. At a thousand dollars a plate, it's simply not worth the investment for a troublemaker."

"Just as well," Leon commented dryly. "We seem to have had enough trouble of late."

"Come on, Leon." Carter grinned. "It could have been a lot worse."

Riley cringed, wondering what they'd say if they knew she'd spent another night with Jake. Or even worse, that she'd been helping him with a story—a story that ultimately might involve her sister. She shook her head, pushing away the guilt. Trouble was par for the course when you were in politics, and her father always said "better offensive than defensive." So that's what she was doing.

And when the time was right, she'd tell him everything.

"All right here's the drill." Maudeen's voice brooked no argument. In the shadow of Maudeen's relationship with her father, Riley often forgot just how good the woman was at her job. They were lucky to have her. "Lunch first. The mayor and the governor will be on the dais with you, along with their wives. Bartlett will welcome everyone, introduce the head table, thank Mr. Turner, since he's the biggest contributor, and then turn it all over to the governor, who'll make some brief remarks then introduce Carter."

"Piece of cake." Carter smiled jovially, giving the thumbs-up sign.

"Have you seen the governor's planned remarks?" Leon wasn't quite as cheerful. "The last time he spoke on our behalf, he mangled our positions on crime and minority rights."

Maudeen nodded. "Way ahead of you." She detached some papers from the clipboard and handed them to Leon. "Here's what he's going to say. I had our people go over it with a fine-tooth comb and I think we're all right."

Leon skimmed the document and handed it back to Maudeen. "Good work."

She smiled at Carter. "I aim to please."

"So how much press time?" This from Carter.

"Fifteen to twenty minutes. There'll probably be some questions on prison reform."

Carter frowned. "Because of the man who died?"

Maudeen nodded. "We're lucky we got a heads-up."

"I've no idea what you're talking about." Riley looked askance at her father first and then Maudeen.

"If you'd made the morning meeting, you'd be up to speed." Leon raised an eyebrow, voicing his disapproval.

"I had another appointment." She felt herself blush, and cringed, watching her father and Leon exchange glances.

"You didn't miss all that much." Maudeen's voice was soothing. "An inmate at the prison died of an overdose last night. A lifer named Bryce Daniels. We got word this morning. With your father's crusade against drugs, and his proactive stance on prison reform, there're bound to be questions."

Riley braced herself against the tremor of fear racing through her. If Daniels was dead, then the trail to Michaels could be cold. And more frightening, there was the distinct possibility that someone had helped the man along in his overdose. "Do you know what happened?"

"Specifically? No. I think prison officials are keeping a pretty tight lid on things until they figure out what happened. But the governor's office got a call, and then they called us."

"Turnabout's fair play. We did a hell of a lot to get the man elected." Carter frowned. "I'm sure I can handle anything that comes up. It's really not my purview. And I've made my platform perfectly clear."

"I agree," Maudeen said. "But it's my job to see that there aren't any surprises. Riley, I suspect there will also be questions about the bombing. So it'll probably be best if you don't take questions at all."

"Fine." She was anything but fine, actually, but there was nothing she could share with them. At least she didn't have to field questions. There was something in that. And as soon as she was out of here, she'd find Jake. He'd know what to do.

"Okay, that's it then." Maudeen smiled. "Any questions?"

"No." Leon stood up. "But I'd like a word with Carter. Will you ladies excuse us?"

The two men walked from the room, leaving an awkward silence behind them.

"It's been a rough couple of days." Maudeen's eyes narrowed in concern. "You doing all right?"

"As well as can be expected, I guess." Riley shrugged.

"How about the dream? Have you had it again?"

"No." She wasn't sure exactly why she lied. Maybe it was to avoid the emotional conversation it would evoke. Or maybe she just didn't want to share it with Maudeen. Either way, she felt guilty. The two women weren't close, but there was no question that Maudeen meant well. Still, Riley was reticent to discuss anything related to Caroline. Even a dream.

"I didn't mean to pry. It's just that I've been worried about you."

"Thanks," Riley forced a smile, "but I'm fine."

"I believe that. But you've been through a lot, and I just want you to know that I'm here. If you need to talk."

Riley's smile was genuine this time. "I appreciate that. But I can take care of myself. I've been doing it for a long time."

"I know. And I'm not trying to butt in, honestly. I just wanted you to know there's a friendly ear if you want to talk about things you might not want to share with your father."

"Daddy means well, but he has been a little overprotective of late."

The older woman smiled. "He's your father. It comes with the territory. And in light of his losing Caroline and your mother, he's just finding it a little more difficult to face the prospect of losing you."

"But he's not losing me." Riley blew out a breath in frustration. They weren't talking about the dreams anymore, they were talking about Jake. "No matter what I do or who I do it with, I'll always be his daughter. And I'll always be here for him."

"I know that, and you know that. It's just harder for him to see it. Especially in light of all that's been happening. His nerves are stretched to the limit, Riley. And I'm not certain he's even capable of seeing things objectively. Everything is tainted in light of the election."

"If it wasn't this it would be something else, Maudeen. He just doesn't want to let go."

"He loves you, Riley. In the end, he'll do the right thing."

"I hope so." There was so much at stake—so much she was going to need for him to understand.

"Trust in him." Maudeen reached over to pat her hand. "And trust in yourself."

Riley met the older woman's gaze, covering Maudeen's hand with hers. Maybe she'd been wrong about Maudeen and her father. The woman obviously loved him. And more important, she seemed to care about what was best for him. Not in a selfish, how-is-this-best-for-me way, but in an honest, loving way.

"Maudeen . . ." She paused, ordering her thoughts. "I hope things work out with you and my father. I know you've hit a rough patch lately. But it's like you said, he's under so much pressure. I know he loves you."

"I know it too." There was pain in her expression. Pain and regret. "But sometimes it's not enough, Riley. Sometimes it's just not enough."

Chapter 20

Jake BANGED HIS hand against the computer in frustration. Every time he got an answer, it only raised more questions, making the puzzle seem more complex. Lenora Hadley's information seemed to confirm Larsen's implication that Michaels had fixed a trial. But he needed corroboration, and the kid Mrs. Hadley had spoken of had disappeared without a trace.

So much for the information highway.

There was still Bryce Daniels, but he hadn't had much luck in that area either. The man he'd talked to at the prison wasn't forthcoming with information. In fact, he'd been downright hostile. Jake's efforts to make an appointment had been stonewalled with absolutely no explanation.

He'd asked Tim for help, hopeful that his editor would be able to put a little more muscle behind the request. So now it was just a waiting game. It seemed odd that he couldn't just arrange a meeting with the man, but then, truth be told, he had no idea what the hell he was dealing with.

That Douglas Michaels had been involved in something shady seemed a foregone conclusion. But what? If Mrs. Hadley was right, Michaels had framed an innocent man. The question was, why? To protect the real killer? Or had it been racially motivated? There was logic in that, since Mrs. Hadley intimated that there had been racial tension during her interview with Michaels.

But that simply wasn't enough to draw a conclusion. And there were a million other explanations, none any better or worse than the others.

Still, nothing happened in a vacuum. Twelve years in the newspaper business had taught him that much. The trick was to find the anomaly. Someone had to have seen something. He just had to find them.

The proverbial needle in a haystack.

Now all he needed was a magnet.

The phone on the desk jangled, the noise jarring him from his thoughts. "Mahoney."

There was silence, punctuated with nervous breathing.

"Hello?" Jake frowned. "Is someone there?"

"Mr. Mahoney?" The voice was soft, hesitant. "This is Amber Northcott, Hank Larsen's girlfriend."

Jake transferred the receiver to his other ear, a tingle of excitement dancing up his spine. "What can I do for you, Amber?" He leaned back in his chair, carefully modulating his voice to keep it casual.

"I . . . well, I didn't exactly tell you everything the other day." She paused, and he heard her sigh.

"And you want to tell me now?" *Go slowly*, his brain urged. She was on the edge of panic, he could hear it in her voice.

"Yes. I mean, no. I want to tell you, but not now. Can you meet me in an hour or so?"

"Sure." He reached for a pen. "Where do you want to meet?"

There was another pause as she considered the question. "How about the food court at Lenox mall? I'll meet you in front of Sbarro."

He frowned. "Wouldn't somewhere more private be better? You could come here."

"No. I want somewhere public."

The excitement changed to concern. "Are you all right, Amber?"

"I'm fine. I've just had a change of heart, that's all." Her answer was quick and bright—too bright. "I'll meet you in an hour."

The phone clicked and went dead.

Jake sat staring at the receiver, trying to make heads or tails of what he'd just heard. Something had obviously prompted Amber to come clean. But about what? And why?

"Interesting phone call?" Tim Pierce leaned against the opening to the cubicle.

"Maybe." Jake hung up the phone. "That was Hank Larsen's girlfriend. Seems she didn't tell me everything the other day. I'm supposed to meet her at Lenox Square in an hour."

Tim raised an eyebrow, taking a seat. "A little shopping?"

Jake laughed. "A light lunch, actually. We're meeting at the food court. You just eavesdropping on my phone conversations or are you here for a reason?"

"A reason. Two, actually. I finally talked to the warden about Daniels. Turns out there's a damn good reason you can't set up an interview with the man."

"And that would be?"

"He's dead."

"Well, shit. I can't seem to catch a break."

"I'd say Daniels was the one who missed the boat in the break department this time."

"One step forward, ten steps back." Jake leaned back in his chair, swallowing his frustration. "So what happened?"

"According to the warden, he died of a self-inflicted overdose."

"In prison?"

"Not unusual. There's a lot of dealing on the inside."

Jake grinned. "You know this from personal experience?"

"Right." Tim smiled in return. "Actually, I covered the correctional system years ago. Anyway, the story is that Daniels was involved in some kind of altercation earlier in the week. Wound up in the infirmary with a stab wound. He was due to be released back into the general population this morning, but when the guard came to get him around five, he was dead."

"They have proof it was an overdose?"

Tim shook his head. "Not yet. They're waiting for the autopsy report. But evidently Daniels had a drug history, and they found track marks."

"And of course nobody saw anything."

"Hey, it's a prison." Tim shrugged. "There was another man in the infirmary, but he swears he slept through the whole thing."

"See no evil, hear no evil." Jake sighed. "And we've got another dead end."

"You're thinking it wasn't an accident."

"I don't know what to think anymore. This whole thing gets more complicated by the minute."

"How did the interview this morning go?"

"Well, if Lenora Hadley is to be believed, it's looking like Michaels framed Daniels. But so far I'm not having any luck digging up someone to support her version of the story."

"What about the other witnesses?"

"Dead or missing in action. Margaret Wallace died in her bed, and the other witness was just a kid. I've used every tool I know of but I can't find him."

"So you're back to Larsen's girlfriend."

Jake nodded, reaching for his notepad. "Looks like she may be the only game in town. You said there were two reasons you wanted to talk to me."

Tim took off his glasses and rubbed one eye, his expression regretful. "Got another call today."

"About Riley." Jake blew out a breath, certain he was right.

"Yeah. Apparently, we're still getting pressure from the O'Brien camp to get you to back off."

He tightened his fingers on his notebook, anger making his blood sing. "You know this hasn't got anything to do with publishing."

"I do. But it doesn't matter. The fact is that Carter O'Brien is a powerful man. And if he calls in favors," Tim shrugged, "then people jump to attention. And for whatever reason, he's decided he wants you kept away from his daughter."

"Tim, you know I respect you. And I respect this paper. But I refuse to let some overly egotistical *politico* dictate the terms of my personal life."

"Carter O'Brien isn't just any politico. He's about to be elected commander in chief of the world's most powerful nation, and that means he's got a hell of a lot of clout. Some dragons you just don't want to be poking."

"Hell, Tim," Jake grinned with more bluster than he felt, "if I don't poke the dragon, how am I supposed to rescue the princess?"

"You tippie-toe, Jake. You goddamn tippie-toe."

The mall was packed. Mothers with children. Lovers. Old, young. Rich, poor. A cross section of Atlanta trapped together in an architectural homage to the almighty dollar. America at its best and worst all under the same roof.

Talk about your one-stop shopping, Jake thought, smiling to himself as he stepped off the escalator, already searching for Larsen's girlfriend. Sbarro was off to his left, stuck amid a cacophony of neon signs advertising chicken, sushi, burgers, tacos, and egg rolls. A veritable smorgasbord of fast food heaven. Normally he'd be a happy man, tempted to have one of everything, but lately his appetite seemed to be on the wane. Too damn much on his mind.

He dodged a stroller and a toddler on a leash, making his way through the tables toward the pizza place. A redhead in stiletto heels and a skintight miniskirt stood in line. Jake started toward her, but she turned her head and he realized it wasn't Amber. Maybe this hadn't been the best place to meet.

He turned to survey the crowd, searching for copper hair. Nothing. He checked his watch and relaxed. He was still a couple of minutes early. She was probably just running late. Or had stopped to window shop. He usually wasn't this impatient, but his mind was still reeling from Tim's revelation that O'Brien was still making waves.

The son of a bitch. He couldn't blame the man for caring about his daughter, but his strong-arm tactics left a lot to be desired. And, in truth, they only served to drive him onward. If the man wanted an all-out war, he had one. Of course, there was the little matter of the daughter to consider.

Riley certainly had her own opinions, and while he was pretty damn certain she was feeling the same sparks he was, he had no idea what else she was feeling. Hell, he didn't really know what *he* was feeling. Other than confused.

He'd thought he had women well and truly out of his system after Lacey'd worked him over, but one look at

Riley had changed everything. Just standing here think-ing about her made him hard.

It was more than that, though. Something way be-yond the physical. And that's what scared him. Scared him silly, to tell the truth. For the first time in his life he was at a loss for what to do. They were so different. He couldn't see her giving up her way of life for his, and he sure as hell wasn't going to give up his for hers.

He hated all that political bullshit. Kissing strangers' asses wasn't exactly his cup of tea. In fact, he didn't even like tea. He was a beer man all the way. Preferably Red Brick, served with lots of boiled peanuts, and if he had to call it, he'd have to say Riley was a champagne and caviar kind of girl.

Maybe Carter was right. Maybe it was best if he let her go. But the idea of giving in to the bastard rankled, and the idea of never seeing her again was unthinkable. For better or worse, she'd gotten under his skin, and he'd be damned if he was getting off before the end of the ride. Wherever it happened to take them.

He looked at his watch again, frustration mixing with other emotions he'd just as soon not identify.

Where the hell was Amber?

Riley rounded the corner, wondering why Jake was meeting someone at the mall. What a godawful place to conduct any kind of business, and the food court was even worse. People jostled each other as they carried trays of fried inedibles, soft drinks sloshing precari-ously as they walked.

She moved among the throng, searching for Jake. His editor had said he was heading for Sbarro. He hadn't wanted to tell her anything at all. In fact, the man had practically sent her packing the minute she'd walked into the office.

But she'd held her ground, insisting that she had information that Jake would want, and finally the man had capitulated, sending her here. It occurred to her suddenly that maybe Tim had lied. That maybe he'd sent her on a wild-goose chase. There was probably some sort of justice in that, considering the big guns her father and Leon had pulled.

She hadn't had anything to do with it, but she could hardly expect Tim to know that. She sighed, wondering if she was here on a fool's errand. Even if Jake were here, it was still possible she'd made a mistake. All morning long she'd debated the wisdom of continuing to see him.

Caroline or no Caroline, she was playing with fire, and she knew better than most that playing with fire got a girl burned. And, in her case, the stakes were a bit higher than just a broken heart.

She bit her lip and stopped moving, letting the crowd ebb and flow around her. She had no business being here. She had no business being anywhere with Jake Mahoney. She'd been over it again and again, and there really wasn't any way out. He was a reporter. The whole purpose of his job was to find trouble and stir it up.

She'd spent the bulk of her adult life doing just the opposite.

He wasn't a political reporter, true. But it didn't really matter. Reporting was reporting. Besides, he didn't seem the type to commit for the long run anyway, and even if he were so inclined, she doubted that he'd choose someone like her. It wasn't as if she could just drop everything and become a regular kind of girl. There was the small matter of her father's election to consider, and if that wasn't enough, there was the fact that every time she saw the man, she wound up featured on *11 Alive News*.

The jury was still out on whether it was his fault the car had exploded, and he certainly didn't cause Michaels to kill himself, but the fact remained that wherever Jake Mahoney went, trouble seemed to follow. And she wasn't exactly in a position to court trouble. Truth was, she needed to stay as far away from it as possible.

Which meant that she was crazy to be standing in Lenox mall surrounded by the masses, looking for a man she couldn't possibly continue to see.

Of course, there was still the matter of Caroline. Her sister's pregnancy, assuming there really was one, and the resulting cover-up, had yet to be explained. But perhaps David was right and it was simply a matter of making the best of what was already an untenable position. Maybe someone in her father's cadre of people had decided to spare him the pain of learning about Caroline's situation. Maybe he or she had changed the documents to protect the family.

She chewed on her lower lip, still searching the crowd. But then again, maybe not. It was all so confusing. And no matter what the reality of the situation was, the fact remained that someone out there wanted the world to believe that Caroline had been pregnant. Someone who most likely wanted to cause trouble for her father.

She needed to make certain that nothing came of it.

And to do that, come hell or high water, she needed Jake.

Jake sighed and looked down at his watch for the third time. The woman was late, and he was beginning to get antsy. He hated crowds, and he hated waiting. But he needed to talk to her. And the only way that was going to happen was if he agreed to her wishes. And that meant staying put, no matter how much he hated it.

A movement off to his right caught his attention, and he turned just as Amber Northcott swung into view. Finally. He lifted a hand, and she nodded, her lips curving into a tenuous smile. He moved forward, and the distance closed between them.

"I was just starting to worry—" He stopped abruptly, watching as her eyes widened and her red lips opened to form a perfect O. She stumbled, and then pitched forward into his arms, her body dead weight against his.

"Jake?" The voice—Riley's voice—came from off to his left. She was standing a few feet away, her face devoid of color, her silvery eyes darting frantically from Amber to him and then back again.

Amber.

His mind clicked back into gear. Dropping to his knees, ignoring the gasps of nearby patrons, he gently rolled her over in his arms. Blood trickled from the corner of her mouth, and his hand brushed against something wet and sticky on her back.

Blood.

"Somebody get help, please," he yelled, hardly recognizing the voice as his own. From the corner of his eye he saw Riley pulling out a cell phone. Bless her.

He focused his attention back on the woman in his arms. "Amber, can you hear me?" he whispered, fingers searching wildly for a pulse, for some sign of life. "Don't you dare die on me."

But Amber wasn't listening. With a little whoosh, she released a breath and was silent, her eyes fixed and staring at the red neon Sbarro sign.

Chapter 21

"WHAT THE HELL are you doing here?" Jake spoke through gritted teeth, his voice lowered to a whisper. Three detectives were conferring in an inner office of the mall's security suite.

"I could ask you the same question." Her voice was laced with anger, red spots of color decorating her cheeks. "You're the one who was dancing with a dead woman. I just came here to tell you about Bryce Daniels."

"I know about Bryce Daniels." He knew he sounded snide, but they'd been waiting in the outer office for more than an hour, and things were getting a bit punchy. "I'm an investigative reporter. Remember?"

"How could I possibly forget? Every time I see you something catastrophic happens."

"That doesn't make it my fault." He tried to sound civil, but that bullet could have easily hit her. She hadn't been two feet away. His heart rate increased with just the thought, the idea of losing her filling him with anger all over again.

She sucked in a breath and released it slowly. "I shouldn't have come."

"No, you shouldn't have." He grabbed her by the shoulders. "You could have been hurt."

"So could you." She met him glare for glare, then

closed her eyes, her anger deflating. "Look, this isn't working, Jake. I can't keep on doing this. Any of it."

She wasn't talking about the investigation anymore, but perversely, he needed to hear her say it clearly. "What do you mean?"

She opened her eyes but refused to look at him. "I mean that I should never have gotten involved with you. My father was right. It's too dangerous."

His grip on her shoulders tightened, his gut churning with emotions—exasperation, anger, fear. "What about Caroline?"

"I don't know. Maybe I'll tell my father. Let him decide what to do. I just know I can't handle this anymore."

"So you're just going to walk away?" He searched her face, looking for some sign that she cared. That this was as difficult for her as it was for him.

"I don't see that I have a choice. Everything I am is tied up with my father and his campaign, and everything about you threatens that, Jake."

"Goddamn it, Riley. I'm not a threat—to you or to the campaign."

She jerked away from him, her eyes sparkling with tears. "Maybe not intentionally, and maybe not with this, but sooner or later there's going to be a conflict of interest. Something you find out that you shouldn't know. Someone that thinks they can get to my father through you. Can't you see that? I can't take that chance with my father's future, Jake. He's worked too hard. This is his moment, and I won't take it away from him."

"You're talking nonsense. I investigate homicides, for God's sake. I don't see how anything I do can affect the campaign." His gaze dueled with hers.

"In just under four days you've involved me in a car bombing, a man's suicide, a near hit and run, and now a woman's execution. I've been in the news daily, and the coverage hasn't been flattering. My father has spent the bulk of his valuable press time answering questions about my escapades. Escapades I would never have had if it weren't for you.

"And the tabloids are just beginning to have fun with it. 'Bomb Explodes: Senator's Daughter Goes Down.' " She waved a hand through the air, her voice rising. " 'Suicide Southern Style: Lovers' Triangle? Candidate's Daughter Goes Under Covers.' Film at eleven.

"Don't you see? It doesn't matter what happens, the press will make a three ring circus out of it and the damage will be done. That I've even allowed myself to be in this position is unforgivable. I owe my father better than that."

"But sometimes things happen, Riley—things we can't control—and that doesn't mean we just throw them away when they become difficult. Life is messy. It comes with baggage, and problems, and dirty laundry."

"Maybe yours does. But mine can't." She lifted her chin, her silvery eyes hardening. "Mine can't."

Pain bit into his gut and Jake steeled himself, letting his anger insulate him against her words. She was rejecting him. It was that simple. She'd rather live in her make-believe castle than in the real world with him. So be it. "Abso-fucking-lutely right. We mustn't let anything sully your majesty's royal name."

"Jake, please. Try and understand."

"Oh, I get it, Riley. Believe me, I get it in spades. So why don't you just get the hell out of here, before something happens you'll really regret. Run home to Daddy, princess. Let him keep you warm at night." He pointed at the door, wishing the words back even before he'd finished the thought.

First surprise, then anger, and finally the stark pain of

betrayal chased across her face. Her jaw tightened and her eyes flashed. "Fine by me. I don't know what I was thinking spending time with someone like you anyway. There are a lot of fish in the sea, Mr. Mahoney, and you're right, I don't have to settle for anything less than the best."

The door slammed shut, and Jake stood there staring at the place where she'd been, his heart ravaged so badly he was finding it difficult to breathe.

The truth was, he was in love with the princess. And she'd just left the building.

Permanently.

"So the woman never said a thing?" Tim's frustration was evident.

"There wasn't much time. Between the shooting and dying, I mean." Jake knew he sounded sarcastic, but he couldn't help it. It had been a hell of a day all in all. He'd realized he loved Riley, and lost her at practically the same moment. His story had hit another solid dead end. And to top it off, it was entirely possible that he might be the next target

"Jesus, I'm not being particularly sensitive, am I?"

Despite the gravity of the situation, Jake smiled. "On a scale of one to ten, I'd say somewhere around a one. But hey, sharing and caring isn't exactly your strong point."

"Seriously, I wasn't thinking. Maybe it's time for you to back off of this thing. We can put someone else on it."

"Not on your life. I started this and I'm going to see it through. I'll be fine. I'm good at watching my back, remember?"

"You're sure?" Tim's look had changed to assessing. "We can always go with what we've got. It may not be substantiated as well as we'd like. But you've certainly bit into something."

Jake ran a weary hand through his hair. "I'm fine, Tim. And I want to get to the bottom of this. Just give me another day. Let me see what I can find. David's still working on the bombing angle. Maybe he's found something."

Tim frowned. "I don't know. I don't like the idea of you getting hurt."

"I'm just asking for twenty-four hours."

"All right. One day. But not a second longer. And if you don't have anything new, we go with what we've got. Agreed?"

Jake nodded, too tired to formulate an answer.

"Good." Tim smiled. "In the meantime, we'll run the Northcott story. We can at least tie that to Larsen's murder." Tim pushed his glasses more firmly onto his nose. "So whatever happened with the information you found on Caroline O'Brien?"

Jake hesitated for an instant. It would be the perfect way to get even. To show Miss High-and-Mighty how the world really worked. But revenge wasn't his style. "Nothing there. Just someone trying to make something out of nothing."

"So all's well that ends well?" Tim as usual had successfully read between the lines, his myopic eyes expressing his concern.

"I suspect I'll survive." Jake tried for a grin but missed, the result more of a lopsided grimace.

"You're better off without her, my friend. Carter O'Brien and his lot aren't exactly in-law material. You know?"

Jake knew that Tim was right. Knew that he was lucky to be out of it all. But somewhere along the way, it seemed his heart hadn't gotten the memo.

• • •

"What I don't understand is what you were doing at Lenox Square in the first place." Riley's father reached for a rose cane and carefully trimmed the topmost leaves.

"I was doing what people normally do at the mall, Daddy. I was shopping." She pasted a smile on her face, wondering if her misery showed. She'd done the right thing in ending it. Whatever *it* had been. But she hadn't expected it to hurt so much.

"And you just happened to run into Jake Mahoney?" Her father's voice was skeptical.

"Yes." One more lie and then it would all be over. She'd just try and forget about all of it. If she could. "I didn't really run into him, anyway. I just happened to be there when . . . when that poor woman was shot."

Her father's look changed to one of concern, and he dropped his pruners and helped her to a garden bench. "I'm sorry, darlin'. I know it must have been awful for you. It's just that I was so worried. What with the press and all."

She wondered peevishly if it was her or the campaign he'd been worried about, then decided she really didn't want the answer. "I'm fine. Really. It's all over now, and I promise you, I'm not going to see Jake Mahoney again."

Her father sat beside her, taking her hands in his. "Riley, you know I only want what's best for you. Unfortunately, sometimes what's best isn't always clear, and then even when you know for certain what has to be done, it can still hurt like hell to do it."

She nodded, tears welling.

"Oh, honey, I'm so sorry." He pulled her into his arms, his voice gruff with emotion.

"It just hurts so much." She tried but couldn't stop the tears. "I . . . I was starting to . . . to care about him."

"I know it's painful, darlin'. But think of it like a Band-Aid. Better to rip it off all at once and get it over with."

She nodded against his chest, still sniffling, feeling all of about twelve again. "I know you're right, but that doesn't seem to help."

"Ah, Riley, if only I could kiss it and make it better like I did when you were a little girl."

"I wish you could too. I've been so stupid."

"No, darlin'. You've just been human, and that's not a fault."

"But I may have jeopardized your campaign." She didn't even want to think about what Jake might do with the information he had.

"I know you feel like that. But I can't imagine that you've done anything to compromise me or the campaign."

"I slept with him, Daddy."

She felt him tense, but his hand on her hair was gentle. "Well, now, princess, you aren't the first woman to fall for a pretty face."

She tipped back her head to look at him. "But it could be blown out of proportion. It's exactly the kind of thing the tabloids have a heyday with."

"It'll be all right, I promise you. There's nothing for you to worry about. It's over now. If there's any kind of storm, we'll weather it together."

She frowned, searching her father's face. "You're not going to do anything to hurt Jake, are you?"

"Not in the way you mean. Although just at the moment, I'd kind of like to go a few rounds with him." Her father smiled, but the gesture didn't quite reach his eyes. "I don't like the idea of someone hurting my little girl."

She shook her head. "Don't do anything, Daddy." The truth was, she wasn't certain who had hurt whom, and the idea of retribution didn't appeal at all. "I just want to put it behind me. Okay?"

"All right, princess. We'll just move on from here. How's that sound?" He tucked a stray lock of hair behind her ear.

"It sounds good." She gave him a watery smile. "I love you, Daddy."

"I love you too, princess. What do you say we don't give Jake Mahoney another thought?" Her father tightened his embrace.

She nodded against his chest, letting his warmth comfort her, wishing he really could make everything all right. The problem was, despite her protestations to the contrary, she still wanted Jake Mahoney.

In fact, she wanted him with all of her heart.

In prison, each day and night had a sameness. A predictability that suckered a man in, until he came to rely on it. To live for it. In the beginning, Haywood had tried to fight it. But like a slowly moving cancer, it had picked away at him, until it was no longer a separate entity, but part of him, necessary for his survival.

The thought scared him. If he couldn't live without the life, what would happen to him on the outside? Not that there was much chance of that.

He rolled over, opening his eyes, the dark almost a palpable, living thing—reaching out for him, calling his name, taunting him. Bryce Daniels was dead. Somehow they'd gotten to him.

He closed his eyes, not sure which was worse—the dark or his nightmares. He'd thought by rescuing Bryce, he'd paid for his sins. Turned some celestial corner that would bring him back into the light. But penance was impossible. Peace unobtainable. And nothing could change that fact. No moment of good could outweigh his evil.

In one arrogant moment, high on life and Glenlivet, he'd slammed his car into an embankment and killed his wife. In a fury of anger and retribution, her brother had seen to it that he'd received the maximum sentence. Incarceration in hell.

Douglas Michaels had made it his goal to see to it that Haywood never forgot what it was he had done. But Haywood knew something his wife's brother had never understood. There was no need for a reminder. None at all. In or out of prison, he'd never forget. *Never.* He'd hear Melanie's screams until the day he died.

Evil always won.

He'd killed his wife and saved his friend. But in the end they'd both ended up just as dead.

He reached out, his hand touching the smooth cardboard of Bryce's box. Bits and pieces of memories. Records of a man's life. Cynicism faded as hope blossomed, spreading up his arm, reaching down into his heart. Maybe all was not lost.

Maybe there *was* something he could do. At least someone he could talk to. There might be no redemption, but that didn't mean he couldn't repay his debt.

Bryce Daniels had been his friend. Not even death could change that fact. Whatever the forces at play here, he had to believe there was hope. For without it, Bryce would be forgotten.

And his friend was worthy of a far greater legacy than that.

Tomorrow, he'd do what he could to set things right.

• • •

Jake opened the apartment door, juggling yet another take-out bag. He really needed to do something about his diet. Like learn to cook.

"There you are. I was about to give up on you."

Startled, he dropped the bag, irritation warring with anger. "Lacey, what the hell are you doing here? You scared the crap out of me."

She lifted one delicate eyebrow. "Now, Jake, is that any way to treat your ex?"

He leaned over to get the bag, fiercely working to pull his emotions into control. "How the hell did you get in here?"

She held out a slender hand, a silver key dangling from one finger. "You never asked for it back."

"And that gives you the right to invade my home?"

"Oh, give me a break. I'm hardly invading. I told you I was going to come by for the boxes."

"You could have called first."

She smiled up at him. "I tried. See, there's the message." She pointed at the blinking light on the answering machine. "I've just never been good at waiting."

Despite his misgivings, he smiled. Lacey was definitely not known for her patience. "The boxes are in the guest bedroom."

It was her turn to smile. "I know. The doorman's just left with them." She eyed the greasy bag with disdain. "I see you haven't changed your eating habits."

He sank into the chair. "I haven't changed at all, Lacey."

"Everybody changes, Jake. Sometimes it's just hard to see the differences." She frowned. "You look tired. I take it things aren't going well with the senator's daughter."

He opened his mouth to deny it, then decided it wasn't worth the effort. "It's over."

"Over as in permanently? Or over as in a brief hiatus."

"Over over, okay?"

"Why don't I believe you?" She leaned back on the sofa, her eyes narrowed in speculation.

"More important, why do you care?" He stood abruptly and walked over to the small alcove that served as the bar. "You still drink gin?"

Lacey nodded.

Jake poured a measure of tonic into her glass. "You haven't told me how you knew about Riley."

"I know you, Jake." She reached up to take the glass from him. "And I talked to David."

"Great, just what I need—a friend with a big mouth."

"He cares about you. And believe it or not, so do I."

"That would be why you slept with everyone in Atlanta but me."

"Ancient history. Everyone makes mistakes. Even me." She shrugged, the gesture making the ice in her glass tinkle musically.

He sighed and sat down again, sipping his beer. "I made mistakes too, Lacey."

"Our relationship is in the past, Jake. It doesn't have the power to hurt us anymore. What's important is that we learn something from all of it."

"And have you?" Jake watched her over the rim of his glass.

"I'd like to think so. I know that I hurt you. And I know I did it to try and get your attention. You keep yourself so segmented off, Jake. Sometimes I just wanted to know that you were in there."

"Believe me, I was present." Even as he said it, he realized that she was right. It was over between them, the hatred vanishing along with the love.

She smiled. "The point is, Jake, you can't keep living

like that. You have to open up to someone. Trust someone. I wasn't the right one. But maybe Riley O'Brien is."

"No." His answer was sharp. A retort.

"I see." Lacey took a long sip, her look knowing.

"You don't see anything. Riley is from a different world, Lacey. She wants the same things in life that you do. Things I can't possibly provide."

She held up her hands. "You have no idea what I want from life, Jake. You never did. And I doubt you know what Riley wants either. If you're running true to form, I'm guessing you're thinking of disengaging. Running away at the first sign of trouble."

"Maybe." He tipped back his head, suddenly feeling tired. "But she was the one who walked away."

"And that means you aren't allowed to go after her?" Lacey leaned forward, her eyes soft with compassion. "Go after your dreams, Jake. Don't let them slip through your fingers. We screwed up our relationship, but the fallout doesn't have to ruin our lives. I've found Martin, and believe it or not, he makes me happy." She set her drink on the table and stood to go. "All I want is for you to have the same thing."

He couldn't explain why, but he believed her. "Thank you, Lacey, but I don't think my happiness is in the cards."

"Sometimes, Jake, you have to fight for what you want."

Jake sighed. "I'm not sure I know how."

She shrugged, smiling as she opened the door. "You do it like everything else in life. One step at a time."

He listened as the door closed, reaching for the bag of tacos, afraid to face the truth in what she said.

Dinner was going to be cold—again.

Chapter 22

SHE'D RUN AWAY from him. It was as simple as that. She'd let Amber Northcott's death scare her. No, truth be told, she'd let it all scare her. The car bomb, the hit and run, Daniels, Michaels, Caroline—Jake. Okay, mainly she was afraid of Jake.

Afraid of her feelings for him. Afraid of his feelings for her. Not that he'd admitted them, but it was there. She could feel it when he looked at her. When he held her, touched her—yelled at her. Riley smiled, then frowned.

What did it matter what they felt? There was so much between them. Her father, the presidency, Jake's job, everything. But maybe that didn't matter. Maybe nothing mattered except the two of them. But then, life didn't exist in a vacuum. She couldn't just ride away into the sunset. There was always a morning after, and she couldn't pretend hers didn't exist. Could she?

God, it was all too much to think about. It made her head hurt.

Which, as excuses went, was rather pedestrian. Riley sighed, and wrapped her arms around herself, looking out at the moon. Maybe everyone was right. Maybe she was letting her father run her life. Maybe she had made his dreams her own. But then again, maybe there was nothing wrong with that.

She rubbed her temples, trying to sort through her tangled thoughts. She hated cowards, hated them with a passion. And she was hiding in her room, hoping against hope that somehow all her problems would just fix themselves. She'd lied to Jake. She'd lied to her father. And she'd lied to herself.

Jake was right. Life was messy. Especially hers.

She'd wanted a life of her own, and now it was right here, within her grasp, if only she had the courage to reach out and take it. But what would the cost be?

Her mother had deserted her father. And Caroline, through no fault of her own, had deserted him too. She knew she couldn't leave him as well. Not after all they'd been through. Not with the presidency hanging in the balance.

And there could be no halfway. Her father would never forgive her defection. He'd made it more than clear how he felt about Jake Mahoney. And if that weren't enough, Leon seemed to have developed an instant dislike for the man, and her father always listened to Leon. No, her father would never see Jake as anyone but the enemy.

It was between a rock and a hard place, if ever there was one. She loved her father, and she cared about Jake. Maybe even loved him. But like Maudeen said, sometimes loving wasn't enough.

She laid a hand on the window glass, beseeching the moon. But there wasn't an easy answer. Any way she looked at it, someone was going to be hurt. She closed her eyes, leaning back against the wall. Why did everything have to be so difficult?

She thought back to her last day with Caroline. They'd been reading fairy tales, discussing happily ever afters. Caroline had believed in them. Absolutely, irrevocably. Riley hadn't been so sure. But she'd wanted to believe. Oh God, how she'd wanted to believe.

Then everything had crumbled to ashes, her sister dead—her family shattered. And Riley had given up on happily ever afters once and for all.

She sighed, wishing that Caroline had lived, that life had been different for all of them. But it wasn't. It couldn't be. And perhaps there was a lesson to be learned in it all. Caroline's secrets had gone with her to the grave. Whatever it was she longed for in life, she'd kept it from her family.

Truth was, if Caroline had been pregnant, and if she'd told their father about her baby—about her lover—he would never have accepted it. No one would have ever been good enough for Caroline. And by default, the same was now true for her.

Riley opened her eyes, the truth hitting her like a stone.

For years she'd battled against the memory of a perfect family struck by tragedy then frozen in time, she and her father forever grieving for what could have been. But it was nothing more than an illusion. There had been no perfect family. Her sister had had secrets. Her mother had been unstable. And her father had been too busy to see any of it.

Had Caroline lived, their world probably would have exploded anyway.

For twenty years, Riley had lived with the pain of her mother's betrayal and her sister's death. She'd spent her life working to make it up to her father. To help him see that he could go on without them. And now she realized that even if Caroline had lived, things would never have been the same.

The thought was liberating—and tragic.

She and her father had lived with a false memory all these years, believing Caroline was something she was not. It didn't make her love her sister any less. In fact, in some ways it made her love her more. But it did make her realize how important it was to live for the now—to make the most of all that you have. Because, like Caroline, it could all be taken away in an instant.

Riley turned from the window, reaching for her jacket, facing the truth head-on. She loved Jake. And no matter how much she wanted to please her father, she couldn't do that at the risk of her own happiness.

There were simply some things more important than a campaign.

He was behaving like a lovestruck adolescent. Or worse still, an insane one. He looked up at the dark windows of Rivercrest, trying to decide what it was he'd thought to accomplish in coming here. It wasn't like he could walk up to the front door and ring the bell.

Even if the good senator didn't toss him out on his keister just for being within a mile of his daughter, it was the middle of the night. Hell, there were probably Secret Service men watching him at this very moment. He tipped back his head, feeling like a colossal fool.

But he'd be damned if he'd let it end like this. Lacey was right. It was time he faced his fears. He loved Riley. And all the differences in the world wouldn't change that. He owed it to himself to face her head-on. To tell her how he felt. They belonged together.

At least he hoped they did. And he wasn't about to let her throw it all away in some stupid attempt to sacrifice her life for her father. If the man loved his daughter half as much as she claimed he did, he wouldn't ask that of her.

Riley was afraid of fallout. She wanted life to be neat

and orderly. But it wasn't. Life was messy and complicated—and wonderful. And he wasn't about to let her off the hook so easily. Any more than he was letting himself off. And nothing, not her father, not his own insecurities, was going to keep him from telling her so.

He stared at the house again, clutching his flashlight, plotting his strategy. He didn't even know which room was hers. There must be fifty windows. Obviously, a little reconnoitering wouldn't have hurt. So much for inspiration. He blew out a frustrated breath.

Moonlight dusted the lawn with a sprinkling of silver, giving the garden a magical feel. He walked toward the house, without a plan, knowing only that he had to see her. A figure emerged from the shadows, the pale light illuminating her.

Riley.

His heart leapt to his throat, his palms suddenly sweaty. He tried to think of all the things he wanted to say, but his mind had gone blank, registering only the moonlight, the magic, and the woman walking toward him.

She made her way slowly, looking behind her to make certain the house was still quiet. Part of her—the logical, rational side—was busy informing her that she was making a huge mistake, that she was letting her emotions get the better of her. And the other side—the free-spirited part of her—was applauding, egging her on.

She fought the urge to tell herself to shut up, and swallowed a laugh, wondering if perhaps she was going a little crazy.

Absolutely, the rational side hissed. *So what's wrong with crazy?* the Gypsy side whispered. It was enough to drive a girl around the bend, or at least make her turn around and go back in the house.

"Riley?"

She jumped about ten feet, her two alter egos heading for the hills. And just as she was about to follow them, her beleaguered brain registered the sound of the voice. "Jake?"

He stepped from the shadows into the moonlight, sending her heart racing all over again, but this time it wasn't from fear.

"What are you doing here?" Her whisper sounded sharp against the soft silence of the night. "You scared me half to death."

His smile was hesitant, his eyes intense. "I couldn't sleep."

"So you wound up over here?"

He took a step toward her, so close now that his breath touched her face. "We left things unfinished between us."

She nodded, her eyes meeting his, giving up all pretense. "I was actually on my way to see you."

His eyes were dark against the night, but she could see the emotion reflected there. "I'm sorry, Riley. I said things I didn't mean. I hurt you."

She shook her head, reaching for him, needing to feel his heart against hers, wanting him inside her, part of her. "I'm sorry too. I was angry and frightened. Oh God, Jake, I was so afraid that it was too late, that—"

His lips found hers, cutting off the words with a crushing kiss, one that drew her in, captivating her with both its tenderness and its power.

There was a difference tonight. Maybe it was the moonlight, or maybe it was because she wanted him so much, but regardless, there was something more to their caresses, something beyond the physical. As if in joining tonight, they were connecting themselves in some deeper, more spiritual way.

The thought should have scared her, made her run for cover, but instead it only made her want him more. This was where she belonged. It was almost as if she'd spent her whole life waiting for this moment—this man.

She broke away, grabbing his hand. "Not here. Someone might see us." Tugging impatiently, she led him toward the shelter of the trees. He followed her wordlessly, his trust in her humbling.

She led them through the trees, impatiently pushing the undergrowth aside, the beam of his flashlight cutting a path, until finally they came to a small clearing. Glass glittered in the wash of white moonlight, making the gazebo seem untouched by time. It was only on closer inspection that damage became apparent.

The gazebo's door hung drunkenly from rusty, broken hinges, rotten boards jutting at odd angles from the frame. Part of the roof appeared to be missing, and vines crawled up the smooth expanse of windowed walls, tangling together to create swaying topiaries of gigantic proportion.

"This was Caroline's retreat." She whispered the words, worried she might break the spell, wondering if the place might indeed be enchanted. "I haven't been here since she died. But I don't think she'd mind us being here."

Together they walked through the gaping doorway, moonlight fracturing through the windows to throw a kaleidoscope of light on the floor, its soft light forgiving. Stars twinkled through two skylights, one of them, long devoid of glass, open to the night.

A cool breeze gently fanned the dry leaves on the floor, adding an undernote to the nearby sound of creek water tumbling over a fall of rocks. Bookcases lined the back wall, shelves in tumbled disarray. A ragged velvet chaise stood in a corner, next to an open book which rested on a table. It was almost as if Caroline had only left for the night.

There was no sadness here. Nothing that made them feel unwelcome. Rather, the opposite. Riley almost felt as if her sister were welcoming them. As if love was always welcome here.

Jake reached out to touch her, one finger tracing the line of her lips. The simple gesture was more sensual than a thousand kisses. She covered his hand with hers, kissing first his palm and then each of his fingers, her eyes never leaving his.

Then, with a slow smile, she pulled off her jacket, throwing it on the chaise behind them. Moving to a rhythm only she could hear, she began unfastening each button on her dress, watching the blue of his eyes darken with need. Wanting her. Only her.

Cool air kissed her breasts, her nipples hardening with excitement as she pushed aside the cool silk, allowing it to billow to the floor. Accompanied by the wind and the soft fall of water, she slid satin panties to the floor, stepping free, ready, her body a silent solicitation.

With a groan, he accepted the invitation, closing the distance between them, his hands running along the line of her shoulders, down the curve of her back, to settle on her bottom, pulling her close, groin-to-groin, his mouth hungrily taking possession of hers.

She opened to his kiss, welcoming him inside her, knowing that tonight there could be no barriers between them. Not in this place. She worked the buttons of his shirt free, relishing the feel of his skin, hot against hers. There was an urgency now, the need for more, always more. She moaned, pressing closer, feeling his hardness through the rough fabric of his jeans.

As if sensing her need, he thrust his tongue deeper,

his hands finding her breasts, his thumbs rasping across her nipples, sending shards of sensation spiraling through her, the pleasure so potent it was almost painful.

Jake felt his desire rising to a fever pitch, and the touch of her skin against his only heightened his need. He bent his head, taking her nipple in his mouth, circling, sucking, until it was taut and hard. She pressed against him, urging him to take more, and he sucked harder, faster, satisfied when he heard her moan, the sound coming from deep in her throat.

He wanted to taste all of her. Wanted to pull her deep inside and keep her there, safe and loved. He trailed kisses up along the line of her shoulder, then moved on to the tiny pink shell of her ear, tracing the gentle curve with his tongue. She shuddered with pleasure, her eyes flickering shut, and his mouth found hers again, taking possession, his teeth tugging at her lips, demanding entry.

He slid a hand along her abdomen, dipping lower to find the soft nest of curls that marked the apex of her thighs. Sliding a finger inside, he began to move in rhythm with his tongue, thrusting deep, feeling her rub against him, responding with abandoned fervor, their bodies perfectly in tune. Moving together almost as one.

"Now, Jake." She tipped her head back, her eyes stormy in her passion, her breath coming in ragged gasps. "Please now."

He felt an answering response deep inside. A need so primal it threatened to unman him. With a growl, he swung her up into his arms, carrying her to the chaise. Their gazes met and held, their hunger almost palpable.

He laid her down gently, then stood back to look at her. The moonlight kissed the gold in her hair, and highlighted the smoky silver of her eyes, its rays caressing the smooth alabaster of her skin, making her appear almost ethereal in the half-light.

Riley.

His Riley.

Needing her now with a desire greater than he'd ever felt, he quickly shed the rest of his clothes and lowered his body to hers, reveling in the feel of her heated skin against his. She arched upward, flesh meeting flesh, and opened to him, the invitation in her eyes, taking his breath away.

With a sure thrust, he found his way home, her slick, hot sheath tightening around him in welcome. Hands braced on either side of her, he strove for a rhythm, his desire meeting hers thrust for thrust, each movement bringing them closer, until there was no beginning and no end.

Only the two of them, joined as one, winging higher and higher, spinning out of control, until, with a hoarse cry, he felt himself shatter, pleasure combining with love to bring an ecstasy beyond anything he'd ever imagined.

And suddenly the night was cloaked with magic, the dark held firmly at bay.

They lay entwined on a bed of discarded clothing and old velvet, stars still twinkling through the broken skylight. The moon had set, leaving the summer house clothed in deep shadow—a comforting darkness that enclosed them like a blanket.

"We need to talk." Jake's voice sounded disembodied in the dark, and Riley burrowed closer.

"I know. It's just that everything is so perfect right now. I hate to spoil it."

"Maybe that's the problem, Riley. Maybe we're both striving for some kind of perfection that doesn't exist.

Maybe we're setting ourselves up for failure before we ever start." He cupped her face in his hands. "All I know for certain is that I love you. I love you, Riley. And nothing else is as important as that fact."

Her heart stopped, her breathing threatened to malfunction. "But there are still so many obstacles." She had blurted out the first thing that came into her head, joy, love, apprehension, and fear all tangling together in one mass of emotion.

"So we take it one step at a time." His eyes searched hers, the question there making her shiver.

"I can't make promises, Jake. I don't know where I'm going. I don't even know for certain what tomorrow will bring. There's still my father, and my commitment to him. I can't just throw all of that out the window, like yesterday's news."

"I'm not asking you to do that. I'm just asking that you give us a chance."

"But my father—"

"Has no place in our relationship, Riley—whatever we decide we want that to be."

She sat up, running a hand through her hair. "I wish it were that easy."

He wrapped his arms around her, pulling her back against him, enveloping her, his breath warm against her neck. "It can be."

She shook her head. "You don't understand. I live in my father's world. I'm part of it, Jake. I can't just walk away."

"I'm not asking you to do that."

"No, but my father is. His whole life is about politics. If he becomes the next President, then my life, every part of it, will be open for public scrutiny." She ran a weary hand across her eyes, wishing that she had a normal life—a normal father.

But she didn't.

"So, what? You're saying that we can't be together?"

"Yes . . . no . . ." She tipped her head back to look at him. "I don't know what I'm saying, Jake. I only know that I don't want to hurt my father."

"I fail to see how your being happy could possibly hurt him." He turned her around, framing her face with his hands. "Riley, you can't keep living your life for other people. Your father is going to be the President, not you."

"But don't you see? I'm part of the package."

He traced the line of her cheek with his thumb. "All I know is that I've waited a hell of a long time to find you. And I'm not going to give you up without a fight."

Her heart tumbled, the blue in his eyes underscoring the truth in his words. It was right there in front of her. Everything she'd ever wanted. All she had to do was take it.

"I care about you, Jake. I swear I do."

"But . . ."

"But it's so complicated."

"Only as complicated as you make it, sweetheart." His voice was warm against her ear, and she shivered with pleasure, running a hand along the hard muscles of his chest. "We'll find a way to work this out, Riley. As long as we're together, we can accomplish anything."

She nodded, taking strength from his closeness. In the dark of the night it all seemed so clear, so easy. But come the morning, everything would be different.

"It's going to be light soon." Again his words reflected her thoughts. "I should go." He sat up, and she shivered, immediately missing his warmth. "I've got work to do."

"Michaels."

He nodded, reaching for the flashlight, turning it on,

and propping it on the table. "Somehow I've got to figure out how he ties into everything that's been happening."

She blinked uncomfortably, the harsh glare highlighting the dilapidated, rotting gazebo, destroying any sense of sanctuary. It seemed morning had come early. "But you're at a dead end."

"There's no such thing," he said, pulling on his jeans. "It's all a matter of how you approach it. There's always a way out. I just have to find it."

She sighed, reaching for her dress. "A new path? But what if you're wrong? What if there truly is no way out?" They were talking about more than Michaels now.

"Then you just have to have a little faith, Riley." He buttoned his shirt, smiling at her, and just for the moment anything seemed possible. "You said this was Caroline's retreat. What did you mean by that?"

"Daddy had it built for her. It was her own private haven. She came to read, to get away. Just to be, I guess. I haven't been in here since she died. It didn't seem appropriate until—" She broke off, embarrassed.

"I'm honored." Jake's eyes met hers, his look sending little sparks of electricity dancing across her skin.

She bent to pick up her belt, her eyes falling to the pile of rotting books at her feet. "Oh, my God." She froze, her heart pounding, her eyes riveted on the floor.

Jake was there in an instant, his arms around her. "What is it, sweetheart?"

She swallowed, trying to find the words, pointing at one of the ragged books. "It's *My Brother Michael*. The book I was telling you about. *Caroline's book*."

Chapter 23

Jake frowned, bending down for the book. "The one you saw in Caroline's room?"

"With the lemonade. And then again in my room. How did it get here?" She ran a trembling finger along the spine, lifting her gaze to meet his.

"It can't be the same one, Riley. This one is warped with age. It's practically ruined. Look at it." He held it out, and she pulled back, almost afraid to touch it.

But he was right. It wasn't the same. The book in the house had been almost like new. The pages yellowed, but otherwise unmarred. This book was bowed, the jacket edges frayed, mildew darkening the spine.

She took it from him and carefully turned to the first page, her heart constricting.

"What is it?" Jake's voice seemed to come from far away. "Riley?"

She swallowed, struggling to find words. "This isn't *My Brother Michael*. It's a journal."

"But the dust cover—"

"Was a decoy. Oh my God, Jake, this is Caroline's diary."

"When is it dated?"

She turned to the front, her hands shaking so hard she could hardly hold the book. The pages were blurred in places, sometimes impossible to read. But she could make out the date. "Jake, she wrote this the year she died."

"Come on, sit down. It's all right. Just take deep breaths." She sucked air into her lungs, closing her eyes, her hands holding onto the journal with a death grip. "Easy now." She felt his arm around her, and forced herself to relax. There was nothing to be gained in hyper ventilating. "Let's have a look at the book." He eased it away from her, and, still breathing deeply, she opened her eyes.

"When does it end?" She bit her bottom lip, watching as he carefully turned the weathered pages.

"I can't tell. The pages are stuck together."

She felt tears threatening. "All of them?"

"No, just the ones at the very end." His hold tightened, his strength comforting. "Shall I read some of it?"

She shook her head, knowing that she needed to face this herself, to read it on her own. "No, I'll do it." She took the book back, opening it randomly, brushing away her tears, concentrated on her sister's spidery scrawl.

March 10

. . . My dearest darling, as ever, I'm writing this to you. Perhaps someday you will read this and know how very much I love you. I think I felt you move today. Although I'm not certain. It seems a bit early. Still, it pleases me to think that you're here growing inside of me.

It's an absolutely glorious day today. Spring is everywhere. In the garden, in the woods, but mostly in my heart. I long to shout the news of you from the highest mountain. It grows harder to be silent every day. And time is working against us.

Before long you'll be making yourself known, a new life anxious to make your mark on the world . . .

The writing faded, a mud stain obscuring the words. Riley turned to another page.

. . . Today I almost told Riley. We were at the river, and it was everything I could do not to sing it all out. But I held my tongue. It's the first time I've ever lied to her. And I don't like the way it feels. Still, I can't trust her to keep my secret. She's only a little girl. . . .

"It's unreadable again." She looked up to meet Jake's solemn gaze and then turned to another page, this one farther back in the book.

. . . I know the time has come to tell him everything—to ask his blessing. But I can't seem to work up the courage. He's so sure of things, your grandfather. And I know he won't believe me when I tell him that I'm in love with your daddy. Madly, passionately, forever in love.

He'll never understand. He'll say I'm too young. That I don't know my own mind. That you're influencing me. But he's wrong. I swear it, my darling. Your daddy completes me, and life without the two of you is untenable. Our love, our little family, is a lifetime thing. And I won't give it up for anyone. Not anyone . . .

This time the writing faded away completely, the pages afterward stuck together in a hopeless mass.

Riley started to try to pull them apart, wanting something more, but Jake covered her hands with his.

"Don't. You'll only destroy what's there."

"But I need to know what happened. I need to know if she wrote something the day she died."

"I know you do. But this isn't the way. Let me have the book. I'll take it to David. He'll know someone who can restore it, open the pages without ruining what's on them. All right?" His eyes met hers, and reluctantly she nodded, letting him take the book, her emotions still roller-coastering inside her.

He carefully flipped through the earlier pages, stopping now and then to read. "These are all letters to the baby."

Riley forced herself to look at the book. "Does she mention the father's name?"

"Not that I can see. But there are obscured passages throughout. The first entry is dated January third. My guess is she started this when she found out she was pregnant."

"So, that's all there is." Her voice came out on a harsh whisper, clouded with tears and grief.

Jake laid the journal aside. "We'll get to the rest. Trust me. For now, it'll have to be enough to know that she was happy. That the baby was loved."

She brushed angrily at her tears. "It's such a waste, Jake. She had everything to live for. It's just not fair."

He turned her to face him, holding her shoulders, forcing her to look at him. "Life isn't fair, Riley. I wish it were. But that's just not the way it is. Things happen. Good things happen to bad people, and bad things happen to good people. The trick is to make something good out of the bad. To find the silver lining. I know that sounds clichéd, but it's all about hope, sweetheart."

"Hope for what? Caroline had hope, and look what happened to her." She tried but couldn't keep the bitterness from her voice.

"For tomorrow. For things yet to come. Maybe we have to make our own happy ending, Riley. Maybe that's what we can take away from all this. You've cloistered yourself behind your pain long enough. It's time for you to start living again. To make peace with your past."

"Easier said than done." She attempted a smile, and failed.

"I'm here." His dark eyes met hers. "Let me help you."

"I wish you could. But this isn't your fight, Jake. It's mine. And before I can do anything else, I've got to find a way to tell my father."

"All of it?"

She didn't pretend to misunderstand him. "Everything. Caroline, you—all of it. I love my father, but I love you too. He'll just have to find a way to deal with that."

"Say that again, please."

"My father will just have to deal with it."

"No, not that part." His gaze collided with hers, the emotion there stealing her breath away. "The other thing."

She smiled, hope blossoming from somewhere deep inside, giving her courage. "I love you, Jacob Mahoney. *I love you.*"

He pulled her close, and she found comfort in the strong beat of his heart. "Then whatever else happens, we'll be all right."

She prayed that he was right, that somehow everything would work out. But somewhere, deep inside her, a little voice still whispered insistently that there was no such thing as a happily ever after.

Riley let the hot water from the shower beat down upon her, her mind sorting through everything that had happened in the past few hours. Jake had told her he loved her. But what did that mean? Commitment? Marriage? Would he move to Washington? Would she stay here? In turn, she'd promised him she'd tell her father. But the thought was daunting. There was so much to sort out. And each answer seemed to raise more questions.

Everything was spinning out of control. Even her memories weren't immune. Caroline wasn't what she'd seemed. She was so much more. And so much less. Riley wasn't even sure how to begin assimilating the fact that her sister had died expecting a child.

It was so tragic. So senselessly tragic. She leaned her head against the tile and closed her eyes, letting the water run over her, soothe her.

Riley. Where are you? Riley . . . Riley?

Caroline.

Riley reached for the taps, turning off the water, her heart pounding. The bathroom was silent, and she strained into the stillness, waiting to hear her sister's voice again. Her mind insisted that she was giving in to her imagination, even as her heart waited, hoping to hear something, anything.

The room was quiet.

She stepped out of the shower, wrapping a towel around her, chastising herself for such foolishness. Her mind was simply overloaded, turning innocent noises into blasts from the past. She laughed at herself, the sound harsh in the echo of the bathroom.

With a sigh, she slipped on her robe and walked into her bedroom, determined to gain control. She was letting it all get to her. And while it might be perfectly understandable, it wasn't acceptable. She had more important things to do, and she wasn't about to let her subconscious get the better of her.

Her bedroom was cold after the warmth of the shower, and she shivered, her mind still caught in the cottony web of her imaginings. She sat on her bed, burying her face in her hands, tears of exhaustion threatening. There was simply too much for her tired brain to process.

With a sigh, she lay back, turning on her side, her arms curling around her pillow. A soft fuzzy pillow. Swallowing a scream, she jerked upright, her eyes locked on the thing in her arms.

Mr. McKafferty. She was holding her sister's bear.

"Riley, honey, what is it? What's wrong?" Adelaide stood in the doorway, her eyes dark with worry.

Tears slid down Riley's face, and without thinking she threw herself, bear and all, into the housekeeper's embrace. "I thought I heard Caroline's voice. And then I found Mr. McKafferty. Oh God, Adelaide, everything's turned upside down. I can't work out what's real and what's an illusion."

"Hush now." They sank onto the bed, the older woman rocking her back and forth, as if she were no more than a baby, Mr. McKafferty smushed between them. And Riley let the tears come. She cried for her sister. For Caroline's baby. For the dreams that had died. She cried for her mother. For her father. For all that could have been. She cried for Jake. For all that had happened. For all that might never happen. She cried for herself, for the life she'd lost and the one that she'd gained.

She cried until Mr. McKafferty's fur was soppy and her nose was stuffy, Adelaide's hand still placidly smoothing her hair. Finally, with a sniffle, she pulled back, still clutching the bear, her breathing ragged, her tears spent.

"Things have a way of working out, honey." Adelaide's knowing gaze was comforting. "You just have to give them time."

"But what if there isn't any time to give?" Riley searched the older woman's face for reassurance.

"Then you have to make choices."

"And if the choices are too hard?"

Adelaide laughed. "They're never that hard, child. Not if you listen with your heart."

Riley sighed, certain there must be a primer to life and that she was the only one missing it.

"You just have to trust in yourself, and everything will be all right." Adelaide squeezed Riley's hands and released them, her voice matter-of-fact again. "So where in the world did you find this bear?" She held Mr. McKafferty up to the light, his tattered bow drooping on either side of his chin.

"I don't know. He was just here." She looked at the little bear, fear reasserting itself. "I think maybe someone is trying to scare me."

"Now why would anyone want to do something like that?" Adelaide reached over to pat her hand. "More likely one of the staff found him and thought maybe he was yours."

"But after twenty years?" She fought against her rising panic.

"Riley, your father wanted the attic cleaned. I'm sure that someone found the bear up there and thought maybe he deserved a better home. I'll check into it, you can be certain of that, but I doubt there's anything sinister in his appearance."

Riley drew in a deep breath, feeling foolish. Of course there wasn't anything sinister about a stuffed bear. She smiled sheepishly. "I guess I sort of overreacted."

"It's to be expected, honey. You've been through a lot in the last few days, and when you add in the stress of the campaign, it's not surprising your imagination is on overdrive." She stood up, reaching into her pocket, and handed Riley a stack of phone messages. "I almost forgot. I thought you might want these."

Riley nodded, her emotions securely under control again. "Have you seen Daddy?" She needed to find him, to tell him about Caroline—about Jake.

"You just missed him, I'm afraid. He and Leon went off to a meeting or something about an hour ago. Said they'd be back by nightfall."

"I see." Disappointment washed through her.

"He'll be home before you know it." She smiled, the gesture warming Riley all the way through. "Anything else you need from me before I go?"

"Go?" She frowned up at Adelaide, her thoughts still muddled. "Oh God, this is your day off. Adelaide, what are you doing spending it in here with me?"

The housekeeper smiled. "Honey, don't you know by now, there's no place else I'd rather be?"

Riley reached up to hug her. "I love you too, Adelaide. But I'm fine now. So get out of here. Enjoy what's left of the day. I'll see you in the morning."

"Remember what I said, Riley." Adelaide's expression grew serious. "Everything happens in its own time. You just have to be patient. Shall I take Mr. McKafferty with me?"

Riley shook her head, reaching for the bear. "No. I'd like to keep him here. A reminder of Caroline."

"Happy memories, Riley. There were loads of them."

"I know, it's just that sometimes, with all that's happened, it's hard to remember that." She held the little bear close, her eyes still on the housekeeper.

"The past is what it is, Riley. You can't change it, and you can't bring it back. So maybe it's time to look to the future. There's a life full of happiness waiting for you, if you'll only open your eyes to see it." Adelaide smiled, and then left, leaving Riley alone with her thoughts.

She wanted the future. Especially if it included Jake. But she couldn't get past the idea that there were secrets she had to uncover before she could move on. Caroline's secrets. With a sigh, she pushed her thoughts aside. She wasn't going to solve anything sitting here feeling sorry for herself.

She flipped through her messages. There were a couple of appointments to confirm for their upcoming road trip, and a call from a newspaper in Ontario. She'd have to run that one by Maudeen. She stopped at the last message. A call from Harv Burkett.

Harv was an attorney friend of her father's, and although Adelaide had marked the message as urgent, Riley couldn't imagine why the man would be calling her. With a sigh, she stood up, reaching for the phone, tossing Mr. McKafferty on the bed. There was only one way to find out.

And, at least according to Adelaide, there was no time like the present.

Chapter 24

"ALL RIGHT." DAVID closed his cell phone with a click, just as the waitress came by to refill their coffee. "Everything's all arranged. I've contacted a friend of mine who's a book conservationist. He's done some restorative work for the ATF before. If anyone can get those pages apart, it'll be him. I'll take it to him as soon as we finish here."

"Sounds great." Jake tore open a packet of sugar and dumped it into his cup. "How long do you think it will take?"

"Not too long. I told him you were in a rush." He shrugged. "Hopefully we'll hear something later this afternoon. Sorry it took me so long to get back to you. We've had a busy morning. But it looks like we've found our bomber."

"Who?" Jake leaned forward in his chair, excitement roiling in his gut. Maybe they were finally getting a break.

"A two-bit thug by the name of Martell Osterman."

"Is he in custody?"

"Not yet. We haven't been able to run him to ground. But we will."

"So you still have no idea why he did this?"

David shook his head. "Nothing definite. He's a hired gun. Fancies himself to be something special, but he's not much more than a two-bit hustler looking to make the big time."

"Not the save-the-babies type, I take it?"

"No. More the how-much-you-gonna-pay-me type."

"Well, that tracks with what we suspected."

David nodded. "I'd say it's looking pretty good. But we won't know anything for certain until we have the son of a bitch in custody."

"And when do you think that will be?" Jake asked.

"Soon. According to his bank records, he doesn't have the wherewithal to get very far. And based on what we know of him, I don't think he has the intelligence to realize how close we're getting. So with any luck, we'll nab him by tonight."

"Which leaves me playing the waiting game."

"Well, unless I miss my guess, you've abandoned the Jake-hates-women school of thought. That ought to give you something to occupy your time." David's grin was just shy of goading.

"Your guess is accurate. But the celebration may be a little premature. There's still the little matter of *Daddy* to deal with."

"The almost President."

Jake nodded. "Riley says she wants to break free of him, but to quote an old adage, I think that's easier said than done."

"It's understandable though. You've got to admit that."

"I suppose." He contained a sigh. "I'm trying to be patient. At least until we get this mess straightened out. But I'm not going to wait forever. Sooner or later she's going to have to choose between Carter and me."

"I'm not sure that's a choice you can expect her to make, Jake. The man's her father."

"Well, I love her too, damn it. And either that means

something or it doesn't." He sat back, running a hand through his hair.

"I think maybe you're preaching to the choir here. The person you need to be talking to is Riley."

"I tried to. This morning. But then we found the journal, and things sort of deteriorated from there. I think she's going to tell her father about us. At least, that's what she said."

"But you're afraid she'll change her mind."

"Carter O'Brien is a persuasive man. And like you said, the man's her father."

"Sounds like you're between a rock and a hard place, my friend."

"More like a rack, with Carter O'Brien turning the screws."

"So you sit back and play the waiting game. I don't see that you have any other choice." David finished his coffee and reached for his cell phone. "In the meantime, maybe we'll catch a killer."

Jake nodded, his mind still on Riley and her father. Waiting did seem to be his best option. Problem was, he wasn't a waiting kind of guy. And push come to shove, he doubted Carter O'Brien was the type to give up the kingdom without a fight. The man was a powerful adversary, and he was after the man's most precious treasure.

And to top it all off, this was the twenty-first century, and these days, princesses got to make their own decisions about where to go and whom to love. And best he could tell, despite all her talk to the contrary, his princess wasn't inclined to leave the kingdom.

Jake sighed. Leave it to him to walk into the middle of a fractured fairy tale.

"I wasn't sure you'd come." Harv Burkett stole a look at Riley as they walked down the prison corridor.

She fought with a smile, trying to maintain her ice queen image. For a woman afraid to make waves, she was becoming quite adept at it. Meeting with a convicted felon was all in a day's work. "I wasn't certain myself, and I still don't really understand why I'm here."

"I actually don't know much myself. Haywood just called me this morning out of the blue and asked me to get you down here."

"And he didn't say anything about why?"

"Nothing more than what I told you over the phone. Just that I should ask you to come for old times' sake. You an old flame or something?" The lawyer was obviously curious.

"No. More like childhood pals. Haywood's family lives near ours. We used to play together when we were little."

Harv nodded, like that explained everything, though it clearly didn't.

"He said he had information for me, right?" She prayed this wasn't a wild-goose chase, that despite the odds against it, there was a connection somehow to everything that had been happening. "About my sister?"

"Yeah. But that's all I know." He stopped in front of a barred door. "This is it."

Riley stopped too, her eyes glued to the door. "You're going in with me, right?"

Harv shook his head. "He wants to see you alone."

She shot a look at the burly guard standing by the door. "Is that normal?"

"No. But not unheard of. And it's what Haywood wants. The guards don't think there's a risk, and frankly, neither do I."

"But . . . ?" She pushed, sensing his hesitation.

"Look, Riley, I urged him to let me be present. I have

no idea what he wants to tell you, but I have to think it's something pretty damn important, and I don't like the idea of him talking about that sort of thing without his attorney present."

She relaxed. If the man's biggest concern was what Haywood might say, then she had nothing to fear. Besides, any discomfort she felt would more than be made up for if he had something to tell her that could help.

"I'm sure I'll be fine." She smiled at Harv, hoping he couldn't see the trembling in her hands. She'd never been in a prison. Let alone in a room with a convict.

Of course, the convict was Haywood. And although she hadn't seen him in years, they had been friends once, and that counted for something, surely. Besides, what harm could come to her in a prison?

She thought about Bryce Daniels, and shivered.

"I'm ready."

The guard opened the door, indicating that she should step inside. As the door clanged shut, her first thought was to try and stop it. The noise sounded so final—so permanent. Her second thought was that, except for a table and two chairs, the room was empty.

Completely empty.

She turned around, ready to bang on the door, to tell the guard that there had been a mistake, when she heard another rattle. This one behind her. Swiveling back around she realized there was another door, and Riley waited as it slowly opened, not certain what to expect.

He was a mere breath of a man. A shadow, really. His blond hair was cropped close to his head, and he was lean to the point of emaciation. There were circles under his eyes, so dark they seemed almost bruised, a startling counterpoint to the pallid white of his skin. But what was most arresting about him was his eyes. They were flat, haunted looking—the pain reflected there almost a physical thing.

Somewhere underneath it all she could see the shade of the boy she remembered and the man he'd no doubt become. A man who had possibly been vibrant. Maybe even handsome. Certainly more alive. It was there in his stance, and in the set of his jaw. But it was no more than a shadow, the essence of what had once been.

Decimated was the word that came to mind, looking at him. And should he lose his tenuous hold, she had no doubt there would be nothing left but the empty shell of what had once been a man. She smiled weakly, uncertain of what to do or say.

"Riley?" Haywood smiled, the gesture transforming him, his eyes lighting with joy. "Is it really you?"

She nodded, and almost as if they had choreographed it, they sat opposite each other at the table, she clutching her purse, Haywood clutching a battered cardboard box. "It's been a long time, Haywood."

"Since we were kids." He ducked his head in a familiar gesture, and she remembered suddenly that he'd been painfully shy.

Riley resisted the urge to touch him, to offer comfort. He seemed so sad. So lost. "I was so sorry to hear about your wife."

His head jerked up, the pain back. "I never meant to hurt her. You have to believe that."

"Of course I do." She met his gaze, willing him to believe her. "It was a horrible accident. Everyone knows that."

"But I'd been drinking."

"And I'm sure you live with that every day, Haywood, but that doesn't mean you meant to kill her. Douglas Michaels was on a vendetta. I never thought you belonged in here."

He nodded once. As if she'd given the proper response to a question she hadn't realized she'd been asked. "I have something for you."

"Something about my sister?" Riley prompted.

Haywood opened the box, reverently removing the lid and laying it on the table. Then, just as carefully, he reached inside and removed a yellowed square of paper, handing it to Riley.

It was old, curling at the corners, browning on the edges, and when Riley looked down, her heart caught in her throat. In the same spidery scrawl that had adorned her journal, Caroline had written on the piece of paper.

I'll love you forever, C.

The date was February 1980—the year Caroline died.

With shaking hands Riley turned the paper over, already certain what she would find on the other side.

Her sister's beautiful face looked up at her, caught for all eternity in a careless grin. Tears filled her eyes, and with a will of their own, her fingers traced the smooth line of her sister's cheek.

She raised her eyes to meet Haywood's, an incredible thought entering her head. "Did Caroline give this to you?"

Haywood's eyebrows rose, a spark of something shooting across his face. "No. No. It wasn't me. It belonged to one of the prisoners."

"You're telling me that someone *in here* had a twenty-year-old picture of my sister?" Her voice rose almost to a shriek, the pressures of the last few days reflected in every word.

"I'm in here. And you didn't think it odd that I'd have

her picture." There was quiet dignity in his voice, and Riley was ashamed.

"I'm sorry, Haywood. That was tactless of me. Will you tell me who it belonged to?" She reached over to touch his hand, and he stared at it as if he'd never seen such a thing. Then he lifted his gaze, studying her, and finally, seeming satisfied, he nodded.

"He was a friend of mine, actually. A real good man. He—" Haywood ducked his head again. "—he helped me out. Kept me out of trouble."

Riley forced herself to hold onto her patience. She needed to know whose photo it was. She needed to talk to him. Find out how he'd come by it. "I'm glad you have a friend."

"Had, actually. He's dead."

"Dead?" Hope died as quickly as it had been born.

Haywood nodded again, his face clouding with grief. It was obvious from his reaction that he cared a great deal about his friend. "He died early yesterday morning. That's why I have the box. The guards gave it to me. Didn't think there was anything there that mattered. But they were wrong, Riley. He'd hidden it in the lid. See?" He lifted the box to expose a tiny slit between the paper lining and the corrugated cardboard. "Nobody thought to look there."

"I still don't see why—"

"He had the picture?" Haywood's expression was thoughtful. "Me either. But I figure if it was important enough to hide away, it must have meaning. Maybe it even has something to do with why he was murdered."

"Murdered?" Prickles of dread danced along the hairs at the back of her neck. "You're telling me your friend, the one who had Caroline's picture, was murdered here, last night?"

"Yes. I can't prove it of course. They're keeping it all hush-hush."

"They?"

"The administration. Word on the cell block is that it was an overdose. But he never used drugs. Not in here anyway. Said you had to stay alert. Watch your back. Evidently, in the end, it didn't matter. They got to him anyway."

Riley leaned forward, her heart pounding. It couldn't be, it was simply too much of a coincidence. "What was his name, Haywood?" She fought for breath, certain that she already knew the answer.

"Daniels. His name was Bryce Daniels." The words hung in the air between them, as if the man himself were in the room.

"Oh my God." Riley felt as if she'd been sucker punched, the air in her body exiting in one fell swoop. She swallowed, trying for words, but there simply wasn't enough oxygen.

"Riley?" Haywood's concerned face swam into view. "You all right?"

She nodded, air finally finding its way into her lungs again. "I'm just surprised."

"That someone could be murdered in prison?" Haywood's laughter was bitter.

"No, Haywood." She covered his hand for a second time. "I was surprised because I know who Bryce Daniels is. Or at least I know the name. I've been helping a friend with an investigation."

"About Bryce?" His face took on a skeptical cast, his eyes wary.

"About his trial, actually. It's possible that it was fixed."

"That would explain a lot. Bryce always said he was

innocent." He frowned at her, his fingers absently stroking Bryce's box. "You got anything else?"

"Not much. Bits and pieces mostly. Although they're starting to fit together. It looks like Douglas Michaels was instrumental in having Bryce framed."

"Why?"

"I don't know. That's a missing piece. But we do know that someone else figured it out, and was starting to put the screws to Michaels. But then Michaels had the man killed. Or at least we think he did."

"So you think Michaels's suicide ties in somehow?"

She frowned, trying to place all that she knew in some kind of logical order. "It's possible. Although there's really no way to prove it. But I'd say it seems a likely scenario at this point."

"But even if you accept all that as true, Bryce was killed *after* Michaels was dead. So he couldn't have done that."

"That's just it. All kinds of things have been happening since he died. A woman was killed, I was almost run down, there was a bomb, and now there's Bryce."

"They tried before." Haywood frowned, his anger animating his face. "With Bryce, I mean. A couple of days ago. Someone stabbed him. With a shank. I saved him. But Bryce was still scared. I've never seen him like that. Talked about it finally being his time. And that some people were just too powerful." He stared down at his hands. "And in the end, I guess, they were." He slowly met her gaze, his eyes full of questions. "This sounds like something a lot bigger than a fixed trial, Riley."

She nodded, all of it almost too much to contemplate. She wished Jake were here. Or her father. Someone to help them sort it through. "And now there's Caroline."

"But how in the world could Caroline tie into all of

this?" Haywood's eyebrows drew together in frustration. "She was just a kid at the time."

Riley looked down at the photograph. "No, she was a woman. We were just too young to see it." She turned the picture to the back again, rereading the inscription. "Caroline was pregnant when she died, Haywood."

"I never heard that." His shock was apparent.

"I only just found out myself. Anyway, the point is, she was in love with the baby's father. And I think, based on this picture, that it might have been Bryce."

Haywood's eyes narrowed as he considered something. "This is probably crazy, but Bryce told me once he worked as a gardener at some big fancy house. You don't suppose . . . ?"

"I don't know. It's certainly possible. If he was, then surely there'll be some kind of record."

"I'd think so. But how does this tie in to murder? Are you thinking that someone had him killed because of his relationship with Caroline?"

She shook her head. "I can't believe that covering up a pregnancy would be worth all that. But it has to fit in somehow."

"It could have been racially motivated."

"You mean that somehow it's worse because Bryce was black? I suppose there are people who would see it that way, but still, it isn't a reason to frame the man. I mean, Caroline was dead."

"But the news wasn't," Haywood said. "Did Bryce know about the baby?"

"I think so."

"So if he did, then he'd have been a threat to anyone who wanted to keep Caroline's pregnancy quiet."

"True, but not enough of a threat to go to these kind of lengths, surely? Couldn't they have just bought his silence?"

Haywood's face hardened. "You didn't know Bryce. He wasn't the type of man to be bought. And people would certainly be less likely to believe what a convicted murderer had to say." Haywood sighed, frustration naked on his face. "But who would do something like that? We know Douglas can't have been acting on his own."

"I don't know. Without understanding what this is really all about, it's impossible to even guess at who might be behind it. Someone trying to protect my father, maybe."

"But protect him from what? There has to be something more, something we're not seeing. Did your father know about the pregnancy?"

"No." A small niggle of doubt worked its way front and center in her mind, but she pushed it aside. There had to be another explanation. Whoever had framed Bryce had also had him murdered, along with Hank Larsen and Amber Northcott. Her father simply wasn't capable of something like that. It was the one thing in all of this she was certain of.

"Well, someone must know what happened. It's possible your father knew about Bryce even if he didn't know about the pregnancy."

"Maybe you're right." She sighed, her eyes meeting his. "Maybe I was wrong not to tell him."

"He doesn't know?"

"I was trying to protect him, but things seem to be spiraling out of control. And if he does know something, that could put him in danger too." She pushed her hair out of her face. "I need to talk to him."

"He'll understand why you kept it from him, Riley. And who knows, maybe he'll even be able to help."

"I hope you're right."

"I am. You'll see." He laid the picture in her hand,

closing her fingers around it. "Take this. Find the answers." His voice broke, his words soft, colored with layers of emotion; relief, regret, remorse, and, unbelievably—hope. "He was a good man, Riley. My friend. And he deserves better than this."

They sat for a moment more, still clasping hands, then Haywood stood up and banged on the door until a guard opened it. He turned to look back at her, his face somehow less shrouded, more alive. "Good luck, Riley. I hope you find what you're looking for. And don't worry about me." His lips curved in the tiniest of smiles. "I'm going to be just fine."

Chapter 25

RILEY LEANED HER head against the steering wheel of her car, trying to still her racing heart. The photograph of Caroline was still clutched in one hand, and her keys dangled uselessly from the other. After everything that had happened, she'd honestly believed that someone would try and keep her from leaving the prison.

She'd walked away from the interview rooms waiting for someone to stop her, to take her sister's picture. But nothing had happened. Nothing at all. Harv hadn't even pushed for details, merely saying he'd talk to Haywood later.

And now she was safe in her own car. With the kind of knowledge that had been getting people killed. With shaking fingers she locked her car doors, the stormy gloom of early evening giving her the willies. The air hung heavy, almost as if it were waiting for something. Something evil.

She shook her head, holding her imagination at bay. She was overreacting, surely. No one had any idea what she'd just put together. Truth was, she didn't even know what she'd put together.

She knew for a fact that Caroline had been pregnant. And if the photograph was to be believed, that Bryce Daniels had been her lover. But the connection between her sister's pregnancy and Bryce being framed was weak, if it existed at all. And there was nothing in any of it that explained why so many people had wound up dead.

She pulled out her cell phone and dialed the paper. She needed to talk to Jake—to tell him what she'd found.

The phone rang three times then connected with his machine.

Damn it.

She debated leaving a message, then hung up. There was no telling who checked his messages. And what she had to tell him wasn't for strangers. She thumbed through her wallet, looking for the card with his private numbers, her stomach sinking when she realized it was lying on her desk at home. Frustrated, she dialed 411 and requested the number.

Unlisted. As was his cell phone.

What kind of a reporter had an unlisted number?

She banged her hand on the steering wheel, wondering what she should do. Her instinct was to go to her father. To tell him everything. He'd help her, she was certain of it.

But she'd feel better if she could talk to Jake first. It was his story, after all. But she'd had just about enough subterfuge to last a lifetime. And it wasn't her fault Jake was unreachable. She needed to talk to someone, and she trusted her father.

Besides, she'd told Jake she was going to tell her father everything this morning. So what if this everything was a little more than she'd bargained for? Her father needed to know. And Haywood was right. Maybe her father knew something that could help.

A sharp rap on the car window jerked her out of her reverie, a shriek of pure fear filling her throat with bile. A uniformed prison guard stood by the driver's window, frowning. Swallowing back her fear, she inched down the window, praying she wouldn't regret it.

"You all right, miss?" The man's eyes seemed kindly, his concern evident, and Riley relaxed slightly, careful to keep the hand holding the picture out of sight.

"I'm fine. Just a little tired. I guess my visit took more out of me than I realized." She shot him what she hoped was a dazzling smile, fairly certain she'd failed miserably.

He nodded, still peering through the partially opened window. "First time?"

"Yeah." She relaxed a little more, her smile more genuine.

"It can be overwhelming." His look had changed to sympathetic. "You best get on home now." He patted the top of the car in emphasis. "There's a storm coming. You wouldn't want to get caught in it."

She nodded gratefully. "Thank you. I had no idea." Stupid statement, considering the clouds and the thunder. "I'm on my way."

She turned the key, and the engine sprang to life.

"Drive carefully." He patted the top of the car again. "And don't worry, it'll be easier the next time."

"There won't be a next time," she mumbled to herself, putting the car in gear. She was in over her head, and if Jake wasn't available to save the day, then she was ready to take the next in line.

And right now her father was at the top of the list.

After traipsing through the centuries exhibited in the museum, Jake was almost startled by the fluorescent lights and stainless steel of the lab. Tucked away in a sub-basement, the room looked more like something out of a Michael Crichton novel than an historical resources department.

A tall lanky man sat at a table in the corner, peering at something through a magnifier attached to a headband. With his dark tan and thatch of blond hair, he looked more like a surfer than a museum employee.

Jake took a step forward, and at the sound of his footsteps, the younger man looked up with a grin. "You must be Jake Mahoney. David said you'd be coming to get the diary. I'm Branson Meyers." The man unwound himself from the stool, towering over Jake once he stood up. "I've had a hell of a time with it. Between the mud and decayed plant matter, it's a wonder there's anything left at all." He reached for the book. "And when you add clay to the mix . . ."

"Clay?" Jake stared down at the book, intrigued despite himself.

"Yeah." Branson traced the edge of the book lovingly. "See how stiff these pages are? They add clay to do that. It's aesthetically pleasing, but when the stuff gets wet, it's worse than Krazy Glue. Fortunately for you, the pages are only stuck in places. Otherwise it would be a complete loss." He looked up and shrugged. "As it is, there are still a lot of passages that are ruined. I did the best I could."

Jake opened the book. The pages were much cleaner, and for the most part they were legible. But Meyers was right, there were entire paragraphs missing. "Did you read it?"

Branson grinned. "Hard not to."

"You didn't come across a name, did you?" Jake stared down at Caroline's writing, willing it to tell him something.

"Her sister Riley is mentioned a lot. But other than that it's mostly familiar names. She talks about her daddy a lot. And of course the baby. And then there's the baby's father. I'd say her husband was one lucky bastard."

Jake jerked his head up, his eyes meeting Meyers's. "They weren't married."

"Sure they were." Branson reached for the diary, carefully turning the pages to the end. "See, she says it right here." He pointed to a faded, mud-stained passage.

> . . . well, it's done. Your father and I are married . . . wonderful feeling to unite with words what was already joined in our hearts . . . together, the three of us. And now nothing can separate us . . . afraid to tell . . . but it's the only way we'll ever truly . . . peace.

It was hard to decipher, the words missing altogether in places, but the meaning was perfectly clear. Branson was right. Caroline had married the baby's father. And if she'd done it in Georgia, there'd be a record. Jake glanced down at his watch, excitement building. If he hurried, he ought to be able to make it to the DHS building before it closed.

"Have I helped?" Meyers's voice broke into Jake's train of thought. He'd forgotten all about the man.

"Absolutely. This is just what I needed."

"Do you want to take the book now? If you'll leave it with me, I can clean it up some more, stop it from degrading further."

Jake thought of Riley. Of her need to make peace with the past. "That would be wonderful. I know the family would appreciate it."

Meyers nodded, already sliding the journal into a Mylar envelope. "I'll just call you when it's ready then, shall I?"

Jake reached out to shake the man's hand. "Thank you. You can't imagine how much you've helped us."

"My pleasure." Meyers smiled. "It's always nice when I can bring the past back to life."

Jake walked toward the elevator, leaving Branson Meyers with his books, wondering what it was exactly they were bringing back to life, hoping it wasn't something with the power to destroy them all.

Leon replaced the phone in the cradle and reached for his whiskey. Thunder rumbled ominously in the distance. A storm was brewing. He could feel it in the air.

"Everything all right?" Carter poured a stout measure of scotch into his glass, his gaze still resting on the phone.

"Just fine." Leon smiled. "Nothing to worry about. We're in the homestretch and everything is looking great." He lifted his glass in salute.

Carter drained his glass and refilled it. "I honestly hope you're right, Leon. There's a lot riding on all this."

"Damn straight there is. But you're making a killing in the national polls, and we're leaving tomorrow for our last whistle-stop tour. You're riding high, Carter, and victory is just around the corner. I can smell it."

"Well, it's good that one of us can." Carter dropped into a chair, looking more like the trailing opponent than the winning one. "All I can think about is Riley. I've already lost one daughter, Leon. I don't want to lose Riley too."

Leon frowned. "Nothing is going to happen to Riley. She's fine. And she'll make a hell of a First Lady."

Carter smiled, the thought apparently cheering him up. "She will, won't she?" He lifted his glass again, but Leon snagged it.

"Can't a man have a drink in the privacy of his own home?" Carter frowned, reaching for the glass.

"A glass, yes, but not the whole bottle."

"I'm just fortifying myself. Nights like this remind me of Caroline."

Thunder boomed outside the window, followed by a flash of lightning. Carter jumped, and Leon sighed. The storm was getting closer. "It was a long time ago, Carter."

"I know, but after today, with Riley, I can't help but think of what life might have been like if Caroline . . ." He trailed off, his eyes reflecting his pain. "Maybe if I'd been a better parent."

Leon slammed Carter's glass down on the table, sloshing liquid every which way. "Jesus, Carter, stop it. Caroline's death was an accident. A twenty-year-old accident. You are on the brink of the greatest achievement of your life. This is not the time for reliving the past."

Carter met his gaze, his own defeated. "Maybe this is exactly the time."

"We're talking about Riley again."

"Leon, if it isn't Jake Mahoney, it will be someone. She can't stay my little girl forever. We've been lying to ourselves to believe that she could."

"Make no mistake, Carter, I want Riley to be happy. Hell, she's like one of my own. But I will not allow her to do that at the expense of the presidency. America is voting for you, Carter. But in some part of their being, they believe they're voting for you and Riley."

"What, a new and twisted Camelot?" Carter's voice was bitter, and he grabbed the glass from the table, filling it with scotch.

"If that's what it takes to win, sure." Leon narrowed

his gaze. "You knew the cost would be high when you signed on."

"But that's just the point, Leon. I knew, but Riley didn't."

"Of course she did, Carter." He tried to keep his voice soothing, but the approaching thunder threatened to drown him out. "We're all in this together. You, me, and Riley."

"And Maudeen." Carter switched subjects like lightning, but Leon was grateful for this one. Riley was essential to their success, and he couldn't have Carter taking his eye off of that ball.

"I take it things are better between the two of you?"

Carter shrugged. "Let's just say we had an energetic night last night."

"Well, I suggest you keep it that way."

"Until after the election. I know the drill, Leon." The lights flickered with the flash of lightning out the window. "Storm's coming."

"It'll be here soon." Leon wasn't certain if Carter was talking about the weather or something else. He could feel it too. The tension building in the air right along with the rain. And it was his job to keep it from exploding.

"I'm trying to play the game, Leon. Keep all the little duckies happy. Hell, I even told Maudeen I was in love with her."

"Are you?" Leon asked, wondering if maybe there wasn't some truth to the idea, despite Carter's earthier inclinations.

"Hell, no." The words exploded from Carter. Whether it was because of the alcohol or because he felt strongly was anyone's guess, but it was dangerous either way.

"It's best, Carter, if you keep that sentiment to yourself until after the election."

Carter blew out a long breath and stood up, squaring his shoulders. "All right. But you're a real spoilsport, you know that, don't you?"

Leon smiled, satisfied, ignoring Carter's jibe. "I left papers in the office for you to sign. Why don't you do it now, before you're too drunk to see the pages."

"Sounds like a plan." Carter emptied his glass again, setting it on the table. "You coming?"

"No. I think you can sign a letter without my holding your hand."

"You going home, then?"

He shook his head. "I'll wait until the storm has passed."

Carter studied him through bleary eyes, his expression almost wistful. "Some storms never pass, Leon. Did you know that?"

Jake drummed his fingers on the counter, waiting. The vital records department was officially closed, but the woman on duty had been willing to stay late. She'd gone to retrieve the certificate, and judging from the time she'd been gone, she'd either gotten distracted and forgotten about him or been swallowed by the archives.

The door opened, and a middle-age woman bustled through it, holding a thin certificate triumphantly. "Here it is. It was misfiled by three days, so it took a little longer to find than I'd anticipated. And then I had to make a copy. Sorry you had to wait."

She handed him the sheet of paper, waiting expectantly.

He scanned the document, noting the date and Caroline's name scrawled at the bottom. It was her signature.

He recognized it from the diary. He glanced up at the woman. "This is it. Thank you."

"Don't thank me. Thank the state of Georgia and their insistence on good record keeping. That'll be ten dollars, please."

He handed her the money, his eyes already back on the other signature at the bottom of the license. It was bold, almost brash, and it made the hairs on Jake's arms rise to attention.

Bryce Daniels.

Caroline O'Brien had married Bryce Daniels.

Martell stood across the street from his condo, watching two men in suits walk to the door. Cops. He could tell from the cut of their clothes and the condition of their shoes. Cops never bothered with nice shoes. Even detectives. And that's what he was looking at. Two bona fide members of Atlanta's finest.

Question was, what were they doing here? Looking for him, obviously. But what the hell for? He threw his cigarette on the ground, listening to the sound of distant thunder. Guess it really didn't matter. Either way his goose was cooked. Best thing he could do was disappear.

But if the boys in blue were on to him, they'd be watching. His bank account was a no go. Not that there was much left of the money he'd been paid. He glanced down at his newest acquisition. Armani. Hand tailored. Worth every penny. But that still left a dilemma.

If he'd been made, he needed a way out of town. Depending on the deed he'd been nailed for, maybe out of the country. And to do that, he needed cash. Bad. And the only person he could think to bail him out of this mess was the person who got him into it.

Except said person was nowhere to be found.

Not at the office, and not at home. He reached into his breast pocket for another cigarette, his hand brushing against the butt of his Glock. Sweet little piece. Always nice to carry a little insurance. He sighed, inhaling deeply, letting the nicotine burgeon his courage.

There was only one place left he could think to look for his meal ticket. Not exactly the kind of place one waltzed up to the door. But still, not impossible. Certainly not for someone like him.

He smiled, feeling better. All he needed to do was breach the fortress, make his demands known, and skedaddle out of town until the fury died down. Simple enough. And if no one was inclined to finance his little journey, well then, he'd just have to do a little persuading. He patted the gun again, satisfied with his plan of attack.

Lightning flashed, underscoring his resolve. After all, he'd more than done his part.

All he wanted now was his just reward.

Chapter 26

THE GODDAMN RAIN was ruining his suit. Martell mentally made a note to add that to his rapidly mounting list of expenses. He stood under the shelter of a magnolia tree, the large waxy leaves giving a little protection. But not enough.

The house was dark except for a light to the left of the first floor. His quarry's car was out front. So that meant he was in there somewhere. The question now was how to get to him without making any more trouble than necessary.

Cursing under his breath, Martell made a dash for a service porch that ran along the far side of the house. He stopped under the awning, searching for new lights, or voices—something that would signal he'd been heard.

There was nothing except the wind and the storm. This side of the house was completely dark. Which was exactly the way he wanted it. After touching the cool comfort of his gun, he reached for the doorknob.

Locked.

He smiled, pulling the small tool kit from his pocket. A man had best be prepared. After selecting a pick, he inserted it in the lock and with a twist of the wrist had the lock open. Next, he felt carefully along the door's edge for a sensor or wiring.

With breath held, he slowly turned the doorknob. No alarm. *Nothing*. Arrogant bastard.

With a sigh of relief, he pulled the door open just enough to allow him to slip inside.

He stood in the half-light, waiting for his eyes to adjust. He was in the kitchen. The room with the light on was in the opposite corner. He'd try there first. Hopefully he'd find his man there, get his money, and get the hell out of here as quickly as possible.

Drawing his gun, he made his way into a hallway that led to the main foyer. It was bigger than most people's apartments. The crystal chandelier glittered almost maliciously in the lightning, casting dancing shadows on the floor. Straight ahead another hallway beckoned, this one with a shaft of light breaking across the floor.

Bingo.

He inched forward, keeping his back to the wall, all his energy trained on willing Leon Bronowsky to be in the room. And to be there alone. He edged up to the door, listening for voices. He could hear a clock ticking and the sound of the rain on the windows, but no voices. Careful to stay out of the light, he tilted his head so he could see inside.

Bronowsky was standing by the window, his back to the door.

Martell smiled. Sometimes things worked out perfectly. Sliding the Glock back into its holster, he drew in a bolstering breath and stepped into the room. "Long time no see, Leon."

Bronowsky spun around, his eyes narrowing. "What the hell are you doing here?"

"I need a little more money." Martell shrugged, walking closer, his hand tensed, ready to grab his gun if necessary.

"I've more than paid you for your work, Osterman."

"Well, now that's what I thought too. But you see, we've hit a little snag." He watched as a variety of emotions paraded across Bronowsky's face. Anger, frustration, and finally fear.

"What do you mean?"

"Seems the police are looking for me."

"How the hell did that happen?" Fear and frustration evaporated in the wake of full-blown anger. "You did the girl, didn't you? Against my express orders."

Martell shrugged. "I couldn't let her talk."

"About what? She didn't know anything, did she?"

"I used her to get to Larsen, and considering the way things have been going down, I figured it was best to take her out."

"And that's what they nailed you for."

"No. Someone tipped them off about the clinic." Actually, according to a colleague, the ATF had made the bombs, and identified him that way. But no need in telling Bronowsky the mistake had been his. "But it doesn't matter what they've got on me, Leon. Murder, arson—either one means prison. And there's no way I'm doing time."

"Of course not." Leon shrugged, and poured a stout measure of whiskey. "Drink?"

"Sure." Martell reached for the glass, watching while Leon poured one for himself.

Leon sat in an armchair behind a small desk, gesturing to the chair across from him. "How much do you think you'll need?"

Martell took a seat, relief flooding through him. "A million."

Leon's eyebrows rose, but there was no other reaction. "Seems like a lot."

Martell shrugged. "I figure I need to get out of the country. And I'll need money to live on."

"So what happened to the money I already paid you?"

"Most of it's gone. The rest is no doubt under police surveillance."

Leon stared into his glass, watching the swirl of color. The storm still rattled behind him, mirroring his emotions. Osterman was a fuck-up. There were no two ways about it. And he had become a serious liability. "Well, there's no way I can get that kind of money to you tonight."

Osterman stirred uncomfortably. "Time is not something I have a lot of. And if I go down, you have to know that you'll go too."

"Easy, Martell." Leon raised a hand. "I didn't say I wouldn't help you. Just that I can't get the money tonight."

"So where does that leave me?" He was close to apoplexy, and tried to hide it behind attitude, but Leon could smell fear on a man. And Osterman reeked of it.

"On a plane out of here tonight."

"They'll be watching the airport."

"Not my private plane."

Osterman smiled, revealing crooked, dirty teeth. Even Armani couldn't make a pig into a prince. "Sounds good."

"I'll call my pilot." Leon picked up the phone and dialed time and temperature, the recorded voice adding a monotonous undertone to the conversation. "Phil, this is Leon Bronowsky."

"The time is 7:24."

"I'm going to need the jet tonight."

"The current temperature is fifty-six degrees Fahrenheit . . ." the voice intoned.

"Yes, a colleague of mine has to make a sudden business trip—to Switzerland." He looked to Osterman for confirmation. The man nodded.

". . . thirteen degrees Celsius."

"Great. His name is Martell Osterman. He's leaving now." He made a play of consulting his watch. "So, I'd say you should be able to leave in an hour."

"If you'd like to make a call, please hang up and try again."

Good advice. "Thanks, Phil." He hung up the phone, his left hand sliding open the desk drawer. "Well, that's it. You're all set. You remember where to go?" Martell nodded. "Fine, I'll wire the money to you in the morning. In the meantime, I'd say you'd better get out of here, before someone else sees you." His hand closed over the cold metal of Carter's gun. Bless the man and his NRA tendencies.

Martell stood up, the relief on his face obvious. "All right. I'm out of here."

"You could say that." Leon pulled back the hammer, the slight click inaudible against the fury of the storm. Lightning flashed as Martell turned to go.

One Mississippi, two Mississippi . . . thunder cracked, echoing through the house, masking the report of the gun. Osterman fell, his body collapsing without sound. Leon wiped the gun with his coattail and dropped it back into the desk.

He'd have to get Carter to help him. Something had to be done with the body. And they'd have to clean the rug. He sighed, heading for the stairs. Why did everything have to be so damn complicated?

"What the hell is this?" Maudeen threw the credit card bill down on the desk, trying to hang on to some modicum of dignity.

Carter looked up from the papers he was reading, a puzzled expression on his face. "I have no idea what you're talking about."

"There are eighteen charges to the St. James on here, Carter. Eighteen."

"What are you doing with my *private* mail?" His eyes flashed dangerously, the telltale flush of his cheeks telling her he'd been drinking.

A little voice in her head warned her to back off, but she brushed it aside, letting her anger push her on. "It was in the pouch Bill sent from Washington. He must have put it in there by mistake. I opened it before I realized what it was. Don't try to turn this on me. This is about you and your indiscretions."

"I'm not trying to turn anything anywhere. You're the one standing here with my mail, accusing me of duplicitous behavior."

"Duplicitous behavior? That's a laugh. I've turned my back on your escapades for years, Carter, but I'm not immune to them, and I don't intend to put up with them anymore."

"I hardly think you have a choice, Maudeen. In case you've forgotten it, *you're* nothing more than an indiscretion." His stood up, his eyes narrowing. "One I'm very much regretting at the moment."

"So what? You're going to throw me out?" Maudeen tried to maintain some level of decorum, but her world was spinning out of control, taking all sense of ladylike behavior along with it.

"Why not?" He shrugged. "Leon wanted me to wait until after the campaign, but since you've called the hand, maybe there's no time like the present."

"Just like that?"

"You've become a liability, Maudeen."

Her heart twisted, plummeting to her stomach. This couldn't be happening. Not now. Not like this. "You don't mean that. You can't mean that. I've put everything that I am into this relationship, Carter. I've worked with you. I've lived with you. Hell, I loved you. And what do I get for that?" Her voice rose to a shriek. "Shown to the goddamned door!"

"Now, Maudeen . . ." His voice was placating now, soothing, but she wasn't buying.

"Don't you dare patronize me, Carter O'Brien. I've been around here long enough to recognize that tone. You just dumped me. And now you expect me to smile sweetly, pack my bags, and walk out of your life?"

"I expect you to behave like a professional."

"Is that what you think I am? A pro? Well, fine then, I'll charge like one." Tears ran down her face, no doubt ruining her carefully applied makeup. Well, to hell with that. "How's two hundred dollars an hour sound?" She clenched her fists, trying for control, but missing by a mile. "Oh, and I'll expect back pay. *Eighteen years worth.*"

"That's not what I meant and you know it."

"Well, that's the implication, isn't it? 'Gee, Maudeen, the party's over. I have to go and be President now.' " She glared at him, her mind trying but failing to find a way out. "God, I wish I'd told Jake Mahoney everything I know."

"What has Jake Mahoney got to do with any of this?" His anger was back.

"Wouldn't you like to know." She smiled, but knew there was no humor reflected in the gesture.

"Maudeen, don't toy with me. What have you done?" Carter's stance was menacing, and she took an involuntary step back, courage deserting her. "Nothing. I was just angry. I said the first thing that came into my head."

Carter's eyes narrowed. "I don't believe you."

She squared her shoulders, facing him with as much bravado as she could muster. "Well, you'll just have to, won't you?"

He crossed the room in two strides, his fingers digging into her shoulders. "I know you better than you think, darlin'. You're hiding something." His grip tightened. "So tell me."

She searched his eyes, trying to find some hint of the man she loved. "It's nothing."

"Maudeen." He shook her. "Tell me." His eyes glittered with anger, and fear rocketed through her.

Fear laced with anger. "I don't deserve any of this, Carter."

He released her, his eyes softening. "No. You probably don't. But unfortunately, that doesn't count for much. I am who I am, Maudeen. And I can't give you what you want."

"Because of the *presidency*."

"It's what we've worked for all these years. In the end, it's the only thing that matters."

"Well, maybe you'd be better off without it." She met his gaze, pleading.

"So what did you do, Maudeen?" He was calmer now, almost relaxed.

She drew in a breath. He was single-minded, but he'd never hurt her, and at the end of the day, she trusted him. She'd just have to make him understand. "I know about Caroline."

Confusion washed across his face. "I'm not following."

"I was there, Carter. I saw what happened to her."

Lightning filled the room, the static electricity almost palpable. "And you told Mahoney?" Carter's voice was deceptively soft.

Maudeen licked her lips nervously, trying to gauge his reaction. "I didn't tell him anything. I just sort of hinted."

"Hinted?"

"Yes. I sent him a copy of her autopsy report."

"I don't understand."

She closed her eyes, searching for strength, then opened them, meeting his gaze squarely. "The real report, Carter, not the doctored one."

"That's impossible. All the copies were changed."

"No they weren't. A copy of the original report was mailed to your office. I found it, and kept it."

"Why would you do that?" He spoke so quietly now, she almost couldn't hear him, the lack of an explosion frightening her much more than if he'd been screaming.

"Insurance. I thought someday I might need it. Looks like I was right."

"So you gave it to Mahoney because you were angry at me?"

"No. I gave it to him because I thought if he found out the truth, you'd turn to me."

"What in hell would make you think that?" His voice reverberated against the storm.

She sighed and sat down, nervously lacing her fingers together. "I saw Leon push Caroline from the balcony, Carter. And I thought—I hoped—that once that little fact came to light, Leon would be out of our lives forever."

"And I'd lose the election."

She shrugged. "I guess part of me hoped that would be the case."

"Then what?" His face was impossible to read, his voice back under tight control. "We'd ride off into the sunset and live happily ever after?"

"Something like that." Right here, right now, it seemed like a stupid idea. "I really believed if I could get Leon out of our lives, things would be better for us."

"Jesus, Maudeen, do you have any idea at all what you've done?"

She stood up, tired of him towering over her. "I did what I thought was best. I held onto this secret for twenty years, Carter. And I did it for you. *For you.* Can you understand that? I wanted you to succeed."

"As long as you were by my side."

"Is that so much to ask? I've given you everything, Carter. My life, my love, everything. All I ever wanted in return was for you to love me. I wanted the full deal, Carter. I wanted you all of the time, day in, day out. No subterfuge, and no Leon breathing down our back."

"Leon wants what's best for me."

"Leon wants what's best for Leon, Carter. He killed your daughter, for God's sake. How in hell was that good for you?"

"It was an accident, Maudeen. The railing broke. I don't know what you think you saw, but it *was* an accident."

"My ass. Leon pushed her, Carter. I know what I saw."

"You don't know anything, Maudeen." Her heart leaped to her throat, making breathing impossible. Leon strode into the room, his gaze fixed on her, his eyes glittering with malice. "Except how to cause trouble. But believe me, it'll take a hell of a lot more than you to bring us down."

Lightning and thunder crashed simultaneously, the entire house reverberating from the impact, and everything went black.

Chapter 27

Lᴵɢʜᴛɴɪɴɢ ꜱᴛʀᴇᴀᴋᴇᴅ ᴛʜʀᴏᴜɢʜ the sky, illuminating the wildly gyrating trees. Rain lashed almost vertically, and Riley ran for the front door, holding her jacket over her head, managing to get soaked anyway.

Leon's car was out front, but she hadn't seen her father's. Odds were he'd parked out back. She fumbled with the door handle, feeling the whole house tremble in the wake of a violent clap of thunder. The storm was in full fury.

Stepping into the foyer, she hung up her jacket and shook the rain out of her hair, grateful to be somewhere warm and dry. And dark.

She frowned, wondering why the lights were off. Then shook her head, remembering that it was Adelaide's day off. No doubt her father and Leon were cloistered somewhere and hadn't realized how dark it had gotten. She reached for the light switch. Nothing.

Obviously, the storm had knocked out the electricity. She reached into the pocket of her jacket to retrieve the photograph, a flash of lightning briefly illuminating her sister's face. She looked so young, her whole life in front of her. And yet she'd had so little time left to live.

Sighing, Riley turned her thoughts to her father. She'd rehearsed what she wanted to say all the way home, but standing here in the foyer of Rivercrest, she suddenly lost her nerve. Her father wasn't going to understand Caroline's relationship with Bryce, and he wouldn't understand why Caroline hadn't told him.

And even worse, he wasn't going to understand why she'd trusted Jake Mahoney with the information and not him.

Riley frowned, wishing things were different. Wishing her father were different. She knew without a doubt that he would never approve of her relationship with Jake. And if he thought Jake was off limits, she could only imagine what he would have had to say about Bryce Daniels.

But it didn't matter. No matter how angry he was, he had the right to know. Besides, someone out there was killing people. Whatever this was all about, it was deadly. And maybe her father could help them figure out who was behind everything. And more important, why all of this had been necessary. The framing, the cover-up, the murders.

Somewhere in the tangle of facts and suppositions, there had to be answers, or at least the key to find them. And it was worth risking her father's wrath to find that. Wasn't it?

She shivered as a brilliant flash of lightning cut through the entry hall, and she wished suddenly that she'd been able to reach Jake. It would be easier if he were here. Thunder followed the flash, the rumble oddly comforting, predictable. She shook her head, firming her resolve. This was something she needed to do on her own.

She started up the stairs, lightning flickering again, thunder shaking the house. Mother Nature augmenting her sentiments. If she were honest, she'd admit that telling her father about Caroline wasn't really the worst of her fears—although she certainly didn't relish the idea. No. What really scared her was the prospect of telling him about Jake.

She reached the landing, almost convincing herself to abandon the entire plan. But thoughts of Bryce Daniels and Amber Northcott spurred her on. She turned into the corridor leading to her father's study, the only illumination intense bursts of lightning coming through the hallway windows.

White light.

She froze, terror blossoming from somewhere deep inside, everything suddenly frighteningly familiar. The hallway, the light—everything. White on black.

The stuff of her nightmares.

Panic threatened to engulf her, and she fought for breath, forcing herself to take a step forward. There was something in facing her fears. Right? And besides this wasn't a nightmare, it was a storm. And the lights were out. Nothing terrorizing in that.

Lightning slashed down the hallway, cutting through the darkness, and Riley steeled herself, heart pounding. What she wouldn't give for Mr. McKafferty. She blew out a breath. There was nothing to be afraid of.

Nothing.

She repeated the thought over and over, letting the rhythm of her litany carry her forward. One step, two . . . a clap of thunder rattled the windows, the rain audible as it lashed against the glass.

Just like last time.

She frowned, wondering where the thought had come from. There'd been no last time. Except in her head. She walked forward again, faster now. The windows at the end of the hall glowed eerily in the flicker of lightning, French doors rattling ominously in the wind.

She cringed, lifting her hands, ducking her head,

waiting for the glass to explode. Eyes closed, she still heard the wind, saw the doors burst open, windows shattering, glass flying everywhere. And in that moment, the lightning split the night, illuminating someone standing on the balcony.

Caroline.

She was seeing Caroline.

Heart still pounding, she realized her eyes were still closed, and slowly she opened them. Wind whistled outside the house, an undernote to the battering rain. But the doors at the end of the corridor were closed, the glass intact, the balcony beyond—empty.

With a hand pressed to her chest, Riley tried to pull air into her lungs, to manually stem the tide of her racing heart.

She'd been there—the night Caroline died—she'd been there.

Her nightmare was based on memory.

She frowned, eyes still locked on the closed doors. There was more. She could feel it. There was something else to remember. Something that her mind had shoved deep into her subconscious.

She fought against her fear, against the knowledge that she might have seen her sister die. Maybe it hadn't been a memory at all. Maybe it had just been a trick of her imagination, the storm resembling her nightmare. She stared into the dark, willing herself to remember something, anything. But there was nothing. Nothing except the sound of rain and the flicker of lightning.

She took another step forward, jumping when light suddenly flooded out of the open door to her father's study, cutting a swath across the hallway. She blinked, her eyes struggling to adjust to the brightness.

Something tugged at her memory but was gone

before she could identify it. She closed her eyes, concentrating, trying to remember. She saw the doors fly open, and saw Caroline, and then . . .

She shook her head. There was nothing there. Whatever she'd seen was lost in time. She rubbed her temples, and stepped into the little alcove outside the study. She needed a moment to bolster her courage, praying that her father would understand everything she'd done. Why she hadn't told him about Caroline. Why she'd stayed with Jake when he'd forbidden it. Why she'd lied to him.

She'd betrayed her father just as surely as if she'd plotted against him. They were a team—a family. And he'd deserved better from her. But she was going to set it right. Tell him everything. She loved Jake in the same way Caroline had loved Bryce. And if her father loved her as much as he claimed he did, then surely he'd understand.

The wind rattled the French doors, the past threatening to break into the house and overwhelm them all. She needed her father. And he needed her. Together they could face whatever happened. She started to step out of the alcove, but froze, as angry voices echoed across the hall. The words clear.

Leon and her father. And Maudeen. She'd forgotten how well you could hear from the alcove. Some anomaly in construction. As a kid, she and Caroline used to hide here and listen to her mother and father.

She chewed on her bottom lip, trying to decide what to do. She should go. Come back when her father was alone. But Leon's voice stopped her cold.

They were talking about Jake.

"I asked you how much Mahoney knows!" Leon's voice was harsh, angry.

"I don't know." Maudeen glared at Leon, grateful for the electricity. With only lightning for illumination, he had looked positively demonic. "Not much, or we'd have seen it splashed all over the paper."

"He could be biding his time. We shouldn't make the mistake of underestimating the man." Carter seemed unaware of the tension flying between her and Leon. Or maybe he was just ignoring it. Either way, Maudeen felt deserted, and very much alone.

"I told you that a long time ago. But it seems, at the moment, Mahoney isn't our biggest threat." Leon met Maudeen's eyes, the animosity reflected there making her shiver.

"Maudeen won't say anything." Carter smiled at her, his voice patronizing. He was so certain of her. If she hadn't been so frightened, it would have been a pleasure to wipe the self-satisfied smirk right off his face.

"I think she's already said too much. Thanks to her, the entire campaign is in jeopardy."

Anger flooded through her, making her careless. "I hardly think I'm the one that put this campaign in jeopardy, Leon. I'd say that honor resides solidly with you. *I* didn't kill anyone."

"And neither did I, my dear." He smiled, his eyes still bitterly cold, the combined effect frightening. "I'm afraid it's your word against mine."

She looked to Carter for support, but he was watching Leon, his expression guarded. So much for help from the gallery. She turned her attention back to her nemesis. "I know what I saw, Leon."

"Come now, Maudeen, the game's been won. And by a better man than you. Why don't you call it a day. In the long run, I promise you'll live longer."

Her knees threatened to buckle and she fought for control. "Is that a threat?"

Leon smiled again. "More a friendly word of advice."

"It's out of my control, Leon."

"Well, I suggest you get it back in control. As you are well aware, I'm quite capable of causing little accidents. And it would be a shame for something to happen to you, now wouldn't it?"

"You'd best listen to him, Maudeen," Carter said. "There's more at stake than you understand."

"Oh, I think I understand just fine. You've made a pact with the devil. Anything for the presidency. Your daughter. Your wife. Even me." She met Carter's eyes, pleading with him to say something to refute what she was implying. But he only shrugged, his eyes sad, his loyalty obviously with Leon.

And in that moment, Maudeen felt her heart shrivel up and die.

With nothing left to lose, she lifted her head, eyes locking with Leon's. "I might have an accident, but that won't be the end of your problems, Leon. You see, I'm not the only one who saw you."

Riley stuffed her fist in her mouth, biting down so hard she could taste her blood. It was the only way she could stop herself from screaming. Leon had killed her sister. *And her father knew.*

Her stomach clenched, threatening to heave up its contents. The rain increased in its fury, echoing the storm inside her. The wind shook the French doors again, and Riley's eyes locked on the balcony, her mind blanching at the vision before her.

Caroline . . . *and Leon.*

She could see him now, on the balcony with her sister. One minute Caroline was highlighted against the railing, and then she was gone. Leon shoving her. Riley had clutched Mr. McKafferty, fighting not to scream. Her mind refusing to believe what she'd seen.

It was a dream. It had to be a dream. But the lightning flashed and she saw him standing there, looking toward the ground. And her sister was gone. *Gone.*

She'd tried to run then, but her legs wouldn't move. She'd tried to call out, to summon her father, but her mouth wouldn't work. Then Maudeen had been there. Soothing her, telling her it was only a nightmare, and that tomorrow everything would seem better. Maudeen had tucked her back in bed and held her, letting her cry, staying with her until at last she could close her eyes and drift to sleep.

And then, somewhere in the night, her mind had erased it all—setting up barriers to protect her, to save her from her pain. And it had worked. For twenty years, except for her nightmares, it had worked.

But now she remembered. And she thought the knowledge might kill her.

Rain slapped against the windshield, the wipers doing little to alleviate the onslaught of water. Jake peered out into the darkness, trying to keep his mind on the road. He needed to get to Riley. To tell her what he'd found. Bryce Daniels was the key.

It had all been about Caroline. About her pregnancy.

Caroline's little secret had had the potential to ruin Carter O'Brien. A love child with a black man wasn't something that would have set well with Atlanta society. Not twenty years ago. And with Carter at the beginning of his climb to political power, the fallout would have been deadly.

Hell, it *had* been deadly.

Caroline's accident had set in motion a chain of events that left a twenty year trail of cover-ups and dead bodies. Bryce, Jensen, Michaels, Amber.

The only question left to be answered was who had been behind it all. Carter seemed an obvious choice, but Riley believed her father was blameless. And Jake couldn't see him orchestrating something this size. Which left one other leading candidate.

Leon Bronowsky.

He had the power, and he had the nerve. But Jake knew he needed proof. Something that would tie Bronowsky to Michaels. Or to Martell Osterman.

Lightning streaked down from the sky, stabbing into the dark, combining with a series of shrill rings, making him jump. He laughed at his reaction. Obviously a little too much excitement of late. The ringing started again, and this time he reached for his cell phone, careful to keep his eyes on the road. "Mahoney."

"Jake, it's David."

Jake opened his mouth with a flip response, but something in David's voice stopped him cold. "What is it?"

"They found a partial print at the D.A.'s office."

"From the other night?" He adjusted the phone to hold it between his ear and his shoulder.

"Looks like it."

"So? Who does it belong to?"

"Martell Osterman."

"Well, I suppose that shouldn't surprise me. Have you found him?"

"No." Jake heard David blow out a breath. "And if Osterman knows he's been made—"

"Then he's bound to be desperate." Jake finished for him, his foot pressing harder on the gas pedal.

"Look, if we're right and everything that's been happening is tied into Caroline O'Brien, then whoever is paying Osterman is someone close to the family."

"I've been thinking the same thing. And my money's on Leon Bronowsky."

"I don't know. I certainly wouldn't put it past him. But the person with the most to lose here is Carter O'Brien."

"I don't know, David. Carter O'Brien isn't the nicest of men, but I can't believe he would do anything to hurt his daughter."

"Maybe not. But I'd bet my life he's involved in this somehow. And if he is, then Osterman might come after him."

Jake trusted David's instincts with his life, and at the moment, that fact scared the hell out of him. "I'm on my way to Riley's now."

"Good. I'm going to request a squad car, just in case. I've been doing this a long time, Jake, and I'm getting a bad feeling."

Jake could taste his fear. If anything happened to Riley . . ." Hopefully, we're wrong, but better safe than sorry."

"Watch your back, buddy."

"I will."

He clicked off the phone, his heart racing in time with the engine. Another bolt of lightning shot out of the sky, splitting the night, and Jake floored the gas pedal, praying that he wouldn't be too late.

Chapter 28

RILEY BENT OVER, trying to hold on to the last tenuous bit of her control. Part of her wanted to run away, part of her wanted to stay and face her father, and still another part wanted to sink into the floor and disappear.

She forced herself to think of Caroline. Of her sister's baby. Of what their last minutes must have been like. She owed it to her sister to find out what had happened. To face her father. No matter how much it hurt. It wasn't just about her family anymore.

There were other people involved. Jake and Bryce. Even Michaels, to an extent. And Haywood Jameson. Bryce had been his friend, after all. Everything in her present was still tied up in something that had happened twenty years ago. It was time to face it and move on.

If she could.

Squaring her shoulders, she stepped out of the alcove into the doorway, the rain still beating down on the roof, the wind rattling the windows.

"Riley." Her father's voice was startled, his expression wary. Maudeen's eyes widened in concern, one hand raised to her mouth. Leon took a step toward her, his expression inscrutable.

"Don't come near me." Riley ground out the words, holding onto the door frame for support.

"How much did you hear?" Leon's look softened, his eyes searching hers.

"Enough. What I didn't hear, I remembered." She shot a glance at Maudeen. "It was you, wasn't it? You put the book there, and Mr. McKafferty."

Maudeen nodded. "I wanted you to remember."

"What are you talking about?" Her father sounded confused, his eyes begging her for understanding.

She swallowed convulsively, forcing herself to meet his gaze, tears pricking her eyes. "I was there, Daddy. In the hallway. I saw Leon push Caroline off of the balcony."

Confusion was replaced by understanding. "Your dream."

She nodded, fighting the urge to run to him.

He took a step toward her, his arms out, and she lifted her hand to ward him off. It would be so easy to go to him. To let him tell her everything was going to be all right. But everything wasn't all right, and he'd known it. She couldn't trust him. Couldn't bear to listen to more of his lies. "You knew about this."

Carter nodded, suddenly unable to meet her eyes.

"He killed my sister and you never said anything to anyone." The tears began to flow in earnest now. "How could you do that, Daddy?" Needles of hot pain spiked through her, stabbing into her, her legs threatening to give way. She clutched the door frame more tightly, determined to face them—to face the reality of who they were.

"Riley, this isn't about your father. It's about me." Leon edged another step closer.

She twisted so she could see him. "It's always about you, isn't it, Leon?"

"You don't know what you're saying, Riley." Her

father's voice was soft, but there was a whisper of authority there.

She swung back around. "How can you continue protecting this man? He's a parasite, Daddy. Living off of people more successful than he. Manipulating things so the game comes out the way he wants it to. No matter who gets hurt."

"You don't understand, anything, Riley." Leon's face was awash with emotion, regret colored by anger. "You've followed your father around for years, enjoying the lifestyle, the perks, the power. If anyone is a parasite, it's you."

Her stomach contracted in horror, the truth in his words cutting deep. "I was a little girl, Leon."

"Well, you're not a little girl now."

"You bastard." Maudeen's voice was low and almost inaudible.

"Maybe." Leon shrugged. "But at least I was honest with myself. I accepted the cost of this presidency, and I paid the price."

"No." Riley's gaze collided with Leon's, anger deadening her pain. "Caroline and her baby paid the price. Bryce Daniels paid the price. Even Douglas Michaels paid the price."

"Douglas Michaels was a fool." Leon spat the words out, his distaste evident.

"You make me sick. All of you." The last was said on a strangled whisper.

Lightning flashed and something moved behind her. She started to turn, but before she could complete the movement, something hard pressed against her head, an arm clamping around her chest.

"Nobody move, or I'll blow her fucking head off." The voice was rough, a low whisper. Her heart hammered in her throat, and she closed her eyes, trying to maintain some semblance of control, fear threatening to overwhelm her.

His hand was sticky, the smell sweet and sickly, almost metallic, and she felt her stomach roil. She swallowed hard, trying not to breathe deeply, her mind scrambling for an explanation. She hadn't heard him approaching until it was too late, her thoughts lost in the nightmare playing out before her.

"Move." The man shoved her forward into the study, one arm still around her neck, the gun still jammed to her head.

The others in the room stood in wide-eyed silence. Maudeen looked frightened, her father terrified, and Leon surprised.

"Osterman." The word was mumbled, Leon's eyebrows drawing together in a confused frown.

"Wasn't very nice of you to shoot me, Leon."

Riley choked on bile as she finally recognized the smell. Blood. The sticky substance was blood.

"Let my daughter go." Her father took a step forward, his face twisted with rage.

"I wouldn't do that, Mr. Senator." Osterman shook his head. "Not unless you want your little girl here spattered all over this expensive wallpaper." He tightened his grip, the gun digging into the soft skin of her temple.

"If you're here for money, name your price. I can afford to pay." Her father was frantic now.

"You have no idea who I am, do you?" She could hear the anger in the man's voice. Anger laced with panic. "Shall I tell him, Leon?"

Leon continued to stare at the man with horrified fascination, saying nothing.

"Cat got your tongue? Well then, I'll just have to enlighten him for you." He pushed her farther into the room, shifting his grip, a soft groan evidence that he was hurt. "I've been covering your ass, Mr. Senator. Odds and ends over the last couple of months. Tailing to arson. I'm a full-service kind of guy."

"You killed Hank Larsen?" Riley squeaked, tipping her head back to try and see her attacker.

"In a manner of speaking." He tightened his arm, forcing her head back down.

"You were paid well for your services, Martell." Leon had found his voice, and it was filled with contempt.

"Up until now. It seems this time," he directed his attention to her father, "your colleague here decided that the best way to repay me for all I've done was to plug me in the back and leave me for dead."

"He was blackmailing us." Leon shrugged, as if killing someone was the answer to everything.

"I just wanted money to get out of the country."

Riley's jumbled thoughts finally fell together in some semblance of order. She shot an accusing look at Leon. "You paid him to blow up Jake's car." The words were out before she'd thought about them.

"It seemed the expedient thing to do."

"But I almost died."

Osterman tightened his grip but made no effort to quiet her.

"You were behind the car bombing?" Her father's anger mixed with disbelief now.

Leon shrugged. "I had no idea Mahoney and Maudeen shared a penchant for Saabs." His gaze shifted to Osterman. "If you'd done your job, Riley would never have been at risk."

"That's right, Leon." He pulled the gun away from her temple and waved it at Leon. "It's always a good idea to antagonize the man with the gun."

Leon ignored Osterman, his eyes still locked on Riley, begging her to understand. "At least you weren't hurt."

She stared at him, feeling like she'd crossed to the other side of Alice's mirror. Reality had been distorted, and nothing was as it seemed. "No, the man you tried to kill saved me."

"Mahoney." This from her father. "If he'd minded his own business, none of this would have happened."

Riley stared at her father in disbelief. Leon had almost had her killed, and her father was blaming Jake.

"Enough. I want my money." Osterman's grip tightened.

Leon's eyes narrowed, his look now speculative. "I think something can be arranged. But I'll need time."

"Why don't we just try the routine with the plane again. Only this time I suggest you place the call. Because if you don't . . ." Riley felt him shrug, and heard the hammer click into place.

Her father held up both hands in placation. "Please, don't do anything foolish. I can have things arranged in just a few minutes. I just need to get to the phone." Osterman nodded, letting the hammer drop back into place, and her father walked closer, exchanging a look with Leon.

Thunder slammed into the house, and they could feel the reverberations. The lights flickered, and Martell's hold on Riley loosened. With a quick intake of breath, she drove her elbow back, slamming it into his chest, praying that it hurt him as much as it hurt her.

Surprised, Osterman groaned and dropped his arm. Riley dove out of the way as Leon rushed Martell, the two men grappling for control of the gun. She saw Maudeen drop behind the desk, and was just wondering where her father was when she felt a solid weight hit her in the back, his body covering hers.

"It's going to be okay, darlin'," he whispered, and despite the absurdity of the statement, she felt comforted. But the feeling didn't last. Almost before she could take another breath, two shots rang out, resonating above the fury of the storm.

Jake dialed her number with shaking hands, trying to see through the downpour, fervently praying that she'd answer. It rang twice and then was answered by an automated voice talking about circuits.

Damn it to hell.

He threw the cell phone down on the car seat and pressed harder on the gas pedal, knowing that the rented Honda couldn't possibly go any faster. He was driving along the perimeter of Rivercrest, but there was no access for another hundred yards or so.

The road was slick with rain, and he felt the car losing traction. He knew he was driving too fast, but his gut told him something was dreadfully wrong and that he needed to get to Riley.

Pumping the brakes, he tried to avoid an out and out spin, but the Honda evidently had other plans. Skidding across the road, Jake fought for control, finally wrestling the car to a stop as it plowed into the undergrowth and slammed into a tree.

After the squealing tires and the noise of the engine, the rain drumming on the roof sounded symphonic, the windshield wipers providing timpani. He mentally checked himself, and except for a small cut on his head, all systems were go. Grabbing the phone, he tried to open his door, with no success.

On the edge of panic, Jake slid across the seat and was relieved when the passenger door opened with only a little coaxing. Dialing David's number, he began to run.

• • •

Riley waited for what seemed an eternity before she dared to move. "Daddy?" She hardly recognized the voice as her own.

"I'm here, darlin'." His voice was low, whispered, and something about it sent a chill racing through her.

"Is everything okay?" She waited, heart pounding, a sick feeling forming in the pit of her stomach.

"Leon seems to have shot Osterman." With a groan, he rolled off her, and Riley sat up, blinking at the sudden onslaught of light. Martell lay sprawled on his back, blood spattered on the floor around him.

"Is he?" Riley asked.

Leon nodded grimly. "This time for good."

Maudeen poked her head up from behind the desk, her face ghostly white, her eyes locked on Martell's body. "Is it over?"

"I think so. But we may still have a little problem." Carter's voice, if possible, was even softer.

"Oh God, Daddy, you've been shot." Riley knelt beside him, fear rocketing through her.

Maudeen lifted her hands to her mouth, stifling a scream, and Leon rushed across the room, kneeling on the floor across from Riley. With gentle hands he pulled back her father's bloody shirt, revealing a pulsing wound in his side, blood spouting like a small fountain.

Riley ripped off her sweater and pressed it to his skin in an attempt to stanch the blood, the white cotton immediately turning an ugly, crimson red.

"Maudeen," Leon bit out, his eyes still locked on Carter, "call an ambulance."

Maudeen picked up the phone, her fingers fumbling with the buttons. "There's no dial tone." She threw the headset down, tears welling in her eyes. "The damn thing is dead."

"I've got a cell phone." He reached for his coat pocket, then mumbled a curse. "It's in my jacket, Maudeen. In the library."

Maudeen stood for a moment, her gaze resting on Carter, indecision holding her cold.

"Go," Leon barked, his words startling her into action. Jumping over Martell's body, she raced from the room.

Riley's eyes met Leon's, anger flooding through her, replacing her fear. "This is all your fault."

Leon blanched, his face suddenly looking old and tired. "I told you, I did what I did to protect your father."

"To protect his bid for the presidency, don't you mean?" Riley pressed harder on her father's wound, not caring anymore what she said. "You selfish son of a bitch. You found out my sister was pregnant, that she was in love with a black man, and so you handled the problem by killing her."

"No."

Riley looked down at her father, arrested by the pain in his voice. Not just physical pain, but heartfelt soul-deep anguish.

"Hush, Carter." This from Leon in a voice so gentle he might have been talking to a baby.

"No," her father said again. "She has a right to know the truth." His voice was so soft, she had to lean down to hear him.

"Let it go, Carter," Leon pleaded.

But her father shook his head, his eyes meeting hers. "Riley, darlin', there's something you need to know. It wasn't Leon who killed your sister. It was me."

Uncertainty warred with shock, followed by a numbing sense of disbelief. "But I saw him, Daddy. I saw him on the balcony."

"That you did, princess. But Caroline was already dead."

"I don't understand . . ." Tears filled her eyes, slipping unchecked down her cheeks.

"Caroline told me about the baby, Riley. That night. Here." He paused, sucking in a shallow breath.

"But I don't see. . . ." Her heart constricted, threatening to blow into little pieces.

He held out a hand, and she closed hers around it. She wanted to wake up and find this all a dream, but the warmth of her father's hand was as real as the look of agony in his eyes. "She wanted to leave here, Riley. To make a new life with *him*." He spit the word out as if it were poison. "I couldn't let that happen. Can you imagine the effect that would have had on my career? My daughter and the gardener?"

His look was tortured, his mind slipping away, lost in the horror of his past. "I told her that," he went on. "Begged her to get rid of the baby, to get rid of Daniels. But she refused. Said she'd married the bastard. The implications were staggering. I lost my temper. She did too. We argued."

He struggled to draw in another breath, a funny wheezing sound accompanying the effort. "I was so angry, I hit her. And she fell against the desk, knocking her head on the corner. One minute she was standing there angry and alive, and then next—" He closed his eyes, remembering, his pain almost a physical thing. "—the next, she fell to the floor, her mouth open in surprise, one hand still reaching for me. She was dead. I killed her." He opened his eyes, his gaze colliding with hers. "I killed my little girl."

She stared into her father's eyes, willing him to say it was a lie, to say that this was some sort of nightmare.

But she knew it wasn't. Knew it from the silence in the room, knew it from the anguish on her father's face.

He squeezed her hand, his eyes pleading now. "I didn't mean it. I swear on everything holy, I didn't mean it. And if I could take it back, I would. But I can't, Riley. I can't."

She pulled away, trying to absorb all that he'd told her. To put it in context with the man she knew. The man she loved. Her father. Oh God, *her father*. He'd killed Caroline. She fought against her sobs, pressing a fist against her stomach, trying to contain her spiraling emotions. "If it was an accident, Daddy, why did you cover it up?"

Her father sighed, the sound lost against his struggle to breathe. "I am not a brave man. I knew that Caroline's death, her pregnancy, all of it would have meant the ruin of me. I couldn't bring her back, Riley. And I couldn't bring myself to commit political suicide. So I called Leon." His eyes darted to his friend, then back to Riley. "He came and suggested a way out. So I let him push her off the balcony, making it look like an accident."

Riley felt her heart shattering.

Maudeen rushed back into the room. "Hang on, Carter. They're coming."

Her father coughed, his whole body shaking. "Maudeen, that you?"

She leaned over him, her hand caressing his face. "I'm right here."

"I lied to you, darlin'. And I lied to myself. I've loved you for a long time. But I was afraid." He covered her hand with his, his eyes full of regret. "And now it's too late."

"Don't say things like that, Carter." Maudeen forced

a smile. "You're going to be just fine. You just hang on. The paramedics are on the way."

"Don't kid a kidder, darlin'." He smiled at Maudeen, then turned his head to Riley, lifting a hand to touch her cheek. "This is it, princess."

"No, Daddy." She shook her head, reaching for his hand, her fingers clasping his, willing him her strength. "Not now. Not like this."

"Riley . . ." He drew in a shallow breath, his fingers tightening around hers. "You have to know that despite everything, I loved your sister. I never wanted to harm her. Things just got out of control." His eyes pleaded with her for forgiveness.

She wanted so badly to fix things. To make them right again. But she couldn't . . . she couldn't. "We'll get through this, Daddy. Somehow we'll find a way."

He nodded, but she could see that he didn't believe her, see that he was already letting go.

She drew in a shaking breath, tears clogging her nose and throat. "I love you, Daddy."

He smiled again, this time so gently it tore at her heart. "I love you too, princess." His hand fell lax and his head dropped to the side, his eyes still open, a single tear tracing its way down his cheek.

"Daddy." She screamed, fumbling for his pulse, pounding on his chest, trying to force him to breathe, to make him live. *"Daddy."*

"He's dead, Riley. He's dead. Let him go." Leon's voice was deceptively calm. She tipped back her head to look at him, her father's head still cradled in her lap.

"Tell me why you let this happen, Leon."

"It was all about protection, Riley. I protected him then, and that's what you're going to do now." He glanced at Maudeen, who was still kneeling beside

Carter, tears streaming down her face. "That's what we're all going to do. This is how it's going to play out." Leon stood up and then leaned down to pick up Martell's gun. "Osterman, here, broke into the house. And your father tried to stop him, getting shot in the process."

"You want us to lie?" Maudeen stared at him, incredulity coloring her expression.

"I want you to protect Carter."

"Protect you, is more like it," Riley said. "My father wouldn't want this. He'd want us to tell the truth. To finally put an end to the lies."

"Haven't you learned anything about your father in the last few minutes?" Leon stroked the barrel of the gun slowly, his eyes seeming to lose focus. "All he ever cared about was winning the game. And he didn't give a damn who got hurt in the process."

"You're confusing my father with you, Leon. Daddy may have been a weak man, and he may have acted out of anger and emotion, but he wasn't capable of cold-blooded murder."

Slowly the barrel came up, pointing at her. "I can't let you drag me into this, Riley. I'm sorry."

The door slammed open as Jake burst into the room, his breathing ragged, his eyes narrowed in anger. "Leave her alone."

Leon swiveled to face him, leveling the gun, and Riley watched, horrified, as he cocked the hammer. "Well, isn't this just perfect. It will play beautifully in the papers. The candidate, his daughter, and her lover all dying in each other's arms."

Rage seared through Riley. So many people had been hurt. But not Jake. *Never Jake.* *"No,"* she screamed, springing at Leon, just as the world seemed to blow apart.

"Riley." The gun's explosion swallowed the sound of Jake's voice, then the room grew strangely silent. Maudeen was standing beside Carter O'Brien, his lifeless eyes visible even across the room. A man Jake didn't recognize lay on the floor in a pool of blood.

It looked like the aftermath of a battle scene. Only the battle hadn't ended. In the center of the room, Riley and Leon still struggled, their hands locked together on the gun, cold steel shining deadly in the fluorescent light.

Jake's breathing stopped, his chest caving inward under the pressure of his fear. "Riley." He said her name again, this time on a whisper. He had never felt so helpless.

Riley and Leon moved in tandem, almost as if someone had choreographed their deadly dance. Jake watched in horror as the gun exploded again. Riley dropped to the floor, the gun clattering from her hand.

Leon dove for it, but Maudeen was faster, grabbing it and leveling it on the older man. "It's over, Leon."

Carter's right-hand man froze, his eyes devoid of emotion, his face crumpled—old. But Jake didn't care. What mattered now was Riley. In two steps he reached her, his hands searching wildly for a pulse.

Silver eyes opened. "Jake." There was a world of hope in the sound of his name, and Jake felt tears against his cheeks.

"Did he hurt you?"

"Not physically." She pushed back her hair with a bloody hand. "I thought he was going to kill you."

"But he didn't. I'm fine."

She touched his face, tracing the lines of his jaw, as if reassuring herself that he was indeed unharmed. "It was all about Daddy." Her gaze shifted to her father's body, pain bubbling to the surface, her anguish laid bare. "Michaels, Larsen . . . all of it. He killed Caroline. Oh God, Jake, he killed my sister." She clung to him, her eyes begging for answers, her body shaking as the sobs ripped through her.

"It's going to be okay, sweetheart. Somehow, we'll make this okay." He rocked her back and forth, pulling her close, willing himself to absorb her pain, wanting only to make it go away. He turned to Leon, hatred threatening to consume him. "Do you have any idea what you've done? How many people you've hurt?"

Leon stared at Riley, his eyes haunted, his face twisted in agony. "I didn't mean for it to end like this."

"You didn't mean for it to end at all." Maudeen waved the gun menacingly. "If you'd had your way, the secret would have stayed buried."

"What the hell is going on in here?" David walked into the room, gun drawn, three uniformed policemen behind him. The cavalry to the rescue. Only they were too damn late.

"Carter killed Caroline." Maudeen sighed, dropping the gun, metal clattering against the wood floor. She sank down beside the senator, her hand stroking his hair. "And Leon was covering for Carter." She looked up at Leon, eyes glittering with regret. "All these years I thought it was you. I would never have sent the autopsy report if I'd known the truth."

"You sent it?" Jake frowned.

Maudeen nodded. "I thought if I could get Leon out of our lives, Carter would be happier."

"And you almost cost him the presidency," Leon barked, a little of his former bluster returning.

"That's all that ever mattered to you, isn't it? The presidency." Riley lifted her head, her eyes still bright with tears, her gaze locked on Leon. "You killed my father with your ambition, as clearly as if you'd pulled the trigger."

Jake tightened his arms around her, her courage making him proud. David bent to pick up the gun, and the policemen moved to flank Leon. "Did Bryce know about all of this?" Jake asked. "Is that why you framed him?"

"No." Leon seemed to be shrinking before their very eyes. Aging as they watched. "He never knew. But he also never believed it was an accident. He started nosing around, looking for answers. I tried to deal with him, but he wouldn't listen." He ran a hand through his hair, his expression resigned. "He left me with no choice. He needed to understand who he was dealing with. To understand just how out of his depth he was."

"So Michaels helped you frame him." Jake frowned, trying to put it all together.

"Yes. Douglas was ambitious. I simply played on that. It was the same with the autopsy report. A promise of money and power will accomplish almost anything." He glanced at Maudeen. "I missed your copy. Didn't even know it existed." There was regret in his voice, but Jake couldn't tell if it was for his failure or the havoc it had caused.

"So why did it all surface again?" David asked. "I mean, you covered your tracks. What happened?" He narrowed his eyes, studying the older man.

"You already know the answer to that." Leon's eyes met Jake's.

"Hank Larsen."

Leon nodded, seeming to relish the telling now that he'd started. "He stumbled on information that proved Michaels had purposefully withheld witnesses in

Daniels's case. He had no idea what he'd stumbled onto. But with Carter so close to election," Leon shrugged again, "we couldn't take a chance."

"So you hired Osterman to take care of Larsen." This from David.

"Yes. And I thought that would be the end of it. But I hadn't counted on you." Leon lifted his gaze to Jake's. "You were the wild card. Larsen told Michaels about you. And Douglas told me. And then when you called him—"

"Michaels?" David asked.

"Yes. When Mahoney called him, he freaked. He thought it was all over. That Jake knew everything."

"So you had Martell try to kill Jake." Riley's voice was harsh, anger bringing color to her cheeks.

"And almost killed you." Leon's voice was sorrowful. "I never meant to hurt you, Riley."

She looked away, laying her head back against Jake's chest.

He stroked her hair, fighting the urge to go for Bronowsky's throat. "So you tried to kill me," Jake said. "And then when that failed, you tried to kill Daniels. Why?"

Leon leaned back against the desk with a shrug. "You were getting too close. And with Michaels dead, I wasn't certain how long I could keep him in prison. He was a good candidate for parole. Between that and your nosing about, I figured it wouldn't be long before he started to talk. From there it wasn't such a big leap to the truth. So I had the threat eliminated. I used some of Michaels's connections. The overdose was staged."

"But it all fell apart anyway." David sounded as disgusted as Jake felt.

"It would have been fine, if Osterman hadn't panicked." Leon's voice almost sounded petulant. "He's the one who killed Amber Northcott. Thought the bitch was going to blow the whistle."

"Christ, Leon, after everything that's happened, you're still trying to blame someone else." Maudeen spat the words out.

"If anyone is to blame, it's you—and my father," Riley said to Leon, her voice soft, her hand still curled in Jake's. He tightened his fingers around hers, his heart breaking at the depth of her pain.

"No matter what else happened here tonight, Riley," Leon said, his voice filled with conviction, "remember that Carter died, saving you. In the end, you were the only thing that mattered to him. He loved you. More than anything. And that has to count for something."

She looked over at her father, a world of emotions chasing across her face—betrayal, anger, love, devastation. The last of these cut into Jake's heart, making him want to kill Carter O'Brien all over again. Slowly, she struggled to her feet, her eyes never leaving her father's body. "It isn't enough, Leon. Nothing will ever be enough."

Jake wanted to grab her, to never let her go, but he knew she needed to be able to stand on her own. To deal with it all in her own way. Perhaps she would choose to put everything—everyone—behind her. Uncertain, he waited, barely daring to breathe.

She turned then, the shadow of a smile at odds with her tears, and held out her hands. In less than a heartbeat he was on his feet, pulling her back into his arms, his eyes devouring her.

"I'm okay," she said softly, framing his face with her hands. Her eyes told another story, but at least she was alive, and he was holding her. It was a start. "And you're here. And I love you. And that's what really counts."

He stroked the soft contour of her cheek, his heart

ready to burst. "I love you too. And we'll find a way to get through this, Riley—together. For Caroline, for her baby—for your father."

She shook her head, reaching up to wipe away his tears. "For us, Jake. We'll do it for us."

He pulled her closer, content just to listen to the sound of her heart beating against his. The moon winked at him from behind the clouds, its dappled light silvering the air outside. The storm had passed.

And they had survived.

Epilogue

HAYWOOD JAMESON SAT in the realty office conference room, marveling at the fact that he was not only a free man, but a moneyed one as well. His release had brought a partial reconciliation with his family.

The prodigal son returned.

Not so much because he'd been forgiven, but more because it looked magnanimous for them to open their home and kill the fatted calf. Whatever the reason, he'd been delighted. He no longer had need of his family or their lifestyle, but he needed their money. So he'd gone back into the fold.

At least in theory. He smiled, wondering what his father would say to his current endeavor.

"I think I've got most everything I need, Mr. Jameson." The pretty real estate agent sent him a flirty smile. And to his great surprise, he returned it.

Maybe he was healing after all. Maybe from all that had happened, he'd be able to find something good. To rebuild his life. To find new direction.

"I need a quick summary of what your plans are for the building."

Haywood smiled again. "I'm turning it into a halfway house. For teenagers in trouble. A place they can stay until they can find their own path. I want to give kids a shove in the right direction. Help them live up to their potential."

The woman smiled again. "What a wonderful thing to do."

Haywood shrugged. "It wasn't my idea, actually. It was the dream of a friend of mine."

"Was?" She tilted her head quizzically.

"He's dead."

"I'm so sorry. I had no idea."

Haywood smiled. "It's all right. He's at peace now. I'm certain of it."

The woman bent over the papers, obviously still embarrassed. "What will you be calling it?"

"Second Chances."

Haywood shot a glance toward heaven, certain that somewhere Bryce Daniels was smiling.

"That's the last of it." Riley watched as the moving men carted away the boxes, leaving an empty house behind. Rivercrest looked alien without its trappings. As though it had already shed the last vestiges of its tragic history, ready and waiting for someone to come along and give it new life.

"You're certain this is what you want to do?" Jake came up behind her, his arms slipping around her, his support feeling as natural to her as breathing.

She turned in his arms, her eyes meeting his. "Positive. The only thing here is the past. And what I want is the future—with you."

Worry drew his dark brows together in a frown. "I can't help but think that you'll miss all this. Life as a reporter's wife won't be as grand as all that you're used to."

She touched his lips with her finger, smiling. "It's just what the doctor ordered. All of this was an illusion,

Jake. It never existed, except maybe in my father's deluded mind. I want something real. Something we can build on together. I want new memories. And I want them with you."

He bent to kiss her, his touch a covenant—the promise of wonderful things to come. She leaned into his arms as they walked toward the front door. Mr. McKafferty sat forlornly in the entryway, his lopsided bow seeming to underscore his dejection.

Laughing, Riley bent to pick him up. There was a card tucked under his chin. She opened it, Jake peering over her shoulder. The writing was Adelaide's.

Everyone should have something old at their wedding. I thought maybe this would do nicely for you. Some memories are worth holding onto.

Riley felt tears welling, and Jake's arms tightened around her. "This is Caroline's bear." She looked up into his eyes, wondering if he could ever understand all that the little bear stood for.

He stroked the side of her face, his smile tender. "Then I think we should take him home with us. Maybe someday give him some kids to play with."

Riley tucked Mr. McKafferty under her arm, linking her hand with Jake's. "Shall we go?"

Together they walked out onto the front porch, surprised at the flashes from photographers. She'd forgotten about the press. They'd been kept out of Rivercrest for weeks, but today there was no one to keep them away.

Carter O'Brien was buried beside her mother. Caroline, her husband, and their baby lay peacefully in their corner of the graveyard. Maudeen was moving up East somewhere. And Leon was awaiting trial.

It was over. And Riley was more than ready to move on.

"Miss O'Brien, Miss O'Brien." Questions assailed her from all angles, and she steeled herself into an assumed calm, Jake's hand tightening around hers, telegraphing his strength and support.

"Miss O'Brien . . ." A man stood a bit away from the crowd, pencil ready. "Are you planning to follow in your father's political footsteps? There's talk that you might run for his Senate seat."

She sucked in a breath, and pasted on what she hoped was a gracious smile. "I have no intention of running for anything. Political life was my father's dream, not mine."

They moved forward, Jake's firm hand guiding her through the throng.

"Miss O'Brien?" She looked up, recognizing the voice, Edna's eyes smiling down at hers with approval. "You just said your dreams aren't your father's. Could you tell us then what your dreams might be?"

She lifted her chin, tightening her hand around Jake's, knowing their whole lives lay ahead of them. One grand adventure. She met Edna's gaze, returning her smile. "I don't know, but I certainly intend to find out."

Read on for a sneak peek at the next novel
of romantic suspense by Dee Davis. . . .

MIDNIGHT RAIN

Coming Winter 2002

Prologue

Coahuila, Mexico

What he needed was a little excitement. Jonathan Brighton shook his head, trying to clear it, to stop the slow incessant onslaught of fatigue, forcing himself to concentrate on the road ahead. It was the sameness that was getting to him. The lack of anything remotely entertaining.

The hazy mountains shimmered in the distance, taunting him, the diametric opposite of the arid hell hole he was driving across. As if in testament to his thoughts, a swirling cone of dust chased a tumbleweed across the road, dissipating when it reached the other side.

What in hell had possessed him to come here? He'd needed a break from the everyday headaches of running Guardian, but surely a nice beach located next to a five-star hotel would have been a better choice of getaway. Instead he was heading for a mountain retreat that was apparently located in the middle of nowhere. Somewhere remote.

Isolated.

Jesus, he'd been insane.

Or rather Florence had. She'd been the one to insist that he needed something different. Something quiet. And his partners had jumped right on his secretary's bandwagon, offering their sage advice. Go here. Go there. Take this road. Take that one.

And he'd listened.

So here he was, in the middle of fucking nowhere, in a rental car that shook if he accelerated past fifty, with a radio that only worked some of the time and an air conditioner that had stopped before he'd gone a hundred miles. Another of his partners' brilliant ideas. "Don't drive your own car in Mexico, Jonathan. Just rent one. It's cheap, it's . . ." *Crap.* The goddamned thing was crap.

Oh yeah, this was the life.

Hopefully the trip would be worth it, but based on the way things were going he sincerely doubted it. He did not feel refreshed. He didn't even feel like he was on vacation—more like he was exiled in hell. Angrily he punched at the fan button, pushing it to high. Sun-heated air blasted out of the vent, and he gritted his teeth, reaching over to roll down the window. Nothing was worth this kind of torture.

Truth was, he wasn't the rough-it-out-in-the-wilds type. He smiled at the thought, glancing down at his pressed jeans and polo shirt. Even they felt odd. He spent his days dressed for success, Armani his uniform of choice. The rest of the world might believe in dress-down Friday's but Jonathan thought it was bullshit. A way for people who couldn't afford the best to justify their situation. And he wasn't falling for it.

With a murmured curse, he pressed down on the accelerator. The little car shook, but held its course. Oh yeah, this was turning into a hell of a day. Hopefully things were going better in Austin. Danny had promised he'd solve their little problem. Get to the bottom of it once and for all. He trusted the man, but sometimes things had a way of getting out of control, and if news leaked out that there was something going on, it could cause the company serious damage. And *that* was something he wanted to avoid at all costs.

He sighed, tipping back his head against the headrest. He put everything he had into Guardian. It was like a child. And he wouldn't—couldn't—allow anything to happen to it. If it died, so did he.

A horn sounded behind him, breaking into his reverie. He hadn't even heard the truck coming up behind him. Three hours in the desert and he was already losing his edge. With a frown, he pulled the rental over onto the shoulder.

The truck, its red paint faded to orangey-brown, started to pass, then slowed, matching its pace to Jonathan's car, a stocky man in the passenger seat smiling, gesturing for him to stop. Jonathan held his speed steady, concentrating on the rutted shoulder. The truck stayed with him.

Just what he needed to top off an already perfect day—a couple of crazy Mexicans in a beat up pickup truck. Jonathan accelerated, the car protesting its mistreatment. The pickup followed suit, the man waving his hand now in agitation, his smile fading.

Something glinted in the man's hand. A badge. The son of a bitch was waving a badge. Jonathan blew out a breath, relief mixing with anger. Where the hell was his siren? Pulling the car to a stop, he turned off the ignition, already reaching for his wallet.

The cop walked up to the car and leaned down, his beefy face glistening with sweat. *"Salga del coche."* Get out of the car.

Jonathan reached for the car handle, but before he could open it, the door jerked outward, the man's beefy hand closing on Jonathan's shoulder.

"¡Ahora mismo!"

He nodded and stepped from the car. The big man's partner joined them, his eyes hidden behind the mirrored lenses of his sunglasses.

"Su licencia, por favor." Despite the word please, Jonathan recognized that the request was in fact an order.

He opened his wallet, digging for his license. *"Yo no hablo el español."* He actually did speak the language, but it had been a hell of a long time, and until he understood what was happening, he thought it best to keep the fact to himself.

The two men conferred for a moment, and then the second man handed the license back, his fat friend heading for their truck. "Where are you going?" Jonathan returned his attention to the policeman in sunglasses. He was speaking English now, his words heavily accented.

"I'm on my way to the mountains. A place just outside of Satillo." He was actually heading for a little village near Torreon, but again it seemed prudent to keep his destination private.

The man nodded. "You are on vacation here in our country?"

"Yeah. I needed a little peace and quiet." Which was turning out to be a whole lot less soothing than advertised.

The policeman smiled, revealing a gold front tooth. "You have come to the right place, my friend. I think we can guarantee you nothing but peace and quiet from now on."

Jonathan smiled back, but the hairs on his neck rose as some part of his body responded to a thread of something else in the man's voice. For the first time he realized that neither of the men was wearing a uniform. Laughter off to his left signaled that fatty had moved, and Jonathan turned, his heart pounding as adrenaline pumped through his body.

The heavy-set man was standing a few feet away, the hot sunshine highlighting the pistol in his hand. *"Duerme bien, amigo."*

There was a flash, and before Jonathan had time to think, let alone act, the sound of the gun's report filled his ears. Then for a moment everything was quiet, the world seeming to move in slow motion. He watched as a bead of sweat dropped from the shooter's heavily jowled face, waiting for the inevitable, and it came—in an explosion of heat and light that obliterated all other thoughts.

He struggled to hold on, fighting to maintain consciousness. There was still so much he wanted to do. Somewhere amid the pain in his head, he heard tires squealing as his assailants' truck pulled back onto the highway, leaving him alone on the side of the road.

If he could have he'd have laughed. It was an inglorious way to die, ironic really. The diametric opposite of the life he'd led. Always pushing for more. As the darkness swirled up to swallow him, his last thoughts were of all that had been left undone.

What he could have been. But nothing—not his money, not his connections, and certainly not his company—could save him now.

With a sigh, Jonathan Brighton gave in to the dark.

Chapter 1

Austin, Texas—Six months later

All he had to do was lift the goddamned pen. Which was easier said than done. John Brighton concentrated on the writing implement, willing his right hand to move. He was halfway there. He'd managed to get his fingers to close around the thing. Now all he had to do was lift it up.

His hand quivered and for a moment rose off the table. He closed his eyes, trying to visualize the action. How could something so seemingly inconsequential be so difficult? Six months of rehab and he was no better than a newborn. Weak and untried.

He swallowed, concentrating on the implement in his hand. This might be the biggest challenge he'd ever faced, but he wasn't about to go down for the count. Some low-life Mexican thugs were not going to get the best of him.

The pen lifted, his fingers shaking with the effort.

"Hey, bro. Ready to blow this pop stand?"

The pen dropped to the bed, then rolled to the floor.

"Danny." John looked up, trying to conceal his annoyance. Maybe he was jealous of the fact that his brother had full use of his faculties. Or maybe he was just in a generally crappy mood. Either way, there was no point in taking it out on Danny.

His brother hung a garment bag on a hook, and dropped into a chair by the hospital bed. "Having a little trouble signing out?" He bent down to retrieve the pen.

"I could have done it." John sounded petulant and he knew it. "You surprised me. That's all."

"Look, Jonathan, there's no need to push yourself like this. Your recovery is nothing short of miraculous as it is. What you need is a little downtime. Let your body come back at its own pace."

"I've had six months of downtime. And believe me when I tell you it isn't what it's cracked up to be." He wasn't surprised to hear bitterness in his voice. So much had been lost. Things he might never recover. Gaping holes in his life. A darkness that sometimes threatened to swallow him whole.

Danny held up a hand in apology. "I didn't mean to ruffle your feathers. I just want you to take a breath and maybe move a little slower. Let me help. It's about time I get the chance to be the big brother." His expression belied the lightness in his voice.

"And how exactly do you propose to do that?" John swung his legs carefully out of the bed, using his left leg to propel his right.

"Well, to start with I can sign these." Danny reached for the dismissal papers. "I doubt anyone will look too closely." His grin was contagious, and John felt his mood lightening. Maybe things would feel more normal once he was home.

"Whatever it takes to get me out of here." He watched as his brother signed the release papers, envying the ease with which he wielded the pen. But then things had always come easy for Danny. The golden boy.

John shook his head, dispelling his thoughts. Danny was who he was, and their roles in life had long since been cast in stone. Except that now he wasn't able to play his part. He fought against a wave of despondency. Life was too damn short for all this wallowing in self-pity. "So what'd you bring me to wear?" he asked, striving to keep his voice light.

"Armani." Danny smiled. "What else? I made a special trip to get it." He unzipped the bag and pulled out the beautifully tailored suit.

John swallowed back a wave of frustration. The suit had enough closures to keep him occupied for a century. He forced a smile. "Thanks. But I think I might have preferred something a little simpler."

Danny frowned. "Yeah, right. This coming from a guy whose friends wager about whether he wears a tie to bed at night."

John winced at the reference. It wasn't the first time he'd heard it. But repetitions didn't make it seem any more real. He supposed people were telling him the truth. After all, *their* brains were perfectly functional. So unless there was a hell of a conspiracy, the reminiscences were bound to be accurate. Unfortunately, they didn't fit with his impressions of himself.

He'd seen pictures, and in some vague way they looked and felt familiar. But the memories lacked emotion. It was as though that part of him had been damaged, twisted—the mirror image of what he'd once been.

And no one seemed to understand. He *was* Jonathan Brighton.

And he *wasn't*.

All at the same time. Hell, he didn't really understand it himself. He only knew he no longer wanted to wear Armani, even if he did have an entire closet of it.

"Well, I hope I'm not an odds-on favorite, because I don't think I'll be tying ties anytime soon." He tried for lightness and missed, fighting to close his hand. Even the simple act of making a fist eluded him. With his good hand he levered himself up, careful to center his weight, slightly favoring his good leg.

"Which brings me back to my original point. You're pushing yourself too fast." Danny reached for the suit coat, sliding it off of the hanger. "Mrs. Tedesky said you were even thinking of coming back to work."

"It's time. I've been out of commission too long as it is."

His brother frowned. "So you're displeased with the way I've been running things?"

"I didn't say that. I just feel like I need to be back at the helm. It is my company after all."

"It's *our* company, Jonathan, and I'm perfectly capable of handling things until you get it all together."

"It's John." He mumbled the words, but Danny heard him.

"Case in point. What kind of man changes his name at thirty-five?"

He managed a shrug, a left-sided affair that still conveyed his feelings. "One that gets shot in the head. Besides, I didn't change it. I shortened it. And one thing has nothing to do with the other. I'm perfectly capable of making business decisions."

"I'm not questioning whether you'll be able to come back, *John*. I'm just questioning whether now is the time. You still aren't a hundred percent. The truth is you may never remember what you've lost." Danny leaned against the bureau, his relaxed stance at odds with his tone.

John sighed, running his good hand through his hair. "So says the doctor. But I haven't lost anything that affects my ability to work. And that's all that matters."

"There's still your physical recovery." Danny's eyes narrowed in thought. "You're moving better, but you're having problems. Hell, you can't even hold a pen." He tipped his head toward the pen on the table.

John swallowed back a retort. There was no sense taking his anger out on his brother. "I'm getting better."

"I know that. I just worry about you." Danny paused, dropping his gaze to study his wingtips.

"I know you do." John closed his eyes, massaging his temple. "But the fact remains that it's my call. And I say I'm ready to come back." Anger, hot and heavy, swelled through him. "What I need now is work. And the work I choose is here." He banged his fist down on the table. "At *my* company. Do I make myself clear?"

Some part of him, deep inside, was appalled at his tone of voice, surprised at the depth of his anger, but it held no sway.

He glared at the man he considered his best friend, waiting for an answer.

Danny sighed, obviously working to contain his emotions. "I just want you to be yourself again. And you have to understand that I have to do what I think is necessary to make that happen."

John dropped heavily back onto the bed. "I know that. I didn't mean to lose my temper. It's just that right now, Guardian is all I have. And for the time being I need to be there. I need to try and make it all work again."

"And I'll be there to help you." Danny's troubled gaze met his. "Look, one way or the other, I swear it'll be all right."

Tears pricked the back of John's eyes. He was so fucking emotional these days. He forced a smile, certain that it was at best lopsided. "I hope so, Danny. Sweet Jesus, I hope so."

Danny sighed, forcing a smile. "All right then, what do you say we start by getting you dressed." He reached for the suit.

"I think Armani might be overkill for a casual afternoon of recovery." The voice was decidedly feminine, deep and smoky. Like aged whiskey, it washed over him, deceptively smooth, ending with a swift kick. He liked it.

A lot.

He swung around, curious to see the woman behind the words. He wasn't disappointed.

She stood in the doorway, dressed in faded green scrubs, the cotton hugging every sweet curve. Neither tall nor short, she simply was. Inhabiting space as if it belonged to her.

A single braid hung casually over her shoulder, her hair brown with golden highlights. Sun-kissed was the word that popped into his head. He smiled at the imagery, wondering if he'd lost his mind, and then ruefully accepted the fact that, woman or no, he was no longer playing with a full deck. Still, he was in the game, and that had to count for something.

"So you guys want to quit staring, or shall I give you a runway turn?" She smiled slowly, green eyes sparkling, and stepped into the room, breaking the spell. He shot a glance at his brother who was standing slack-jawed, eyes riveted on the new arrival. Evidently he wasn't the only one attracted to their visitor.

Danny closed his mouth with an audible click, his smile

turning predatory. Jealousy surged through John, surprising him with its force. Yet another emotion out of control. Hell, he didn't even know the woman.

But then neither did Danny.

Almost as if they had choreographed it, they moved toward her, like two awkward adolescents. Or moths to the flame. John closed his eyes, fighting to keep his balance. His leg was much better, but walking required his full attention, distraction almost certainly spelling disaster.

And this woman was definitely a distraction.

She moved before he had a chance to think about her intent, steadying him with gentle hands, the soft smell of her surrounding him with tantalizing hints of vanilla.

He reached up with his good hand, planning to push her backward, to protect his space, but she'd already moved, standing again in the doorway, one shoulder propped against the door frame.

"Who the hell are you?" His words came out sharper than he'd intended. The woman's scrubs marked her as a hospital employee. A nurse of some kind, no doubt. He shouldn't have snapped, but he wasn't a man who liked to be coddled and he was more than capable of standing on his own two feet.

"Apparently your dresser." She held up a pair of sweats and a T-shirt. "Can you lift your arm?"

Shooting her what he hoped was an indignant look, he slowly raised his arm, stopping when it reached shoulder height, the effort costing him more than he wanted to admit. "How's this?"

"It's a good start. Can you get it any higher?" She watched him dispassionately, but he could see a spark of something in her eyes. Pity or maybe compassion. It didn't really matter. Either sentiment was abhorrent. And he wasn't about to tolerate it from a stranger—hospital staff or no.

He let his arm drop. "I don't see that it matters."

She shrugged. "It doesn't—to me. But I'd think sometime in your life you'd like to be able to pull something off the top of a shelf, or hang the star on the Christmas tree."

He studied her through narrowed eyes, responding to the challenge in her voice. "And you care about this because . . ."

She smiled, the gesture changing her from formidable to impish in an instant. "I get paid if you touch the stars."

There was a world of meaning in her words, but only in John's imagination.

"Does that go for me, too?" Danny's tone was a cross between wistful and wolfish.

John shook his head, pulling himself back to reality. The woman was a witch. He'd completely forgotten his brother was in the room.

"Only if you've suffered major head trauma." Her gaze brushed over Danny, dismissing him. "I'm John's physical therapist."

Nonplussed by the brush-off, Danny grinned. "Hey, I'm the patient's brother. Surely that gives me the right for consults or something."

John took a hesitant step forward, pleased when his left foot obeyed. "You have a name?" His voice was still brusque. A combination of irritation and embarrassment. When it came to women he'd never been able to compete with his brother. But he'd at least been able to hold his own. Now, he was more like the invisible man. Still, she was here for him.

Not Danny.

Even if there was nothing personal in it, it gave him a delicious sense of victory. And these days he'd take what he could get.

"My name is Kathleen." Her words tickled his ear, and he realized she'd moved again, this time flanking his bad side. "Kathleen Cavanaugh."

"Irish?" The word popped from his mouth before he had time to think about it.

"Boston Irish." Her eyes crinkled at the corners, and his heart rate ratcheted up a notch.

"That explains the accent." Danny moved to his other side, and together they helped him toward the bathroom.

"Take these." She handed him the sweats when they reached the door. "You ought to be able to get them on yourself."

His eyes met hers, and it felt as if they were locked together in a world all their own, the soft intake of her breath assuring him that he wasn't alone in the feeling. "And if I can't manage?"

Her smile was slow and sure. "Then I'll just have to come in and help you."

She'd lost her freaking mind. Katie stared at the closed bathroom door, trying to ignore Danny Brighton's blatant stare. It bored into her back. But he wasn't the source of her discomfort.

No, indeed. It was much worse than that. She was having less than pure thoughts about Jonathan Brighton. And she wasn't supposed to be thinking about him like that. Heavens, she wasn't supposed to be thinking about him at all.

She was a professional. And this was a routine situation. All she had to do was observe the man, and based on what she saw make recommendations to her superiors. Simple as that.

The door opened and he stepped out of the bathroom, every muscle outlined by the T-shirt she'd provided. His dark hair curled against the neckline, his face shadowed with the hint of a beard.

He looked unkempt. And dangerous. A far cry from the button-down workaholic she'd been briefed about. This was a man with an edge.

And she'd always liked men who walked the line.

"You're staring." His tone was mild, but the current running between them was reflected in his eyes.

"I wasn't actually. I was just thinking about where we ought to begin."

"On the bed?" His smile sent shivers trailing down her back.

She swallowed, struggling for composure. "I beg your pardon?"

Danny laughed behind her, a hint of something protective in his voice. "I think he means that he needs to sit down."

She pulled her mind out of the gutter and focused on the man in front of her. Really focused. He was holding himself together by sheer willpower, but a sheen of sweat glazed his face, and his jaw was twitching with the effort to look at ease.

"Oh God, I'm sorry. What was I thinking?" Five minutes and she'd compromised his health. Her training had been rushed, but it had been thorough. She wasn't here to hurt him. On the contrary, she needed Mr. Brighton fully operational. Again her over-eager mind flooded her brain with vivid images having nothing to do with her job or Jonathan Brighton's recovery.

Danny joined her, and they helped John to the bed. He sat down with a sigh. "I'm the one who should be sorry. Getting dressed never used to be an all-day affair. Although this get-up," he gestured to the faded sweats, "beats the hell out of that." He tipped his head toward the suit, shooting her a grateful smile.

"I thought John already had a therapist."

Katie regretfully pulled her attention away from John, turning to face Danny's skeptical gaze. "He does. Or rather he did. Linda Osborne was his P.T. here at the rehab clinic, but now that he's being released, he needs someone at home. Someone to watch over him, to work with him to continue to improve his mobility."

"And that would be you." His eyes narrowed as he studied her. This time there was no hint of playfulness. Danny Brighton was all business. And the business was protecting his brother. For all their physical differences—the one dark as sin and the other almost angelic—the brothers obviously had a deep bond. And right now Danny Brighton was assessing her.

"Exactly. Linda doesn't do home care." She met his gaze square on, unflinching. "I do."

"And you're good at what you do?"

"So I've been told." She fought to keep her tone level. She'd never responded well to unspoken threats. And there was no question that John's brother was baiting her.

"Give the woman a break, Danny. She's just trying to do her job." John's voice was laced with laughter, but there was an underlying note of authority.

Danny studied her for a moment longer, then relaxed. "I'm sure you can understand my concern, Ms. Cavanaugh. My brother has been through quite an ordeal. And I just want to be certain that he has the best of everything."

"What he means, Kathleen," her name tumbled off his lips like warm wine, caressing her from the inside out, "is that he likes to think he's running the show. And you were a curve he hadn't expected." He smiled at his brother, then returned his attention to her. "I assume you were assigned by my doctor?"

"Your insurance company, actually." She shrugged, leaning over him to straighten his pillow. "Your doctor orders in-home care, but your insurance company is responsible for assigning someone."

"I see." He nodded, his expression thoughtful. "So you're with me for the duration."

"Duration?" She straightened, trying to read the subtext of his words.

"Yeah. I need to know that whoever I'm working with will be around to see things through to the end."

"You mean a full recovery." He was testing her again, but she wasn't exactly sure how.

He shrugged. "Or as full a recovery as I'm likely to get."

"You get what you work for, Mr. Brighton."

"John." He smiled again, the tension dissipating with the gesture. "And I always work for what I want, Ms. Cavanaugh. Always."

"Now there's an understatement." Danny's words were mumbled, but there was a wealth of information in his tone.

"Looks like I'll fit in just fine, then. I expect my patients to work hard. But I assure you in the end it's more than worth the effort." She shot a look at first one brother and then the other, noting again the contrast between them.

Women were more likely to respond to Danny's pretty boy looks than to John's dark mystery. There was something off-putting about the older Brighton boy. Something that she had absolutely no intention of investigating. She was here to do a job.

Period.

"So where do we start?" John's question pulled her out of her musings.

"I'd think the first thing to do is get you home." Danny's voice was proprietary again.

"Sounds like a plan." John's smile included her as well as his brother, and warmed her all the way to her toes. "I suppose I have to wait for a wheelchair?"

It was Katie's turn to smile. "Actually, if you're up to it, you can walk. Since this is rehab, and not a hospital per se, we like for our patients to feel like they're leaving in better shape than they've arrived. I'd say you've earned the right to walk out of here." She was babbling. But it was better than letting her mind wander free. "Of course if you'd rather have the wheel-chair . . ." she trailed off, already certain of his response.

She wasn't disappointed. He held up a hand, shaking his head. "Not on your life. They wheeled me in here. They're sure as hell not wheeling me out." To illustrate his point he pushed himself off of the bed, wincing with the effort. Without think-ing, she slid an arm around his waist, feeling his muscles bunch in rebuff.

"I can do it myself." His words vibrated through her, his body warm against hers.

"I know you can." She tightened her grip, steadying him. "But sometimes it's all right to ask for a little help." She told herself that she needed to gain his confidence, and to prove to him she knew what she was doing. But the truth was she just wanted to touch him.

And the thought scared her to death.

If you enjoyed DARK OF THE NIGHT
you won't want to miss these other fabulous
novels of romantic suspense by Dee Davis...

AFTER TWILIGHT

After her husband's awful death, Kacy Macgrath uncovered secrets about him she was better off not knowing, so she ran away to a small cottage in Ireland. Now someone is watching her. Braedon Roche has traveled across an ocean looking for justice—to expose Kacy Macgrath as a master forger who had nearly destroyed his career as an art dealer. What Braedon doesn't expect is his undeniable attraction to the fragile widow hiding behind a web of deception. But Braedon isn't the only man following Kacy. A savage killer stalks from the shadows, chipping away at her sanity, and trapping her in an unspeakable nightmare. . . .

JUST BREATHE

For aspiring travel writer Chloe Nichols, escorting a tour group of wealthy old ladies through Europe was supposed to be anything but thrilling. Then she is rescued from an assassin's bullet by a stranger on the train—a perfectly handsome, charming stranger who saves her life with a kiss and asks her to pose as his fiancée. Chloe believes Matthew Broussard is trying to protect her, until the seductive charade becomes part of a lethal international conspiracy in which no one is what they seem—including her captivating hero. . . .

Published by Ballantine Books.
Available in bookstores everywhere.